ACCLAIM  GLENN COOPER

"Smart and entertaining, every page is pitch perfect. A terrific story, terrifically told." —Steve Berry,
New York Times bestselling author,
on *The Fourth Prophecy*

"Cooper's name on a book's cover guarantees two things: an elaborate story with plenty of twists and turns and a swift pace that carries the reader through to the end." —*Booklist*

"Cooper's intelligent, heart-pounding homage to *Raiders of the Lost Ark* and *The Da Vinci Code* will appeal to fans of action, thriller, and conspiracy genres." —*Booklist* on *The Debt*

"[Cooper] is no ordinary thriller writer, but one who asks big questions." —*Sunday Telegraph* (UK)

"The debut of a startling new talent. Here is a story both incandescent and explosive. A seamless blend of modern-day thriller and historical mystery with an ending that left me breathless." —James Rollins,
New York Times bestselling author,
on *Library of the Dead*

ALSO BY GLENN COOPER

The Fourth Prophecy

THE
LOST POPE

GLENN COOPER

GRAND
CENTRAL

New York Boston

Copyright © 2023 by Lascaux Media LLC

Cover design by Ben Denzer. Cover images: Saint Mary Magdalene, c.1524 (oil on panel) Luini, Bernardino (c.1480-1532) from Bridgeman Images; Vatican and background texture from Getty Images.
Cover copyright © 2023 by Hachette Book Group, Inc.

Grand Central Publishing
Hachette Book Group
1290 Avenue of the Americas, New York, NY 10104
grandcentralpublishing.com
twitter.com/grandcentralpub

First Edition: June 2023

Grand Central Publishing is a division of Hachette Book Group, Inc. The Grand Central Publishing name and logo is a trademark of Hachette Book Group, Inc.

The publisher is not responsible for websites (or their content) that are not owned by the publisher.

The Hachette Speakers Bureau provides a wide range of authors for speaking events. To find out more, go to www.hachettespeakersbureau.com or call (866) 376-6591.

Library of Congress Cataloging-in-Publication Data
Names: Cooper, Glenn, 1953- author.
Title: The lost pope / Glenn Cooper.
Description: First edition. | New York : Grand Central Publishing, 2023.
Identifiers: LCCN 2022053121 | ISBN 9781538721261 (trade paperback) | ISBN 9781538721278 (ebook)
Subjects: LCGFT: Thrillers (Fiction) | Novels.
Classification: LCC PS3603.O582627 L67 2023 | DDC 813/.6–dc23/eng/20221115
LC record available at https://lccn.loc.gov/2022053121

ISBNs: 9781538721261 (trade pbk.), 9781538721278 (ebook)

Printed in the United States of America

LSC-C

Printing 1, 2023

THE LOST POPE

1

Northern Oasis, Egypt, 67 CE

Brown was her color and the color of this place.

Her eyes were brown, and though her hair was graying, it still showed streaks of its original bronze. When she was young, her skin was light enough to go pink as a newborn mouse at the blush of love, but the sun had been baking it for over fifty years, rendering it the shade of tiger nuts. Her old linen robe, her second skin, was the same nut-brown even after she washed and beat the cloth.

Her coloration matched the arid land, for it too was brown beyond the green fertility of the oasis. Near to the oasis, the soil was dark as cedar bark, but as one moved away from its spring, the terrain lightened from copper to mustard to the bleached tan of the desert sands. The cluster of houses she came upon were companions of the earth, rising organically from the desert floor, their walls of limestone blocks, rough and tawny.

She arrived by mule when the sun was burning near the horizon and northerly winds were whipping fine sand into the air. One of her fellow travelers knocked on the rough door and stepped aside for her.

An old man showed himself and, in Aramaic, asked who she was.

The woman responded, "I am Mary."

The man, Isaiah, looked at her hard and said, "My hearing is poor. Did you say Mary?"

She lowered her hood, revealing sunken eyes and cracked lips, and said, "Yes, I am Mary. Mary of Magdala. I seek sanctuary."

Old eyes widened. "From whom do you flee, My Lady?"

"All of them," she said. "Christians, Jews, Romans, all wish me dead. I am told this is the house of Leah."

Isaiah escorted Mary and her three male companions to the largest house and asked them to wait in a dimly lit room of generous proportions. The floor was hard-packed dirt. Wooden bowls were stacked on a long dining table. The shutters had been closed to keep the swirling sands at bay, but fine yellow grit penetrated the gaps, coating the table and benches, and the gusting wind set the candles dancing and flashing.

A woman rushed in from an adjoining room. Mary thought she must have been sleeping because her blinking, foggy eyes searched the chamber before settling on her. This woman was younger than Mary, taller, with finely chiseled, patrician features. She had the look of a lady who once might have draped herself in mantles of silk, but here and now she wore a coarse gown that brushed the tops of bare feet. Mary's days of vanity were long gone, but this woman, with her unlined, lovely face, made her bitterly feel her years.

The woman bowed deeply and said, "I am Leah. Is it true you are Mary Magdalene?"

"I am."

Leah cried, "The Blessed Matriarch!" and tears moistened her cheeks.

"I have traveled long and far to meet the deacon Leah," Mary said, using the honorific Greek word, *diakonos*. "You are known to the Christian world."

Leah dropped to the ground and kissed Mary's feet. "Blessed Lady, your presence in my house is a gift from the Lord."

Mary pulled her up by the shoulders and gazed tenderly at her face.

"Tell me, why have you come to my house?" Leah asked.

"I am old, and I am weary of running for my life. The Lord knows my days are numbered. I want my story told before I die. I would have you tell it."

Hearing of visitors, the community of some twenty souls spilled from their houses and peered through the cracks in the shutters until Leah invited them inside. Then, one by one, the adults fell to their knees, and they too kissed Mary's feet while their children watched in wide-eyed curiosity. After hasty preparations, the visitors were served a simple meal of bread, boiled vegetables, and diluted wine, and apologies flew over the lack of meat. Mary expressed gratitude for the hospitality on offer, but Leah dispatched a lad to buy a goat so they might have a feast on the morrow.

At the communal table, Leah asked Mary to give the blessing.

"This is your house," Mary said. "The blessing should be yours."

The travelers were not pressed into conversation, for it was evident they were hungry and weak. Yet, fortified by food and drink, one of Mary's men, Quintus, a brawny young fellow with long ringlets of golden hair, responded robustly to a boy of ten who could no longer contain his curiosity at the muscular presence.

"Where are you from?" the boy asked.

"Me? I am from Rome. Do you know where that is?"

The boy shook his head.

"The lad was born here," Leah said. "This place is all he knows."

"Perhaps you will see it one day, boy," Quintus said.

A man at Leah's side sneered across the table. "I can tell by your accent that you do not speak your born tongue. I think maybe you were a Roman soldier," he said, dipping the last word in poison.

"That is true, brother," was the cheerful reply. "I was a Praetorian guard who served the emperor. It was three years back when I met Simon Peter and Mary. Mary hated me before she loved me, for I was Simon Peter's jailer."

Mary reached out to touch Quintus's hand lightly. "Oh, how I love him now."

"When I heard Simon Peter speak of the Christ, he opened my eyes as never before," Quintus said. "He baptized me in the name of the Father, the Son, and the Holy Spirit, and I abandoned my post. Renouncing my past was easy." His lips curled into a smile. "Learning Aramaic was hard."

Leah returned the smile. "Our children were born Christian, but the rest of us are converts, Jews from Jerusalem."

Mary looked up from her bowl and said, "It was Paul who converted you, was it not?"

"Yes, it was Paul, seventeen years ago. We congregated with him for a time, and when he departed Jerusalem for Antioch, Jacob, my husband, founded our own Christian house. From the beginning we suffered vile persecution at the hands of the authorities, and then one night the Romans took Jacob away and executed him. It fell upon me to lead the house. I persuaded my brethren to leave for Egypt, and we settled here, in this far-flung place, so that we might worship the Lord in peace. For us, it began with Paul. A day does not pass when I do not think of him and pray he is well."

Sadness fell over Mary's face like a veil. "Paul is dead, dear lady. Nero beheaded him in Rome, three years after he crucified Simon Peter. We heard this from a Christian traveler who stayed with us in Antioch."

Her words cast a pall over the room, and the women began to sob, all but Leah, who nodded solemnly and said, "The Lord has surely welcomed Paul to his side in Heaven. We forgive his executioners, and we will pray for their souls."

When they had eaten their fill, Leah invited Mary to walk with her. Swathed in shawls, they ambled, hand in hand, through a grove of olive trees, the stillness of the cool night broken by cricket song and the occasional bleating of the newly purchased goat.

"It is terrible you had to flee," Leah said. "My heart aches for you."

The woman's empathy touched Mary. "For much of my life, I was so loved and cherished. It has come as a shock to become despised."

She felt Leah's hand tighten around hers. "Who despises you, Blessed Lady?"

"First, it was the Romans. After they killed Simon Peter, we feared we too would be taken to Nero's Circus for the cruel pleasures of the mob. We left Rome hastily for Antioch, where we had dwelled before. We rejoined the Christian community there, and we established our house of prayer among them in the Kerateion, the Jewish district. I am pleased to say we convinced many a Jew to follow the path of Jesus Christ, but therein lay a problem. The rabbis were angered, and we learned that brutes had been pressed into foul service to murder us. And so we fled once again to Galilee, my homeland, where the Jewish and Roman war had subsided."

"Pilgrims have told us there are many Christians in Israel now," Leah said.

"That is so, and among them are elders who can remember the days when Jesus walked the Earth, teaching and making miracles. Oh, it was good to be home again. For well nigh a year, we were happy there, and crowds thronged to hear us preach the word of the Lord. Then one dark day, we received an emissary from Rome who caused us to flee once again."

"Who sent this emissary?"

"The wretch, Linus. Word reached him of the adulations heaped upon our ministry, and his message to me was a terrible one. Cease your ministry or die by the sword. So-called Christians prepared to carry out his orders. We could understand why Romans and Jews wanted us dead, but our fellow brothers in Christ? It was too much to bear."

"Envy must have darkened Linus's heart," Leah said. She squeezed Mary's hand again. "My poor lady. May I tell you something? You have been my inspiration. Not Simon Peter. Not Paul. You. If not for your life and deeds, I could not have found the strength to establish this house and lead this community. When I was a young woman, I felt my voice stifled by the rabbis and the elders. They wanted us only to keep house and make babies. We could not recite the Torah. We could not worship with men as equals. When I became a Christian, I learned of your life and how precious you were to Jesus and his ministry. Though we never met, it was you who gave me the courage to preach the word of our Lord after they killed my Jacob."

It had been a good while since Mary felt the flutter of joy in her breast. This warm hand in hers was precious flesh. It had been an arduous journey from Jerusalem across the scorching desert to reach the oasis. Many wanted to follow her, but Mary insisted that families should not be uprooted and sent to an uncertain fate. At her final meal with her flock, she hugged each member and wept with them, and before dawn on the Jewish Sabbath day, she bade farewell to her homeland. Only Quintus and two other stalwarts accompanied her, and truth be told, there was nothing Mary could have said or done to keep the faithful Quintus from her side. Mile after grueling mile, Mary rocked on the swayback of her mule and felt her life force draining, and she was sure that death would come to her in Egypt, the ancient land of pharaohs that Moses had fled. But the melancholy that befell her on the journey was at once washed away by the cold, clean, anointing water that was this woman, Leah.

"You and I are much alike," Mary said, her voice strengthening. "We have both lost loved ones to the wickedness of Rome. We both had the fortitude to take our places at the head of the table. We are truly sisters in Christ. There is no time to waste.

In the morning, I would begin my account of my life in the service of Jesus of Nazareth."

Leah said, "I will listen in rapt attention, Blessed Matriarch. We have papyrus, and we have ink. Isaiah will be your scribe. He can write in Greek, the language of the world, for Christians everywhere need to know about you and your acts. In the years to come, they will sing the praises of the three pillars of our faith—Jesus Christ, our Lord and Savior, Simon Peter, the rock upon which the Church was built, and Mary of Magdala, the mother of the Church." She let go of Mary's hand and clasped hers together in prayer. "We shall call your story the Gospel of Mary."

2

The present

Although most of the passengers on Delta flight 124 from Boston to Rome were American, Portuguese was the language that ruled the roost that night.

Cal Donovan estimated that three-quarters of his fellow travelers were of Azorean descent. As the plane streaked over the Atlantic, they burst into traditional Azorean folk songs every few minutes, creating an atmosphere more like a soccer match than an international flight. Cal had given up on sleep. Although business class was a little less raucous than economy, the curtains separating the cabins did nothing to dampen the festivities. Not that he minded. He was in a partying mood himself.

It wasn't every day you were heading to the inauguration of one of your closest friends to become the next pope.

The flight attendants discovered that Cal spoke Italian like a native, and one of them leaned over and said in a husky Milanese accent, "There seems to be a problem with your glass."

"And what problem would that be?"

"It's empty. Same again?"

He answered with a smile.

She returned with another Grey Goose on the rocks and declared the problem solved.

"Temporarily," he replied.

"You had an accident?" she said, pointing at the walking cast poking from under his trouser leg.

"It was a fight, actually. You should have seen the other guy."

She took it as a joke and went about her business. It wasn't. The other guy was dead.

Most people with a broken leg gain weight from inactivity. Cal had lost a few pounds, and for the first time since he was a skinny kid in the army, his cheeks were hollowed out. He wasn't the type to dwell on emotions or blame a poor appetite on stress. He just cinched his belt a notch and got on with things.

If anything, a lighter Cal was even more handsome than his recent cover shot in *The Improper Bostonian*'s issue on Boston's most eligible singles. His jawline was sharper, and his dark eyes sunken deeper were even more penetrating. He seemed to have something of the night about him.

The lavatories in business class were occupied, so he headed to the rear, unaware that a priest had left a mid-cabin seat to follow him. When he finished up and unlocked the door, the priest, a portly middle-aged fellow with a toothy grin, was waiting for him in the galley.

"Professor Donovan," he said.

Cal couldn't place him. "Yeah, hi, how are you?" he said, hoping the fellow would identify himself.

"You probably don't remember me. I'm Father Manny

Cardoza. We met a few years ago when you gave a lecture in New Bedford on the Portuguese Inquisition. You were there with Cardinal Da Silva—oh my goodness, it's still so fresh—I mean the Holy Father."

The best Cal could muster was a vague recollection of a sea of nuns and priests inside an overheated community center. "Oh yes, Father Cardoza, it's good to see you again. It is fresh, isn't it?"

Only five days had passed since the cardinal protodeacon had appeared on the Benediction Loggia of St. Peter's Basilica, leaned into a microphone, and addressed the massive crowd at St. Peter's Square. "I announce to you a great joy! We have a pope! The Most Eminent and Reverend Lord, Lord Rodrigo, Cardinal of the Holy Roman Church, Da Silva, who takes to himself the name John the Twenty-Fourth."

On the second ballot of the conclave—the shortest conclave on record—Cal's dear friend Rodrigo Da Silva became the two hundred sixty-seventh pope of the Catholic Church, the second born in Portugal, and the first American pope.

"You're limping. You were injured?"

"I fell in a library. Occupational hazard."

"At Harvard?"

"No, I was in England. I hadn't been home for long when the conclave concluded. There aren't too many things that could've gotten me back on a plane. This was one of them."

"We are so very excited," the priest said. "Many of my parishioners have hardly slept. I have hardly slept. A son of the Azores is the pope!"

"Looks like you brought most of New Bedford with you to the party."

"And all the other Portuguese communities. We are over-joyed."

Cal looked at the floor and mumbled, "Yes, it's wonderful."

The priest caught himself and said apologetically, "I'm sorry, Professor. I know you were also close with Pope Celestine. His death—such a tragedy."

"That it was."

When the priest returned to his row, his traveling companion, an assistant priest from his parish, asked him, "Who was that?"

"His name is Calvin Donovan. He's a famous professor of religion at the Harvard Divinity School. He's going to the inauguration too."

"How do you know him?"

"We met once. He remembered who I was. I was quite pleased."

"He knows the Holy Father?" the younger priest asked.

"More than that. They've been friends—good friends—since Da Silva was bishop. Donovan was also friendly with Pope Celestine. I think it's a good thing for our highest clerics to have people outside the Church with whom they can confide. It takes them out of the Vatican bubble."

"So, then. He's a pope whisperer."

"I like that," Father Cardoza said. "Cal Donovan, pope whisperer."

Cal reclined his seat and curled his hand around an icy glass. As soon as he closed his eyes, unpleasant things streaked through his mind, the same images that had been plaguing him these past days. An assassin stalking him through the dark passages of an English manor house. The killer's crumpled body lying beside him on the library floor. Pope Celestine's waxy body in repose at the Vatican Apostolic Palace. Elisabetta's heavily bandaged hands.

He extinguished the grim highlight reel by lifting his eyelids and the glass of vodka, his anesthetic of choice.

He blamed himself for the pope's death. Celestine had been warned about a planned assassination. A hidden document held the key to the plot. Celestine had asked Cal to find it, and he succeeded just as time ran out. His last-second warning may have prevented Celestine from perishing in the fireball that burned Elisabetta's hands, but it couldn't stop the heart attack that took his life. The act would go down in history as an assassination attempt, but that was splitting hairs. It was the violent removal of the leader of over a billion Catholics. Cal was a student of the Church, and he knew its brutal history well. As far as he was concerned, you could add the name of Celestine VI to the long list of murdered and martyred popes.

As the plane flew toward the dawn, the folk songs kept coming, and Cal kept drinking.

Cal's preferred hotel in Rome was the Grand Hotel de la Minerve. He loved the roof terrace overlooking the Pantheon, the elegance of its seventeenth-century architecture, and its long history as a gathering place for visiting artists and intellectuals. And it didn't escape him that the hotel had a particularly topical connection. It had been built as a mansion for the Fonseca family, Roman aristocrats of Portuguese origin.

Tourists were snapping photos of Bernini's *Elephant and*

Obelisk statue in the piazza outside his window. Cal pulled the curtains, showered, and sank into a blissfully soft bed.

The hotel phone caught him mid-dream. The glowing clock surprised him—he'd been asleep for hours.

"Pronto," he said.

He heard an exhalation as if the woman had been holding her breath. "Cal," she said.

"Elisabetta. Hello."

"I do hope I didn't wake you. I saw your flight was on time."

"No, I'm up. It's good to hear from you. How are you? How are your hands?"

"Better. The skin grafts went well. I only have to wear these little gloves. How is your leg?"

"It's fine. I only have to wear this little cast."

Her laughter tickled his ear.

"Emilio and I were wondering if you were free this evening for dinner. We thought Tonnarello, where we went before."

Rome was magnificent on a late-summer evening such as this— the setting sun drenched the ancient cityscape in mellow, amber light. Cal's orthopedic surgeon had advised him to take it easy, but it was called a walking cast, so Cal was damned well going to walk. He was itching to get back to his routine of running by the Charles in the morning and sparring with the Harvard Boxing Club—he'd been its faculty advisor for years. Cal had learned to box in the army during his wayward years between high school and buckling to his father's will by enrolling at Harvard College, where Hiram Donovan was a professor

14

of biblical archaeology. Boxing had always helped Cal blow off steam, and he badly needed to throw some punches right about now.

The low, slanted light managed to make even the muddy Tiber sparkle a little. He crossed it on the Ponte Garibaldi, ignoring his aching shin. The faster he walked, the faster he'd see her again.

He had been in and out of countless relationships in his forty-eight years. He never had to be alone—his looks, his charm, and his glittering academic career guaranteed that. But there was one unobtainable woman, who had captivated him the first time he saw her, and years later, he was still simmering with longing. He wasn't the first man to wonder how Elisabetta had found her way to nunhood. It wasn't just her rare beauty—he found her intellect as stimulating. He had been in a relationship for much of the time he knew her, but recently his girlfriend had gotten fed up with his faltering commitment and voted with her feet. Unfettered, Cal found himself falling hard for Elisabetta, but loving her felt like running into a brick wall, and it left him bloody and raw. The last time he saw her was at Pope Celestine's funeral Mass, and since then she was constantly front of mind. He had been searching for a reason to return to Rome and, perhaps, muster the courage to show his affection when the news of the conclave broke.

He stopped for a moment to rest his throbbing leg and caught sight of his reflection in a shop window. *What an idiot,* he thought. *What the hell is wrong with you? You can't be in love with a nun.*

Elisabetta had grown up on the west bank of the Tiber, and the ancient Tonnarello restaurant in the heart of the Trastevere neighborhood was her family's favorite. When Cal arrived, he found her alone at a corner table.

A nun's shapeless habit drives attention to the face, and hers was lovely. When Pope Celestine broke centuries of tradition and named her the first female private papal secretary, the Italian press discovered that her face sent newspapers and magazines flying off their shelves. La Bella Suor, they called her, the beautiful nun. She wore the black-and-white habit of her order, the Augustinian Sisters, Servants of Jesus and Mary. Their garb was somewhat less restrictive than other orders. She did not wear a wimple, so her cheeks and neck were uncovered, and Cal could see them redden when he reached to brush her gloved hand. Her black veil and white cotton cap were set back more than usual, exposing a silky band of black hair. Until then, he had never seen her hair, though he had fantasized about how it might look, flowing over her bare shoulders.

She spoke in Italian. "Cal, it's wonderful to see you."

"It's wonderful to see you too, Eli."

The day she finally consented to use first names with him was a breakthrough of sorts, or so he had imagined.

"Do you like my little gloves?" she said, wiggling her white fingers. "They're like my first communion gloves when I was a young girl."

"I like them a lot. What do you think about my little cast?" he said, pulling up his trouser leg.

"It suits you." She laughed.

She was treated like royalty here, and the restaurant owner descended on them with a bottle of wine. "Compliments of the house, Sister. Bramito Antinori, from Umbria. It's a very nice one. May I pour for you and your guest?"

"Thank you, Aldo."

"How is the new Holy Father?"

"I would say that he is serene."

"We'll miss having him here. He came often."

"Cardinals can eat out," she said. "Popes not so much."

"I'll make his favorites so you can take them back to the Vatican tonight."

Cal proposed a toast. "To new beginnings," he said, and they clinked glasses.

"Emilio sends his regrets," she said. "He had to meet with the chief of the Polizia di Stato to coordinate some aspects of the security operation for the Mass. It's been nonstop meetings. After what happened—well, we don't want to lose another pope."

Elisabetta's brother, Emilio Celestino, was the inspector general of the Vatican Carabinieri and had been the last pope's personal bodyguard. Cal had gotten to know him during some tense days in Sicily and found him a decent, honorable man.

"We do not," he said.

"He does want to see you while you're here. He talks about you all the time. He'll call."

"Has Emilio's role been clarified?"

"The Holy Father wants him to carry on as before."

"I think that's a good decision."

"Me too, although I'm biased."

Cal capitalized on the unexpected pleasure of being alone with her to open this chess match of the heart with a gambit he'd been contemplating.

"Has he decided about you?"

"I've made the decision myself. He needs his own person as private secretary. I've been helping him during the transition, but we haven't talked about it yet. I plan on asking for my old job back at the Pontifical Commission for Sacred Archaeology. If that can't happen, I'll happily return to teaching. I showed you my old primary school on the Piazza Mastai the last time you were here."

He wet his mouth with wine, swallowed, and leaned in. "Or—" he said.

"Or what?"

"You could try something different."

She laughed. "That sounds mysterious."

"Instead of teaching children, why not teach at a university?"

"Italian universities aren't very interested in having a nun on their faculty."

"It's not so uncommon in America," he said.

"And what would I teach?" He could tell by the lightness of her tone that she wasn't taking him seriously.

"You were trained in Roman archaeology. You're an expert on the catacombs. You had a seat at the table when Celestine divested Vatican art for his charity. You know the Vatican as well as anyone. You shattered its glass ceiling. I can think of a dozen undergraduate courses and graduate seminars you could teach."

"Okay, I'll go home tonight, make a curriculum vitae, and mail it off to American universities," she said with a mocking tone.

"You don't have to do that. I can get you a position as an adjunct professor at the Harvard Divinity School tomorrow."

Her smile dissolved, and their eyes met for an uncomfortable moment until she suddenly blinked in relief, looked toward the entrance, and waved.

"Ah, there's Micaela. When Emilio couldn't come, I invited her."

Elisabetta's sister was a live wire—funny, volatile, opinionated, a woman who lived on the borderland of conventionality and nonconformity. Her spiky, fire-engine-red hair, short skirts, and giant hoop earrings set her miles apart from the other doctors at her hospital.

"Micaela, what a nice surprise," Cal said, hiding his disappointment at the collapse of an intimate evening. "It's good to see you again."

"Lovely to see you too. How's your leg?"

"It's coming along."

The waiter filled her wineglass, and she said, "It looked like you two were having an intense conversation. Sorry to interrupt."

"If you must know, Cal was just inviting me to become a professor at Harvard."

"You should do it," Micaela said without hesitation. "The hell with the Vatican."

"You and I have very different views on the Vatican," Elisabetta said.

"Mine are correct. Bunch of medieval sexists."

"Pope Celestine wasn't," Elisabetta said.

Cal inserted himself into the melee. "The new pope isn't either. I know his views. I think you'll see him push for more inclusivity for women."

"Female priests?" Micaela said, glancing at the menu.

"That might be a stretch," Cal said.

"Well, I don't think it should be," Micaela said. "I'd rather confess to a woman. So, are you going to accept Cal's offer?"

Elisabetta avoided two pairs of probing eyes. "Let's get through the inauguration first. Are we ready to order?"

The dinner conversation bounced along pleasantly. They talked about Carlo, the sisters' father, a mathematician with a lifelong quest to conquer the Goldbach conjecture, one of the most famous unsolved problems in math. The sisters lived in fear of waking up one morning to read that someone else had solved it, depriving the old man of his raison d'être.

Cal regaled them with stories about his friendship with the new pope, how they had met when Da Silva was bishop of Providence, Rhode Island, and how they nurtured their friendship by indulging in the prelate's favorite pastime—fine dining.

Over dessert, Micaela chatted about life as a consultant gastroenterologist at the Gemelli University Hospital. Her husband, Arturo, was an emergency room physician there, but she cast a pall over the table when she said, "Cal, did you know that Arturo was on duty when they brought Pope Celestine in? He knew he was gone, but they worked on him for an hour anyway. Arturo even massaged his heart—can you believe it?"

Elisabetta abruptly got up and left, saying she had to use the ladies' room.

"I think I put my foot in it," Micaela said. "I do that sometimes."

Elisabetta didn't sit when she returned. She had a bag of Tonnarello dishes for Pope John.

"I took care of the bill," she said. "We can go."

"I'm sorry," Micaela said.

"Don't be. It's okay. I've got work to do. I have a driver if you and Cal need a ride."

"I think I'll walk," Cal said. "Nice evening, good for my leg."

"Your hotel is close to where I live," Micaela said. "I'll go with you."

The sisters pecked their goodbyes, Cal got to touch Elisabetta's gloved hand again, and she let him know that a courier would deliver his VIP ticket for the inauguration Mass.

Cal and Micaela were halfway over the Ponte Garibaldi when Micaela stopped and looked over the railing toward the dark river coursing underneath. "You're in love with her, aren't you?" she said.

"Is it that obvious?"

"Yeah, it's obvious."

"Does she know?"

"Of course she does. She had a life before she became a nun. She had a lot of boyfriends. The boy who got killed when she was in graduate school—she was going to marry him. She knows men, believe me."

"Has she told you her feelings about me?"

"I won't answer you. She's my sister. I will say that none of us in her family would be unhappy if she renounced her vows, but she's a strong woman. She does what she wants. So, if you asked me what she's going to do about the Vatican, about your job offer, about you, I would answer: God only knows."

Cal was shaving when his cell phone rang from a blocked number.

"Hello, Cal."

"Rodrigo—I mean, Holy Father. How are you?"

Cal enjoyed the deep chortle rumbling through the line. "Listen, Cal. You're my best friend outside the Church. You must continue to call me Rodrigo, at least in private. It will help keep me grounded."

"That's a tall order."

"Consider it a papal command."

"All right, you're on."

"What are you doing this morning?"

"I was going to swing by the Vatican Archives."

"Could you stop by to see me at ten?"

"Absolutely. Where?"

"I'm still using my office at the Secretariat. After tomorrow, I think I get kicked out."

Cal laughed. "After tomorrow, you can use any office you want."

The Swiss Guards at the Vatican Apostolic Palace checked Cal's name off an authorized visitors' list, wanded him, and escorted him to the main elevator. He got off on the third floor, one above the marbled Clementine Hall where Pope Celestine had suffered his heart attack and where his body had lain in state. A left turn led to the door of the papal apartments that Celestine had eschewed during his pontificate, opting instead for humble rooms in the Vatican guesthouse.

Cal turned right toward the offices of the Secretariat of State, where Monsignor Mario Finale was waiting for him.

Finale had been Da Silva's private secretary at the Secretariat and was fulfilling interim duties. Like the new pope, Finale enjoyed his food. His jovial, round face and volleyball belly gave him a passing resemblance to a younger Da Silva.

"It's a pleasure seeing you again, Professor," Finale said. "The Holy Father is expecting you."

Cal liked to joke that he needed sunglasses whenever he visited these rooms. The furniture was gilded. The brass fixtures gleamed. The wallpaper was gold-flocked. Since his last visit, the only thing that had changed was that his friend now wore white instead of red. He sprang from behind his desk, his white zucchetto sticky-taped to his bald dome, and made a beeline to give Cal a bear hug. Cal had to bend to reciprocate.

"Sit, sit," the pope said. "You want a coffee?"

"I'm good, Rodrigo. Thanks."

"Excellent. You're obeying the papal command. How was your journey?"

"It was noisy. Half of New Bedford was on the plane."

"Marvelous. So many friends have sent felicitations. I wish I could see them all. By the way, I've sent your email for framing: *Second ballot! That's like the Sox winning 16–0 in a no-hitter!*"

"How are you doing?" Cal asked.

"You know, you're the first person to ask me that. It's been a whirlwind—nonstop audiences with diplomats, the press, Curial officials subtly or overtly lobbying me for this and that."

"Well, you look healthy," Cal told the sixty-eight-year-old, "and has anyone told you that you look good in white?"

"That's a relief. One less thing to worry about. Are you on the mend?"

Cal rapped on his cast. "Healing nicely."

"Thank God for that." The pope puckered his mouth, the way he always did when he had something important to say.

"How many years have I known you?"

Cal did the math. "Fifteen."

"And how many meals have we had together in Massachusetts, Rhode Island, Italy, Portugal?"

"Incalculable," Cal said.

Pope John patted his middle. "Yes, incalculable."

"And how many times have we seriously disagreed on a theological, ecclesiastical, or political issue?"

"Not very often. That's probably the reason we've stayed friends."

"Indeed. And that is why I want to tell you about a decision I'm pondering. If you seriously disagree, I might be persuaded to change course. Do you know Cardinal Tosi? Giuseppe Tosi?"

"By name."

"Tosi is the cardinal camerlengo. He's been inside the Curia his entire career, a born administrator. Knows the place inside out. Savvy politician. The camerlengo, as you know, organizes the conclave, and he was the key person during the interregnum. He reports to the College of Cardinals, but he's essentially been governing the Church since Celestine's death. I've seen more of him since the conclave than in all my years as secretary of state. He's been buttering me up something fierce. He wants my old job, wants it badly. He tells me, and it seems true, that after the first ballot failed to give any hope to a conservative candidate, he was instrumental in pulling together a winning coalition that evening."

"You have reservations about him?"

"I do. He's a bit of a wolf in sheep's clothing. He cast himself as a progressive to curry favor with Celestine, but behind the scenes, he was one of the figures who worked to stymie some of his Curial reforms. I fear that he'd be in a position to do my papacy significant damage if I made him cardinal secretary."

Cal shot him a quizzical look. "This can't be your difficult decision, Rodrigo. Of course, I agree with you. You can't promote someone who's going to compromise your agenda."

Seemingly out of the blue, the pope asked, "What do you think about Sister Elisabetta? I know you've had frequent dealings with her."

Cal forced out a quick answer. "I think she was an excellent private secretary. She was a bold and controversial choice for the role. That put her under the microscope, and I think she handled the pressure well and did Celestine proud. I can't say enough good things about her. So if your question is, do you keep her on as your private secretary, I think you'd be pleased with the choice."

"I want Monsignor Finale for that job. We've worked together very efficiently. I'm comfortable with him. No, I've got something else in mind for the good sister. I want to make her my secretary of state."

Cal heard him perfectly well, but he found himself asking, "What?" as a way to gather a few seconds to collect his thoughts.

"Secretary of state," the pope repeated.

"I'm sorry, Rodrigo, if I'm not mistaken, since the seventeenth century, only cardinals have occupied the office."

25

Cal's blank look of disorientation seemed to amuse the pontiff. "No, you are not mistaken. They've all been cardinals."

"To state the obvious, she isn't a priest either," Cal sputtered.

"She is not."

"So, what am I missing? Putting aside any consideration of her qualifications, how can you do something like this?"

"I've done my homework. I can say with certainty that the role of secretary of state is not bound to the sacraments or the priesthood. It has merely been a matter of tradition to bestow the post upon a cardinal. It's been a glorified old boys' network."

"What about canon law?" Cal asked. "There must be some issue embedded in the code."

"I've spoken in confidence with some of our most eminent canon lawyers. The only possible issue is that the secretary of state traditionally exercises authority in the pope's name. Some believe that to do so, the secretary must be ordained. This is a matter of inference, not the black letter of the law. Even if one were to take this position, relatively minor procedural workarounds could be enacted via proclamation. No, it can be done."

"But *why* do it?" Cal asked in exasperation. "You're my friend. I want you to succeed. You have the intellect and humanity to become one of our truly great popes. Doing this will unleash a firestorm. It will, without a doubt, consume the early days of your pontificate, if not all of it."

The pope's chair had some give to it, and he rocked as he answered. "As soon as Celestine died, we both knew there was a chance I could be elected. I've been on all the lists. I've been papabile ever since he made me cardinal secretary. During his reign, Celestine appointed enough electors to the College of Cardinals to ensure the deck was stacked with like-minded progressives. So I began contemplating what I might wish to accomplish if I wore the fisherman's ring. I wonder, was that hubris or pragmatism?"

"Pragmatism, of course."

"Thank you, but maybe a little of both. I know how things work around here. The Curia is designed to throw grit in the gears of change. To achieve something truly transformative, one must strike quickly and boldly. The window of opportunity closes fast. My calculation is that I need to make my move during the first days of the pontificate."

"But why this move?"

"Because I want my legacy to be this: Pope John the Twenty-Fourth did more to elevate the role of Catholic women than any pope in history. The Church has weaponized ordination and used it as a shield to keep women from positions of authority. You know my views better than anyone. How many bottles of wine have we consumed discussing politics?"

"More like, how many cases?" Cal chuckled.

"Exactly. So you know that I do not and will not support the ordination of women into the priesthood. Some to my left would disagree, but I firmly hold that women priests would fundamentally change the nature of Catholicism and would drive a wedge through the Church, perhaps leading to a schism. However, we can begin to refocus the role of female Catholics by elevating a nun—an eminently qualified nun—to the Vatican's most important administrative position. Think of the effect on dioceses all over the world. Nuns and laywomen alike will find a greater voice."

"I'm all for a pope addressing gender inequality," Cal said. "I'm just a little worried to hear that you'd be the one placing his head on the block."

The pontiff put his hand to his throat and said, "I'm so fat I have no neck. It's difficult to chop off my head." Then he pointed toward the frescoed ceiling and the heavens beyond it. "My mother, God rest her soul, was the strong one in my family. My father was a wonderful man, a funny man, but she was the one who put steel in my spine. She will be looking down on me, and she will give her blessing. And besides, for those critics who say this is an act of symbolism only, I will say, no, Sister Elisabetta is completely qualified for the job."

When the pope pounded his desk for emphasis, Cal saw his dream of luring Elisabetta to Cambridge flying away.

"Celestine gave her great authority, and she wielded it with force and grace," the pope said. "When he disagreed with something happening in the Secretariat, he dispatched her to straighten things out with me. She was always respectful to a fault, but she usually got her way. She's tough. We saw that when she was at the Pontifical Commission for Sacred Archaeology as its first female leader in a role that had always belonged to a bishop. She made the hard decisions and took the heat for divesting Vatican treasures for Celestine's charity. She completely understands how the Curia works, so I'm confident she'll naturally adapt to the internal affairs function of the Secretariat. When I took the job, I was an outsider, and it handicapped me for a long while. I've no doubt she'll learn the diplomatic functions quickly. Besides, I appointed many of the bishops and nuncios who'd be working for her, and they are able men. They respect me, so they'll respect her. Or else. We say that the secretary of state's task is to be the eyes, the heart, and the arms of the pope. I would be most comfortable with her in this seat."

The intercom buzzed, and the pope mumbled, "That will be Monsignor Finale." He picked up the phone, told his secretary to give him a few more moments, and began rapidly tapping his fingertips together in a sign of urgency. "So, that's it, Cal. I've made my case. Now I want to hear from you. Should I do this?"

Cal was tied in knots. If he could persuade Elisabetta to come to Cambridge, far from the Vatican mothership, secular forces might chip away at her sacred core. He had stayed up late, drinking and thinking about Micaela's reply to his question about her sister's feelings. *I won't answer you*, she had said. Trying to divine the meaning of this non-answer drove him from despair to elation and back again. With one swing of the pendulum, he imagined Elisabetta moving in with him and loving him. With the opposite swing, he imagined a bottomless pit of unrequited love. But in the here and now, he owed his friend honest counsel.

"I think you should do it, Rodrigo," he heard himself saying. "It's a courageous move. It's the right thing to do, and she'll be amazing at the job. You'll have a formidable partner to make your reforms happen. Will you make some powerful enemies? Yes, you will. Will you make a lot of friends? You'd better believe it. Many Catholics and non-Catholics are going to be very happy with you. And needless to say, I will support you in any way I can."

The pope smiled broadly and pushed himself from his chair.

"I'm pleased you see it the way I do, Cal. Extremely pleased. You've made my next appointment easier."

"Who's it with?" Cal asked.

The pope winked at him mischievously. "Sister Elisabetta, of course. She's waiting for me in the anteroom. Say hello to her on your way out."

3

Northern Oasis, Egypt, 79 CE

Shakir, the mask maker, usually kept his workplace tidy, but the tragedy that had befallen the civil servant Senbi and his family had thrown him into a tizzy, and his workshop looked ransacked. Wooden molds of all sizes—large ones for men, medium for women, small for children—were off their pegs and scattered on the benches. Jars of paint and gilding and strips of linen were everywhere. Shaping tools were strewn about. A pot of lime plaster had spilled, and a puddle of gesso was hardening on the dirt floor.

The mask-making shop was in the center of Bawiti, the most populous and wealthiest town in the oasis. During the day, when Shakir looked up from his workbench, he saw shoppers and merchants and carts of goods passing by his open door and heard constant jabbering and haggling.

Night had come, the street was quiet as a tomb, and Shakir was still at his bench. He worked by oil lamp, saturating the linen strips in gesso and applying them to a mold, building up layer after layer of what would become

31

Senbi's hair and forehead. All the while, he listened for the return of his apprentice. Jabari had been gone since the first light of day, and Shakir was worried—not for the boy's safety, but his own. If the masks were not ready for delivery in a fortnight, the priests could shut down his business, and he might be beaten, maybe even imprisoned. Shakir's mask-making rival, Ahmose, had initially received the commission, but a fire in Ahmose's shop destroyed all the works in progress, and the priests turned to Shakir. They demanded a guarantee that he could finish the job in time for the entombment. The seventy-day mummification was nearing its completion. The carpenters had made the coffins. Stonemasons had carved the sarcophagi. The burial chamber had been cut and plastered, and the grave goods, including dozens of mummified cats and ibises, were assembled. Because of Senbi's nobility, there was speculation that the vizier himself would attend the ceremony. Such an enormous task, Shakir had said, stroking his pointy beard, so little time. And he hemmed and hawed until the priests did what he hoped they would do—they raised the price.

Now he wished he had declined the commission. A promised delivery of bolts of linen had failed to materialize, and without linen, the remaining masks simply could not be made. He had molded only two of the small ones, and he was halfway through Senbi's, but there wasn't enough cloth to finish it. And there were five more to do! Such was the scope of the massacre. One of the slaves serving in Senbi's noble household had gone stark raving mad, stabbing Senbi, his wife, and their six children in a frenzy of rage as they lay in their beds before turning the bloody knife on himself.

Shakir's mouth was parched with worry. Eight funeral masks commissioned, and not enough linen to make them.

Finally, he heard the braying of a mule, and he ran to the door and peered into the night to see if the animal was laden with bolts of cloth. His jaw went slack.

"Nothing! You found nothing?"

Jabari stood by the animal, afraid to approach his master. "I went to all the merchants in the town you told me to see, sire. None had linen to sell. So I rode the mule to Qasr and inquired there. No linen, they said. So then I went to Harrah. Also, no linen. Everyone said there was a problem with the flax plants. Bugs, they said. Bugs ate the crop."

"Useless boy! Idiot!" Shakir raged. "Where is my stick?"

"Please do not whip me, sire. I tried my best."

Shakir couldn't find the switch in the darkness, and a thought distracted him from corporal punishment. "I could fashion the masks in the old way, the way my master and those who came before made them."

The apprentice took a few cautious steps forward. "What is the old way, sire?"

"Instead of linen, they mixed papyrus with the plaster."

"Do you wish me to buy papyrus in the morning?" the boy asked.

"These days, it is far too dear. If I had to buy it, I would lose money on the job."

"Then where shall we get it?"

"Do you know the Christian houses in the desert? They have a room filled with papyrus scrolls. Once, when I was passing by, I saw them with my own eyes. Go there now. Sneak in when they are sleeping. Fill a sack with scrolls, and bring them to me."

The boy began to tremble. "What if they catch me? They will beat me to death."

Shakir raised an arm. "If you do not do as I command, I will beat you to death."

Mary Magdalene had been gone for eleven years. The scribe Isaiah had passed away in the spring. At Mary's burial, Leah had invoked Isaiah's name. "Thanks to our beloved Isaiah, we have copies of the Gospel of Mary in our scriptorium. We have given visiting pilgrims codices to carry into the world, and we will continue the practice into the future. Thus, Christians have learned the truth about the Blessed Lady, and she will take her rightful place in history."

Since Mary's passing, Leah's community had grown in size, and the congregation could no longer fit inside her house. The solution was a church built of limestone with a simple altar and low wooden benches. The roof had a steep pitch, giving volume to the interior and bringing a sense of Heaven to the space above their heads. When the boy, Jabari, approached the compound, the church and other buildings were dark and quiet. He tied the mule to a bush and crept closer on foot. His master had described the scriptorium, and he looked for a low, rectangular structure with a large, eastward-facing window to let in morning light. On a clear night such as this, a full moon was both friend and enemy. It helped him find the scriptorium, but it also made it hard to conceal himself.

He prayed no one would leave their dwellings to empty a bladder.

Jabari pushed the scriptorium door gently and was relieved it was not bolted and the hinge pegs did not squeal. The moon was high, so the window did little to brighten the room, and he had to wait for his eyes to adjust to the murk. Soon, shapes emerged. A long table with benches. Pots of ink. Jars of quills. And against one of the walls, a row of wooden cases, packed with scrolls and codices. The boy ran a finger over a pile of papyrus scrolls and then pulled open the drawstring of his hemp sack. He began grabbing and stuffing scrolls, depleting an entire section before moving on. The next set of shelves was full of codices, some unbound, leather-clad, and he shoveled all of them into the sack. When the bag was full, he tested its weight and could not hoist it over his shoulder. He had to drag it to the door, and with the moon revealing his great crime, he tugged the sack across sandy soil to his waiting mule.

When the boy appeared at the workshop door, Shakir rushed over and snatched the bag by its drawstring. "Were you seen?" he demanded.

"No, sire. I saw no one, and no one saw me."

The mask maker lugged the bag to his workbench and grunted as he lifted it. "It is heavy. That is good."

"Did I do well, sire?"

"Let us see."

Shakir began greedily grabbing codices and scrolls as if he

were starving and these were loaves of bread, and he made a mound of papyrus on his bench.

The boy repeated his question.

"Yes, yes, you did well," Shakir replied. "I might even let you sleep a little longer in the morning. Now, watch what I do. For tomorrow, you will perform this task. Then I will complete the mask of Senbi and begin the remaining masks."

He unfurled a scroll and began ripping it into strips. "You see the size of this?" he said, holding the fragment above the oil lamp. "The length of my hand and as wide as four fingers. That is the best size for mixing with gesso. Show me you can do it."

The boy took hold of one of the leather-bound codices. "Why are some in leather, others not?"

"I cannot say," his master said. "I am not a Christian."

Jabari opened it and scanned the peculiar, slanting symbols on the first leaf. "Do you know what it says, sire?"

"I have no earthly idea," Shakir said. "Go on, make the pieces as I have done."

The boy tore the first page from its stitched binding and ripped a length of papyrus from it. "Is this good?" he asked.

Shakir plucked it from the boy's fingers and inspected it. "That will do. Tomorrow morning, you will fill the sack."

He dropped the piece of papyrus into the open mouth of the sack, and as it fluttered down, they were oblivious that slanted symbols on the fragment bore the Greek words THE GOSPEL OF MARY.

Leah was in her house, attending to her morning ablutions, when she heard a bloodcurdling scream coming from the scriptorium. She ran outside and found the scribe, Amos, running toward her, his face contorted in anguish.

"Gone! Gone!" he cried.

"What is gone?" Leah asked.

"Our sacred texts, all of them! Stolen!"

Amos's howls carried in the wind, and by the time Leah entered the scriptorium, the entire community had assembled, crowding through the door. Leah inspected the bare shelves and the few scrolls left behind on the ground.

She said, "Who would have done this?"

Quintus pushed his way inside. After Mary's death, the former Praetorian guard and Mary's loyal protector had been insane with grief, but in time, he transferred his full devotion to Leah. He was still as strong as a team of oxen and was the community's volatile protector. Whenever the Egyptian traders in Bawiti cheated them or the Roman overlords subjected them to harassment, Quintus was the one who called for retribution. And it always fell to Leah to calm him by imparting the teachings of Jesus.

"You know what our Savior taught, Quintus," she would say gently. "He said, 'Blessed are the peacemakers, for they will be called children of God.'"

Quintus's face would burn, and he would counter that this merchant was patently dishonest or that Roman soldier had pushed one of their lads into a dung heap, and he could not let the transgression pass. Leah would place a small hand on the slab that was his shoulder and say, "You have been blessed with great strength and courage and a sense of righteousness—

more than any man or woman among us. And whenever you can quench the fires within you and turn the other cheek, you will find yourself closer to the Lord than any of us."

"I will tell you who did this," Quintus roared. "It was the wine merchant Flavius and his sons."

The Egyptians were avid beer makers and consumed it liberally. But the Christians preferred wine, so they had to trade with the local Roman merchants who imported it from Rome. Wine diluted with water or sweetened with honey was a staple at Leah's table.

"Why do you say it was Flavius?" Leah asked.

"Last week, we went to his shop to buy one amphora of Falernum and one amphora of Albanum. The price he wanted was double the last time. He said it was because a merchant ship had foundered and its wine cargo was lost. When products are scarce, the prices go up, he said. We argued, but we paid. Later, we talked to a man leaving the shop with an amphora of Falernum. We asked him what he paid. It was half what we were charged!"

"What did you do?" Leah asked.

"We confronted Flavius and demanded he return the money we overpaid. He refused. I may have pushed him to the ground."

"May have?" Leah asked.

Quintus dropped his head. "I pushed him."

"Oh, Quintus," she said.

Another man said, "The six sons of Flavius came to his defense and began beating us. We had to protect ourselves, but we quickly left on our own accord. That is when Flavius threatened us."

"What did he say?" Leah asked.

"That he would have his revenge."

Quintus raised his head and pushed ringlets from his eyes. "And here is his revenge. The sacking of our holy scriptorium. Our manuscripts, gone. The work of Amos and Isaiah, gone. So now, I think it is our turn for revenge."

The younger men mumbled their approvals.

Leah said, "We have no proof it was Flavius. And if we did, it would be a matter for the Roman soldiers. True Christians do not engage in violence. Jesus said, 'All who take up the sword will perish by the sword.' You may speak with people in Bawiti to see if anyone knows who committed this crime, but you must do no violence."

Quintus set his jaw and said, "Yes, My Lady."

Amos, the scribe, was getting on in years and suffered from headaches. He sat upon his writing stool, holding his forehead between ink-stained hands. "What shall we do about our manuscripts?"

Leah lifted her voice so that all might hear. "Today, we will rest and pray. Tomorrow, we will buy fresh papyrus, and, God willing, Amos will begin anew, setting down that which we know by heart: the teachings of Jesus, his apostles, and Mary."

That night, Quintus could not sleep. He rose from his rush mat, crept away from the house where the unmarried men lived, and made for the church and the small storeroom within it. He lifted an amphora of wine kept there, poured ruby liquid into a sacramental cup, downed it, and filled it again. After his sixth cup, his anger got the better of him.

He arrived on foot at Bawiti in the dead of night, only a little less drunk than when he had left the church. Flavius's wine shop was a mud-brick building in the Roman quarter, crammed between a harness maker and an apothecary. Quintus sniffed the air and followed the scent of smoke across the empty lane, where he found a smoldering campfire on a piece of barren ground. Blackened goat ribs, remnants from a late-night feast, lay in ash and embers. Leah's words of peace echoed in his head. With fists clenched, he fought the dueling sides of his nature. But his anger prevailed, and he tore a strip of cloth from the hem of his pallium and lit it from a glowing chunk of wood.

The door to the shop was latched from within, but it took one push from his battering-ram shoulder for the latch to splinter. The strip of cotton was burning close to his hand. He looked for something else to light and found a stack of papyri on the countertop. At first he mistook them for some of the stolen codices, but they were only the shop's accounts. As the flaming cloth reached his fingers, he set the paper alight.

Quintus pushed the flaming papyri off the counter toward the wall where barrels of wine and amphorae were racked, and he exulted as the first barrel caught. Soon the flames were leaping toward the rafters. Before the ceiling ignited, he grabbed an amphora of wine and calmly walked across the lane to watch his handiwork from the barren piece of land. As he drank, he could see Flavius and his sons arriving from their houses to the rear of the shop. Their shouts of alarm and feeble attempts to quench the blaze amused him. He was unbothered when the flames jumped to the harness shop. The whole Roman quarter could burn down for all he cared. Rome killed Jesus. Rome killed Simon Peter and Paul. He raised the amphora and poured a river of wine into his mouth. Rome could go to Hades.

At the first light of day, the extent of the devastation was apparent. An entire row of buildings had burned to the ground, and a gaggle of distraught shopkeepers surveyed the damage. Then, after a time, one of the Romans spotted a figure lying on the ground across from them. The fellow went for a look and scampered back to alert Flavius and his sons.

"Isn't that Quintus, the Christian you squabbled with last week?"

The sons picked up rocks and surrounded Quintus, who was snoring and cradling one of their amphorae.

One son, Manius, a muscular twenty-two-year-old man, kicked his leg and said, "Quintus, wake up, you dog. We will not kill a man in his sleep."

Quintus heard someone shouting in Latin in his dreams, and he imagined he was back in Rome, back in the army. He opened his eyes at the next kick and saw a fist with a rock coming toward his face.

In the slice of time between the first blow and the one that killed him, Quintus had a memory of the night they arrived at Leah's house after crossing the Egyptian desert. He had lifted Mary from her donkey, and as her feet were touching the ground, she looked at him with sad, dry eyes and said, "Dear Quintus, we are home."

It took two weeks for General Gaius Aeterius Fronto to reach the Northern Oasis after learning of the arson in Bawiti and the uproar among the Romans. Fronto, it must be said, had grown bored with city life, and turmoil in the countryside seemed like a fine reason to stretch his legs. And so he mobilized a legion of one hundred twenty men to ride to the oasis.

He met with the ruined merchants and heard their complaints upon his arrival.

"Before he became a Christian dog, the man who did this was a Praetorian guard," Flavius, the wine merchant, said. "Did you know this?"

The general nodded. "I was told."

"He was the biggest troublemaker," one of Flavius's sons said, "but there are others among them."

"The apothecary perished in the fire," Flavius said. "Burned to a crisp. Did you know this too?"

"I was informed."

"Only the gods know what goes on there, out in the desert," the harness maker said.

"They come to town, and they are arrogant, and they expect us to cut our prices for them," said the cloth merchant.

"They need to pay for what they did," Flavius said. "They destroyed my business. "Who knows when my next shipment of wine will arrive. How am I to survive?"

Manius, who had bashed Quintus's head, said, "They must be punished."

The general, an imposing man with a red beard, arose from his crouch and said, "That is why I am here."

On the ride to the Christian enclave, General Fronto had a question for the local commander. "Tell me, Sextus, what do they call their abode?"

"Before, it was called the House of Leah. Now, they call it the Monastery of Mary Magdalene. She died here some years ago."

The general said, "I saw her once, in Rome. A plain woman." The greenery of the oasis was behind them. Fronto surveyed the featureless desert from his saddle and said, "The gods have forsaken this place."

The legion came upon the monastery, and Fronto ordered it encircled. Children playing in the dirt ran to their houses. Women cried out, and men impotently bolted doors and latched shutters. Some of the younger men, friends of Quintus, entered through the rear of Leah's house and told her they would fight if they had to.

"Do not provoke them," she said. "I will speak to their commander."

"We knew this day would come," one of them said.

"That is so," she replied.

Fronto towered over Leah from his white steed.

"I am General Gaius Aeterius Fronto, prefect of Egypt," he said in Latin. "You are Leah, the matriarch of this community?"

She answered honorifically in his language.

"Your man, Quintus, did great damage to the Romans of Bawiti. I am here to collect just recompense."

"Quintus paid for his sin with his life," she said.

"More is owed. The apothecary was killed. Merchandise was lost. Buildings were destroyed."

"What would you have us do?" she said.

"How many live here?" he asked.

"There are about seventy."

"How many are young men?"

The question alarmed her, and her jaw began to tremble. A gust of wind blew the veil from her head. "There are a dozen."

"Here is my judgment," the general said. "Deliver to me forthwith five thousand silver denarii and five strong men. The men will be sold into slavery at one thousand denarii per head. Thus, all told, the Roman citizens who were barbarized will receive ten thousand denarii as just compensation."

Leah eyed the sea of soldiers and said defiantly, "We have a few coins here, and you can have them, but you cannot take any of our sons. The sins of one man are not the sins of the entire community."

"Did Quintus, the Roman, have a family?"

"We were his family."

She had fallen into his trap, and the general smiled. "Under Roman law, it is the responsibility of the family to compensate victims of a crime."

"We are not Romans," she said. "We are followers of Christ."

"Like it or not, this is Roman territory, and I am the representative of the emperor. I will enforce the law as I see fit."

"We will give you every coin we have. You cannot have our men," she said.

The general turned his horse to confer with Centurion Florus. "She is a strong woman and pleasing to the eye," he said. "It pains me, but we must do what is right. Round up the young men and put them in chains. Burn the buildings. Put all others to the sword."

"Children too?" Florus asked.

"Children too."

"What will be given to the aggrieved Roman citizens?"

The general turned his horse. "The men as slaves, the livestock, and this."

He drew his sword, kicked the flanks of his steed, and took Leah's head in one stroke while she was in the middle of a silent prayer.

4

The present, Cairo, Egypt

When Samia Tedros returned to Cairo, she secured a position as a junior conservator at the Egyptian Museum. The job was beneath her qualifications, but it was the best she could find under the circumstances. During her undergraduate years, the papyrus restoration laboratory had been her home away from home, and returning to it was bittersweet.

While she had been abroad, the gleaming Grand Egyptian Museum in Giza had opened its doors. The old museum in Tahrir Square took on a more prosaic role as an antiquities storehouse and research facility. The tourists were gone, the exhibitions hollowed out. Even her old papyrus lab was a shadow of its former self because the administrators had moved the bulk of its collection to the modern facility in Giza. When she was a student, her supervisors had allowed her to work on important texts. In her new job, she was lucky to work on scraps.

On a Saturday such as this, the old museum used to be thick with visitors and bristling with security, but when she flashed

46

her staff credentials, the listless guard let Samia and her guest enter with little more than a grunt.

Their footsteps echoed in the emptied-out great hall, and her companion, Dodo Shamoun, a sprig of a man in skinny jeans and untucked shirt, turned to her and said, "That was easy."

Back home in Egypt, Samia dressed conservatively in a headscarf and a long, baggy dress that hid her shapely figure.

"It's not a target for terrorists anymore," she said. "And all the great treasures are gone."

"Let's pray we find some little treasures," Dodo said.

She used her keycard to enter the papyrus lab and flicked the lights.

"No security cameras," Dodo said, looking around.

"When it was busy, the staff, mostly women, objected. They thought the male guards would watch them. There's no point now."

Dodo wandered to a rack of drawers and pulled one out. Inside were plastic boxes, each with hundreds of tiny papyrus fragments. "What about this stuff?" he asked.

She rushed over and angrily shut the drawer. "Believe me, everything's been picked over, and all the important pieces went to Giza. There's nothing that would interest you."

"Too bad," he said. "It's easier than cartonnage. Where are the masks?"

"Down the hall. Stay here and don't touch anything. I'll check to make sure no one's working in the storeroom."

Samia had received her undergraduate degree from the Cairo University faculty of archaeological conservation. As a member of Egypt's Coptic Christian minority, she gravitated to Coptic manuscripts and wrote her senior thesis on third-century biblical papyri. Her ultimate goal had been to get her PhD abroad and emigrate to the United States, where one of her uncles had settled, and her wish had come true six years earlier when Harvard accepted her into a graduate program.

She returned to the papyrus lab and took Dodo to a temperature-controlled room with floor-to-ceiling storage.

He greedily surveyed the racks. "Where do we start?"

The time had come for words to turn to deeds, and Samia froze. How had things come to this? Not long ago, she had been flying high. She had earned her doctorate and had high hopes of getting a job at a prestigious American university. Her family in Cairo was healthy, and despite a bad economy, they were afloat. Then the rejection letters started to arrive one by one, until the last rejection sealed her fate. Her student visa was expiring, and without a job, she had no choice—she had to pack her bags and leave for home. Not long after she returned, her little sister got ill, and Samia's unhappiness turned to desperation.

She was never sure who led Dodo to her, but it must have been someone who knew about her situation. Now she wished she'd hung up the phone when he explained what he wanted, but she was ripe for his entreaties. She needed money, and he offered it. What he wanted her to do was a crime, and worse, a betrayal of trust, but she asked herself, what was more important, a few middling artifacts or her sister's life?

"What's the matter with you?" Dodo asked.

She had come to loathe this diminutive man with his coarse mannerisms and his incongruously dainty beard. "I don't know if I can do this," she said.

"Too late for that, sister. How much did you say the private hospital wants for a transplant?"

"Twenty-five thousand dollars," she said.

"You can make that with one good piece. If we get lucky and find something nice today, you'll never see me again. So, where do we start?" On repetition, his question sounded like a threat. Her quivering lip did nothing to soften Dodo's tone. "Believe me. You don't want me as an enemy."

Her chest heaved. "We'll look here first."

The funeral masks of pharaohs were made of gold, glass, and precious stones. Non-royal Egyptians were afforded more mundane treatment. Their masks were humble papier-mâché, but because of their method of construction, they were as good as gold to certain collectors. Ancient mask makers used strips of linen or recycled papyrus, mixed them with gesso, an amalgam of animal glue, chalk, and white pigment, and pressed them in layers onto molds in the form of a face. The artisans then overlaid this compressed structure, the cartonnage, with plaster, and lastly, painted the face of the deceased on it. There was a lucrative market for these masks, for if the papyrus strips bore writing, these fragments of contracts, financial records, philosophies, scriptures, poetry, and proverbs were highly desirable to researchers, museums, and private collectors. Dodo Shamoun, the antiquities broker, was after these snippets of history.

Samia pulled out a drawer and lifted the lid from a cardboard box, revealing the face of a woman with golden skin tones, flowing brown hair, black eyes lined in blue, and a red, gold, and azure breastplate.

"Look how beautiful she is," she muttered. "Do you even know why they made the masks?"

Dodo growled a non-response.

"It was to help the soul find the body in the afterworld so it could return to it," she said softly.

"All I want to know is how old it is."

Samia consulted the index card in the box. "Second century CE."

"Too recent," he said.

She returned the mask and opened another box to find another female face.

"Third century CE," she said.

"Too recent," Dodo said.

She kept going through drawers until she discovered an older mask from the second century BCE of a pale young boy with royal blue eyes.

Dodo lit up. "Give it to me."

Samia hesitated.

"What's the matter? Let me see."

"He's such a precious boy," she said mournfully.

"It's a mask, not a boy," he said, grabbing the box.

He turned the mask over and opened the blade of a small folding knife.

"Please don't," she cried.

He pointed the knife at her. "Listen to me. You knew what you were getting yourself into. Think about your sister. You want her to get well, don't you?"

Samia mutely watched him scrape the underside of the mask with his blade and look through a magnifying loupe into the gouge he had made. "Yes," he hissed. "There's writing. I can't tell the language. You look."

She took the loupe and bent over to inspect the exposed

bit of papyrus. "It's hieratic, what you'd expect for something this age."

"Good, we'll take this one," he said. "Find one more. We'll do two at once."

Samia sorted through masks that were all too recent until she came upon a face so lifelike it almost made her gasp. It was a man with a serene gaze, large searching eyes, a natural, flesh-colored complexion, and a traditional chisel-shaped false beard. The index card said that his mummy was one of six found in 1989 in a tomb at the Bahariya Oasis. The Egyptian Museum had procured this mummy. The others went to Alexandria. His remains were radiocarbon dated to 70–80 CE, and his sarcophagus bore the name Senbi.

Dodo perked up when she announced the date.

"First century is always interesting," he said.

"He's too recent," she said protectively. This face emanated power and charisma, and she didn't want the loathsome man to touch it. "The practice of using recycled papyrus in burial masks ended with the reign of Emperor Augustus in 14 CE," she said. "They switched to linen. Cartonnage made with papyrus has never been found after Augustus. Don't waste your time."

"First century is always interesting," he repeated in a sing-song. "Maybe the dates were off a little." He ignored her protestations, took the box from the drawer, and set about scraping and examining the underside of the mask. "What do you call that?" he cried triumphantly, handing her the magnifying glass.

Samia had a look and choked on her words. "I don't

understand how this is possible. The museum carbon dating is very reliable."

"I think there's writing on it," he said. "What is it?"

She had another go at the loupe and said, "My God, it's Greek."

Dodo raised a fist into the air and said, "Do you know what first-century Greek can mean?"

She nodded that she did.

"I've dreamt of a day such as today. You may be able to buy your sister a kidney after all."

Samia slowly shuffled to the sink as a condemned prisoner might and filled a basin with soapy water.

"We can do this without destroying it. There's a technique for extracting the cartonnage from the overlying plaster."

"I know, I know," Dodo said, "but it takes a week. I'm not waiting. I'm here, and I want the papyrus now. You are not inspiring trust, sister. I fear your commitment is wavering. Please don't make me force you."

Senbi stared at her as she slowly lowered his face into the basin. He spoke to her. *Why are you doing this to me? I died once. Must I die again?* She felt as if she were holding a man underwater until he drowned, and she choked on tears as the plaster and cartonnage softened in her hands and turned into formless brown mush.

Dodo was hanging over her stooped shoulders. "Good," he said. "There's no turning back. Keep going."

Samia had never before gone fishing in cartonnage goop, but she was an expert in handling papyrus and knew what to do. She began gently peeling layers apart and laying them out on blotting paper.

"It's mostly linen," she said.

She was immersed in her task and unaware that Dodo had stepped aside to make a video while she worked.

"The papyrus is in there somewhere," Dodo said. "We both saw it."

"Let me work," she said.

The outermost layers were all linen. Samia kept peeling until she saw the unmistakable fibrous texture of papyrus. She used forceps to separate it from a layer of linen. The fragment was the size of her hand.

"Is that it?" Dodo asked.

"Yes, that's it," she said, laying it on a fresh piece of blotting paper.

"Tell me it's Greek."

She spent long moments studying the four rows of angular, reddish letters. "It is Greek."

Dodo closed his eyes and mouthed a silent thank-you. "What does it say?"

She lied to him. "I don't read Greek."

"A scholar like you?"

She snapped back, "I read hieratic, Demotic, and Coptic. What can you read?"

"I read the language of money. If this is biblical, it will be a language writ large."

"I'm sorry, I can't help you."

He kept recording his video as he talked. "Give it to me. It would be perfect for an American collector I know who specializes in biblical texts. He will have people who know Greek."

She remained hunched over the workbench. "You can't take it. It's too fragile. It will fall apart. There are procedures I must perform to preserve it, but they take some time. I also need to prepare a sample for dating. You want dating, don't you?"

"Fine," he said, sounding like a child told he must wait to open a present. "Out of my way so I can take a picture."

He elbowed her aside and held his phone over the wet papyrus. There was nothing she could do to stop him.

The night before the inauguration Mass, Cal was at a cocktail party at a friend's apartment in Rome, where the guests, a collection of academics, literati, and journalists, were gently and not so gently pumping him for insights into the new pontiff. A particularly aggressive reporter had him backed into a corner when his phone chimed. He would have used a spam call to get out of this fellow's clutches, but the caller was known to him, and he gladly excused himself.

"Samia," he said. "How are you? Are you in Cairo?"

"Yes, I am. Am I bothering you, Professor? It sounds like you're with people."

"I'm at a party in Rome, but I can talk."

"Oh, I'm so sorry. I thought I'd find you in Cambridge. I wouldn't have called so late if I knew you were in my time zone."

"I came over for Pope John's inauguration."

"Of course. Your good friend. How marvelous, Professor."

Samia had been the only grad student who refused to call him by his first name, and her formality still amused him. He thought her thesis work had been rock-solid, and he enthusiastically endorsed her applications for faculty positions elsewhere. However, she had ignored his advice to broaden her job search to include some lesser universities, and he wasn't surprised when she came up empty.

"How can I help you?" he asked.

"If you recall, I'm working at the Egyptian Museum again, and I've happened upon quite an early Greek papyrus."

"Oh yes? What is it?"

"I'm working on it, but I need help interpreting two words I've never come across. As you know, my Greek takes a backseat to my Coptic. I thought there was no one better to ask than you."

"What words?"

"They are ?ρχιερε?ς μέγιστος."

Cal effortlessly rolled into teaching mode. "You've got yourself an interesting couplet, Samia. If you were to romanize them, you'd have *archireús mégistos* — *archireús*, meaning archpriest, and *mégistos*, meaning highest. So, highest archpriest. It's what the Romans referred to as *pontifex maximus*. That's a fascinating term for an early papyrus. How early is it?"

"Possibly 70–80 CE."

"What's the provenance?"

"Cartonnage."

"Makes no sense. That's too late for papyrus to be in masks."

"I know. I'm trying to figure it out. I've sent it for dating. Can I get back to you when I know more?"

"You're not going to tell me what the rest of it says, are you?"

"I promise to call you as soon as I've figured out this puzzle, Professor. I'm most grateful for your help."

Samia stared at the timer on the lab's drying oven. There were a couple of hours left, so she called home.

"Mama, I'll be working at the museum until eleven or so. Don't wait up for me."

"Be sure you take a taxi. I don't want you on the bus so late."

"I will. How was Paisi's dialysis today?"

"The same problems as always, poor thing. She's been sleeping since she came home."

Samia switched off most of the lights, sat at her workstation in near darkness, and thought, *How can I let Dodo Shamoun, this heathen, take this treasure? Which is more valuable—my sister or this papyrus?* And she pondered that question until she dozed off, head on arms.

A ding from the timer woke her, and she wearily opened the oven door to check on the papyrus gently desiccating between sheets of blotting paper. The fragment was dry as a bone and brittle, and its thick brushstrokes had turned a deeper shade of rust.

She slowly reread the four lines, although she had already memorized them. Then, lingering over the word Μαγδαληνή, the woman from Magdala, she thought, *Samia, look what you have found! Does this not change everything? How can the world ever be the same again?*

5

Cal's plan had been to fly to Boston the day after Pope John's inauguration, but under the circumstances, he lengthened his reservation by a couple of days. The Vatican was about to be under verbal assault, and he wanted to be there to help in any way he could. At the post-inaugural reception at the Paul VI Audience Hall, Monsignor Finale found him in conversation with Cardinal Macy of New York and said, "The Holy Father would like a word."

Macy, a sequoia of a man who towered over everyone in the hall, seemed to think the summons was directed at him and told Cal they should continue their conversation later. When Finale politely told him that it was Cal whom the pontiff wished to see, the cleric pointed toward another cardinal and said, "Yes, yes, I meant I needed to speak with Cardinal Marcolini."

The pope was sequestered in a small speaker's preparation room off the hall with a nattily dressed man with graying temples. As the pontiff made introductions, Cal noticed the fellow was running his thumb in a circular motion over the pads of his adjacent fingers, a nervous tell if ever there was one. Silvio Licheri, the director of the Press Office of the Holy See, had joined the section directly from university and had worked his way through the ranks. The Press Office was an organ of the Secretariat of State, so Licheri and the new pope already had a working relationship.

The pope's Italian was good, but he was more comfortable in English. "We're going to announce Sister Elisabetta's appointment tomorrow morning at eight. A private message will be sent to cardinals shortly beforehand."

"She accepted," Cal said.

"This morning, after a prayerful night. She let me know before the Mass, a nice gift."

Cal clamped his lips. He had been hoping for another outcome but was prepared for this one. "How much time are you going to give the cardinals before the press release goes out?"

Licheri said, "We've been debating this. Of course, the Holy Father wishes to be respectful and provide some time for contemplation, but there will be leaks, if not from certain eminences who might not support the appointment, then from their staffs."

"Silvio tells me we can expect tweets within minutes," John said.

"That is why I recommend notifying the cardinals no earlier than fifteen minutes in advance," Licheri said.

"Not a long time, but it's the thought that counts," Cal said, eliciting a belly laugh from the pope.

"Tell him, Silvio! Isn't that exactly what I said?"

Licheri smiled weakly. "It is, indeed, Holy Father. We could make an embellishment by giving the Council of Cardinal Advisers a longer heads-up."

The Council, also known as the C8, were the eight cardinals handpicked to form the inner circle of the papacy.

"I can't do that," John said. "Celestine appointed everyone on the C8. I haven't decided who among them I'll reinstate. I don't want to send a false signal. No, we'll treat all the eminences equally."

"I think that's the right decision," Cal said.

"Silvio has a draft press release that's a good start. Cal, I'd be grateful if you could take a look at it. I'd like to have the perspective of someone outside the firm, as it were. Every word will be scrutinized to divine whether her appointment is an isolated move or a prelude to a more radical overhaul of Church practices. Can you work with Silvio on this?"

"I'm at your disposal, Silvio," Cal said.

"Thank you, Cal," the pope said, checking to see if his zucchetto had shifted. "I believe I'm obligated to mingle a while longer, at least until my rooms are ready and I can put my feet up."

"This is another, smaller, but highly symbolic issue," Licheri said. "Pope Celestine made a conspicuous show of modesty. His residency at the guesthouse was emblematic of that. People will ask if your choice to occupy the papal apartment represents a philosophical shift."

The corners of the pope's eyes crinkled. "Simply tell your journalist friends the truth, Silvio," he said. "Tell them I refuse to take all my meals at the guesthouse cafeteria, as wholesome as their cooking may be."

"Yes, well, I'd prefer to frame the matter as an homage to

tradition," Licheri said humorlessly. "It will help balance the Sister Elisabetta announcement."

"Whatever you think best. After you and the professor finish massaging the press release, please let me see it."

⌾══════⌾

Cal wasn't sure that Licheri was delighted to have a copy editor assigned to him, but the fellow kept his private opinions close to the vest and comported himself professionally. On their brief walk from the Apostolic Palace to the Press Office on Via della Conciliazione, Cal tried to engage him in some chitchat.

"Interesting times," Cal said.

"Indeed," was the bland response.

"How do you think the announcement will be received?"

Licheri swiped his keycard and politely held the door to his building open. "It will be a catastrophe."

The Press Office staff looked on with curiosity as their boss led a stranger to his inner sanctum and deployed the privacy blinds. The office was a window into Licheri's personality— he organized books by subject, laid papers and folders on his desk at perfect right angles, and kept a spare dress shirt and tie on a hanger on the off chance he stained them over lunch. There was a conference table in the corner, and he offered Cal the chair facing the street where stragglers from the Mass continued to vacate St. Peter's Square.

Licheri slid a folder toward him containing the draft press release and said, "The Holy Father told me you support this initiative. Clearly, he takes your counsel."

"We respect each other's views. I told him that I endorsed

the reasons behind his decision, but I made it quite clear that there would be consequences that might eclipse or imperil other elements of his agenda."

Licheri removed his suit jacket, placed it on a hanger, and frowned as he flicked a crumb from a lapel. "There will be chaos."

"That's a bit dramatic, don't you think?"

Licheri took his seat and looked hard at Cal. "Whatever we say, however much we tell people that this move isn't a prelude to allowing women to become priests, conservatives within the Church will not believe us. I fear this issue will stir the beast of schism."

Cal chose his words carefully. "I believe the pope when he says that he intends to empower women to have greater roles in the life of the Church, not to change the landscape of the priesthood. You don't believe him?"

"Certainly, I do," Licheri said. "However, his views might change throughout his papacy. The far left and the feminists will applaud the news, and they will shower him with adulation. The liberal press will line up in support. The Curia, as you know, employs many gay priests. They may not be ardent supporters of women, but they will hope that a pope who appoints a woman as secretary of state might be a pope who will allow the ordination of openly gay priests.

"The Vatican is an echo chamber. The Holy Father will hear his supporters more clearly than his detractors who, by and large, do not live and work within our small realm. He may be emboldened to go further in years to come. Perhaps he will come to support women becoming deacons. Perhaps he will eventually change his mind on women priests. Meanwhile, in dioceses around the world where real people live, conservatives will lose their minds. The anger will boil over."

"Real people?" Cal asked.

"I think you know what I mean," Licheri said.

Cal didn't disagree with anything he said, but he felt compelled to ask, "Are you one of these real people?"

"I love my work, I love the Vatican, but most of all, I love the Church. It's my job to see the big picture, and with this appointment, I see unprecedented discord. Pope John is the third pope I've served. I've survived, and some would say thrived, in this office because I am a man in the middle, a centrist who can see the concerns of either pole. So, whether or not I am one of these real people, I understand them." He leaned back and smiled. "Regardless, I will do my utmost to support Elisabetta Celestino in her new role. After all, she will be my boss. Shall we review the press release? The Holy Father thinks my draft is overly long and defensive. Less is more, he said."

Her family had no idea why Elisabetta asked to meet them at her father's apartment the night of the inauguration. She deflected their questions, so they assumed something was awry. Micaela and Emilio arrived before her and asked their father if he knew what was happening.

Carlo Celestino was nearing eighty. He had an agricultural worker's robust body and ruddy complexion and a mathematician's elite mind. When he socialized with neighbors at the dairy farm in Abruzzo left to him by his parents, he was a fish out of water. Likewise, he had been odd man out at his old Department of Theoretical Mathematics among pale, gangly colleagues. The only place he felt perfectly at home was in Trastevere, in his spacious flat on the top floor of a clay-white apartment block on a narrow, sloping street.

"Papa, do you know what this is about?" Emilio asked, removing his suit jacket and looping his shoulder holster over an arm of the coat tree.

"She told me nothing," Carlo said, puffing on his pipe and filling the kitchen with Cavendish fumes. "I see you've got a new boss."

"The Mass went well," Emilio said. "A few pickpockets, a few demonstrators, no significant incidents."

Micaela shooed her father toward the sitting room and waved a magazine to clear the air.

"Is she sick?" Emilio asked.

"She's not sick. If she were and didn't tell me about it first, I'd kill her," she said.

"Well, what, then?" he said.

She waved her head from side to side like she had done as a girl whenever she knew a secret. "Maybe it's got something to do with Cal Donovan."

"What the hell are you talking about?"

"You know what, Emilio, men are as stupid as a bag of rocks. You've never noticed how he looks at her?"

"No, dear sister, I haven't. How does he look at her?"

"Like a man in love, for Christ's sake."

"She's a nun!" he cried.

"She wasn't born a nun, and she doesn't have to die a nun."

"Are you saying she's got feelings for him?"

"I'm not going to divulge conversations among sisters, Mr. Policeman, but hypothetically, it's possible to love two men at the same time."

"What? There's another man too?" he asked in exasperation.

"I'm so happy I'm not the dumbest one in the family," she said. "One of them is Jesus."

Emilio sat down heavily. "It's been a long day. We had ninety thousand pilgrims. Now this. Be a good doctor and get me a beer."

Elisabetta arrived, apologized for her lateness, removed her head coverings, and gave them quick kisses.

"Everyone's eaten, yes?" she said. "If not, I can call for a pizza."

"We've eaten, Papa's eaten," Micaela said.

"Where is he?"

"Follow the smoke."

"Well done today, Emilio," Elisabetta said. "Everything went smoothly."

"Thank God, my men did well. The Swiss Guards did well. It's a good start to the pontificate."

"I'll just freshen up," she said. "Then we'll talk."

Elisabetta went to the bedroom she had shared with her sister, now preserved as a museum to two contrasting teenagers—Elisabetta, the serious reader and lover of art and history, and Micaela, a girl besotted by pop music and fashion. She gazed at the poster over her bed of a giant stag from the Lascaux cave, thought about the twists and turns her life had taken, and was adrift in memories until her sister called out, "Let's get this show started, Eli!"

Carlo put his pipe on an ashtray atop a stack of mathematics journals and asked the question on everyone's mind. "So, what the hell is up with you?"

She sat across from them and said, "I'm sorry for the drama. I have something to tell you. It didn't feel right doing it over the phone."

When her father said he didn't like the sound of this, Micaela shushed him and said, "Let her speak, Papa!"

The tension on Elisabetta's face was infectious. Emilio scooted to the edge of the sofa and worked a fist.

"Last night, the Holy Father offered me a new position," she said.

"Good. I hated that my daughter, with all her education, was a secretary," Carlo said.

Emilio threw up his hands. "To this day, you can't get into your head that being the papal secretary isn't the same as the lady who typed your papers at the university."

"Would you let the woman talk?" Micaela said before continuing to talk herself. "What position did he offer?"

Elisabetta let out the breath she'd been holding. "I'm afraid it's another secretarial position. He asked me to become the secretary of state, his old job."

Carlo reached for his pipe and lit it again in the silence that followed.

It was Emilio who spoke first. "I know that you're not joking, because you don't make jokes like this. But this can't be. It's a job for a cardinal."

"That was my reaction, too," Elisabetta said. "It seems there is no such requirement. One doesn't even have to be a priest. He thinks I'm qualified and, in his view, the best person to take on the brief of the Secretariat."

"This, I wasn't expecting," Carlo said. "I was hoping you were going to tell us you were leaving the Vatican, that pit of vipers, and returning to academia. If you had stayed at the university instead of foolishly becoming a nun, you'd be an associate professor by now, maybe even a professor."

"Papa," Elisabetta said quietly, "surely we're not having this conversation again."

Micaela's eyes welled up. "What did you tell him?"

Elisabetta wedged in between Micaela and Emilio on the sofa and hugged her sister. "Why are you crying?"

"Because I think you took the position."

"You're right. I slept on it and told the Holy Father shortly before Mass began that I'd accept. He was pleased. He has a mission to empower Catholic women to participate more meaningfully in the life of the Church and thinks a female secretary will send a powerful message."

"I'm scared for you," Micaela said. "They'll try to crucify you."

"Who will?"

"All the assholes and Neanderthals, that's who."

"Well, don't worry. It so happens that I know the man in charge of the Vatican Carabinieri, and he's more than up to the task of protecting me."

Emilio stood to relieve his tension. "It's true that I can protect you physically, but you'll also be the target of psychological assaults. I can't protect you from those."

"I'm strong, you'll see," Elisabetta said.

"I know you are, but I don't think you realize how tough it will be," he said.

Carlo's incessant puffing produced a layer of smoke that hovered over his head like a rain cloud. "Your sister is tough as nails," he said. "She'll make her critics look like fools. Secretary of state. Wow. It's a very big job, bigger than a professor, for sure. I wish your mother were alive to see this day. Can you imagine how proud she'd be?"

Elisabetta went to him to kiss his cheek. His approbation had been a long time coming. "Thank you, Papa."

Emilio said, "Papa, you've still got the bottle of prosecco in the fridge I bought last Christmas. It's time for it to see some action."

After a toast, Micaela pulled Elisabetta toward the piano in the corner and asked, "Did you tell Cal yet?"

"Not yet."

"He'll be disappointed."

Elisabetta took a sip from her fluted glass. "I know he will, but I also know he'll understand. The Holy Father told me he asked Cal for his advice."

"What did he say?" Micaela asked.

"He agreed that the Holy Father should make the offer. He said it was a courageous move, and I'd be amazing at the job."

Micaela teared up again and positioned herself in front of an antique mirror to dab herself with a tissue and curse her smeared eyeliner.

"Why are you crying again?" Elisabetta asked.

"Because Cal would have made a great brother-in-law."

Cal was at the club lounge at the Fiumicino Airport awaiting his flight to Boston when his phone blew up with news alerts. Nothing about the announcement was unexpected. After all, he had wordsmithed the press release. Yet seeing it in print set him into a funk, and if it hadn't been so early, he would have poured himself something from the self-service bar.

He waited a few minutes for the news to trickle down, and then checked the major Italian news sites for commentary. *La Reppublica* was first out of the blocks with an article that began, "In an announcement of historic proportions, Pope John, on the first full day of his pontificate, has taken the highly controversial step of appointing a woman as Vatican secretary of state." Soon Twitter was on fire. Cal routinely followed the feeds of Catholic groups across the political spectrum, and as he scrolled from one account to the next, the emerging picture was predictable. Progressives were ecstatic, and conservatives were incandescent, some of them rage-tweeting about the end of the Church as we know it.

At the preboarding announcement for Boston, Cal gathered up his newspapers and electronic devices. Once he was airborne, every hour would take him five hundred miles from her. It occurred to him that he hadn't sent a congratulatory message. He was a few words into a text when he abandoned it, thinking it too impersonal. A voicemail would be better, provided he could gin himself up to sound chipper. He called her mobile phone, betting she'd be caught up in the hoopla and unavailable. But there she was on the fourth ring.

"Cal," was all Elisabetta said.

"I wasn't expecting to get you in person. I was going to leave a voice message."

"I saw it was you and stepped out of an interview. I was

glad for the break. I've been doing them on embargo since six this morning. Ten down, about twenty to go. Silvio Licheri is a taskmaster. He told me you worked on the press release with him. Thank you."

"I was happy to help. Look, I'm at the airport, and I just wanted to tell you how pleased I am you accepted the post. It's wonderful for you, the Vatican, and the entire Church. It's Harvard's loss you won't be taking my offer, but it's the world's gain."

There was a tantalizing pause on the line before she said, "Can I tell you something?"

"I wish you would."

"Before the Holy Father offered me the job, I was close to telling you that I should like to teach at Harvard. The notion of starting anew with a clean slate—well, it was exciting. But I couldn't refuse him, could I?"

There was something devastating in her revelation. A road not taken, the course of lives altered. "Of course you couldn't," he said. "You're making history, Eli. You are going to inspire girls and women all over the world, and you are going to be a great secretary of state. That said, I have to admit I'm disappointed."

"I know you are," she said softly.

"Tell you what. Why don't I keep the offer open? One of these years, you might want to know what a clean slate feels like. If so, I'll be there for you."

He could hear Silvio Licheri in the background, telling her they were falling behind schedule.

"Cal?" she said.

"Yes?"

He hoped that she wanted him to hear her breathy sigh. "Thank you," she said. "I wish you safe travels."

Cardinal Giuseppe Tosi described himself to friends as a born Vatican insider, an enforcer of rules and traditions, and a warrior for Christ. Having spent most of his career at the Vatican under three—now four—popes, he was one of those members of the Curia who thrived by being something of a chameleon, changing his ideological appearance to suit the times.

Under Pope Celestine's conservative predecessor, Tosi led the Congregation for Catholic Education, where right-wing elements lauded him for his traditional orthodoxy. However, Celestine wanted someone on the education front more aligned to his liberal views and moved Tosi to head up the Pontifical Commission for the Cultural Heritage of the Church. In that position, Tosi sat across the table from Sister Elisabetta, who had led the Pontifical Commission for Sacred Archaeology when decisions were made on Celestine's divestiture of Vatican cultural treasures. Privately, he opposed the selloff, telling confidants it made him physically ill, but publicly he offered only limited resistance, describing the initiative to like-minded prelates as a runaway train.

Celestine got wind of Tosi's lack of ideological commitment and kicked him upstairs to the camerlengo role. On paper, the camerlengo is responsible for administering the property and revenues of the Holy See, but the office staff were real estate and financial experts, and the supervising cardinal had little to do.

It was on a pope's death that the camerlengo entered the limelight. He was responsible for formally declaring the pope dead, taking the Ring of the Fisherman from his finger, and cutting it with shears in the presence of the cardinals. During the *sede vacante*, the interregnum before the new pope is elected, the camerlengo served as the Vatican's acting sovereign, and now that Pope John was in place, Tosi's heady days of service had come to an end. Having positioned himself as a kingmaker during the conclave, he was just settling back into obscurity when, to his amazement, Elisabetta Celestino was named as his boss.

Tosi had the protruding face of a lean hound. He had inherited the tendency among men in his family toward heavy beards, and every afternoon he had a second shave. He spoke with a clipped enunciation, an artifact of the technique he had employed to conquer childhood stuttering. Now seventy-six, the cardinal felt the weight of time on his shoulders. In four years, he would be aged out from being a cardinal elector, and as the new pope was relatively young, he had likely participated in his last conclave. He assumed that Pope John would keep him on as camerlengo as a reward for wrangling votes for his speedy election. But following this bombshell announcement, anything was possible.

The one man with whom Tosi could always be his authentic self was the Spanish cardinal Manuel Navarro, the prefect of the Congregation for the Evangelization of Peoples. They had been seminarians together at the Pontifical Roman Major Seminary at the Archbasilica of St. John Lateran. Both were natural theologians and administrators born for the Curia, not pastoral care, and their careers had progressed in lockstep. Tosi was made bishop a year before Navarro was; Navarro was made cardinal two years before Tosi. The Spaniard was also a bit of a political shapeshifter, but unlike Tosi, he was readily identifiable as a traditionalist. As soon as he read the press release, it was Navarro whom Tosi called, and both men agreed to continue their commiserations over supper.

Absent a Vatican subsidy, Navarro could not have afforded his luxurious apartment on his monthly salary of five thousand euros. He enjoyed five well-appointed rooms overlooking the Tiber near the Ponte Sisto footbridge and the services of an elderly Capuchin nun from his home province of Galicia who lived in his guest room and tended to the cooking and housekeeping chores.

Tosi sniffed the air in the hall and asked his host, "What is that marvelous smell?"

"Ah," Navarro said, "Sister Valeria has made paella. Come, have a drink."

"I've been counting the minutes," Tosi said. "I need something strong."

The men settled into antique chairs by a non-working fireplace and sipped orujo, Navarro's favorite Galician brandy.

"I must say, Giuseppe, I am quite angry with you," Navarro said.

"Why is that?"

"Because you persuaded me to vote for Da Silva."

"He was going to win within four or five ballots anyway, regardless of how you or I voted. It was expedient for us to get behind him openly."

"Always politics with you."

"And not you?"

"Guilty as charged," Navarro said, "but not as guilty as you, my friend."

Navarro had a sagging face with puffy eyelids. He was one of those men whose weight had crept up on him, a few kilos a year, hidden under the loose robes of a high cleric. He hadn't quite come to grips with his state of health until his last irregular checkup, when his doctor diagnosed high blood pressure, early diabetes, and arthritis of his hips. A few years earlier, Navarro had invited Cardinal Da Silva to his flat to talk about a diplomatic matter and proceeded to show the cardinal secretary his pill bottles. "You're heavier than me, Rodrigo," Navarro had said. "Which of these do you take?" Da Silva had chuckled and replied, "I take nothing beyond good wine and port. I'm in perfect health. You should adopt my Portuguese diet, Manuel. More fruits of the sea. That's what you need."

Tosi banged back the rest of his brandy and rasped, "So, what are we to do?"

"Do?" Navarro said. "We bite our lips and work with her. What else can we do?"

"I cannot believe you can be so passive," Tosi said. "When something threatens the Church we love, we must act. Perhaps we are obliged to operate in the shadows, but we must act."

"I take your point, Giuseppe. We can certainly mobilize elements of the Curia to resist any dangerous initiatives she puts forward. We are masters of that game."

Tosi pounded the arm of his chair. "No! That is not enough. Her initiatives will not be the problem. *She* will be the problem. It is bad enough that Da Silva filled the position with a non-cardinal. Putting a woman in charge of the Secretariat takes the Church on a path of ruination. If this stands, it is only a matter of time before this pope or another sanctions the ordination of women."

The Capuchin sister announced that dinner was served.

"What, then?" Navarro said, struggling to lift his bulk.

"We need a savior," Tosi said.

Navarro pointed a fat finger into the air. "I believe we have one."

"An earthly savior. This will require more than prayer."

"Who is this savior?"

"He is a modern crusader. I am hopeful he will help us."

6

When Tommy Cunliffe purchased what was known as Villa Parini back in 2005, his real estate broker assured him it was the largest house in the state of Pennsylvania. However, shortly after closing on the Bell Acres mega-mansion, he learned that a pile in the Philadelphia suburb of Gladwyne was bigger. Tommy was a Pittsburgh man through and through, and it didn't sit well to be upstaged by some old-money bastard from Philadelphia. So Tommy got a builder to add an extension, bringing the house to forty thousand square feet on seventy-four acres. "Who the heck is ever going to build something bigger in Pennsylvania?" Tommy had crowed. "My bragging rights are never going to expire."

Sam Parini, the upstart who had built the neo-Gothic castle near Pittsburgh, had wound up bankrupt and in jail for tax fraud, and the trophy property was going to seed when Tommy swooped in. It needed a billionaire's checkbook to make it truly glorious, and when the renovations were done, Tommy renamed it Heartland Manor and settled in with his wife, six children, two nannies, husband-and-wife butlers, personal assistant, four dogs, fifteen cars, and a helicopter.

The children were grown now, and all but a middle-born son, Evan, had flown the nest. An estate with thirty-six rooms, eleven bedrooms, and twenty bathrooms was a bit much for three members of a family, but Tommy liked to say that the word *downsizing* wasn't in his vocabulary. Besides, at the rate things were happening on the baby front, there would be dozens of grandkids to fill the mansion and parklike grounds one day.

For the moment, Evan, a hulking thirty-year-old, rattled around in his own wing of the castle. When he wasn't doing work for his father, he spent his time in the gym complex and entertaining an entourage of Pittsburgh friends in the sports pavilion, facsimile English pub, and screening room.

The tennis court was a hike from the mansion, so Tommy kept his rackets and tennis clothes in a summerhouse down the hill. He was old school to a fault and, even at home, played in whites. It was September, but summer was still going strong, and the mercury on the court hit ninety. Evan was kaleidoscopic in a blue T-shirt, red shorts, and yellow sneakers, but he was wilting in the heat, unlike his father.

"Tell me again why we're playing at the hottest time of day?" Evan panted at the net.

"Because I'm in between meetings, and it's healthy to sweat," Tommy said. "Let's go. Your serve—three-five."

It was an odd inversion—most adult men who persisted in calling themselves Tommy were Tommys when they were little. His parents had insisted that he always be called Thomas, and he obediently went along with them until he left for college at the Colorado School of Mines. There, his new roommate, a kid from Tulsa, took one look at him and said, "The fuck I'm going to call you Thomas, Tommy-boy." Tommy wound up fitting better in the world of tobacco-chewing drilling crews he was entering, and it stuck.

He was sixty-three now, and there wasn't a person in his orbit who didn't call him Tommy. The juvenile moniker also conjured a man-of-the-people sort of informality helpful for his next project. He had a PowerPoint deck in his office that his consultants had prepared after focus-testing various messages with voters. The winning slogan was "Tommy Cunliffe—Pro-Worker, Pro-Life, Pro-Pennsylvania." After a stint as governor, if all went as planned, "America" would be substituted for "Pennsylvania," and he'd be off to the big race.

His son was taller and stronger, but Tommy was a machine. He was able to return almost every ball, sending them back with angle and spin, and he drove his opponents nuts with consistency and stamina. Around his country club, members would say, "You can't beat the son of a bitch. It's like playing against a backboard."

He was trim and muscular, with a deep tan kept year-round with the help of a tanning salon in the sports pavilion. He wasn't handsome. His eyes were too close together and his chin was too small. But his whiskey-toned skin, bright dental veneers, and sandy hair that boyishly flopped over his forehead made him pleasantly photogenic.

Now he flashed a threatening smile across the net and exercised his habit of calling out the score even if he wasn't the one serving. "It's 30–40," he said, shuffling in the ready position and mumbling encouragement to himself.

Evan hit a booming first serve long and sliced a second serve to Tommy's backhand. Tommy hit a cute return, dinking it with backspin. Evan came charging from the backcourt and uncorked a forehand with heavy topspin that looped toward the baseline.

"Out!" Tommy shouted. "Game, set, and match."

"C'mon!" Evan yelled. "That was in."

"Dream on."

Evan strode around the net, inspected the baseline, and circled a ball mark in the clay with the end of his racket. "In by two inches, for Christ's fucking sake."

His father was already covering his racket, wholly uninterested in litigating the matter. "You're looking at an old mark," he said. "And you know I won't tolerate juxtaposing profanity with the Lord's name."

His son shook his head. "Sorry, but it was in."

The sight of Barbara Cunliffe speeding down the lawn in a golf cart saved them from further confrontation.

"What's your mother doing?" Tommy asked.

Barbara drove to the gate and ratcheted the brake to the floor. "I see you're done," she said.

She was her husband's age and equally fit and tanned. When she wasn't playing tennis herself, she was on the golf course at their club, where she was the perennial women's champion. She sprang up, her bottle-blonde coif immobile in the breeze. She always dressed sportily during the day. Her white golf shirt had little pink palm trees that matched the pink of her shorts.

"I won," Tommy said. "The kid can't touch me."

"He cheated," Evan said.

"Your father doesn't cheat, at least at tennis," she said. "I tried calling you."

Tommy glanced at his phone. "The ringer's off. Anything wrong?"

"I emailed you a link. I think you should see it."

"I left my glasses in my dressing room. Read it to me." He tried to get her to take his phone, but she refused.

"I don't want to see what's on your phone," she said, crossing her arms over her chest. "She probably sends you pictures."

"Stop it," Tommy snapped. "Not the time or place. Evan, would you please read me whatever it is that's so urgent?"

His son took the phone and clicked through to the link. "It's a Vatican press release," he said.

"Go on," his father said.

Evan scanned the text and said, "You're not going to like it."

"What's our new man gotten up to?" Tommy asked.

"The headline is 'The Pope Appoints New Secretary of State,'" Evan said. "'Today, the Holy Father John announced that the next Vatican secretary of state will be Sister Elisabetta Celestino. Sister Elisabetta was formerly first private secretary to Pope Celestine and the President of the Pontifical Commission for Sacred Archaeology. "Sister Elisabetta is eminently qualified to lead the Secretariat," the pontiff said. "While a cardinal has traditionally held the post, there is no bar to a non-ordained person occupying the position."'"

Tommy cut in, "This isn't from some kind of sick parody site, is it?"

"Nope. Official release from the Vatican Press Office."

"Christ Almighty," Tommy vented. "Is there more?"

"Mostly her bio, a few quotes."

Tommy snatched his phone back. "I knew Da Silva was going to be trouble, but this? It's a provocation that will not stand. Barbara, give me a ride back to the house, assuming you're sober."

The whirring of the electric motor was her reply as she pressed on the accelerator and sped away.

"Tell you what. I'll walk," Tommy called after her. "Evan, have Beth Ann meet me in my office. I've got calls to make."

Beth Ann Feeney had been Tommy's assistant for only six months, and she was still getting used to her boss's quirks. For the most part he was courteous and gentlemanly, but he showed fangs on occasion, and this was one of them.

Tommy was too worked up to shower and change out of his tennis gear, and his sweaty thighs stuck to the chair leather. His office, with a sweeping view over manicured acres, was the size of a small suburban house and had multiple seating areas. The photos that hung everywhere had a common feature: He was in every one of them, consorting with politicians, celebrities, presidents, and popes. The bookcase held an extensive display of plaques and medals awarded by civic and religious organizations.

Beth Ann stood at attention before his desk, holding a corded phone to her ear. She was attired in her standard wardrobe of pleated skirt hemmed just above her knees, satin blouse, faux pearl necklace, flesh-colored panty hose, and medium-height heels. When Tommy had extended an offer upon her graduation from the Cunliffe Catholic Bible College, his wife invited the young woman for tea, gave her a check for two thousand dollars to buy clothes, and explained how to dress as Tommy's assistant.

"Well?" Tommy said.

"I'm still holding," Beth Ann said. "They're trying to reach Archbishop Stockwell's secretary. She's at lunch."

He half-shouted, "Is she the only person at the diocese of Pittsburgh who knows when Stockwell's plane lands?"

"I'm not sure," she replied.

"Forget about her," Tommy barked. "Get me the auxiliary bishop. What's his name again?"

"I'll have to look it up," she said.

"It's your job to know these things. Do you like your job?"

She was already scrolling through her contacts with her free hand. "I do," she said. "It's Bishop Curtin."

"Yeah, Curtin. Get him on the line."

Beth Ann got herself transferred back to the receptionist and connected with the auxiliary bishop. "Your Eminence, please hold for Mr. Cunliffe."

"Bishop Curtin," Tommy said with his usual telephonic ebullience, "Tommy Cunliffe here. How are you?"

"I'm fine, Mr. Cunliffe. How are you?"

"Well, I could be better. Have you seen the announcement from the Vatican?"

"I'm afraid I haven't. I've been in a meeting. What's been announced?"

Tommy shook his head contemptuously. "I'll let you read it for yourself. Do you know when Archbishop Stockwell is returning from Rome?"

"I'm afraid I don't. Shall I check with his secretary?"

"It's all right," Tommy said. "When you see the archbishop, just tell him to give me a call."

He hung up and said to Beth Ann, "There's a reason I can never remember his name. Get me President Pfeiffer at the college. I can't believe he hasn't called me yet."

The office line rang, and she plucked the phone from its cradle. "Mr. Cunliffe's office. This is Beth Ann." She listened and replied, "Please hold."

"That's Pfeiffer, isn't it?" Tommy said.

"It is."

"Gareth," Tommy said, "I was just about to call you."

"It's a black day, Tommy," the president said.

"Tell me about it. I mean, who would have thought? How's it being received on campus?"

"There's confusion. Consternation. We'll have to provide a forum for students and faculty to vent. Perhaps a town hall. I need to think our response through."

"Let me know what you decide. I'll make myself available."

"Thank you, Tommy. I don't suppose there's anything you can do at this point. I mean, it's a fait accompli, right?"

"I wouldn't call it that. What's done can be undone. You're buddies with Bishop Molla at *Catholic Shield* magazine, right?"

"I am indeed."

"Give him a call, would you? Tell him I want them to fire a broadside. Tell him it's their Lexington and Concord moment, the first shots fired in a revolution."

"I'll do that."

"Meanwhile, let me work my address book. We'll talk soon."

Tommy noticed that Beth Ann was absorbed with her phone. "That better not be Instagram," he said.

"I was just checking the reaction on Twitter," she said. "It's crazy."

"I assume you're as outraged as I am," he said in an inquisitorial tone.

She nodded like a bobblehead. "Absolutely. I mean, a woman?"

"Right. Stay focused, kid. It's battle stations. Our Church is in trouble. Cancel my CEG meetings and see if you can track down Cardinal Rowe from Houston and Archbishop Rice from San Diego. Come on, chop-chop."

The next day, it rained sheets, so Tommy took his morning swim in the indoor pool. He had an awkward swimming stroke that he insisted was an asset when his family teased him. His engineer's mind calculated that the inefficiencies of his mechanics meant he had to work harder and therefore burn ten percent more calories.

Beth Ann was under orders to hold routine calls, but as he prepared to push off on a new lap, he saw her holding a phone and a towel.

"It's a Cardinal Tosi calling from the Vatican. Do you want to take it?"

"I most certainly do. The mountain comes to Mohammed." He climbed out, dried himself, and took the call off hold. "Cardinal Tosi—how nice to hear from you."

"Is this a good time?" the cardinal asked.

"Anytime I get to speak with the cardinal camerlengo is a good time."

"Ah, you're too kind. Although we've never met, I feel I know you."

"How's that?"

"I've read your opinion pieces. I've viewed your speeches on YouTube. You are an important figure in American Catholicism."

"Well, that's good to hear. I spend about as much time thinking about the Church as I do about pulling energy out of the ground. How can I help you, Cardinal?"

"I assume you've seen the news."

"I have indeed. It doesn't sit well, which is about the mildest thing I can say about it. I understand you're partially to blame for it."

The longish pause that followed made Tommy wonder if the call had dropped, but Tosi finally replied, "I am not sure I grasp your meaning."

"Well, I heard you lobbied hard and pulled together the votes Da Silva needed for a second-ballot victory."

"How can you possibly know that? Conclave deliberations are secret."

"In my line of work, information is the single most valuable commodity. I talk to people. People talk to me. I'm not wrong, am I?"

"His victory was inevitable. I merely read the room."

"The Sistine Chapel is quite the room. Well then, I admire your political acumen. You're now in a unique position. Pope John must believe you're an ally. Are you?"

"When I can agree with the Holy Father on a position, I will be an ally. When I disagree, I will cease to be an ally, but I will exercise my disagreements discreetly."

"People say that's how you handled Celestine."

"The people who talk to you."

"Now *you're* talking to me, and I'm listening."

"This business with the nun," Tosi said. "I, along with some of my colleagues on the College of Cardinals, are concerned."

"As well they should be," Tommy said. "Celestine created the monster by putting her in charge of the Archaeology Commission—we saw what she did there—and he compounded it by making her his private secretary. Now this. The next thing we know, we'll be taking communion from someone in a dress. Did you have any inkling Da Silva would be a bomb-tossing revolutionary?"

Tosi grunted. "No one saw this coming. He is a known progressive, but he was never considered a fire-breather. I regard this action as the thin edge of the wedge. With the stroke of the pen, he is taking the Church in a radical new direction. If we are not vigilant, the ordination of women and perhaps other inappropriate initiatives on sexuality and gender might come to pass one day."

"Vigilance is a passive activity, Cardinal. I don't like passivity, not with something vitally important. No, this requires active measures. I've already spoken to every sympathetic American cardinal and bishop. As you know, it's not a large universe— Celestine was around long enough to elevate his liberal pals to the available slots. Everyone I contacted talks a good game, but none of them have a handle on how to play a good game. Am I making myself clear?"

"Mr. Cunliffe, I believe we see eye to eye."

"My friends call me Tommy."

"And my friends call me Giuseppe. So, Tommy, my

colleagues and I believe that there is only so much we can do from within the Vatican. We require a champion from the outside, a crusader to come to the defense of the Church, a man like yourself with strong convictions and, if I might say, deep pockets."

Tommy caught Beth Ann's attention by pointing at his phone and smiling broadly. "So, Giuseppe, as I understand it, you're asking me to find a way to knock off Sister Elisabetta."

Tosi sniffed. "Not literally, of course."

"I was speaking metaphorically," Tommy said. "I wish the good sister a long and healthy life, just not as secretary of state. Let me get to work on some ideas. We'll communicate by phone. No electronic messages, no notes to file, all right?"

"Certainly."

Tommy said, "With the Good Lord's help, we'll send Sister Elisabetta back to teaching elementary school, where she belongs."

7

D odo Shamoun stared at the pair of emails sitting in his
sent folder and wondered why he had not received a
reply. After the first went unanswered, he sent another a day
later, marking it urgent, and still there was nothing. Dodo
double-checked the email address. The messages had not
bounced back, so they must have gone through. He had a
phone number, but he was hesitant to use it, fearing his English skills weren't up to the task.

There were other potential buyers, but none better. This
group was known to pay handsomely, sometimes outbidding
competitors by an order of magnitude, but they only bought
quality. Dodo had a strong feeling that his merchandise was
golden, but he couldn't be sure what he had at this point.

He was at a sweltering outdoor café in Cairo, having a
morning coffee and watching cars whizzing by on the broad
avenue, when he finally sucked up his courage. A street cart
vendor on the corner was already preparing kebda eskandarani,
and the air filled with the aroma of grilled beef liver. It was

midafternoon in the buyer's time zone, a respectable time to call. He steeled himself as the phone rang through.

"Yeah?" was the clipped answer.

"Oh, I am sorry," Dodo said. "I am wishing to speak to Mr. Evan Cunliffe."

"Who's this?"

"I am Dodo Shamoun from Egypt. I sent you emails about a papyrus I find. Maybe a very important papyrus."

"Do I know you? Have we done business?"

"Unfortunately, no. I never had a good enough item to make present to you. This item is very, very good, I think."

"You're a broker?"

"Yes, yes. Antiquities."

"How'd you get my number?"

"From a colleague. A Mr. Mansour who sold something to you before."

Dodo suddenly heard loud, thumping pop music, followed by Evan shouting at one of his friends, "Turn it down, jackass! Can't you see I'm on a goddamn call?" The music stopped. "Sorry about that. You say you sent me an email?"

"Two."

"Hang on, let me check. What did you say your name was again?"

"Dodo Shamoun."

"I don't see them. This was to my company email at CEG or the museum email at AMF?"

"AMF."

"Okay, I see them. They were in spam. Hang on a sec."

"Yes, yes."

"So you say this is first century, from a mask?"

"Yes, mask was first century."

"What's the provenance?"

Dodo's lies rolled off his tongue. "A private collector I meet. Maybe his father's father bought mask many years ago in a bazaar."

"You have paperwork?"

"Yes, yes. Bill of sale. Testimony of seller. All perfect."

"I'm looking at your photo. The papyrus is awfully dark."

"Before it dries. Photo is from right after being found in cartonnage. My colleague, she's an expert in papyrus. She tells me it is dry now."

"So, this was just found?"

"Yes! Only two days ago."

"You say it's Greek?"

"Greek, yes."

"What's it say?"

"I don't read the Greek. My colleague no reads either. I am hoping you have people to make good translation."

"It could be someone's shopping list."

"No, no, I don't think. Could be Bible."

"But you don't know."

"I think, don't know."

"Has it been dated yet to confirm the mask date?"

"My colleague, she say, maybe tomorrow we have carbon date."

"All right, Mr. Shamoun. I get the picture. I'll pass this along to my expert. If you don't hear back from me, we're not interested, okay?"

"Yes, yes. Fair man. Thank you very much."

Bill Stearns liked to say that it was the hand of God that steered him to Pittsburgh. Born in Tulsa, Oklahoma, to a Bible-thumping family, he grew up loving football and God. The strapping lad played fullback on a state champion football team in high school. He was good enough to get an athletic scholarship to Texas Christian University, where he promptly blew out a knee during the first week of practice.

Fortunately, he was a pretty good student. He regrouped and majored in business, figuring it would set him up for a career in industry. When his scholarship evaporated, he became one of those kids who had to take out loans and find on-campus jobs to make ends meet. In his junior year, he landed a gig in the laboratory of a biblical studies professor who needed to catalog a donated collection of papyrus texts.

These little bits of antiquity with squiggles of writing instantly captured his imagination. He pictured ancient scribes hunched over their tables, dipping quills into pots of ink and scratching out contracts and inventories and, most thrillingly, the precursor texts and earliest copies of the Old and New Testaments. Yet he felt as helpless as an ape, unable to make sense of the squiggles, and he asked the professor how he could learn the ancient languages.

"Take Introduction to Ancient Greek next semester, and if you like it, you can take the intermediate course next year, and if you're gung-ho, the beginner's course in Coptic or Aramaic."

He liked the Greek course, and he wound up taking the others, but a panic set in over his student debt as graduation approached. Instead of pursuing his passion for early biblical texts, he took a job as a junior financial analyst at a company he had never heard of, Cunliffe Energy Group in Houston. It wasn't a colossus, but it was large enough that he only saw the blond and charismatic founder and CEO, Tommy Cunliffe, from afar.

Bill did well in Houston, got a few promotions, steadily whittled down his debt, and met his future wife at a church potluck dinner. He told his Friday night poker buddies, "Being a financial analyst isn't my dream job, but I consider myself a lucky guy. CEG's a good company, America needs to get energy-independent, and fracking is the way we're going to get there." Biblical studies were relegated to the status of a hobby. That is, until the day the hand of God intervened again.

That day, Bill was taking his lunch in the company cafeteria at a table overlooking the courtyard. It was a blazing summer in Texas, and despite the air-conditioning, the thermal panes were hot to the touch. He often ate alone to read, and he was fully absorbed when he noticed that someone was looking through the window at him, none other than Tommy Cunliffe. He didn't quite know what to do, so he gave the CEO a sheepish wave. Tommy held up a finger as if to say wait there and fast-walked to the nearest door.

Bill wasn't sure if he'd done something wrong, so he held himself stiffly, waiting for the big cheese to appear. Tommy headed toward his table and extended a callused hand.

"Tommy Cunliffe. How are you?"

"I'm fine, sir. Bill Stearns, from finance."

About twelve years separated them. Stearns was twenty-six at the time. Tommy had been that very age when he founded

CEG. Tommy Cunliffe was considered a true wunderkind when he opened up a small energy exploration shop in Houston straight out of a graduate program in petroleum engineering from the Colorado School of Mines. What twenty-something kid had a dozen scientific publications and a raft of patents for wellbore heads and new types of fracking additives?

Tommy lived up to the hype, and CEG quickly became a success, drilling a portfolio of its own wells and licensing its technology to other companies. Some said that Tommy Cunliffe would become a billionaire, and on that hot summer day in Houston, he was well on his way.

"I couldn't help notice what you were reading," Tommy said.

Stearns felt his face getting warm. A young financial analyst should have been using his lunch hour to read company reports or trade publications, not this.

"Oh yeah," he said. "It's a hobby, I suppose."

Tommy reached for the journal. *"The Bulletin for Biblical Research* is pretty heavy-duty for a hobbyist, I'd say."

"I majored in finance but minored in biblical studies."

"Where?"

"TCU."

"Good school. Mind if I join you?"

Stearns was aware that nearly everyone in the cafeteria was staring, undoubtedly wondering how a peon had messed up enough for the CEO to be targeting him at lunch.

"Please do."

"What's the article you're reading?" Tommy asked.

"It's about a new translation of something called the Bodmer Papyrus, Number Ten. It's—"

Tommy finished the sentence. "Paul's Third Epistle to the

Corinthians, found in Egypt in the 1950s. It dates to about AD 200. It's in Greek, am I right?"

Bill was dumbfounded. "How do you know about the Bodmer Papyri?"

Tommy grinned. "You're not the only guy with a weird hobby. I'm a bit of a collector. I own a few bits and pieces. Nothing spectacular. Yet."

"Papyri?" Bill asked.

"That's right. I don't have much disposable time, but I dabble in the antiquities market. How'd you like to see what I've got?"

"I'd love to."

"What's your church, if I can ask?"

"My people are Baptist," Stearns said.

"I'm Catholic," Tommy said, getting up, "but I won't hold it against you. I'll send you an invite—Sunday evening if that works. It'll be great shooting the breeze about something other than oil and gas."

Tommy's house in the tony River Oaks community didn't hold a candle to the grandeur of his future estate in Pittsburgh, but it was the most magnificent home Bill Stearns had ever seen. It was a redbrick neo-Georgian backing onto the River Oaks Country Club, where Tommy was a member.

In an instant, Bill realized he had overdone it with a blazer and slacks. Tommy and his wife were hanging out in shorts and golf shirts. Tommy was hunched over the grill in the back-yard, and his wife, Barbara, a woman who still resembled the cheerleader she had been, drank something potent from an iced pitcher. Bill, a teetotaler, sipped a soda and watched golfers hit approach shots to the green on the long tenth hole.

"It's nice here," Bill said, unsure how to converse with the wife of the company's CEO.

"You think so?" she said.

"Oh yeah. I'll bet your kids love it. I mean, look at the size of your lawn."

"How did you know we have children?"

He sheepishly pointed toward a sandpit off to the side, littered with buckets and spades and toy trucks.

Barbara looked askance at the play area and apologized that the nanny hadn't put away the toys.

The young man was desperate to keep the chat going, as she asked nothing about him. "Will they be coming down for the barbecue?"

"Oh God, no. This is our time of day."

Bill's stomach was in a knot before he ate, and after a half hour of stilted conversation with his hosts and an overdone cheeseburger, he was in a full cramp. He didn't relax until Barbara floated away on a tide of whatever was in her pitcher and Tommy invited him to his study, a clubby space with cherry paneling and plaid chairs.

"Let me show you what I've got," Tommy said, opening a cabinet and presenting a glass-topped display box.

Bill feasted his eyes on a few dozen papyrus fragments, the smallest the size of a postage stamp, the largest a file card.

"This one's Hebrew," Tommy said, tapping on the glass with a pen. "I'm a New Testament guy, but I couldn't resist picking this one up. It's a snippet from Deuteronomy, found in Egypt, second century before Christ, but who knows—I could have been sold a bill of goods. I got it in a package deal with the stuff I was especially interested in."

He tapped the glass over a cluster of papyri.

"Koine Greek," Bill said.

"Hey, you know your stuff," Tommy said. "This one's a fifth-century fragment of Mark 4. Can you make it out?"

Bill suspected this was a test. He sounded out the words and said, "'Again, Jesus began to teach by the lake.'"

"Bingo!" Tommy said. "Have a look at this one. It's Acts 12, fourth century."

Bill studied it. "There's a couple of words I don't know."

Tommy urged him on.

"'The apostles performed many signs and wonders among the people. And all the believers used to meet together in—'"

Tommy consulted a notebook that held all the translations. "Solomon's Colonnade," he said. "'—meet together in Solomon's Colonnade.' You're the real deal, Bill. How many years of Greek do you have?"

"In college, just one. I was a business major and crammed in a few electives. I've tried to keep learning, you know, on the side. On weekends."

"And during your lunch break."

"Caught me red-handed."

Tommy had him join him on a couple of overstuffed club chairs. The young man accepted a cigar, aping his host by sniffing the wrapper and using a guillotine on the tip.

"Permit me to tell you my dream, Bill," Tommy said. "I've been fortunate. The company's been a success. We're pulling a lot of energy out of the ground, and it's only the beginning. I've got a wonderful family, and as you can see by this little window into my world, we're enjoying the fruits of our labor. Do you want to know who I credit for my good fortune? I credit our Lord and Savior, Jesus Christ."

"Amen to that," Bill said, letting out an aromatic puff of smoke. The strong tobacco was making him lightheaded, and he blurted out, "If you don't mind me saying, you sound more like a Baptist than a Catholic, sir."

Tommy let out a belly laugh. "I am grateful I was born a Catholic, but I do envy the zeal of you evangelicals. So listen, here's my dream. I want to dedicate the rest of my life to honoring the word of God. One day, I want to build a museum that will teach people, young and old, about the glories of the Bible. I want to pack that museum with artifacts of Christianity—artwork, statues, relics, icons, and especially its foundational texts. My motivation for buying these papyrus fragments was an investment—I won't tell you how much I paid, but it was obscene. But they've come to mean a lot more to me than money. They are a connection to the early days of Christianity, and I feel as if they bring me closer to Christ.

"My dream is to one day own as much of this heritage as I can for good people to come and marvel over it. Problem is, I'm a babe in the woods. I'm a petroleum engineer. The little I know of the antiquities world is that it's full of snakes. I don't know what's real and what's fake. I need experts who are one hundred percent loyal to me and my mission. I want to be able to buy the best at fair prices. See where you might fit in?"

Bill blinked through the smoke and told his host that he did not see.

"Do you like your job?" Tommy asked.

"Yeah, I like it a lot. It's interesting work. The people I work with are great."

"But do you *love* it?" Tommy didn't give Bill a chance to answer. "The way I see it, a fellow who reads a scholarly biblical journal over lunch is declaring his true love. How come you didn't pursue it?"

"I needed to make a living. Besides, I couldn't afford grad school."

"Bill, there are thousands of financial analysts out there. I'm sure you're good at what you do, but it's a fungible role. What I need is a biblical expert I can trust."

Bill shifted uncomfortably in his chair. "Mr. Cunliffe— sir—I only had a few college courses."

"Sure, I understand that. But what if I paid for your grad school and gave you living expenses to boot with the proviso that, when you're trained up, you come back and work for me on this museum of mine? I already have a name for it: the American Museum of Faith. What do you say, Bill? Can I get you to change the course of your life for the better?"

Three decades later, Bill Stearns was at his desk at the American Museum of Faith, studying a photograph of a purportedly first-century papyrus recovered from Egyptian cartonnage.

Everything that Tommy Cunliffe had promised him that long-ago day in Houston had come to pass. He had paid for his tuition and expenses during the five years it took for Bill to get his PhD in religious studies and ancient languages at Yale, the repository of one of the great papyrus collections in the world.

When Bill returned to Houston, Tommy put him to work at his newly formed Cunliffe Foundation to lay the groundwork for the museum to be built one day on the grounds of another passion project, the Cunliffe Catholic Bible College in Pittsburgh.

Over the ensuing years, Tommy's business empire grew on the back of shale gas extraction. He became one of the largest frackers in Texas, Louisiana, Ohio, West Virginia, and Pennsylvania. He joined the billionaire club and became the environmentalists' public enemy number one. Both designations delighted him. His foray into energy exploration in his home state was the catalyst for moving back to Pittsburgh and buying Heartland Manor, much to the distress of his wife, a fixture on the Houston philanthropy scene.

One of his children became a doctor, one went to work at his charitable foundation, three joined Cunliffe Energy where they advanced mostly on merit, and Evan, the college dropout, lived at home and worked at the museum, ostensibly overseeing acquisitions. Everyone at the museum, with the possible exception of Evan himself, saw him as a figurehead with a director's title. Bill Stearns signed off on the bona fides of acquisition pieces, and Tommy signed off on the payments, leaving Evan to field inquiries and shuffle papers.

Bill stared at the papyrus for a good while, printed the photo, and then stared at the printout some more. He was fine-tuning his translation when Evan called.

"Hey, did you get my email?"

Bill was still a large man, but muscle had given way to fat. He was an amiable goateed presence around the museum, padding around in comfortable shoes, khaki pants, voluminous shirts, and an unzipped safari vest. Most would say that Bill was the most contented man they knew, even after he struggled through his wife's cancer death. Employees wondered how a man as accomplished as Bill could report to a nonentity like Evan Cunliffe, but Bill was so grateful to Tommy for the life he'd been given that dealing with Evan was a small price to pay.

"I got it, Ev. I've been studying it."

"You ever hear of this guy, Dodo Shamoun?" Evan asked.

"He's a minor player, as far as I can tell. We've never done business with him. He's not on our watch list of forgers and scoundrels."

"Is it a forgery?"

"I can't begin to tell you that from a photo, but it has all the appearances of being genuine. Of course, if the mask was validly dated at 70 CE, the cartonnage story doesn't seem to hold water. By then, linen had replaced papyri in mask production."

Bill heard laughter in the background and a feminine scream as someone jumped into a pool.

"Could you translate it?" Evan asked.

"Indeed I could. It's—well, let me just say this—it's extraordinarily interesting."

"Bill, c'mon, don't hold out on me."

Bill ignored his pleadings and asked, "Where did Mr. Shamoun say the radiocarbon dating was being done?"

"Hang on. I wrote it down. The IFAO in Cairo."

"French operation. Top drawer. When will they have the result?"

"He says tomorrow. Don't know why he didn't wait to show it to us until he had the date."

Bill had some tea and said, "If you were part of a forgery scheme, you'd probably present all the manufactured data in a neat, compelling package. If anything, this ass-backward approach is a sign of naïve enthusiasm, not artifice."

"So what the fuck does it say?"

Bill, like Tommy Cunliffe, couldn't abide swearing, but it wasn't his place to police Evan's manners.

"Why don't we see if your dad is available?" Bill said. "It would be good to discuss this together."

"Why get him involved now?"

Bill glanced at the translation he'd made. "Because if this is authentic, Ev, it's the single most important biblical papyrus ever discovered, and it's worth a fortune."

8

During the ensuing videoconference, Evan had to work hard to keep himself in the picture. After he recounted his call with Dodo Shamoun, the conversation essentially became a dialogue between Bill Stearns and his father. Bill was his usual cautious, phlegmatic self, but Evan rarely saw his father get this worked up. Tommy was taking the meeting from the company headquarters in Houston, where he typically spent two days a week liaising with his senior team and, as his wife suspected, his mistress. Tommy kept his voice raised in excitement and anger. At times he seemed on the verge of violating his no-swearing edict, substituting faux oaths at the last second.

Tommy leaned into his camera, filling their screens with his tanned face. "How in Hades is this possible, Bill? This son-of-a-gun, nonentity of a broker cold-calls us from Egypt, peddling a provocative piece of garbage. It has to be fake, right?"

Bill replied slowly in his sonorous radio voice, "Well, I think we have to be circumspect at this time. We have a photograph, nothing else. Does it look authentic? On the face of it, it does. But we all know that collectors of biblical papyri, including us, have been scammed in the past. Forgers look at you and your checkbook, Tommy, and they drool all over themselves. All we have to go on for dating is a wholly unsupported statement that the burial mask that was the source of the cartonnage was 70–80 CE, which doesn't fit with a papyrus matrix. However, the lab they claim they sent it to for dating is a good one. It's the one we use for Egyptian material. Once we have the report, we'll know more."

"If it comes back first century, then what?" Tommy demanded.

"I suppose I'll have to take a trip to Cairo and have a look at it," Bill said.

"Who's this Dodo character supposed to follow up with?"

"That would be me," Evan said.

His father blew his nose into a tissue. "Let's have Bill take over. The stakes are too high on this one."

Evan's cheeks flushed in indignation. "I'm the business guy! I deal with brokers."

Ever the peacemaker, Bill said, "We can double-team this, Tommy. Ev and I make a good pair. We'll get this figured out and let you know our recommendation."

Tommy exited the frame for a few seconds and reappeared with a cigar. Cunliffe Energy was a non-smoking facility, except for the chairman's office.

"All right, you handle the preliminaries as you see fit, but do not mess this up. If it's a fake, I want you to let every museum and auction house know this broker is a con man selling toxic goods. But if this papyrus is real, then we've got to own it. And once we own it, we've got to bury it. My God, can you imagine what our enemies would do with this? It can never see the light of day. Do I make myself clear?"

***

Samia hated going to the dialysis center, but she had no choice today. Paisi could take herself to her thrice-weekly dialysis appointments, but the sessions so debilitated her that she needed assistance getting home. Their mother or auntie usually accompanied the girl, but they had other obligations.

Samia left work at the Egyptian Museum and arrived at the Heliopolis Kidney Clinic near bustling Heliopolis Square with an hour left in Paisi's five-hour dialysis. The girl had developed lupus in her early teens, and by eighteen, lupus nephritis had destroyed her kidneys. At first she tolerated dialysis reasonably well, but after a few months she began to experience dialysis-induced hypotension at every session, requiring fluid support and drugs to boost her blood pressure and leaving her weak as a kitten for the rest of the day.

On arrival, the dialysis nurses told Samia that Paisi's pressure had stabilized, but she was still nauseous and throwing up. Samia held the moaning girl's hand, listened to the humming of the ward machinery, and prayed for a new kidney to deliver her from her miseries.

An aide put Paisi into a wheelchair and pushed her outside to a waiting taxi. The usual afternoon Cairo gridlock turned the five-kilometer drive to El Zeitoun into a twenty-minute slog. The district was home to a thriving Coptic community centered around St. Mary's Coptic Church. The sisters had been raised in the family's three-bedroom apartment on Toman Bai Street overlooking the five domes of St. Mary's.

"Here we are," Samia said, gently nudging the pale, dozing girl. "Do you want me to get the wheelchair?"

"I can walk," Paisi said. "Thank you for coming today."

"You never have to thank me for doing what sisters do."

The two Tedros sisters, the two beauties, the church members had called them when they were growing up. As pretty as Samia was, Paisi had been even prettier, with full cheeks like a doll's, rosebud features, and smooth, unblemished skin. Now her cheeks were hollowed out and her skin was blotchy and mottled. Her illness had cruelly aged her.

The apartment was empty, but Paisi's favorite post-dialysis sweet, a basbousa semolina cake drenched in syrup, was on the kitchen table. They were having seconds when their mother came home, took one look at the decimated cake, and scolded them for ruining their supper.

She hung her headscarf on a peg and asked, "How was it today?"

"It was the same," Paisi said. "It's always the same."

"As usual, she was very brave," Samia said.

"I'm sure you were," Mrs. Tedros said.

"How was your appointment?" Samia asked.

Their mother sighed, pulled up a chair, and cut herself a small piece of cake. "It's like banging one's head against the wall," she said. "I waited for hours to speak to the man from the Curative Care Organization. He said it didn't matter that Daddy is a pharmacist at El Ezaby. It wouldn't help us get a kidney faster."

"Did they say where Paisi is on the list?"

The woman wiped syrup from her lips. "At first he couldn't even find her name. Then he said he was looking at the wrong list. He said maybe a year, maybe two."

"They have more than one list?" Samia said.

Their mother shrugged, got up, and started taking out pots. "Daddy will be home in an hour. Let's get supper going. Baby, lie down. Samia will help me."

When they were alone, Samia asked her mother, "Did you tell him that every time she gets dialysis, there's a crisis?"

The woman tied her apron around her waist. "He said he would make a note of it."

"That's all?"

"That's all."

When Samia's phone chimed with an email alert, they had liver sizzling in a pan with bell peppers, onion, and garlic. She had a quick look at the screen, excused herself, and withdrew to the lounge, the room with the best view of St. Mary's. She gazed at its domes and crosses, said a prayer, and settled onto the TV sofa to open the message from the French radiocarbon lab.

The email included a photo of the small square of blank papyrus she had snipped from the corner of text for processing. She skimmed over the usual methodological descriptions and jumped to the conclusion.

Date of Sample: 65 CE +/- 10 years

She still couldn't understand why a mask maker was using papyrus half a century after the practice had been abandoned, but it didn't matter. Senses dulled by her sister's suffering came to life. The smell of liver and onions filled her nostrils. Traffic sounds filled her ears. She felt the skin of her forearms tingle. This papyrus that materialized when the beautiful mask of Senbi ceased to be had real value—not a value measured in Egyptian pounds, American dollars, or euros, but the value of life.

This astonishing papyrus would buy a kidney.

Dodo was inside a tiny antiquities shop in Alexandria trying to negotiate the purchase of a minor collection of looted Fourth Dynasty burial goods when he received a text from Samia to check his email. He stubbed out his cigarette and told the shopkeeper he had another matter to see to and that his last offer was final. He read the lab report under the awning of a nearby cobbler's shop and thanked God for bestowing such good fortune upon him.

He eagerly placed a call and said, "Hello, Mr. Cunliffe, this is Dodo Shamoun calling you from Cairo. How are you, sir?" There was a whooshing noise on the line. "Hello, can you hear me?"

Evan was in his car, a Corvette convertible, on the way to the Bible College in Pittsburgh's Squirrel Hill neighborhood.

"I hear you. I've got the top down."

The term confused Dodo, but he persisted. "Okay, fine. I just received the good news on the date. I sent you report."

"Oh yeah, when?"

"Just now."

"I'm driving. What did it say?"

THE LOST POPE

"First century is confirmed. Carbon date is 65 to 70 CE."

Evan slowed to a red light. "That *is* good news."

"Did your expert make the Greek translation?"

Evan had rehearsed the response to this question with Bill Stearns. "He did. It was a kind of a strange passage. It didn't make a lot of sense."

"What did it say?"

"I'll send it by email."

"It is from Bible, yes?"

"It looks like it's biblical, but it isn't from the Bible. We don't know where the hell it's from."

The cobbler stood at his door, suspiciously watching the slight, bearded man in skinny jeans talking loudly in English.

"Maybe it is from one of early texts they didn't put into official Bible. I not Christian, but I must know some things for my job."

"Yeah, I'm not sure about that."

"Mr. Cunliffe, you want to buy or no buy?"

Evan delivered his practiced reply as the Corvette leaped off the line. "I would say that we are interested in principle. We are prepared to pay a good price, provided you negotiate with us exclusively."

Dodo excitedly jumped in. "Yes, yes. No problem. How long for exclusive?"

"Until we come to Egypt and evaluate the item in person. We'll want to meet your papyrus expert. We can probably fly over within a week."

"Yes, fine. A week is good. Exclusive."

"If you show this to any other buyers, the deal is off. Understand?"

"Yes, understand."

Evan concluded, "You'll be hearing from me soon," and hung up without further niceties to demonstrate to the broker that he was very much the one in charge.

Evan immediately called his father. "Dad, the guy in Egypt just sent the dating report. It's confirmed. It's late first century."

"Then you and Bill better get your posteriors over there. Take Spooner too."

"Why him?"

"Use your head. We have no idea who's working with this Dodo character. Could be some bad hombres. If we buy the thing, as soon as we transfer funds, they could snatch it back, and you and Bill could wind up floating in the Nile."

Evan laid it on thick. "Aw, that's sweet. You care about me."

"Don't flatter yourself. Did you tell Dodo he's toast if he shows it to anyone else?"

"I told him."

"Where's the lab report?"

"In my email. I'm on my way to the museum. I'll show it to Bill."

"Let me know what he says. And tell Bill to keep his fat mouth shut. I know how he likes to brag to his friends in academia."

"Keep fat mouth shut—check."

Tommy refused to engage his son in sophomoric banter. "Listen to me, Evan," he said sternly. "If the piece is authentic, we've got to own it. The Church is going through a crisis. This is a perilous time for a text like this to become public. Don't screw this up."

It was late, and the household was asleep. The walls in the apartment were thin, and Samia could hear her father snoring. Moving back to her childhood bedroom was only one in a series of humiliations. Her phone dinged from its bedside charger, and she smiled for the first time that day.

The text from Danyal had a teenage charm.

U up?

She missed everything about her life in America, including even Danyal. They had met the way expats often met—through a mutual friend. During her first year at Harvard, Samia encountered a Coptic student at the law school who invited her to dinner to introduce her to other Egyptians. The woman was a natural matchmaker. It didn't take long for her to declare that she knew a great Egyptian guy who attended the same church as she and her husband did. Samia had done enough research to learn that none of the six Coptic churches in Massachusetts were easily reachable without a car. She was more interested in attending Divine Liturgy than meeting someone, but one Sunday morning, she accompanied the couple to the Boston suburb of Wayland to attend a service at St. Philopater Mercurius & St. Mina Church, a modest chapel nestled in trees.

It was Samia's first New England autumn, and she took pleasure in crunching through the yellow and ochre leaves blanketing the chapel walkway. Her friend pointed out the young man by the entrance speaking to the long-bearded priest, Father Sidarous.

"That's Danyal," her friend said. "Come. We'll introduce you."

Danyal was clean-shaven, with a gentle smile. His bulbous

GLENN COOPER

nose supported a chunky pair of black eyeglasses with thick lenses that magnified his eyes. His sweater was a size too small, making him seem plumper than he was. Samia was a sheltered young woman who had little experience with men. The introductions passed in a blur of embarrassment, but she knew right away that he was not going to be the man of her dreams. She tried to concentrate on the service, but during the two-hour liturgy in Arabic, she caught Danyal sneaking glances at her across the pew.

He asked her on a date, and despite her demurrals, he persisted until she broke down and eventually accepted his invitation. Over dinner in Harvard Square, she learned that his parents had emigrated from Egypt when his father took a software engineering position at a Massachusetts company. Danyal had been a lonely only child, a math nerd who finally came into his own at his high school coding club, where he won a national award for an app to help people connect with kids for driveway shoveling and lawn mowing. He went to college at MIT to study artificial intelligence and machine learning. When he and Samia met, he was a second-year grad student at MIT, aspiring to become a professor with his own lab one day.

Danyal was smitten with her and eager in his courtship, but Samia always pumped the brakes. She came to love him more like a brother than a boyfriend and used their mutual religious conservatism as an excuse for taking things exceedingly slowly. When she finally succumbed to his advances, it was not out of love. Moving in with him during her last semester at Harvard was not her proudest act.

Samia texted back, In bed. Awake

110

RU ok?

I'm ok

U don't sound ok

She smiled. How did you know?

Psychic powers

Worried about Paisi and some things at work

I'm all, he texted with an emoji of an ear.

She did think he was the sweetest man.

With her student visa expiring and no employment offers on the horizon, she had pushed him toward marriage so she could remain in the country. He countered that he would agree in a heartbeat if he thought she loved him. She was willing to enter into a marriage of convenience. He was not. Trapped by the situation, he had something of a meltdown before she let him off the hook and returned to Cairo.

I think I found a way to get Paisi a kidney at a private clinic

You have the $$?

Maybe

Maybe??

It's complicated

Is it legal?

I've always been a good girl

You mean until now?

You're too smart

If I were smart I wouldn't have let you leave

She stared at the text and began to cry and then froze over the keyboard.

Still there?

Her phone vibrated with a call from Dodo Shamoun.

She texted Danyal back with a heart.

I have to take a call

Danyal ended the chain with an emoji of a gold ring and a question mark. She gasped at it and took the call.

"I spoke to the American buyer today," Dodo said. "They translated the Greek."

"Oh yes?"

"I'm sending you their translation right now. I don't understand it. You're Christian. Maybe you can make sense of it."

She already knew what it said, but she looked at Dodo's email to see if their translation comported with hers. It did.

"It's non-canonical," she said. "It's not from the established New Testament Gospels and other books of the Bible. It's hard to know what it is and what it means."

"The guy sounded very interested. I think they're going to buy it."

She thought of Paisi asleep in the next room.

"He said they would come in a week to look at it."

"Where did you tell him it came from?"

"I told him a mask from a private owner. I'll need to make some documents to show an ownership chain. They want to meet you when they come. We need to get our story straight."

Samia swung her feet onto the floor in alarm. "Why me?"

"They want to hear how you treated it and how you prepared the sample for carbon dating."

"They must not know my name! They'll find out I work at the museum!"

"No problem," Dodo said. "Tell them your name is Cleopatra. Everyone in this business lies."

She steadied herself and asked, "How much will they pay?" she asked.

"If they are satisfied, God willing, I think they'll pay a lot."

Emboldened, she asked, "Will I get more than you said?"

"One kidney," Dodo answered. "That was our deal."

Samia didn't know what *a lot* meant, but surely this American would understand the monumental significance of the text, even if Dodo Shamoun did not.

"That doesn't sound fair," she said.

Dodo scoffed at her. "Listen to yourself. What will you do? Go to the police and get yourself put in jail? Be happy if you get one kidney from this affair. It is better than no kidneys."

9

Pope John was enjoying his breakfast in the dining room of the papal apartment when Monsignor Finale knocked and entered with Silvio Licheri in tow.

"Holy Father—" his secretary began.

The pope, who was mopping the last of his eggs with a piece of toast, looked up and said, "Finale, is this an emergency?"

"It is not."

"Then why don't you and Silvio have some eggs? Mario, show them the beautiful eggs."

The papal butler, Mario Santovito, a dignified man in a black suit who might have been mistaken for an undertaker in a different context, dutifully raised the lid on a chafing dish.

Both men politely declined but agreed to sit for coffee.

John said, "Silvio, you must have dinner with me soon. Bring your partner—what's his name again?"

"Paolo."

"Yes, Paolo. Our new chef is a revelation. It's hard to believe that this young fellow was languishing as an assistant in the

Vatican cafeteria. He went to a good culinary school, but he has a young family and didn't want the restaurant life. Mario, have Eduardo come out and take a bow."

Eduardo, the young chef, made a humble appearance and scurried back to the kitchen.

The papal apartment had been sealed during Pope Celestine's pontificate, and it required a good scrubbing and airing before the new pontiff moved in. The prefect of the Papal Household, an Italian bishop anxious to keep his position, offered to commission a refurbishment of the ten-room apartment, but John refused. He was perfectly happy with the accommodations as they were. The apartment had undergone an essential remodeling for Pope Benedict that updated dangerous wiring, replaced leaky pipes, restored the sixteenth-century marble and inlaid floors, and installed a modern kitchen and medical studio. All John had to do was move clothes, books, personal items, and his mattress from his old secretary of state apartment, located one floor below.

"So, gentlemen," the pontiff said. "How can I help you?"

Licheri's tone bordered on pleading. "Holy Father," he said, "we have been inundated with requests for additional comments and clarifications regarding Sister Elisabetta and the implications of her appointment. The volume of inquiries is such that it has become quite difficult to conduct the normal operations of the Press Office. I believe the most effective way to deal with this situation is to have you sit for an interview."

John dabbed his lips and tossed his cloth napkin onto the table. "I thought that Sister Elisabetta's interviews were quite good. When asked about the so-called implications of her appointment, she was circumspect, as I would be. I don't see what I could add at this point."

"Yes, I agree she did well," Licheri said. "The principal way she dealt with questions about future initiatives concerning Catholic women was to defer to you. I feel that if we can get a single definitive interview from you on the record, we can turn down the heat, at least for a time."

The pontiff signaled his openness through a combination of shoulder and facial movements. "You have something in mind?"

"I do, Holy Father. I was thinking about *L'Osservatore Romano*."

John smiled. "I fail to see how an interview with the Vatican newspaper will satisfy our critics."

"Actually, my recommendation would be to have the interview conducted for the monthly magazine supplement of the paper *Women Church World*. The interviewer would be its editor—"

The pope finished his sentence. "Analisa Paciolla."

"You know her?"

"I know *of* her. I read her articles with great interest. She's tough on the Church, very tough, but she's right most of the time. Her article on how cardinals and bishops at the Vatican treat nuns like unpaid servants was quite powerful. Paciolla has shaped my thinking. On women's issues, I would even say she is my muse. Finale will tell you that we have not employed nuns to do the cooking and cleaning in the papal apartment because of her."

Monsignor Finale said, "It's true. We had to hire a cleaning service. It's an extra expense, but, well."

"Yes, I'll do an interview with Analisa Paciolla. Set it up, Silvio. Now, Finale, let's get to our first meeting. I want to get moving on appointments to my Council of Cardinals."

Suddenly, they heard a bullhorn-enhanced voice in the distance and muffled shouting.

"What is that?" the pope said.

Monsignor Finale went through to the study and peered out the louvered window where popes deliver the Sunday Angelus to the faithful. He returned with an answer.

"It appears to be a demonstration regarding Sister Elisabetta. The police are dealing with it."

"For or against?" the pope asked.

Finale clasped his hands at his waist. "The loudest voices are always against, Holy Father."

Antonio Solla had been inside his stuffy car in the Testaccio neighborhood of Rome for four hours, darkly contemplating his life while he stared at the entrance of an upscale apartment building. This was the kind of work he had been obligated to perform when he was breaking into the game. It was not an assignment for the firm's managing director, a man in his prime. However, bookings had been sluggish, and the client on this particular ticket was a large manufacturing company that had been the source of considerable business in the past. They asked for him specifically, so he couldn't say no.

He understood the company's outrage over suspicions that a key employee was defrauding them with false claims that a lingering illness prevented him from returning to work. Yet to

Antonio, this was an insignificant drama beneath his capabilities. All he wanted to do was get the claimant on video playing football with his mates or cycling through Rome like a madman and be done with it.

His stomach gurgled, and he turned to his sandwich, shedding crumbs on his polo shirt. Visitors to his website, Investigazioni Solla, found a noirish black-and-white photo of a craggy-faced private investigator in a dark suit and a trench coat. Of course, he wouldn't be caught dead in a getup like that for a real job. He was chewing a piece of salami when a call came in from his office.

His younger partner, Monica Magnani, asked, "How's it going?"

"The asshole hasn't left his flat yet, not even for a coffee."

"Maybe he's sick after all," Monica joked.

Antonio said, "More likely, he was out dancing and drinking all night, and he's sleeping it off."

"Then you'll have to get off your ass and follow him around at night."

He took another bite of his sandwich. "There isn't enough money in the world. Are you calling for something or just busting my balls?"

"I got an interesting inquiry this morning about a very tasty piece of business," she said.

"You've got my attention."

"The guy who called is an American named Joel Spooner. He's the head of corporate security for an energy company, CEG, based in Houston. I looked him up. He's a serious guy. He used to be some kind of special operations officer for the US Defense Department. His boss, the head of CEG, wants to speak to us about doing what Spooner described as a significant investigation in Italy."

"How did they find us?"

"A personal recommendation from some company we did work for. He wouldn't say which one."

"What kind of investigation?"

"He wouldn't say that either."

"What do you mean, he wouldn't say?"

"They wanted us to sign a nondisclosure agreement before they'd even talk about the nature of the matter."

"That's bullshit."

"I know it's bullshit, but I checked out CEG. The CEO, Tommy Cunliffe, is the seventeenth richest person in America."

Antonio perked up and said that this was a good fact.

"Here's another good fact," she said. "If you can commit to being exclusive to the investigation, they'll pay triple our usual rate."

"Pinch me. Am I awake?" he said. "What about the NDA?"

"I showed it to our lawyers. They said it's heavy duty. Iron-clad language, massive financial penalties for breach. Their advice was to sign it only if we're one hundred percent sure we'll never violate it."

"Whatever it is, it's got to be better than sitting in my car and waiting for this asshole to prove he's an asshole. Sign it."

"I already did. They're waiting for our call."

He loved Monica for being the pistol she was. When it was time to hang up his metaphorical trench coat, the firm would be hers. "What now?" he asked.

"Yes, yes. This minute. I'll conference them in. And please stop eating," she said. "All I can hear is chewing."

Antonio waited on hold, now hoping his target stayed indoors a while longer. The call began with Monica confirming that everyone was on the line.

"As you know, Mr. Spooner," she said, "we have executed your NDA. Antonio Solla and I are anxious to hear the nature of the investigation you wish to conduct."

Spooner said, "Mr. Cunliffe is going to brief you."

Tommy Cunliffe started with a honeyed declaration that Solla came highly recommended, and based on their due diligence of Italian private investigation agencies, Solla was the first choice. Antonio received the praise dispassionately. Assignments usually started with kind words all around. When problems arose, as they invariably did, words tended to sour. He was no expert in American accents, but he tried to place Tommy's. Was there a bit of Texas twang?

"I am flattered, Mr. Cunliffe," Antonio said.

"Everyone calls me Tommy."

"Then you must call me Antonio."

"All right, Antonio. Here's the long and the short of it. We want you to do a deep dive into someone who's been in the news lately. It's ultra-high-profile and ultra-sensitive. You get my meaning?"

"Of course, Tommy. You've come to the right place. At our core, we are professional and discreet. We have done many sensitive investigations into so-called boldfaced names."

"Have you ever investigated the Vatican?"

The question startled Antonio. For a moment, he considered lying and saying yes to burnish his image, but he answered that he had not.

"Would you have a problem doing so?" Tommy asked.

"No, I don't see any problem. Monica, do we have any conflicts in this regard?"

"I see no conflicts," she said quickly.

Tommy performed the big reveal. "The target of our investigation is the new Vatican secretary of state, the nun, Elisabetta Celestino."

Antonio was glad this wasn't a videoconference because it was easier to keep his surprise from showing. He wasn't a religious man, but culturally he had always put the Vatican on something of a pedestal. He understood corporations and governments and the motivations of their employees. To him, the Vatican was a different animal—impenetrable and inscrutable.

He collected himself and gave an anodyne rejoinder. "What would you like to know about her?"

"Everything," Tommy said. "But focus on the negatives. I'm sure she loves God, children, and little furry animals, but everyone has negatives. A man in your line of work knows this to be true, am I right?"

"For sure, Tommy. I've yet to meet someone who is the pure embodiment of good. There are always undesirable situations that can be elucidated with enough effort and skill."

"Specifically, what are you looking for?" Monica asked. "What do you suspect?"

Tommy chortled. "I'm starting from a position of ignorance. I don't know the woman, so I don't have any particular suspicions. What I want you excellent people to do is cure my ignorance. I want to know everything about her. I want you to find skeletons in her closet sufficiently damaging, embarrassing, or criminal to force her to resign her position."

"May I ask why?" Antonio said.

"Is that something you need to know for this assignment or human curiosity?"

"Curiosity, I would say."

"Then I'll just keep my reasons to myself. Mr. Spooner will be your contact from here on out. He's more formal than me—not a first-name type. I expect his mother calls him Mr. Spooner."

"You've got my contact information," Spooner said humorlessly. "I'll need weekly reports at a minimum and my approval in advance for all expenditures over five thousand euros."

"That won't be a problem," Monica said. "We will get to work immediately."

"Say, one more thing, Antonio," Tommy said. "It's also on the curiosity side of things. I looked at your website. You don't really wear a trench coat, do you?"

"I rented one for the photo shoot."

The first large-scale event staged by Sister Elisabetta was an extraordinary session of the Diplomatic Service of the Holy See. The Section for Relations with States was the wing of the Secretariat she was least familiar with, and she was determined to get up to speed quickly. In her view, there was no better way of doing so than meeting her ambassadors, the Vatican nuncios.

The Holy See conducted formal diplomatic relations with one hundred eighty-three sovereign states, most of which hosted apostolic nunciatures in their capitals. The majority of

European and North American nuncios traveled to Rome to attend her conference in person, but given the short notice, many ambassadors from other continents participated via video link. When Elisabetta took the stage at the Paul VI Audience Hall, she was met with a standing ovation that left her visibly embarrassed.

She used her hands to urge the audience to sit and began. "My dear colleagues, welcome to Rome. We gather today to mourn Pope Celestine's loss and celebrate the new pontificate of Pope John. Leaders change. Such is life. But the Church endures, as it has done for two millennia. And the mission of the Diplomatic Service of the Holy See endures. The first papal representatives, the apocrisiarii, were sent to the emperor of Constantinople in 453. By the fifteenth century, it had become usual and customary for states to accredit permanent ambassadors from Rome. So our vital work has been ongoing for centuries. For an institution so rooted in history and tradition, you may ask whether there is anything new under the sun."

When she had rehearsed the speech, she had paused at this point and wondered how she might handle a deafening silence, but her worries were unfounded. With a few exceptions among older nuncios appointed by Pope Celestine's conservative predecessor, the audience sprang up and began to clap wildly. Elisabetta smiled broadly and blushed, but she alone was responsible for this small act of hubris. She had addressed the elephant in the room, and no more needed to be said. She wore a nun's black, not a cardinal's red. She was a woman, not a man. But she was their leader nonetheless.

After the lectures and breakout sessions were done for the day, the chairs were removed, and the hall was reconfigured for a wine and cheese reception for the nuncios, the Rome-based staff of the Diplomatic Service, and various senior Vatican clergy. While Elisabetta flitted from group to group, three cardinals congregated around a cocktail table, speaking in hushed voices.

Cardinal Paul Montebourg, the prefect of the Congregation for the Doctrine of the Faith, was a lean Frenchman with a shock of white hair and matching eyebrows, as thick as caterpillars. His congregation, the oldest of the nine congregations of the Roman Curia, was tasked with promoting and defending sound Catholic doctrine in all corners of the world. It was fitting that an august and sober churchman led an august and sober department. None of his colleagues could recall hearing him crack a joke or acting flippantly. His stern demeanor so disquieted fellow members of the College of Cardinals that he was rarely invited to purely social gatherings.

Cardinal Tosi asked him, "Were you here when she gave her opening speech?"

"I was not. How was her performance?"

Cardinal Navarro positioned a piece of cheese on a cracker and said, "It was credible."

"I would say the entire spectacle was incredible," Tosi said scornfully.

"Incredible and, no doubt, dangerous," Montebourg said.

"How have the priests within your congregation reacted to a woman at the helm of the Secretariat?" Navarro asked.

"I've no idea," the Frenchman replied. "I do not engage in office gossip. You gentlemen, I am certain, are more approachable than I am. What do your people say?"

"I would say it is generational," Tosi said. "The younger men are supportive. The middle-aged ones are circumspect. The older ones are appalled. Are you finding that too, Manuel?"

"With some exceptions, but yes."

"It pains me to hear this," Montebourg said. "Our seminaries are to blame if the younger generation of priests is blind to the erosion of foundational Catholic doctrine. What are we to do about this? Sit back and watch the Church be debased in front of our eyes? Wait for female deacons and priests? A woman as pope?"

"Ask Giuseppe," Navarro said. "He's the one taking decisive action."

"What kind of action?"

"Can we trust you?" Tosi asked.

"Trust me?" Montebourg asked in surprise. "I never cast a ballot for Da Silva, as I believe both of you did. I wonder if I should trust you?"

"With the power of hindsight, we made a mistake," Tosi said. "Have you never made a mistake, Paul?"

The cardinal set the white caterpillars moving above his eyes as he considered the question. "Never one of this consequence." He considered his answer. "You can trust me on this matter."

Tosi leaned in and came close to tipping his wineglass. "I reached out to an influential man, a great friend of the Church with considerable resources at his disposal. He is horrified at her appointment and is anxious to help."

"Who is he? Would I have heard of him?"

"His name is Tommy Cunliffe, an American billionaire."

"I believe I have heard of him. He's the one with the Bible museum, no?"

"That's him."

"From what I've read, he's ideologically sound, although he's rather evangelical for my tastes."

"We must forgive him for the sin of being an American," Navarro said.

"What can he possibly do?" Montebourg asked.

Tosi said, "With a man like this, the question is what can't he do?"

Excited murmuring overtook the hall as Pope John entered and waved to the delighted nuncios. The pontiff's entourage included a videographer, who captured the moment John found Sister Elisabetta in the crowd and made a very public showing of engaging her in congratulatory conversation while clutching both her hands.

"A made-for-TV moment," Navarro said.

The French cardinal puckered his mouth and asked Tosi, "Your American—you believe he can solve our problem?"

"I pray he can. He seemed confident."

"How will he do it?"

"Paul, if you are like me, you enjoy eating sausage, not witnessing how it is made. I have every confidence that the nun is already in the grinder."

10

Samia received a text while she was waiting in the hospital lobby that sent her reeling.

It was from Dodo: Buyers arriving Thursday. Call me.

In contrast to the hubbub and overcrowding of Cairo public hospitals, the waiting area of the private Saudi German Hospital was a model of tranquility and quietude, save for the rumbling of jets taking off from nearby Cairo International Airport.

Her first instinct was to ignore Dodo's text and run from the crime she had aided and abetted. But what would happen to poor Paisi? Could she let her sister suffer and maybe even die for lack of a kidney? She could not. In her mind, she and her sister shared one body and one soul. Samia would take all Paisi's suffering and transfer it to herself. It would take a different form. Her agonies would be guilt and fear, but Paisi would be well, free to live her life and achieve her dreams.

Dodo answered her call. "You got my message?"

She said in a low voice, "Thursday, you say."

"Speak up," he demanded. "I can barely hear you."

GLENN COOPER

"I'm in a hospital."

"Shopping for a kidney?" he asked wickedly.

She ignored the question and asked about the meeting.

"Noon at the Four Seasons Hotel in the Giza district," he said. "They'll have a meeting room."

"Who is coming?" she asked.

"The buyer's son, a papyrus expert, and one other guy—I don't know what he does."

"What is his name—the expert?"

"Bill Stearns. He works at the American Museum of Faith in Pittsburgh, Pennsylvania. You know of him?"

"I heard him speak at a conference. He's controversial. Not everyone likes the idea of a private museum. Did you speak to him?"

"No, only the son. I think he's a rich boy who doesn't know much or he is very stupid, or maybe both. I flattered him about how important he must be and let him talk and talk and talk. They want the papyrus very badly. He keeps asking for assurances that we're not offering it to other parties. I got the idea they're not too worried about its provenance. They want the ownership paperwork, but they're not going to look at it too closely. I think they don't care if it's stolen, only that it's real."

"How can this be?" she asked. "Museums are obsessed with provenance. The Museum of Faith was fined a lot of money by the US government and had to return artifacts to Israel and Syria because they accepted falsified documents."

"I'll tell you the answer," Dodo said. "This fellow, Evan, says that, if our papyrus is genuine, his father will make sure no one will ever see it. It will sit in a vault forever."

128

"But why?" she asked, although, in her heart, she knew the answer. The buyer was scared. The papyrus terrified him. To some people, a buried truth is no longer the truth.

"I don't know why, and I don't care," Dodo said. "As long as they pay. Oh, and this is important. They want to be sure that we don't keep any photos, documents, or notes of any sort about the papyrus. We must burn all paper records and delete everything digital. They will ask us questions, and we need to satisfy them."

"But you have a video and photos on your phone," she said.

"The video will prove how we recovered it from the mask. I'll delete the file in front of them if they want."

Samia heard her name called from the reception desk, and she waved an arm.

"When will I get the money?" she asked.

"If they transfer funds on Thursday, you'll have what you're owed on Friday," he said. "Just make sure you're at the hotel on time, Cleopatra."

Samia was escorted to the office of the business manager, a stout man in a short-sleeved shirt. He shuffled some papers and said, "We received your sister's medical records. Our doctors looked at them. They say they can definitely do the transplant."

"Thank God," Samia said. "When can it be done?"

"Soon, very soon. They are already looking for a good match. You couldn't donate?" he asked.

"I had hepatitis. I was told I couldn't."

"No other family?"

"Only my parents, and their health isn't so good."

"Okay, no problem. They'll find a nice kidney for your sister. All we need is payment in advance. Can you pay today?"

"Not today. Is Thursday okay?"

"No problem," the manager said, stacking the paper-work.

Tommy personally greeted his visitor at the gargantuan en-trance to Heartland Manor. The walnut door was two stories high. It was a gimmick, conceived by the original owner, but Tommy enjoyed showing it off. It was wholly impractical to fully open it for routine comings and goings, so a normal-sized door was cut into it for everyday use. The full behemoth was powered by motors and hydraulics that lowered it vertically, evoking a drawbridge.

"Stay there," Tommy told his guest, Gil St. John. "Let me show you something. Step back a little."

Tommy ran inside, pushed a button on the wall, and the door slowly descended until it touched the stone pavers of the driveway.

"Will you look at that?" his visitor marveled. "All you need is a moat."

"I wanted to do that when we bought the place!" Tommy enthused. "My wife nixed the idea—thought we'd find one of our brood in it, facedown. Come on in, Gil. I'll give you the nickel tour."

They eventually settled into Tommy's study, where coffee, iced tea, and chocolate chip cookies were on offer. St. John, a beefy septuagenarian who seemed to have a cushion of fat under every inch of skin, piled cookies onto a plate and sank into a leather chair.

"Well, thanks for making the pilgrimage to our humble abode," Tommy said.

"I've seen humbler," Gil said with a Tennessee drawl. "Let me tell you, Tommy, I've been chomping at the bit to pitch you. I most certainly have. I know you've been talking to my competitors. I'm here to tell you to look no further."

Tommy stirred his coffee and said, "I like your directness, Gil. You've got quite the reputation. I'm hoping I've saved the best for last."

St. John started talking again with half a cookie in his mouth, thought better of it, and held up a finger while he finished chewing.

"Excellent cookies," he said. "Here's a question for you. What do Fletcher, Pillsbury, Westfall, and Allenby all have in common?"

"I'm going to say they're all politicians."

"Yes, they are. Governor Fletcher. Governor Pillsbury. Congressman Westfall. Senator Allenby. All successful first-time candidates. All new to politics. All managed by yours truly. There are dozens of Republican political consultants out there, Tommy. There's only one Gil St. John. And I will tell you right here, right now, there's only one Tommy Cunliffe.

"I've done my homework. I've had my pollster do some work at my own expense. If you decide to run in Pennsylvania, with the right positioning and a deep war chest, you can beat Governor Henkes and sweep her and her liberal cronies out of Harrisburg."

Tommy gestured expansively toward the window and the vast acreage on display. "I've got the war chest. Let's talk about positioning."

"All right, let's get into it," St. John said. "Gimme your gut answers to these questions. Don't overthink them. Why do you want to be governor?"

Tommy looked to the coffered ceiling. "I want to bring common sense and dignity back to the state, and I want to get the government's hand out of people's pockets. Let freedom ring, I say."

St. John smiled approvingly. "Let freedom ring—three beautiful words. What would you say is the biggest problem facing the citizens of this state?"

"The loss of freedoms. The government is making too many decisions, and it's bleeding hardworking people dry with excessive taxation to fund socialist agendas. I want parents to decide what their kids learn at school. I want people to be able to make choices about their health. I want folks to be able to speak and worship freely without fear of political correctness and cancel culture coming down on them."

The consultant nodded while polishing off another cookie. "You've never held political office. Why do you think you'll be able to march into Harrisburg and successfully hold on to the reins of the highest office in the state?"

"Being governor is an executive function. You're the CEO of the state. I've built a world-class company from scratch. With Tommy Cunliffe at the helm, CEG has become one of the most important players in the domestic energy space. I know how to lead, and I know how to motivate. I can do for Pennsylvania what I've done for my company."

"As a leader, how does your faith inform you?"

"I'm deeply religious. Unabashedly so. With every tough decision I face, I ask myself, what would Jesus do? The Bible is a gift from God. It lays out a roadmap for righteous and ethical living. It has never let me go astray."

132

St. John began slowly clapping his meaty hands. "I do believe I'm looking at the next governor of the Commonwealth of Pennsylvania. I want to comment on your religion—something interesting came out of my pollster's focus-group work. Every single member of the group knew about your Faith Museum. It's a huge positive. But they all thought you were a Bible Belt Christian, not a Catholic."

"I get that a lot," Tommy said. "Just call me an evangelical Catholic."

"You've got a new pope, I see."

"Yes, we do."

"He surely is making waves already. The nun and all."

Tommy spat out his opinion. "Obviously, not a fan of the decision. Yet another erosion of traditional values."

"A lot of people agree with you on that score. Well, listen. Let me be candid. It probably doesn't matter who you choose to run your campaign because you're that good. But you don't want to just eke out a victory. You want to crush Henkes by double digits because you and I both know that being governor is a logical stepping-stone to the White House. Hire me, and we'll get Tommy Cunliffe all the way to Pennsylvania—1600 Pennsylvania Avenue, that is."

Tommy leaned across to shake the man's hand. "I assume you're expensive," he said.

"Extremely."

"Send me the paperwork, and let's get this party started."

St. John grinned and got up to explore Tommy's vanity wall of photos with luminaries. "How many of these folks can you count on for support?"

"Most of them," Tommy said. "All the Republicans, at least.

That wall cost me a few million. I always expect a return on my investments."

St. John pushed his pointer finger onto one of the pictures. "Your wife, Barbara. How's she feel about your running for office?"

"She's not overjoyed."

"You're going to need her. It's the way the game is played."

"She'll be a trouper," Tommy said.

"She isn't around, is she? I'd like to meet her."

Tommy checked his watch and frowned. The bottle usually opened about now. "Let me see."

He found her in the lounge of her bedroom suite, feet up, listening to Broadway music. There was a half-empty glass of something on the end table.

"What?" was all she said.

"I've got the campaign manager I'm going with downstairs. He wants to meet you."

She pulled tan legs to her chest protectively. "Tell him I've got a headache."

"Do you?"

"You're my headache."

"Come on, Barbara, not now."

"You always say that. 'Not now, Barbara.' It's never a good time for me to say what's on my mind."

"That's what your shrink is for, not me," he said, bending over her chair and sniffing her breath. "Forget it," he said. "You won't be able to put your best foot forward."

"Well, that's a fucking euphemism."

"Please don't swear."

"Please don't fuck your girlfriend."

The house was of a size that he didn't need to keep his voice down for the sake of his downstairs visitor. He got himself ramrod straight and snarled at her: "I am running for governor, and I will have my wife by my side during the campaign, as wives do. My wife will be sober, and she will be smiling, and she will project adoration. I give you an unlimited expense account. I support your parents and your ne'er-do-well brothers and sisters. Cross me on this, and I will cut you off, and I will throw your family out of all the houses and cars and boats that they don't own because I do. Am I making myself clear?"

Barbara comforted herself with her half-empty glass. "Perfectly clear," she said. "You're always perrr-fectly clear. I *was* talking to my therapist a few days ago about something on my mind. I was wondering if the girl in Houston also has an unlimited expense account."

Tommy turned his back on her, fashioning his right hand into a tight fist, driving fingernails into his soft flesh.

Elisabetta was not comfortable with her workspace at the Secretariat. She felt ill at ease sitting behind the imposing desk amid all the Renaissance finery. Yet eschewing the trappings of office would signal that she was not as worthy as the long chain of previous secretaries, cardinals all. It was safer to go with the status quo.

She was in between meetings, reading a voluminous report on Church finances, trying not to drown as she drank from a firehose of information, when her new personal secretary, Monsignor Gus Thompson, knocked to say that Archbishop

Cloutier had arrived. Thompson, a laconic Englishman with a wry sense of humor, had been her assistant at the Pontifical Commission for Sacred Archaeology, and she had been eager to work with him again.

"He looks like he's been sucking on a lemon," Thompson said.

Elisabetta nodded and said, "Duly noted."

Pope John had hinted that Archbishop Cloutier, the head of the Section for General Affairs of the Secretariat of State, would be a challenge but didn't offer much in the way of commentary. In her role as papal secretary, she had only infrequent interactions with Cloutier and had the impression that he was being kept under wraps. "You'll figure him out," the pope had told her. At their first substantive meeting, Elisabetta formed the impression that the prickly Canadian Francophone cleric was one of these grand old men of the Curia, a repository of decades of information, much of it existing solely within his head. Secretaries of state came and went; men like Cloutier endured.

"Madame Secretary," Cloutier said, sitting stiffly, fingering the red piping of his black vestments.

"Archbishop," she said, "I wanted to discuss with you the enactment of Pope Celestine's *motu proprio* regarding reformed guidelines for Peter's Pence."

In her previous job, Elisabetta worked with canon lawyers to draft the law Pope Celestine had promulgated in an apostolic letter issued *motu proprio*—on his own impulse. The law intended to set forth new regulations for the oversight of Peter's Pence, the annual collection of worldwide donations from the dioceses that supported the pope's charitable mission.

Scandal-fueled audits had revealed that millions of euros of Peter's Pence monies had found their way into a slush fund to cover losses on ill-advised property deals in London and Paris overseen by the Secretariat. Celestine's solution was to transfer the administration of Peter's Pence funds into safer hands, from the Secretariat to the Holy See's treasury and sovereign wealth manager, known as APSA.

"Ah, yes," was Cloutier's Sphinxlike reply.

"The new law was enacted a year ago," she said. "However, I don't believe that the accounts held by the Secretariat have been transferred to APSA. Why is that?"

As Cloutier launched into a convoluted and labyrinthine monologue on the technical complexities of effecting the new law, Elisabetta hit upon what disquieted her about the archbishop. Unlike Italians, who spoke with their entire bodies, the only muscles that moved when Cloutier talked were around his mouth. The rest of him was lifeless.

"When the Holy Father sat in your chair as cardinal secretary," Cloutier said, "he understood that everything regarding Peter's Pence needed to be handled with precision."

"The language of the new law is quite precise," she countered. "In my view, twelve months is more than enough time to perform the necessary documentation and audited transfers."

"We wouldn't want our haste to lead to mistakes that engender further investigations and embarrassments, would we, Madame Secretary? Cardinal Da Silva understood this."

Whether or not he was conscious of it, he retracted his eyelids and lifted his brows suggestively. She knew this stare, the stare that said *you don't belong here.* She had seen it countless times since becoming the most powerful woman in the Vatican.

She checked her anger. It would only fuel back-office gossip if she lost her temper and behaved like their stereotypical image of a hysterical female.

She painted on a smile and said, "Why don't we reconvene in one week? We'll meet with the auditors, the treasury officials, and the lawyers, and you can lay out a precise timetable and plan for enacting the law. It will be good to put this behind us, don't you think?"

She stood, forcing the desiccated old man to his feet.

"Very well, Madame Secretary, but I would suggest you consult with the Holy Father, who wisely took his time with the law's implementation."

Monsignor Thompson informed his counterpart, Monsignor Finale, that Sister Elisabetta wanted a moment with the Holy Father, and not an hour after her meeting with Cloutier, she was with the pope in his library office at the Apostolic Palace.

John looked up from his simple trellis desk flooded in afternoon light and asked if she was all right.

"Of course, Holy Father. Why would you think otherwise?"

"Because you look peeved."

"I suppose I am peeved. I've just met with Archbishop Cloutier on Peter's Pence."

"Come, sit. Oh my goodness, Cloutier! No wonder you're upset. The expression—'can't live with him, can't live without him'—was invented for Cloutier. I've never had anyone tie me in so many knots. He is the personification of the Curia, an institution that protects itself through ossification. I thought about dismissing him, but he knows everything about everything. Of course, if you can't work with him, feel free to put him out to pasture."

"We do need to get this sorted out," she said. "It's been a year."

John sighed. "The people at the Secretariat can behave like children with too many cookies who don't want to give any away. They view the Peter's Pence funds as theirs. It pains them to give up control. But of course, the time has come to abide by the law. I look forward to seeing how you make it happen. You're perfect for the job. You're tougher than me."

Monsignor Finale appeared and whispered into John's ear.

"Put him through," the pope said. "Sister Elisabetta won't mind." He drew his phone closer and told her, "Cal Donovan is returning my call. I'd like you to hear the conversation."

"It's line one, Holy Father," Finale said.

"Cal!" the pope boomed. "I've got you on speakerphone. Sister Elisabetta is here with me."

Elisabetta took note of the momentary silence preceding Cal's response.

"Hello to both of you," Cal said. "I'm sorry I wasn't available when you called. I was teaching a class."

"What subject?" the pope asked.

"It's an undergraduate course on the history of early Christianity—Jesus to Constantine."

"Is it popular?" Elisabetta asked.

"Very. I'm an easy grader. Is there something I can help you with?"

The pope said, "I haven't spoken to Elisabetta about this yet, but if you have time in your busy schedule, a brief background document will help us counter some of the rather vigorous pushback we're receiving on her appointment."

Elisabetta got the question out before Cal could. "What sort of document?"

"I was thinking about a historical perspective of the role women have played in the Church," the pontiff said. "Something we could provide to journalists and politicians to help them frame the issue—as I said, brief—maybe bullet points. I'd like people to understand that what we've done here isn't necessarily an anomaly. It's marvelous that you're teaching a course on early Christianity, Cal. I don't believe there is full awareness of how women contributed to the early Church and indeed the vitality of Church life over the centuries." The pope paused and took in the nun's stony face. "Elisabetta, do you think this is misguided?" he asked.

"I think I should just get on with my job. Isn't that the best way to calm the storm?"

"Yes, certainly," the pope said. "I just thought that if we can shape the narrative a tad, perhaps we can divert the storm offshore. So, Cal, what are your thoughts?"

Cal was at his desk in Swartz Hall on the Harvard campus. His Divinity School office was tidy and organized, with books and boxes of file cards arranged by topic. The Peabody Museum, a block away, had been good enough to lend him artifacts his archaeologist father, Hiram Donovan, had found on Holy Land digs a half century ago, and he displayed them with pride. His office overlooked a library courtyard filled with Divinity School students basking in the afternoon sunlight. He imagined how it might have felt watching Elisabetta on one of the benches, a book on her lap, shielding the sun to gaze up at his window.

He put the call on speaker and began plucking books from shelves. "I'd be happy to pull something together that you can use in any way you like. It's reasonably well documented that the early Christians welcomed women into leadership roles. Paul's letter to the Romans, written in the first century, describes Phoebe as a deaconess of the Church. Hang on, let me get the direct quote—here you go, Romans 16:1: Paul asked that Phoebe be received 'in the Lord as befits the saints, and help her in whatever she may require from you, for she has been a helper of many and of myself as well.'

"He goes on to mention two other prominent women as 'co-workers in Jesus Christ.' One is Priscilla, who hosted a church house with her husband. The other was Junia, who's of particular interest. Paul writes, 'Greet Andronicus and Junia, my fellow Jews who have been in prison with me. They are outstanding among the apostles, and they were in Christ before I was.' It's not ironclad, but several scholars, myself included, believe that Junia is the Roman name of Joanna, a woman referenced in the Gospel of Luke. Can I read you a passage from Luke?"

"Please do," the pope said.

"Okay, it's Luke 8. 'After this, Jesus traveled about from one town and village to another, proclaiming the good news of the kingdom of God. The Twelve were with him, and also some women who had been cured of evil spirits and diseases: Mary Magdalene from whom seven demons had come out; Joanna the wife of Chuza, the manager of Herod's household; Susanna; and many others. These women were helping to support them out of their own means.'

"Junia makes other key appearances in the Gospels. She's

141

with Mary Magdalene, who visited Jesus's tomb and found it empty. She's with the group of women to whom Jesus first appears after the resurrection. The First Council of Nicaea in 325 CE declared that deaconesses were laywomen and couldn't serve at the altar, but Nicaea probably didn't stop the practice.

"There are some fascinating artifacts from the fifth century—an ivory reliquary from Rome and a stone sarcophagus from Constantinople that depict women serving with men at altars, raising chalices in the liturgical poses of priests. At the end of the fifth century, Pope Gelasius I, in a letter, is still trying to crack down on women serving the Mass."

Elisabetta said, "Other than wild conspiracy theories that I've already been secretly made a priest, our present concern isn't with the ordination of women. I suppose what interests me is whether there are any historical examples of women in leadership roles at the Vatican. Wasn't there a nun some years ago? Pascalina?"

"You're one step ahead of me," Cal said. "I was about to fast-forward to the twentieth century and mention her. Madre Pascalina Lehnert was a Bavarian nun who was Eugenio Pacelli's housekeeper and secretary from his early years as a nuncio in Germany through his time as secretary of state. When he became Pope Pius XII, Pascalina continued to live and work in the Apostolic Palace as his right-hand woman until he died in 1958. It was said that she was the power behind the throne. Some called her the Godmother. I really can't think of a better comparator to your position, Eli."

The pontiff practically squealed with delight. "The world needs to know about Pascalina," he said. "It helps put our situation into a historical context. Cal, I know it's a big ask, but could you memorialize this conversation in a memo?"

"I'll have it to you tomorrow."

"I do hope no one refers to me as Godmother II," Elisabetta said.

"I'll be sure to leave that part out of the memo," Cal said. "By the way, you can visit her. She's in the Teutonic Cemetery at the Vatican."

"Thank you, Cal," Elisabetta said. "I think I'll pay my respects this evening."

Samia texted Danyal to see if he was free, and her phone immediately lit up with his call.

"I wasn't sure you'd be awake. It's after midnight for you," she said, closing her bedroom door for privacy. The apartment was fully occupied—her mother was in the kitchen, her father watching the news in the lounge, Paisi in the next room, sleeping off her dialysis.

"I'm marking homework. What's going on?"

"I've got a problem."

"The private clinic can't do the transplant?"

"No, they think they can do it. I just have to pay."

"Is that the problem? I mean, I have a little saved."

She choked on her reply. "That's very sweet, Danyal. I can get the money. That's the problem."

She sensed he was standing now. He always stood when he got frustrated or irritated, and her oblique responses were surely winding him up.

"Why don't you just tell me what the situation is?" he said.

"I found something," she blurted out. "Something valuable. Someone will pay us for it. I'll get enough for the kidney."

"Us?"

"There's another guy."

"Who?"

"He's a dealer. He found me, and I found a papyrus for him."

"Let me ask you this, Samia," he said. "Is what you've done legal?"

She answered with tears.

"Oh," he said quietly. "Are you sure you won't be caught?"

She managed to speak again. "I'm not sure of anything. All I'm thinking about is Paisi. But no, I was careful. I don't think I'll be caught."

Danyal had a deep, velvety voice that had a calming effect. "I'm trying to understand," he said. "If you're sure you won't be caught, take the money, get the kidney, and move on. Pieces of papyrus get sold all the time."

"This papyrus is special," she said. "It's important. It can change the world."

"That's a big statement," he said.

"I know it is, but it's true."

"I still don't understand the problem. Whoever buys it will put it on display and let scholars study it, no?"

"I've been told that the buyer doesn't want the world to know about it. He's going to hide it in a safe."

"Good Lord, Samia, won't you tell me what the papyrus says?"

"I don't want to get you involved. The buyer is a very powerful man."

"Look," he said, exasperated, "take a picture of it. Leak it to the press, maybe not right now, but eventually. Then the world will know what it says."

"If scholars don't have access to the original papyrus, there's no way it can be authenticated. It will be dismissed as a forgery."

"So what are you going to do?"

"I don't know what to do. If it weren't for Paisi, I'd go public, admit what I did, and accept my punishment. But I can't let my sister suffer and die."

He was quiet for so long that she asked if the call had dropped.

"No, I'm still here," he said. "Samia, I've seen what you can do with papyrus and a brush. Maybe you could do it here."

The guards at the Egyptian Museum on Tahrir Square were incurious why the young woman was coming to work so late at night. Al Ahly SC and Zamalek were playing in the Cairo Derby, and the men were glued to the TV in their guard booth watching football. Samia went to the Papyrus Restoration Lab and gathered everything she needed for the job.

The linchpin for her plan was finding a suitable piece of blank papyrus, preferably dated to the first century. After a search through drawers, the best she could come up with was a fourth-century piece about twice the size of her cartonnage fragment. She had the original tucked into her Bible, placed it side by side with the blank, and began shaping it by tearing away pieces with a pair of forceps. She worked slowly and methodically until she had an identically sized and shaped copy.

She had made facsimile ink before, often for schoolchildren visiting the museum lab on field trips. It was a simple enough process if one knew the technique. The cartonnage papyrus was written in reddish ink, so she retrieved a jar of finely ground red ochre from a cupboard and spooned some into a dish, to which she added a little hot water from the tea kettle and a few drops of white vinegar as a binding agent. When she had the right consistency, a paint that would flow nicely—not too thin, not too thick—she chose a brush that would make perfectly proportioned strokes. She was an accomplished copyist. She had shown Danyal papyri she had made in the lab at Harvard, and he couldn't tell the fakes from the authentic texts.

Samia worked for hours under a magnifying stand, carefully drawing each Greek letter to match the brushstrokes of the original. She finished at nearly four in the morning, but further tasks remained. She snipped a small square of papyrus from one corner, corresponding to the piece she had cut from the real one for radiocarbon dating, and then placed the forgery in the drying oven.

An hour later, she removed her brittle papyrus from the rack and inspected it alongside the genuine article. It looked good to her, but would it fool the buyers?

Outside, the sky was lightening to a muddy pink. The Bible in her bag held one real and one fake papyrus between its pages. At the taxi rank at Tahrir Square, she saw a squad sweeping the steps around the Ramses II Obelisk with hand brooms. The lives of these low men seemed so simple. She almost envied them, for surely, none of them were playing a game as dangerous as hers.

11

The dense fog that rolled into Cairo overnight led to fender-benders that snarled traffic and delayed Dodo's arrival. Samia had the hotel room number but refused to go up alone. This was Dodo's show and she was, hopefully, merely a prop. So she remained in the lobby of the Four Seasons, biting her fingernails and vaguely listening to a pianist in a tuxedo playing Chopin etudes on a concert grand.

Dodo finally blew into the lobby, spotted her, and muttered a thanks to God, "Nishkur Allah." He was dressed more formally than usual, with his shirt tucked into his skinny jeans, a tight-fitting sports jacket, a narrow tie, and shiny shoes.

"You got my text," he said. "I was an idiot. I left my house without thinking about the traffic. I was worried you would go to their room on your own."

"I wasn't going to see them without you. I wouldn't know what to say."

"You have it, right?"

She patted her shoulder bag by way of reply.

"Okay, do you remember how I told you to answer their questions?"

"You may be an idiot. I am not," she said indignantly.

He smiled and shook his head playfully. "Don't be angry with me, sister. We make an excellent team. Come on, let's make a deal with these guys so that you can buy your sister a kidney."

Evan Cunliffe filled the doorframe of the Presidential Suite on the fifteenth floor. He clapped a large hand on Dodo's shoulder and said, "Mr. Shamoun, I was wondering if you were going to show up."

"I'm very sorry, sir," Dodo said deferentially to the younger man, who looked sloppy and unprofessional in a tracksuit, baggy T-shirt, and white socks. "The foul weather. Everything is backed up."

"This must be your colleague," Evan said, sticking his hand out for Samia. "I'm Evan Cunliffe."

"Very pleased to meet you," she said. "I am Samia."

"Is that a first name? Last name?" he said.

"First name," Dodo said, jumping in. "Samia needs to be discreet, so only first name today."

Evan showed his bemusement. "All right. Whatever works for you. Come in and meet team Cunliffe."

The vast living room was decorated in fine Empire-style furniture and silky Persian rugs to suit the taste of globetrotting guests. The fog robbed them of the grandeur on display outside the tower. The Nile was dark and hazy, the pyramids on the Giza Plateau merely ghostly shadows.

Another oversized American was already on his feet. If Evan was underdressed, Bill Stearns was in full business attire with a gray suit and a red tie, the brightest object in the room. He came across as a hail-fellow-well-met, with a generous smile. "Folks, I'm Bill Stearns, from the American Museum of Faith."

"Hello, sir. I am Dodo Shamoun, the dealer."

"Pleased to meet you, Mr. Shamoun." He turned to Samia. "And you are?"

"Samia," she said, shaking his hand.

"Well, hello, Samia. How do you fit into all this?"

"I have some technical expertise. I've worked with papyri in the past."

"May I ask where?"

When she hesitated, Evan said, "She's going incognito today, Bill. First name only. That was the deal. Samia's an international woman of mystery."

"I apologize," she said. "I don't wish to be rude. My employer shouldn't know about my activities away from work."

"Well, I do understand," Bill said. "Sometimes these situations can be delicate."

The living room was large enough for a second seating area a fair distance away. There were two other men. One of them looked like he might be another American, judging by the sharp part of his blond hair, his tan trousers, blue blazer, and brown loafers. The second fellow was darker-complexioned, smaller, with a thin leather jacket and sneakers.

Evan saw his visitors eyeing the men and said, "Don't mind them. Mr. Spooner works for us at the company and the museum. Ahmed's a local, helping us with logistics. Why don't we get down to it?"

They arrayed themselves on either side of a marble-topped coffee table that Bill had cleared of a floral display and small objets d'art. Dodo cued Samia, who reached for her shoulder bag that she had placed by her chair. She put a plain laboratory notebook on the table, opened it to reveal blotting papers, and carefully lifted the top sheet.

Bill whistled appreciatively and laid out the tools of his trade: a high-intensity LED lamp, a quartet of magnifying stands from low to high power, and extra-large cotton gloves.

Donning the gloves, he said, "She's a beauty, isn't she?"

"She?" Samia asked, drawing a glance from Dodo as if to say, *I told you not to speak unless asked.*

Bill switched on the lamp. "Where I come from, beautiful things are always feminine. Let's have a look at her."

What followed were minutes of wordless inspection as Bill studied the papyrus under the naked eye and with varying degrees of magnification. Finally, he sat back and rubbed his eyes.

"You said you had a video of you fishing it from a mask?" he asked.

"Yes, sir," Dodo said, pulling out his phone. "Let me show it to you, please."

He set it down so everyone could see, although Samia looked away. She couldn't bear to watch the face of Senbi dissolving in her hands.

"That's a lovely mask," Bill said. "You said you got it in a private sale?"

"Yes, yes," Dodo quickly said, unzipping his clutch. "Private owner from Alexandria. Mr. Hamdi. He says his grandfather bought it in a shop in Alexandria in 1953. I have bill of sale from Mr. Hamdi and his affidavit signed by notary. Here are originals for you, if you buy."

Evan took the papers and gave them a sneering once-over. "I'm sure your Ministry of Antiquities would bless these if we were to apply for an export license."

"Papers are good," Dodo said defensively, but he added, "Export licenses are very, very difficult to obtain these days."

"We're aware of that," Evan said with a laugh. "If we go forward with this, it'll come with us in checked luggage."

Bill was fixated on the video, watching Samia peel away layers of papyrus from the soupy cartonnage. "Good technique," he told her. "You've done this before."

She mouthed a guilty thank-you.

"This mask had an intrinsic value, more than what you paid for it," Bill said. "What made you take the chance and destroy it?"

"I scraped the back and saw Greek letters," Dodo said. "I thought, okay, mask is supposed to be first century. Greek papyrus. This is worth the risk."

Bill grunted. "Well, it was a pretty good call, I'd say. All right, here's where you found her. It's like watching a baby being born, all slimy and wet. Very, very nice."

The video ended with the dark, soaking papyrus laid out on a piece of blotting paper. Bill sat back in his chair, looking toward the Great Pyramid of Khufu rising from the gloam.

"Who decided to use IFAO for the C-14 dating?" he asked.

Samia said she sent it, and Bill asked, why them?

"They are the best in Egypt," she answered.

"I completely agree," Bill said.

Evan looked impatient. "Come on, Bill, what do you think? You wouldn't want to play poker with this guy."

Bill ignored him and kept going with Samia. "Did you know what you had?"

She looked to Dodo. This wasn't one of the questions they had rehearsed. "We were unsure. Neither of us could read Greek. Obviously, we hoped it was biblical."

"And now?" Bill said. "Do you know what you have now?"

She swallowed before answering. "Yes, I saw the translation you made. It seems very interesting."

"That's one heck of an understatement," Bill said.

"I'm not an expert," she said.

Spooner got up just then and walked past her on his way to the kitchen without making eye contact. He returned a moment later with a can of soda.

"So, Mr. Shamoun, who else knows about this?" Evan asked.

"No one, sir. Just Samia and me. I am honoring your request for exclusive."

"Yeah, but you must've talked about it to friends or acquaintances."

"No, no one," Dodo said.

"How about you, Samia?" Evan asked.

"Not a soul."

"All right," Evan said, yawning loudly. "Still waiting for your verdict, Bill."

Bill leaned over the papyrus and said, "I think it's genuine, and I think it's extraordinary. It's the find of a lifetime. I only wish—"

"What?" Evan said.

"Nothing. I've told you what I think."

"Let's have a little huddle," Evan said.

As they headed toward one of the bedrooms, Spooner

summoned Evan and Bill with a crooked finger, and they paused to exchange a few whispers. Dodo took the opportunity to tell Samia in Arabic that she had done well. Everything was looking solid for them, and hopefully, they would hear good news.

Spooner got up again and was passing by their chairs when a clatter and cry rang out from across the room. Dodo and Samia turned their attention to Ahmed, who was cursing at his glass of ice water, tipped over on his coffee table. He complained that he'd drenched his trousers and asked if Samia could get him a towel from the bar.

Samia complied, and the instant she left her seat, Spooner bent over, had a few seconds' look inside her purse, and joined the Americans in Evan's bedroom.

"What was that?" Evan asked.

"Ahmed dropped something by accident, on purpose," Spooner said in a smooth South Carolinian drawl. "I saw that the girl had a ribbon hanging out of her handbag, you know, like the kind used for employee badges, so I snuck a peek at it. Her name is Samia Tedros. She works at the Egyptian Museum."

"Nice work, Spoons," Evan said. "Tasty piece of info."

Spooner nodded and left them.

"He hates it when you call him that," Bill said. "You know that, right?"

"I know," Evan said. "Guy takes himself too seriously."

"He is a serious guy, Ev. That's why your dad hired him. I'm in the camp that believes he killed people in Iraq."

"Yeah, whatever," Evan said. "I think we've got the picture here. The provenance is bull crap. The docs are fake. The mask came from the museum."

"It did look like a museum-quality mask," Bill said.

"We're dealing with a couple of crooks," Evan said.

"But the papyrus is spectacular."

Evan chuckled. "Put it back in your pants, Bill, and try not to come. You know you're not going to be able to publish it, display it, or even brag about it to your homies in bow ties. Dad wants it disappeared."

"We've got to buy it first," Bill said.

"Sit back and watch me do my thing, Billy boy."

In the living room, Evan rubbed his hands together and said, "Mr. Shamoun, why don't we see if there's a deal to be made? I don't think Samia needs to stay for this."

Dodo pointed toward the table, and on cue, Samia put the papyrus between the sheets of blotting paper, tucked it inside into her notebook, and slipped it back into her bag.

"If we make a deal, you can take possession of the papyrus when funds are deposited," Dodo said.

Evan escorted Samia to the door, exchanged goodbyes, and said, "You take care of that, Samia, the mystery woman. It's a valuable piece of paper."

Dodo was waiting expectantly. The fog was clearing, and the full glory of the Cairo cityscape was coming into sharper focus, but Dodo was only interested in the rich man's son.

"We're prepared to pay you one million dollars, but here's the thing, Mr. Shamoun, the offer is good for five minutes. That's how much time you've got to make your decision, and it's not negotiable."

Dodo slowly shook his head and looked at Bill, cross-legged and expressionless on the sofa.

"Don't look at him," Evan said, "look at me. I'm the guy with the checkbook."

"I'm sorry, Mr. Cunliffe, but I don't need five minutes. One million dollars is not enough. This is a very rare and very fantastic papyrus. You heard what your colleague says. The whole world will be interested in it. Many people will come to your museum to see it. No, I need ten million."

"You're out of your mind!" Evan exclaimed. "I don't think you understood me. I said non-negotiable. Should we get a translation dictionary?"

Dodo's smile looked forced. "I know what means non-negotiable. I think we are still negotiating."

"Here's the thing," Evan said, spreading his legs boorishly. "We are careful and sophisticated buyers. Your provenance is camel dung, excuse my Egyptian. Mr. Hamdi, if he even exists, is probably some guy you paid a hundred bucks. We think the mask's been stolen, probably from one of your fine museums. We are nevertheless interested in the item, but the price has to reflect the deficiencies in provenance. One million five hundred thousand dollars. Best and final."

Dodo immediately countered, "Five million, and we can have a deal. Mr. Hamdi is a real man, the real owner of the mask. You can meet him if you want. He is in Alexandria. I can call him."

"I don't want to speak to your Mr. Hamdi," Evan said, putting air quotes around the name.

Dodo knew how the game was played. It was his game too. He stood and buttoned his jacket. "I want to thank you, gentlemen, for coming so far to see my papyrus. I am sorry we were not able to make deal. We can agree, I think, that the exclusive time is over. I have many other buyers to call."

Evan stayed seated. "I like you, Mr. Shamoun. You're good. Three million. Done deal."

"Number is five," Dodo said.

Evan sucked on his lip, looked to Bill, and across the room to Spooner and Ahmed. "All right, you've got your five. It's got to be done in crypto, that okay? We don't want a money trail."

"Bitcoin is good. No problem." Dodo had a piece of paper in his jacket pocket. "Here is my account number."

"Look at you! Crypto account ready for action. Call Samia and tell her to come back," Evan said.

"I will call her. She is waiting in the lobby."

"You are one sly dog, Mr. Shamoun. All right, I'll get the transfer done."

Evan and Bill returned to the bedroom, where Evan opened his laptop and pulled up the museum's bitcoin wallet.

"That's a lot of money," Bill said.

"Dad gave me a limit of eight, so he'll be ecstatic. Everyone's a winner today, especially Dodo. It looks like crime does pay."

Samia got the call from Dodo, and with trembling fingers executed her plan, switching the real papyrus for the forged. She returned to the Presidential Suite, her heart thumping so violently against her ribs that she worried it could be heard. Dodo told her everything was good, and she delivered the papyrus into Bill's waiting hands. While he reexamined it, she found it impossible to breathe, and when he remarked how wonderful it was, she filled her lungs and fought against tears.

Evan clapped his hands in a slow cadence. "All right, Mr. Shamoun and Miss Samia, our mystery woman. We are done. Go in peace. And don't forget what we said about your obligation to destroy all copies of documents, photos, videos, physical and electronic, about this transaction. And you are expressly forbidden to talk about the papyrus or us to anyone else. You've been put on notice. We don't bother with written nondisclosure agreements. We find them too difficult to enforce, especially on foreign soil."

He cast his hand toward Spooner and Ahmed, still lurking in the corner of the room. "Those men over there enforce our verbal nondisclosure agreements. If you ever see them again, you have seriously fucked up."

12

Everything about Analisa Paciolla was practical. Her short gray hair required little attention. Her public uniform of a white blouse, dark midi skirt, dark blue button-down sweater, and flat shoes never varied. Her reading glasses were always ready at the end of a chain. Her only makeup was a trace of blush to animate her deathly pallor. A small woman, she was an unwitting acolyte of Theodore Roosevelt's adage: Speak softly and carry a big stick, although in her case the stick was her biting intellect.

Silvio Licheri stage-managed the papal interview and decided that the optics would be best if Sister Elisabetta appeared alongside the pontiff. Pope John would join her at her office at the Secretariat, sending a non-subtle message about the nun's new stature.

Paciolla arrived by taxi from La Sapienza University and met Licheri at the Press Office a few minutes before the interview began, armed with several demands. She seemed taken aback when Licheri not only anticipated but acceded to them.

"Analisa," he said, "I completely agree that your next issue of *Women Church World* should be entirely devoted to Sister Elisabetta and the broader contexts of her appointment. And I've already gotten a commitment that *L'Osservatore Romano* will publish the magazine supplement two weeks earlier than scheduled if your articles are ready."

"The articles will be ready," she said. "I'll need photographs."

"We'll have a photographer take some pictures at your interview today, and you can suggest any other settings for additional shots of Sister Elisabetta."

"You're making me suspicious, Silvio," she said.

"How so?"

"You're being so cooperative that I suspect you're in a defensive crouch. Is the blowback from conservatives scaring you?"

"Analisa," he said, "the only one in this world who scares me is you."

"Yes, well, I very much doubt that. You know I'm very happy about our new secretary of state, Silvio, but I hope you aren't expecting a puff piece from me."

"My only expectations are that you will do your usual excellent job."

He asked why she was sniffing the air, and she replied, "Because we are in the middle of a city, and yet I can smell bullshit."

They arrived at the Apostolic Palace to find the pope and Elisabetta waiting.

"Ah, Professoressa," the pope said, "so good to meet you. I am an admirer of your work."

Paciolla responded with a slight genuflection. "Your Holiness, allow me to extend my congratulations on your election."

"Welcome to my old office," he said. "I'd like to introduce you to the present occupant, Sister Elisabetta Celestino."

Elisabetta shook Paciolla's hand, and the two women locked eyes.

"And please accept my congratulations as well, Madame Secretary," Paciolla said. "It's a great pleasure to meet you."

"We've met before," Elisabetta said. "When I was a student at La Sapienza, I took one of your courses on postwar Italian feminism."

"How did you do?"

"Ottimo."

"I don't hand out many highest honors. A sign of greatness to come, perhaps?"

Elisabetta said modestly, "My goodness, I don't think so. I did nothing but study in those days."

Her subjects sat for photos, and Paciolla got to work. "Holy Father, tell me why you decided to make this historic appointment."

The pope said, "I was guided by a principle attributed to Saint Augustine. *Ecclesia semper reformanda*—the Church is always in need of reform. We have neglected to modernize our approach to women within the Church. Women make up half the faithful, yet men occupy almost all our leadership roles within the Curia and our dioceses—popes, cardinals, bishops, and priests, of course, and rectors of seminaries, college presidents, diocesan chancellors, advisory board members. I could go on. Between my election and inauguration, I thought about this issue. I considered appointing women here and there within the middle layers of the Curia, but after prayerful reflection, I decided to make a bolder decision to send a clear signal on this vital issue."

Paciolla arched a brow. "So, are you saying, Holy Father, that this was a symbolic appointment?"

"Far from it. It was the appointment of a woman who is completely qualified for the high office and has already been a trailblazer as the first woman to lead a pontifical commission and the first woman to serve as papal secretary. Nevertheless, I welcome the attention that Sister Elisabetta is receiving, and I hope that women see this as a sign of inclusivity."

"What do you think of the attention from the conservatives? I wonder if you've read Bishop Molla's rather vicious article in *Catholic Shield* magazine. He describes you, Holy Father, as someone who seems hell-bent on precipitating a schism within the Church. And he describes you, Madame Secretary, as being not only unqualified but disqualified for the job."

"I haven't read it," the pope said, "but Silvio was good enough to make a little summary for me. The only ones who think about schisms are certain bomb-throwers on the far right and their billionaire backers."

"Would you care to name these billionaires?"

"There is no necessity to do so," he said.

Elisabetta added, "As to my qualifications, I wouldn't have accepted the position if I felt I could not perform the duties at a high level."

"I understand that an American group is preparing to file a challenge under canon law to the idea that a Vatican secretary of state can be a non-ordained person," Paciolla said.

"Let them challenge us," John said with a toothy smile.

"The best lawyers looked at this before I took action. I have no concerns."

Paciolla turned to Elisabetta. "And you, Madame Secretary? How do you see your appointment?"

Elisabetta smoothed her habit and rested her hands on her lap. "I see it as a great honor, and I am grateful to the Holy Father for allowing me to serve."

"You must have more to say than this," the professor said.

"Well, of course," Elisabetta said. "I accept that this is a significant milestone for the Church. I do hope that Catholic girls and young women, in particular, are inspired to take on greater responsibility within the Church in the future."

Paciolla paused her note-taking and pointed her pen at Elisabetta. "Will their responsibilities in the future include service as ordained deacons and priests?"

Elisabetta said, "That is not a question for me."

"Holy Father?" Paciolla asked.

John said emphatically, "I have made it clear before, and I will make it clear again. I support the elevation of women, but I do not support the ordination of women. However, I cannot say, and indeed, no one can say, what will occur in future pontificates. During this pontificate, I can only pledge that I will actively consider qualified women for other positions within the Holy See as openings become available."

"But not as priests," the professor said.

"Not as priests," John repeated.

"Madame Secretary," Paciolla said, "can you foresee a day when a woman becomes a priest, a cardinal, even a pope?"

Elisabetta laughed. "I'm not very good at predicting the

future. I never foresaw a day when a woman could become secretary of state."

⊷━━━⊶

Samia was regretting her honesty. She had told Dodo exactly how much a kidney cost, and that's what he gave her, not a penny more. It would have been easy enough to inflate the figure so there would be some money left over, but she was new to larceny and didn't have the appropriate mindset. Dodo never revealed how much the Americans had paid for the papyrus, and Samia didn't want to know. It would have upset her to find out how much this odious little dealer had made, and besides, thinking about Dodo and the Americans made her too anxious.

She prayed her forgery would never be discovered. If the Americans did what they claimed and consigned the papyrus to the inside of a safe, then it would not be the subject of further scrutiny, and her secret would be safe. And yet she had another problem—figuring out what to do with the real papyrus. The world needed to know about it, but if she let the cat out of the bag, her family would be disgraced, she would incur the wrath of the buyers, and she would go to jail. She gave a thought to hiding it someplace safe and bequeathing it to a museum upon her death, but she put it out of her mind for now. She needed to concentrate on getting her sister better. Everything else was secondary.

She entered the Saudi German Hospital arm in arm with Paisi and told the receptionist, "My sister is here for her kidney transplant."

163

When Tommy Cunliffe was planning the American Museum of Faith, he commissioned a bake-off among famous architects. Most of the designs were modern, with sweeping walls of glass. One had a touch of whimsy with an evocative nod to Noah's Ark. The winning one was solid and traditional, steel and red brick.

"This one says Pittsburgh," Tommy had said. "This is my museum."

Bill Stearns was a good soldier, but he was also a curious academician. When he examined their new five-million-dollar acquisition on his return to Pittsburgh, he had no intention of disobeying the directive to entomb the papyrus inside a museum vault. However, he was bothered by a few niggles in the Greek lettering on reinspection. Why did one of the alphas look a little boxy? Why did one of the mus lack a tail? How could he have missed these anomalies in Cairo? He referred to the photo that Dodo Shamoun had first sent Evan, but that was taken when the papyrus was still soaking wet, and it was hard to compare. So he did what any good papyrologist would do—he performed some tests. Now, sitting with the reports at his desk, he made a panicky call.

"Ev, where are you?"

A TV was playing in the background. "At the house. What's up?"

"Where's your dad?"

"I don't know. Somewhere. Did you call him?"

"I need you to come to the museum."

"I'm working out."

"Stop working out and get in your car."

"For fuck's sake. Can't you tell me what's going on over the phone?"

"Now, Ev. We've got a problem."

Evan arrived in his workout clothes, smelling ripe.

"A couple of small things bothered me about the Cairo papyrus, so I did some tests."

"What do you mean, bothered you?" Evan said, his throat suddenly raw. "You looked at it at the hotel."

"And I looked at it again when we got back. I spotted a few inconsistencies in the lettering that I'm a hundred percent sure I wouldn't have missed before. Let me show you."

Evan sat down at Bill's table, gulping like a fish out of water. "Come on, Bill, would you please get to the point? What tests did you do? What did they say?"

"I re-ran the radiocarbon dating on a piece I snipped from the edge. It came back 380–400 CE."

"What the hell? It's supposed to be the first century."

"I realize that."

"Maybe our lab fucked it."

"Our lab is infallibly accurate. When I got the result, I had them repeat it twice."

"Do you think the lab in Cairo got it wrong?"

"All I can say is that it's a highly reputable organization. Anyway, there's more. I sent a scraping of ink for analysis, and there's a problem there too. Egyptians began writing with ink about 3000 BCE, and they used the same ink-making techniques through the time Egypt was under Roman control, namely the period when our papyrus was created. Black, carbon-based inks and red, ochre-based inks were the most common, but they always mixed in lead particles to help bind the ink to paper. That's why the inks hold up so well after thousands of years. Guess what our lab found?"

"No lead?" Evan asked.

"No lead," Bill said.

Evan got up and began pacing around the table like a trapped animal looking for a way out of the room. "Are you telling me that you gave the green light to lay down five million bucks on a fake papyrus?"

"No, Ev, I'm telling you that I gave the green light to buy an authentic papyrus. They pulled a switch on us. We got conned."

"Motherfuckers!" Evan shouted. "Dad's going to kill us."

"I know. It's not good."

Evan began to spout. "Jesus, Bill. We can't tell him. He'll crucify us. He'll fire me. He'll cut me off."

"We have to tell him."

"He wants to bury it anyway. Just stick it in the vault, and let's keep our mouths shut. It's the only way to save ourselves."

"You're not thinking this through, Ev. What if they sell the real one to someone else? Any other museum or private collector would make it public. Then what happens to us?"

Evan sat down again, his tree-trunk legs no longer able to bear his weight. "Oh Christ, oh Christ. This is bad, Bill. This is bad."

"Your dad's a reasonable man," Bill said. "Let's talk this through and work out a plan. It's the only way."

Evan stabbed the air with his forefinger and exploded in anger. "All right, but this is on you, Bill! You're the goddamned expert. I relied on you, and you fucked it."

Tommy Cunliffe's assessment was that they both had fucked it, although that word would never have passed his lips.

"I'm very disappointed in you," he said. "Evan, you should have kept the sellers in the suite until the money cleared and not allowed them to pull a switch. And Bill, you should have studied the papyrus more carefully the second time. This was amateur hour."

His son and his employee took the licking stoically. There was no point in pushing back and making excuses. Their expressions of pathetic helplessness probably helped to defuse the situation, because Tommy transitioned fairly rapidly from incandescence to disappointment to problem-solving mode.

"I didn't pay five million dollars to display a new bright, shiny object in the museum," he said, weary from his tirade. "I paid the money to save the Church I love by making sure it wouldn't see the light of day. In the wrong hands, the Cairo papyrus will challenge the bedrock principles upon which Roman Catholicism is built. I won't abide that. Here's what you're going to do."

When the call came in from Evan, Dodo was shopping for a new Mercedes at the El-Khalig dealership. He had just positioned himself on the buttery-soft driver's seat of a Maybach S-Class sedan with an eye-watering price tag of almost six million Egyptian pounds. His dreamy smile faded when he saw the caller ID.

"Hello, sir!" he said as cheerfully as he could. "How may I help you?"

Evan was on one of the lawns of Heartland Manor with leaf blowers whining in the distance. He affected an aggressiveness absorbed from watching genre movies and said, "Mr. Shamoun, the question isn't how you can help me. It's how you can help yourself."

"I am sorry, sir. I don't understand what you are saying."

"The papyrus is a fake. It's a forgery. Can you understand that?"

Evan heard the clunk of an expensive car door closing, followed by street sounds as Dodo retreated from the dealership.

"No, no, Mr. Cunliffe. The papyrus is good. It is completely perfect. I was there when we found. You saw video for yourself."

"The papyrus you gave us is a fake. You pulled a switch on us. We had it tested in our labs. It dates to the fourth century, and the ink is all wrong. You took a blank fourth-century papyrus and forged the Greek onto it."

Dodo almost screeched. "No, no, that is impossible. Your lab must make a big mistake. The papyrus is good, and you get a very good price."

"Listen to me, and listen carefully," Evan growled. "There are only three possibilities: You and Samia are in this together, you did it alone, or she did it alone. That's not for me to say. That's for you to say."

"No, I am honest broker. I would never do something bad like this."

"Then you'd better have a talk with Samia."

"Yes, yes, I talk."

Evan's phone dinged with a text, and he went on speaker to open the attachment. "Here's what's going to happen, Mr. Shamoun. You are going to put the original papyrus in a very safe place. You are not going to sell it again to another buyer. We are going to return to Cairo to pick it up, and you will transfer two and a half million dollars back to us as a penalty for being a thief."

Dodo filled his lungs with diesel fumes from the cars barreling down the Nile Corniche. "I will speak with Samia and tell you what she says, but sir, my sales are always final. You came with expert. You should ask him."

Evan sent the attachment to Dodo and said, "I just texted you a photo. You should look at it, Mr. Shamoun. You're not dealing with some assholes from the British Museum or the Metropolitan. We are serious people you cannot cross. Look at the photo."

Dodo opened his messages and was overcome with a queasy sort of confusion. The photo showed him exiting the Mercedes dealership a few minutes earlier. "I don't understand," he whimpered, furiously looking across the boulevard toward the bank of the Nile where someone had taken the shot.

"We know where you are, Mr. Shamoun. We know where you live. Understand that unless you make this right immediately, we will make you wish you were never born. Samia, the mystery woman, needs to hear the same message. Call me back in one hour."

Samia received Dodo's call from the surgical waiting room at the Saudi German Hospital. Paisi was several hours into her transplant, and Samia, her parents, and her aunt were anxiously watching the door for the surgeon.

She left the room when Dodo began describing his call with the Americans and found a bench in the corridor to stop herself from collapsing.

"I don't know why they are saying what they are saying," she said weakly. "Their lab must be mistaken."

"Sister," Dodo said, "tell me you didn't give them a copy, because if you did, we're going to be in jail, or we'll be dead."

"I didn't do anything," she moaned. "They shouldn't say such things. I should see the report from their lab."

"They sent them to me. I'll text you. Call me back when you read it. Where are you?"

"I'm out," she said. "I'll call you when I get back."

When the line went dead, Dodo rang her again, but this time it went to voicemail, as it did the next ten times. He fled the dealership and drove his old car to his apartment in Heliopolis, checking his mirrors to see if someone was following him. He was packing a bag when Evan rang.

"It's an hour, and you haven't called," Evan said.

"Mr. Cunliffe, sir. I checked with the girl," he said. "She say the papyrus is good. She say your lab is the problem."

Evan was in the back of an SUV with Bill Stearns and Joel Spooner, heading to the Pittsburgh airport.

"All right, Mr. Shamoun. You've made a very bad decision. My jet is being fueled as we speak. We'll be in Cairo in the morning. We'll be seeing you very soon. Don't try to hide. You can't."

Dodo had grown up on the narrow streets of El Hadara, a gritty neighborhood of Alexandria where tourists rarely ventured. He inherited his boyhood apartment when his mother passed, and he used it as a place to sleep when business took him to the northern city. Under the circumstances, he felt safer there than in Cairo. He had made the three-hour drive from the capital the day before. Except for a trip to the supermarket, he remained indoors with his phone off on a high floor of the building.

On his second night there, at one in the morning, he was in the midst of a dream where he was running wildly through dark alleys when a blinding light made him skid to a dead stop. He jolted awake, unsure if he was still dreaming. A flashlight was shining in his face.

"Hello, Dodo," Ahmed said. "I'm going to speak in English, so my friend can understand what we are saying. Do you remember me? We met at the Four Seasons."

Dodo sat upright with his back pressed up against the headboard. "How did you find me?"

"Before I helped international clients make their business in Egypt, I was a National Police officer. Finding you wasn't hard. Did you buy that Mercedes?"

"Please turn off torch," Dodo pleaded.

"No problem," Ahmed said, finding a wall switch.

Dodo blinked at the men at the foot of his bed. Spooner's arms hung at his side. Ahmed had a handgun.

"It's time for you to right your wrong, brother," Ahmed said. "Where is the real papyrus?"

"I swear, I don't know anything," Dodo croaked. "I'm an honest guy. We found a good papyrus, and I swear to God that I believe I sold you genuine piece. The girl, Samia, she stopped taking my calls. If something bad was done, she did it, not me. You have to believe what I say."

"Get up," Ahmed said.

Dodo was too scared to keep laboring in English. "Why?" he said in Arabic. "What are you going to do?"

Ahmed responded in kind, "It doesn't matter if the reason you won't tell us is that you're stubborn or you don't know. Either way, this will be the end for you. The only way to stay alive is to give us what we need."

"I swear, I don't know what the girl did," Dodo blubbered.

Ahmed said to Spooner, "He says—"

"I got the picture," Spooner said. "Hold him there while I toss the place."

It was a small flat, and even though Spooner was methodical, it didn't take long to rifle through every conceivable hiding place. He returned to the bedroom and opened the window when he was done.

"Please, no," Dodo begged.

"Listen, brother," Ahmed said. "Don't scream and don't fight. I'll only have to beat you up, and it will hurt a lot. When you hit the street, you'll be so smashed up that no one will know you were beaten, so I don't care either way. You can say your Du'a al-Faraj if you want or you can skip it. It's up to you."

Dodo began to sob and soak his underpants.

"Don't forget the bitcoins," Spooner said.

Ahmed told the trembling man, who reeked of piss, "Transfer the Bitcoins back to the museum or I'll cause you unimaginable pain. You have a brother and a sister. I'll hurt them too, I promise. The faster you do it, the faster you'll be at rest."

Dodo took his phone from his bedside, turned it on, and sat on the bed to do the transaction. It wasn't long until Spooner received a confirmation text.

"It's twenty-five thousand dollars short," he said.

"The girl, I gave her money."

Spooner said, "For what you paid her, I'm not surprised she screwed you over. Go ahead, Ahmed."

"What about his prayers?"

"He's a piece of shit. Forget his prayers."

They were surprised how easily the end came. Dodo slipped off his underpants, mumbling about not wanting to be found wet. Then, sobbing and shuddering, he put one leg out the window, then the other. He fell into the darkness without crying out. No one saw him slamming onto the empty street. There was a sickening thud, and then the night returned to silence.

Ahmed said, "Okay, we go back to Cairo to the girl. She will have your papyrus."

The worst was over, but Paisi had endured a rough couple of days. Her surgeon declared the transplant a success, but the bottom dropped out of her blood pressure in the recovery room, and they had to re-operate to tie off a leaking blood vessel. Next, she spiked a fever and had to be put on antibiotics. She remained in intensive care in her second post-op night, but she was awake and breathing on her own. Samia and her parents maintained their bedside vigil while Samia's aunt returned to their apartment on Toman Bai Street to take a nap and prepare food for the family.

Samia was asleep in a chair, her head on her mother's shoulder, when the pale light of sunrise gently woke her.

"Mama," she whispered so as not to wake her father, "it's nearly six. I have to go to work this morning. I can't miss another day. Call me if there's any news."

"I will, sweetheart," her mother said. "Are you going home first?"

"To shower and change," she said.

"Give your auntie a kiss for me."

The moment that Samia stepped through her apartment door, she knew something terrible had happened. The chest in the front hall was pulled away from the wall, and the contents of the drawers were scattered.

She took a few tentative steps and weakly called out, "Auntie?"

The lounge was turned upside down. All the furniture was overturned, and someone had slit the fabric and pulled the stuffing from the sofa and her father's recliner.

"Auntie?"

She shuffled numbly from room to room. She had seen images of what houses looked like after tornados struck. That's how the kitchen and bedrooms looked. Clothes and books were everywhere; furniture was splintered. There was only one room left to see. She crept toward the bathroom and called out for her aunt one more time.

The woman was in the bathtub, and the bathtub was full of blood. She was fully clothed with a hand towel stuffed in her mouth. Wherever skin showed, there were superficial stab wounds and a deep gash in her neck.

Samia knelt by the tub, too scared to cry. She could only stare at the lifeless body and let go of everything she held dear. Her bag was over her shoulder. She reached inside for her Bible, not to pray but to look at the papyrus pressed between the pages of the Gospel of Matthew.

This is my reward for saving you, she thought. *I've killed my auntie. I've ruined my life. Were you worth it?*

It was a knee-jerk reaction to call Danyal. She had been dwelling on his text—If I were smart, I wouldn't have let you leave—and she thought about it again. Standing in her wrecked bedroom, she heard the US ringtone.

"Samia, hi," Danyal said. "How's your sister?"

"She had the operation. The new kidney is working."

"Then how come you sound terrible?"

"I don't want to get you involved. They killed my auntie."

Danyal shared a small office at MIT. He closed the door and locked it in case his colleague came back. "Samia, tell me, please, are you in danger?"

"Yes."

"I want to help you. Tell me how I can help you."

"I did what you suggested. I made a copy and kept the original. After they paid the money, they discovered my forgery. They came looking for me, Danyal," she wailed. "They killed my auntie."

"Where are you?"

"At my apartment. My parents are at the hospital with Paisi."

"All right, listen to me," he said. "Get out of there right now. Do you have your passport? Credit card?"

"Yes," she said.

"Come to me. I'll take care of you."

"Why?"

"Because I love you, Samia. I should never have let you leave."

"Danyal—"

"It's okay. You don't have to say anything. Just go. Now."

"What about my family?"

"Call your parents. Tell them you did something bad. To help Paisi. Tell them what happened to your aunt. Tell them you have to hide, but don't tell them where. Ask for their forgiveness. Are you listening to me?"

"Yes."

"Call the police from the airport to come to your apartment. And then call Professor Donovan."

"Why him?"

"Because you can trust him. He'll know what you should do with the papyrus."

13

Samia had the presence of mind to book her flights before doing anything else. That done, she packed a small bag, picked at clothes scattered on her bedroom floor, and gave her apartment one last look. It wasn't a moment tinged with nostalgia. The space had been desecrated.

Toman Bai Street was thick with morning traffic. Drivers were pounding their horns to gain small advantages. Motorbikes dodged pedestrians on crosswalks. Commuters scrambled to get onto microbuses. Samia was enraged by the ordinariness of the day. How could everyone be going about their business when her aunt was lying murdered in the bathtub?

Near the taxi rank at St. Mary's Church, she gulped back tears and placed the most harrowing call she had ever made. She had no idea what she was going to say. Instinct would have to carry her along.

"Mama, it's me. Are you still at the hospital?"

"Where else would I be?"

"Have you seen her yet?"

"Not yet. The nurses are with her. Why are you calling, sweetie? Is everything okay?"

All her mother heard was sobbing.

"What? What happened?"

The words somehow spilled out. "It's Auntie. Bad men came. They were looking for me."

Her mother fed off her anguish and said with rising hysteria, "Why were bad men looking for you?"

"I stole something. For Paisi. For her kidney."

"You said your friend in America, Danyal, gave you the money."

"I lied, Mama."

"What did you steal?"

"I can't tell you that. I have to run away. I'll call you in a few days."

"Where are you going?"

"I can't tell you that either. I don't want you to tell a lie when people ask. I know you hate to lie. I'll call you soon, I promise."

"Please don't leave, Samia," her mother begged.

"I'm sorry, I have to. There's something else I have to tell you. Auntie was there when the men came. She's dead, Mama. They killed her. Don't go back to the apartment until later. I'm going to call the police. Forgive me, Mama. This is all my fault. I did it for Paisi."

She hung up before her mother could respond. She knew it was cowardly, but she couldn't bear to hear the wailing.

The taxi driver asked if she was all right. The ticket agent at the Lufthansa desk asked the same question. In a monotone, she told them she was okay. At the departure gate, she called the police, reported that a woman had been killed at her address, and hung up.

She knew the fall semester had begun at Harvard, and the professor was likely in Cambridge. It was the middle of the night, but you never knew with him. Sometimes he would return emails at all hours.

When her call went to voicemail and with boarding about to begin, Samia left a message: *"Professor Donovan, this is Samia Tedros. I have a big problem. I'm hoping you can help me and advise me what to do. It's about the first-century papyrus I told you about, the one I found inside a burial mask. I can only describe the text as incredible. It completely changes our knowledge of early Christianity. Here is my problem—I was desperate. I needed money for my sister to get a kidney transplant. I stole the papyrus from my museum. I know it was a terrible thing to do, but what's done is done. A dealer I know sold it to a rich American for a lot of money. When I found out the buyer was going to suppress the papyrus for political reasons, I made a forgery and kept the original. You see, the world needs to see it. They discovered what I did and came for me when I wasn't home. I'm very scared. I'll try to contact you again soon. Thank you, Professor."*

Cal's morning ritual involved getting a cup of coffee as soon as he awoke and taking it back into bed while he read mail and news on his phone. A voice message from Samia Tedros jumped the queue.

He listened to the message several times with growing alarm.

Surely, this was a matter for the police, not him. As her thesis advisor, he had learned how she dealt with the pressures and frustrations of grinding out her magnum opus. Samia was a dedicated and competent grad student, but she wasn't worldly, and because of that, he always felt protective. It sounded like she had done something unforgivable and that she was now floundering in troubled waters. Her academic career was over, but that wasn't the worst of it. When he tried calling her back, the call went straight to voicemail.

"Samia, this is Cal Donovan," he said. "I got your message. I'm sorry you're in this mess. Call me when you can." He hung up and gulped down his cooling coffee.

What the hell did she find?

Cal carried on with his day and taught his undergraduate course on the history of Christianity. When his morning lecture was over, students swarmed him with questions. His two teaching assistants, both grad students at the Divinity School, marveled at the scrum.

"They treat him like a rock star," one said.

The other replied, "You know the old saying. Men want to be him. Women want to be with him. It's not a problem you and I are ever going to have."

When Cal dispatched the last of the students, he left Sever Hall and turned his face to the autumn sun. Harvard Yard always elevated his mood. Students heading to class or the library seemed full of promise. Tourists took pictures of the old brick buildings and snapped selfies at John Harvard's statue.

His phone buzzed in his pocket again, as it had been buzzing all through his lecture. This time he looked at the screen and took the call from his office. His secretary wanted to know if his old student Samia Tedros had managed to reach him.

"She said she's tried to get you a few times," she said. "It sounded urgent," she added.

"Yeah, I picked up a message this morning and tried to call her back," he said. "We're playing phone tag. Hey, I'm getting my cast off later."

"I'll miss the early-warning system," she said.

"How's that?"

"Hearing you clomping down the hall."

He sat on the steps of Widener Library and found a new voicemail from Samia. It was perfunctory—sorry to bother you again, will try later, etcetera. An errant Frisbee banged into a step near him. He waved off the apology and sent it back toward Memorial Church with a perfect line drive.

The kid who caught it yelled, "Great throw!"

Once again, his call to Samia went to voicemail, and he left a barebones message.

When he stood, the Frisbee guy called out to him, "Lemme see you do that again," and hurled it in his direction.

Cal's house on Lowell Street was a short walk from campus in one of the leafy areas in Cambridge favored by senior faculty members. It was a rambling Victorian on a tight lot with just enough room in the backyard for a small patch of grass and a patio where he had his first drink of the evening when the weather was good. His landscaper was in and out so fast that he used to tell him, "Prof, you don't need me. You could do the job yourself with a pair of scissors."

Cal bought the house with trust-fund money when he became a tenured professor. In the years that followed, the values in the neighborhood skyrocketed, and now he was sitting pretty in a multimillion-dollar bachelor pad with enough room for all the books and objets d'art he could ever accumulate. For a time, he had fantasized about showing the house to Elisabetta, but the door to those kinds of thoughts was closed.

He threw his mail onto the hall table and rang his secretary to tell her he'd be working from home and that he was still having trouble reaching Samia. He suggested digging up her old Divinity School application for a contact number in Cairo.

His secretary came through—as she always did—and gave him Samia's home telephone number and address on Toman Bai Street. He rang the number with low expectations, but a man picked up and answered in Arabic.

Cal's Arabic was rudimentary, and after serving up a "good evening," he tried his luck in English. "Masa' alkhayr, this is Professor Calvin Donovan calling from America. I'm trying to reach Samia Tedros."

When the man answered in English, Cal immediately recognized the tension in his voice. "You were Samia's professor. This is her father. She spoke about you often. Samia isn't here. We don't know where she went."

"She called me earlier and said she might be in some kind of trouble," Cal said. "She asked for my help. I've tried to reach her, but she isn't picking up."

"Yes, we have big trouble. Samia did something bad to get

money to help her sister. The police are here. People came to our home, you see. Samia's aunt, my sister-in-law, was killed — stabbed to death. We are in a terrible situation. My wife —"

A lengthy silence gave both men time to compose themselves. Cal had difficulty imagining that an innocent like Samia had gotten herself entangled in something like this. "I'm so sorry, Mr. Tedros. You have no idea where she was going?"

"No idea. None. The house is wrecked. Maybe she took some things with her like her passport, maybe not. The police won't let us touch anything. Please, Professor Donovan, if she calls you again, tell her to call us. We are very worried and sick in our hearts."

⊙═══╤═══⊙

Cal was at his orthopedist's office, waiting for way longer than acceptable, but his desire to rid himself of the wretched cast outweighed his impatience. Finally, the nurse looked in and said, "He's on his way. His surgery went longer than planned."

Cal had come with a book. He grunted and returned to it.

The afternoon had become the evening when the surgeon finally flew in, waving Cal's x-ray.

"Hey, Cal, the bad news is I've kept you waiting. I got an emergency case, a car accident. This kid's got enough plates and screws in his leg now to open up a hardware store."

"Is there a good news part?" Cal asked.

"You bet. Your x-ray looks fantastic. Let's get you over to the cast room, and Lila's going to cut that sucker off. Leave your stuff. It'll be safe here."

Before landing, Samia went to the lavatory and locked the door. Sitting on the toilet, she took her Bible from her bag, carefully extracted the papyrus, and laid it on the book cover. She framed a shot with her phone and blinked at the bright flash. Back at her seat, she composed a text to Cal, attached the photo, and waited for a signal. At two hundred feet above sea level, the bars popped up.

It was worth the wait. Walking back to his car, Cal felt light and free. His doctor told him he could start with some gentle activities, but he was already planning on ignoring him and having a morning run. Before starting the ignition, he checked his phone and puffed his cheeks in frustration. He'd missed a text from Samia.

Professor, this is Samia again. I'm somewhere safe now. I'll try reaching you again soon. I wanted you to see what is at the heart of my problem.

There are certain moments in life so traumatic or beautiful or miraculous that they burn their way into your brain and make you relive them over and over until the day you die. For Cal, this was one of those moments. He opened the attached photo, read the Greek text slowly, and whispered, "Oh my God."

...and Peter said unto his wife, Mary from Magdala, when I am dead, you will take my place as pontifex maximus. You will spread the word of our Savior and proclaim the Gospel of Mary. And when Mary became pontifex maximus...

The doorbell rang at Danyal Tamer's apartment on Lawrence Street in Cambridge, one half of a two-family house in a cozy residential neighborhood. He answered it, shirtless, in sweatpants.

"Hi, Danyal," Samia said. "I don't have a key anymore."

14

P ope John was finishing his breakfast of whirled eggs on buttered toast, hash browns, and sausage when Elisabetta arrived at his residence.

"Have you eaten?" he asked.

"Thank you, Holy Father, I have." She failed to mention that breakfast had been a cup of coffee and a glass of orange juice.

"Do you know why Cal wanted to speak with us?"

"I've no idea," she said.

Monsignor Finale was hovering nearby. "The email I received in the middle of the night said it was an urgent matter. Shall I phone him for you?"

Finale got Cal on the speakerphone and retreated to another room.

"Cal, you have Sister Elisabetta with me on the line," the pope said. "What's going on?"

It was a wet, windy day in Cambridge, and Cal was at his Divinity School office, waiting for the call and watching rain and autumn leaves lash his windows.

"One of my former grad students has made an astonishing discovery in Egypt," he said. "It's a first-century papyrus with four lines of Greek text. If it's confirmed to be authentic, I think it will mightily shape the discourse on women in the Church. Eli, can I text you a photo?"

Her phone dinged a few moments later. She opened it and shared it with the pontiff.

"My Greek is somewhat lacking," the pope said. "Frankly, it's completely lacking. Tell us what it is."

"It's biblical," Cal said. "It's about Mary Magdalene."

"An interesting woman," the pope said. "Look, Cal, I rarely doubt you, but how can a snippet of text about Mary Magdalene shape our current discourse? I pray you're not going to tell us that it says she was married to Jesus, à la *The Da Vinci Code*."

"Dan Brown should be so lucky," Cal said. "Eli, I'm sending you my translation."

Elisabetta and Pope John read the text together and fell silent, prompting Cal to ask if they were still there.

"We are," Elisabetta said. "I'm in shock. I think we're trying to process this."

"It's a lot to take in," the pope said. "How do you know this isn't a fake? It wouldn't be the first biblical hoax."

"We won't know for sure until we get our hands on it and subject it to a battery of tests. I've only seen the photos. What gives me the confidence to raise it to your level is that the woman who found it is a highly credible scholar. It doesn't have a murky provenance. It hasn't passed through multiple sets of hands. This woman, Samia Tedros, literally found it herself in cartonnage, the papier-mâché used to make Egyptian funerary masks."

"Where is the papyrus now?" Elisabetta asked.

"Okay, here's where the story gets a little difficult," Cal said. "Samia told me that she was desperate for money to fund a kidney transplant for her sister and stole the mask from the Egyptian Museum where she's been working."

"A little difficult?" the pope quipped.

"I know," Cal said. "It's a problem, but it doesn't mean it's not authentic. A broker sold the papyrus for, as Samia put it, a lot of money, to an American collector. She subsequently learned that this collector intended to suppress the papyrus for political reasons. In any event, Samia recognized the earth-shattering implications of the text and made a facsimile copy. She says she wants the world to know about it. I've seen her copy work. She's a masterful papyrologist. The collector has the forgery. Samia has the original. It seems the forgery was discovered, and someone came looking for her and killed her aunt. She reached out to me on the run. I'm waiting to hear from her again."

"My goodness," Elisabetta said quietly. "This is all very disturbing. Is this the kind of thing we wish to be involved with?"

"The circumstances are distasteful," Cal said, "but that doesn't detract from the importance of the papyrus if it's authenticated. I mean, there've been many landmark finds sold out from under the nose of the Egyptian government. You know the Nag Hammadi codices?"

"The largest trove of non-canonical Gospels ever found," Elisabetta said.

"That's right," Cal said. "One of the Nag Hammadi codices wound up being illegally smuggled to Zurich in the 1940s and sold to the psychiatrist Carl Jung. It didn't make the manuscript any less important."

The pope said, "Let's assume for the moment that this papyrus is real. Tell us how we should think about it?"

"This could very well be a missing passage from the non-canonical Gospel of Mary," Cal said. "The papyrus manuscript of the Gospel of Mary surfaced in 1896 in an antiquities market in Cairo. It had probably been looted from a graveyard in Achmim. A German scholar named Reinhardt purchased it and brought it back home, where it became known as the Berlin Codex. It was written in Coptic and was dated to the fifth century. It was almost certainly a copy of an earlier Greek manuscript. We know this because two small third-century Greek fragments that perfectly match passages in the Coptic manuscript were found in Egypt in the early twentieth century. It's long been thought that the original was written sometime between the late first century and the second century.

"The Berlin Codex was eighteen pages long, so it's a short Gospel. However, the first six pages and pages eleven to fourteen were missing, so we have less than half the manuscript. The existing text is quite remarkable. For one, it explodes the erroneous view that Mary Magdalene was a prostitute and a minor member of Jesus's circle. On the contrary, it provides a convincing argument that Mary had an important leadership role in the early Church."

"It's been ages since I looked at it," Elisabetta said.

Cal had the text of the Berlin Codex on his desk. "The setting is a discourse among a group of Jesus's followers that happens at some point after Jesus's death," he said. "The named followers are Peter, Mary, Andrew, and Levi. In it, the disciples say they are fearful of spreading Jesus's gospel lest they share his terrible fate. It's Mary who rises and comforts them, saying, 'Do not weep and do not grieve or be irresolute, for His grace will be entirely with you and will protect you.' Then Peter says to her, 'Sister, we know that the Savior loved you more than the rest of women. Tell us the words of the Savior which you know, but we do not, nor have we heard them.'

"At this point, Mary goes on to describe a vision where Jesus tells her to win the battle against the wicked powers that seek to keep the soul entrapped in the world. When she's finished, Andrew says that Mary's teachings are strange ideas, and he doubts the Savior said these things to her. This is all too much for Peter, who admonishes Mary, 'Did he really speak privately with a woman and not openly to us? Are we to turn about and all listen to her? Did he prefer her to us?' Mary gets upset with Peter, starts weeping, and says, 'Do you think I have thought this up myself in my heart, or that I am lying about the Savior?'

"It's Levi who comes to her defense. He tells Peter, 'You have always been hot-tempered. Now I see you contending against the woman like adversaries. If the Savior made her worthy, who are you indeed to reject her? That is why he loved her more than us.' And it ends, 'And when they heard this, they began to go forth to proclaim and to preach,' followed by the phrase 'the Gospel of Mary.'"

Pope John said, "It's a remarkable text as it stands, even before this new revelation of yours."

"It is," Cal said. "The non-canonical Gospels, like the Gospel of Mary, the Gospel of Thomas, the Gospel of Peter, the Gospel of Philip, and others that didn't make the cut for inclusion into the New Testament, tend to be held in lesser regard. But they're important historical documents and provide windows into early Christianity. In the Gospel of Mary, we see Mary assuming the functions of Jesus himself. She comforts the disciples. She gives them special teachings. And then she boldly challenges the apostles, including Peter, who reject a woman's mastery. It shows that the authority in the early Church wasn't solely vested in a male hierarchy. Women were in the leadership mix."

"I've always been touched by Mary's central position in the story of Christ," Elisabetta said. "She accompanied Jesus throughout his ministry. She was at his crucifixion and his burial. She discovered the empty tomb. In the Gospel of John, the risen Jesus gives her special teaching and has her announce the resurrection to the other disciples. I've always found it curious that she was never specifically called an apostle."

"Yes, but she fulfills the role, doesn't she?" Cal said. "There's another mention of her in one of the Nag Hammadi codices, the Dialogue of the Savior. She's having a discussion with Jesus on a theological matter, and the narrator says of her, 'She spoke this utterance as a woman who understood everything.' Some scholars have called her the apostle to the apostles.

"And here's another way to think about her: The Christian faith is founded on the belief that Jesus was raised from the dead. Who was it who first proclaimed this belief? It was Mary Magdalene. You can make the case that Mary was the founder of Christianity."

"And yet the tide of history turned on her, did it not?" the pope said.

"Very much so," Cal said. "In Western art and literature,

Mary is portrayed as a repentant prostitute. Mary was belittled and denigrated by a male hierarchy interested in diminishing her role and, hence, women's position within the Church from the fourth century on. Theologians began to claim that she was the unnamed sinner in Luke 7 who anointed Jesus's feet. They pointed to her being the first person to receive Jesus's redemption after the resurrection, not as a sign of her importance but of her weakness. They positioned her as a second Eve, a woman who brought sin into the world and whose faith in Jesus overcame her offenses.

"Pope Gregory the Great put the nail in her coffin in one of his sixth-century sermons." Cal put his phone on hands-free, rustled some papers, and said, "Listen to this: Gregory says of Mary, 'It is clear, brothers, that the woman previously used the unguent to perfume her flesh in forbidden acts. What she, therefore, displayed more scandalously, she was now offering to God in a more praiseworthy manner. She displayed her hair to set off her face, but now her hair dries her tears. She turned the mass of her crimes to virtues, in order to serve God entirely in penance, for as much as she had wrongly held God in contempt.'"

"My goodness," Elisabetta said. "He's rewriting history."

"It's pure fiction on his part," Cal said. "He's killing two birds with one stone. He undermines the critical roles that Mary plays in the Gospels by portraying her as a harlot, and at the same time he erodes the capability of women to take on leadership functions. He's painting all women with the same brush, and he's erasing not only Mary but all the other women in the New Testament who held prominent positions in Jesus's inner circle.

"As I wrote in the memo, let's not forget that Paul, in his letter to the Romans, described Phoebe as a deacon in the Church of Cenchreae. He describes Priscilla as supporting a congregation in her home, Tryphaena, Tryphosa, and Persis as his co-workers for the gospel. And he remarkably names Junia as foremost among the apostles. Women likely played a prominent part in early Christian communities because worshippers met in their homes. Later, when Christians began to assemble in public churches, men became dominant, and women were removed from positions of authority.

"By the time we get to the sixth century, all these early female Christian leaders were essentially forgotten, and Mary Magdalene had become a harlot. The exception to the narrative that Mary was a prostitute comes from the Eastern Orthodox Church, where Mary has always been venerated for what she was—a witness to the resurrection."

"And now we have your papyrus," the pope said. "What are we to make of it?"

Cal leaned into the speaker and said, "The declaration that Simon Peter was married doesn't break new ground. Mark 1:30 says, 'Simon's mother-in-law was in bed with a fever, and they immediately told Jesus about her.' Then there's 1 Corinthians 9:5, which refers to Peter by his Aramaic name, Cephas, for rock. 'Don't we have the right to take a believing wife along with us, as do the other apostles and the Lord's brothers and Cephas?'

"Again, if this is authenticated, the new information is that his wife was Mary Magdalene, which is astonishing in its own right. What follows is the even more remarkable disclosure that Peter designated Mary to succeed him as pontifex maximus.

If we believe the papyrus is real, the world needs to come to grips with the revelation that Mary Magdalene was the second pope."

Cal stared at his phone, waiting for one of them to speak.

"My head is spinning," Elisabetta said.

The pope said, "But Cal, history teaches us that Linus was the second bishop of Rome, the second pope."

Cal said, "That comes from the writings of the Greek bishop Irenaeus in the late second century and the historian Eusebius in the fourth century. Both were far removed from events in the first century. It's conceivable that Mary's pontificate was brief and lost to history or that it served the male hierarchy of the later Church to suppress her role. Almost nothing is known of Linus's life. I don't have reason to doubt that he was a pope, but maybe he was the third, not the second."

"This leaves us in a precarious situation," the pope said, affecting an assertive tone. "Unless and until the papyrus is deemed to be genuine, we cannot give it any weight."

"I don't disagree," Cal said. "However, if we prove that this is a true first-century document, and can reach a scholarly consensus that it's a missing fragment from the Gospel of Mary, then it will have profound implications for our appreciation of Church history and the controversy around Elisabetta's appointment. If a woman could serve as pope at the dawn of the Christian faith, it seems to me it's untenable to oppose a woman serving as secretary of state in the twenty-first century. This papyrus could be a two-thousand-year-old message in a bottle washed up on our shores, teaching us that authority within the Church wasn't intended to be vested in males alone."

"Yes, the implications are profound," the pope said gravely.

"It will surely elevate the debate to a fever pitch. It has been foundational dogma that the ordained ministry originates in Jesus's choice of the twelve male apostles."

Cal said, "This papyrus takes a can opener to the dogma."

"This must be why this collector wants to suppress it," Elisabetta said, her voice turning husky. "It must not be suppressed." Cal imagined she was close to tears and wished he could comfort her.

"It speaks to the power of the papyrus," Cal said. "As a historian and as your friend, I'll be damned if I'm going to let someone bury it."

There was a time when Monica Magnani considered this kind of work grubby, but that time had long passed. When Antonio Solla first approached her to join his firm as a junior associate, he told her that no one grew up wanting to be a private investigator. It's something you fall into, not like a pothole, he joked, but as a better alternative to your current line of work.

In her case, she had been chained to a desk as a bored claims adjuster at an insurance company. Antonio had met her while working on a case, thought she would make a good PI, and coaxed her to make a move. He had a crush on her back then, and he still did, but he was always a gentleman. She was married, he was married, and their relationship had never strayed from professional.

Her first assignments skewed heavily toward surveillance of wives suspected of straying on their husbands, some of them complete bastards as far as Monica could make out. Who could blame these women for looking for a little sunshine? After work, she would often spend an inordinate amount of time under the shower, literally and metaphorically cleansing herself of the day's dirt. But as time marched on, she became inured to the work, and her evening showers were shorter.

She and Antonio agreed she was the better of the two to investigate Elisabetta Celestino's formative years and interview old friends. She began by tracking down classmates at Elisabetta's upper secondary school in Trastevere and her university, La Sapienza. Posing as a journalist writing a flattering article for a feminist website, she collected mostly glowing anecdotes about Elisabetta's character and deeds while gently probing for chinks in the nun's armor. Did she do any drugs in those days? Could there have been a hidden abortion? Her boyfriend's stabbing death—was it possible there was some kind of love triangle going on? Yet more than two dozen friends and acquaintances had nothing negative to say about her. On the contrary, the young Elisabetta had been good as gold, pure as the driven snow—pick your cliché.

Monica was left with one last door to knock on. She had a photo of the girls' volleyball team published in the school's student newspaper that showed Emanuela Sordelli standing next to Elisabetta. The two girls smiled for the camera, arms around each other's shoulders. Emanuela was last on Monica's list because she had been the most difficult of Elisabetta's contemporaries to track down. She never married or had children. She changed her residence frequently, often without leaving a forwarding address with the post office. Her employment history was spotty—mostly waitressing and bartending jobs, and she was repeatedly fired for being late or missing shifts.

Her trail led to a drug-infested neighborhood in the Ostia district of Rome. Monica would never have gone to Piazza Gasparri alone at night, but she was willing to poke around in the light of day. Rival clans there dealt drugs, collected protection money, and warred. The dilapidated high-rise apartment blocks had views of the Tyrrhenian Sea the rich would die for, but they could be dangerous places when the sun went down. Using shoe-leather methods, Monica had discovered that Emanuela's last known address was an apartment on Via Franco Storelli. As she entered the building lobby, she heard sharp whistles from a rooftop lookout, warning drug pushers that a suspicious stranger was afoot, and she endured a few hard stares and a crude remark from a pimply teenage boy in the stairwell. Monica turned tough with the kid, told him to fuck off, and arrived at a door on the second floor that needed paint. She knocked, saw the peephole darken, and knocked again.

"Hello," she called through the door. "I'm looking for Emanuela Sordelli. My name is Monica. I'm not with the police or the tax authority. I'm a journalist. I'm doing a story about your old pal Elisabetta Celestino. I've been talking to all her school friends. You played volleyball with her, I think."

The door opened slowly, revealing a gaunt woman with raccoon eyes and stringy hair, barefoot in torn jeans and a tube top.

"How'd you find me?" she said.

Monica smiled as warmly as she could and said, "I look things up. I follow my nose. It's what I do as a journalist. Do you have a few minutes for me?"

"To talk about Eli?" she asked.

"Yes. Just a few questions."

The apartment had only a few pieces of furniture, the kind of threadbare and beat-up pieces that people leave on the sidewalk. There were open tins of food and pizza crusts on the kitchen counter, and the sink was filled with dirty dishes. Monica took a seat on the side of the sofa that didn't have a hole in the cushion while Emanuela hastily brushed some items from the coffee table into its drawer. It was a quick maneuver, but Monica spotted a spoon and a rubber hose. The woman's pupils looked normal, and she wasn't all that jittery, so she figured she had caught her at a good point in her cycle.

"I ran out of coffee," Emanuela said.

"I just had one," Monica said.

"What do you want to know?" Emanuela asked, throwing a long leg over the arm of her chair.

"When was the last time you saw her?"

"I don't know. A long time ago. Some kid threw a party a year or two after graduation. She was at university. I wasn't. I'm not even sure we spoke that night. That was the last time. She went on to great things. I went on to shit things."

"What was she like? At school, I mean."

Emanuela's eyes narrowed into something of a squint. "Sorry, why are you here? What's the purpose of this?"

Monica replied with her standard explanation. "I write for a feminist publication. As you can imagine, our readers are thrilled with Elisabetta's appointment as secretary of state. They want to know about her path from childhood to the Vatican. Their curiosity is natural, don't you think?"

"What do you want to know about her?"

"Well, you were her school friend, her teammate in sports.

Anything you think our readers would be interested to hear—anecdotes that show her strengths and even her weaknesses. I mean, no one is perfect, right?"

Every interviewee had at this point launched into reminiscences about Elisabetta's kindness, sense of humor, studiousness, etcetera, but not Emanuela.

"How much are you paying for these anecdotes?" Emanuela asked.

This one is street smart, Monica thought. *She's going to play the angles.*

"Well, a lot of the people I've spoken to have said the same things about her," Monica said. "If you have some more unusual stories to tell, I could give you some cash."

"How much?"

"I suppose it depends on how unusual the stories are."

There was some kind of commotion on the street, and Emanuela sprang to the window to check it out.

"This place is full of assholes," she said. "It's the worst place I've ever lived, and that's saying something. You're not a journalist, are you?"

"Why do you say that?"

"A female journalist wouldn't come to this neighborhood alone."

"I'll show you my card."

"Don't bother. You said that no one is perfect. I think maybe you're looking for dirt. Do you care if it's the truth?"

I'm entering dangerous territory, Monica thought. She had paid for information in the past—it was part of the business. She had never paid for disinformation. She opened her purse and waggled her voice recorder. "What I care about is your willingness to go on the record about Elisabetta Celestino's imperfections. Some imperfections may be worth more than others."

Emanuela said cockily, "Did you bring cash?"

"As a matter of fact, I did."

———⁂———

On her way back home, Monica called Antonio from her car.

"How did it go?" he asked.

"This last girl was a train wreck."

"Sometimes we like the train wrecks," he said. "What did she say?"

"The same as all the other ones who knew her from school days and university. Even before she was a nun, she practically walked on water. If I had been so perfect, I wouldn't be interviewing drug addicts in Ostia for a living."

"So, nothing?" Antonio said. "We've got nothing?"

"I didn't say that. I've got her on the record saying some interesting things. Whether or not they're true, partially true, or false, I can't say. Here's the recording."

She hit play on her voice recorder and let her boss listen.

"Not bad," Antonio said when it was over. "It's a start. We'll give it to Chiara to write it up for her online rag. But you and I know it probably won't be enough to satisfy our client. Spooner is calling me twice a day for updates. What you have delivers a flesh wound. We need a kill shot. I'm working on something much bigger. It will be expensive, but the client tells me that price is no object."

"Is it real or fabricated?" Monica asked.

"These days, it's hard to know the difference." Antonio laughed.

"What the hell are we doing, Antonio? Elisabetta Celestino sounds like a good person."

"I'll tell you what we're doing," he said. "We're doing our job."

15

Galilee, 36 CE

Jesus was dead, and times were hard, but at least they were together in the land of their birth.

Mary was from Magdala, a village of about four hundred on the shores of the Sea of Galilee. Simon Peter was from Capernaum, a larger seaside village a three-hour walk north. Their early lives revolved around fish. The people of Galilee called their water a sea because of its vastness, but it was a freshwater lake, teeming with Galilean tilapia (that would come to be known as St. Peter's fish), sardines, carp, and catfish.

Mary's family were not fishermen—they were middlemen who met the boats, bought the catch, cleaned the fish, dried them on racks on the beach, and sold the preserved flesh to merchants at a profit. Mary learned how to gut and scale a fish when she was five, and she worked her short-bladed knife throughout her childhood, six days a week, whiling away the hours by singing songs with her brothers and sisters.

Simon's people had been fishermen for generations. By the time he was eight, there was nothing of the trade he could not do. He mastered net making and repair, trawling, rowing, and sailing, and when he came of age at thirteen, he was already tall and muscular with the first stubble of a beard and the bright blue eyes of his lineage.

Although they were not far apart, the villages of Magdala and Capernaum might as well have been on different planets. Their peoples had little reason to mix, other than chance encounters at sea when squabbles broke out from time to time when nets tangled. Yet on one fine Sabbath day ten years before, when springtime showers had turned the countryside green, Mary and Simon Peter, known only as Simon in those days, met. She was fourteen; he was twenty-five.

Mary's parents drove their cart and mules to Capernaum, hearing that a preacher and healer of some renown would be holding forth in the village square. They arrived to find a crowd gathering around a flat rock upon which stood a man, perhaps thirty, whose fraying linen robe hung loosely on his bony frame. Mary did not understand why people would be interested in hearing an itinerant preacher, but she was excited to spend an afternoon in a village not her own. She was far too old for her father to lift onto his shoulders, so she secured her vantage point by wriggling her way to the inner circumference of the circle, where she found herself standing beside a tall stranger whose clothes, like hers, reeked of fish. However, she took no note of him because the preacher, a fellow with a wispy reddish beard and scraggly hair, instantly captivated her. This man, Jesus of Nazareth, didn't rant and rave, or jump about, or shout like most of the seers and magicians she had seen coming through her village. His voice was soft and sweet as honey, but the words he uttered had an inherent volume.

She heard him say, "Happy are you who are poor, for yours is the Kingdom of God. Happy are you who hunger now, for you will be filled. Happy are you who weep now, for you will laugh. Happy are you whenever men hate you, and when they exclude you and reproach you and denounce your name as wicked for the sake of the Son of Man. Rejoice in that day and leap for joy, for look, your reward is great in Heaven!"

He spoke for an hour, and when he was done, he climbed down from the rock and let the people touch his arms and shoulders as he passed. Mary's fingers tingled for a while after grazing a rough sleeve.

The tall stranger muttered, "Do you know what we have just witnessed?"

She looked up, uncertain the question was aimed at her. "Are you speaking to me?" she asked.

"Who else is standing by my side?" He laughed.

"Oh!" she said. "What have we witnessed?"

"The Son of God," Simon said. "We have been blessed by the presence of the Son of God, of that I am sure."

"His words," she replied. "I never heard such words."

"How did they make you feel?" he asked.

"I do not know. No, that is not true. I do know. I feel happy."

Simon laughed and said, "Happiness is good. What is your name, child?"

She quickly retorted, "I am not a child. My name is Mary."

"Are you not? Let me have a look at you, Mary."

She had a light complexion, for though she toiled in the burning sun, her mother had taught her to protect her face with a scarf. Her high cheekbones gave her a regal look, and her lips were pleasingly plump. Bronze hair flowed to her shoulders from under her scarf. Although her robe was shapeless, the cinch rope she wore tightly around her waist gave her a decidedly feminine silhouette.

"I apologize," Simon said. "You are certainly not a child. My name is Simon. Where are you from, Mary, who is not a child?"

"Magdala. Do you know it?"

"Only its shoreline. I am a fisherman, you see."

"Perhaps it is your fish I cut and dry," she said.

"Well then, don't we make a pretty pair? Are you here on your own?"

"My parents are here."

"Take me to them, if you will. I would like a word with your father."

"What about?" she asked.

"Why, about you, Mary, who is not a child. I would like to see you again if it does not displease you."

She smiled into his rugged face. "It does not displease me."

Within a month, Simon and Mary were man and wife. Mary's father became ill shortly after her betrothal, and he coughed up blood in the week leading to the wedding ceremony. He just managed to see his daughter off, and his funeral came on the heels of her nuptials. Some said his death cast a pall on the newlyweds, and in time, Mary and Simon would have to agree. Mary was barren, and the lack of an heir would weigh heavily on Simon until the day he died.

They lived in Capernaum at the house of Simon's father.

A room with a high window and a burlap door was their private space, but that privacy was short-lived. Mary's widowed mother, Sarai, went to live with her eldest daughter, the only of her children who remained in Magdala, but the daughter's husband couldn't get along with his mother-in-law and forced her to leave. And so Mary and Simon took Sarai in, and Simon used his skills to fit a net and burlap partition in their room to preserve a little modesty.

The weeks passed. Simon fished with his older brother, Andrew. Mary and Sarai cleaned and dried their fish and did a small business in Capernaum, trading on their skills. Then, one day, word came that the preacher Jesus of Nazareth, who was making a circuit of all the towns in Galilee, was returning to Capernaum to teach at the synagogue.

Ezra, the old village rabbi who taught the Torah to the young men on the Sabbaths, had been skeptical of this itinerant rabbi from Nazareth since he first appeared in the village square. Like most Torah teachers, Ezra only had the authority to educate students on the accepted interpretations of the laws.

This preacher, Jesus, was different. Seeking to arouse the entire nation, Jesus boldly professed that he had the authority to make new interpretations of the law. He told the poor and oppressed that he was the Messiah, the shepherd who would seek the abandoned and save them. You are one of God's lost sheep, he would say to them. He still loves you. And he repeatedly demonstrated his divine bona fides by cleansing the lepers of their affliction, restoring sight to the blind, hearing to the deaf, and mobility to the lame. He admonished the chief priests swaddled in riches and told them that they had scattered and harmed God's flock and should expect to receive God's retribution.

Ezra did not have the fortitude to take a stand against this rabble-rousing rabbi and prevent him from preaching at his synagogue. The people of Capernaum wanted to see Jesus, and Ezra let him come.

The synagogue, a simple meetinghouse with benches and a reed roof, was filled that Sabbath morning. Mary, Simon, and Andrew arrived early enough to secure seats in the front, but most had to stand. Sarai, too, had wanted to attend, but she had been suffering from a fever for the last few days and could not easily lift herself from her bed. There was no denying that this man, Jesus, had captured Mary and Simon's imaginations. They often spoke about the teachings they had heard when they first saw him preach from the flat rock in the village square. The dry lessons of the Torah paled in comparison to Jesus's evocative rhetoric about fair dealings for the poor and salvation for all who embraced God's word.

As Jesus spoke in the synagogue that Sabbath, Mary felt her spirit soar, and when she looked toward her husband, she could tell that he too was in the thrall of this rabbi. There were times during his sermon when she was convinced that Jesus was speaking directly to them. And she was amazed that, when he finished, he came to her, looking down on her upturned face, and told her that she seemed burdened.

Mary said. "My mother, Sarai, has a fever."

Jesus asked where she was.

"In my house," Simon said. "Sarai is my mother-in-law."

And then Jesus said he would heal her.

All who had been in the synagogue, except for the rabbi, Ezra, who sulked off, followed Jesus to Simon's house and waited in the courtyard as he ministered to Mary's bedridden mother. Jesus took Sarai by the hand, and the fever soon left her body. Infused with vitality, she rose from her bed and began to prepare a meal of thanksgiving.

The crowd marveled when Sarai emerged from the house to announce her recovery and began firing her oven and kneading her bread. While they ate, Andrew asked Jesus where he was going next. Tiberius was his reply.

Mary and Simon whispered eager words to one another, and then Simon said to Jesus, "Master, we are but simple fishermen, but we would like to come with you and help you spread your good words."

Andrew chimed in, "I too would follow you."

Jesus smiled at them and replied, "Come follow me, and I will make you fishers of men," and then he resumed munching contentedly on one of Sarai's freshly baked loaves.

Ten years. Ten tumultuous years.

Jesus traveled throughout Galilee and Judea preaching, teaching, and performing faith-affirming miracles, followed and nurtured by Mary, Simon, and a burgeoning band of acolytes who believed with every fiber of their being that he was the Messiah, the Son of God. In the evenings, Jesus and his inner circle dined collectively, bantering and arguing over his teachings as he pushed them toward a purer understanding of how best to live a righteous life. There were many strong voices among his disciples, but none stronger and more passionate than Simon, whom Jesus began calling Petrus, his rock, and his wife, Mary of Magdala. Mary was at times Jesus's mother, and at times his sister, making sure he was fed, washing his feet and applying unguent to his cracked heels, and singing him to sleep when he was restless.

Simon Peter was as protective of the master as his wife, but he could not fully contain his jealousy, as no man enjoys sharing his wife with another, even in the absence of carnality. When Mary and Peter (as even she began to call her husband) were alone, they often quarreled until they were both exhausted, neither of them giving the other an inch. If they could steal a few moments of privacy in the nook of a borrowed house, they would sometimes find earthly pleasure in making hasty love, hoping beyond hope that their union would bear fruit.

Their Nazarene movement grew, threatening the authority of the Romans who ruled Judea with their Jewish client kings. One poor man could be swatted like a fly. Thousands upon thousands of them could not be so easily dismissed. In the way that men in power have always done, the kingdom's rulers reasoned that killing the leader of a rebellion would cause the movement to collapse. Or so the theory goes.

In the year 32, Jesus was tried, condemned, and executed, but the miscalculation of the Roman generals, the Jewish kings, and the Temple's high priests was of an epic proportion. The death of Jesus was the beginning, not the end, of the revolution, for when Mary went to the rock-cut tomb to tend to the body of the martyred Jesus, she found it empty. His resurrection was akin to a lightning strike in a parched forest— the fire it started was unquenchable. At first, the Nazarenes were anguished and reeling. Their beloved teacher was dead, but lo, he was risen, then once again gone. It was left to them to keep his teachings alive, but every movement needs a leader. Although there were rivals such as James, the brother of Jesus, and John, the youngest of the disciples, Peter, the rock, assumed the mantle of their pontifex maximus. In time, the Nazarenes became known as Christians, an homage to their anointed master, Jesus Christus.

"It falls upon you," Mary told her husband in the days following the resurrection and ascension.

"And you," Peter said. "I was his rock, and you are mine."

"We must leave Jerusalem," he said. "It is too dangerous. Others will die upon the cross. We must spread the joyous news of the Master's resurrection throughout the land."

And Mary recalled Ruth's words from the Jewish Bible. "Wherever you go, I will go. Wherever you stay, I will stay."

Some of Jesus's apostles spread the gospel in Damascus, Antioch, and Rome, but for four years, Peter, Mary, and a group of their followers remained in Judea and Galilee preaching in large towns and small villages, picking up stakes whenever angry local rabbis summoned the Roman authorities or the high priests of the Temple to threaten their arrest. In the year 36, Peter and Mary returned to their marital home of Capernaum and preached from Peter's family compound. One day, a stranger arrived on a donkey, a short, pugnacious man with the arrogant bearing of someone who had grown up in privilege. He was seen having words with Ezra, the rabbi, who pointed him toward Peter's house.

Finding Peter and Mary in their courtyard mending fishing nets, he asked in an officious tone, "Are you the one they call Peter?"

"I am, friend," Peter said. "Who would you be?"

"I am Linus of the tribe of Benjamin, a Pharisee of the Temple, here to give you a warning."

The Pharisees, a sect holding rigid views of Jewish law, had been harassing Jesus and his followers from the beginning of their movement. Peter saw Mary's mouth curl, and with a hand to her shoulder, he stopped her from delivering a tongue-lashing.

"You have traveled a great distance to deliver this warning," Peter said.

"I would not have undertaken the journey if it were not a serious matter," Linus said. "Your preachings violate the laws of the land. They corrupt the minds of the weak and feeble, and they anger the rabbis."

"Ezra, our rabbi here in Capernaum, was born angry," Peter said lightly.

"This is not a matter for jest," Linus said. "Your illegal teachings must cease."

Mary could not contain herself. "How can the divine teachings of the Son of God be illegal?"

"Jesus of Nazareth was no child of God. He was a mortal Jew, as I am, as are you," Linus said.

"A mortal man does not arise from the dead and ascend to Heaven to sit at his Father's side," Peter said.

"Yes, yes, I know the tales you people tell," Linus said dismissively.

Mary wagged her finger at him and said, "It was I who found his tomb empty. It was I to whom he appeared after his resurrection. I saw him ascend to Heaven. These things I have witnessed with my own eyes are not tales."

Linus turned away from her and addressed Peter. "I did not

come here to debate a woman. I am here to warn you that you are breaking Jewish law. If you persist, I will have the Romans arrest you as they arrested and crucified Jesus of Nazareth. You are not the only ones receiving this warning. Pharisees have been sent hither and yon to find your lot and bring you to heel. My great friend, Paul of Tarsus, a fellow pupil of Rabbi Gamaliel in Jerusalem, is on his way to Damascus to arrest James, the brother of Jesus. Be thankful that you will not be arrested today. The rabbi, Ezra, will be watching how you go. If you persist in your folly, the next time you see me, I will be with Roman soldiers."

When they were alone, Mary sighed and said to Peter, "So, my husband, we must leave Capernaum."

"It is a pity," he said. "We were happy here."

"As long as we have each other in the flesh and the spirit of Jesus in our hearts, we will be happy anywhere," she said. "Where shall we go next?"

Peter gathered up the fishing net he was repairing and said, "Let us leave the land of the Jews and join with my brother Andrew who is preaching in the land of the Gentiles. Let us go to Antioch."

16

Danyal's apartment was familiar and unfamiliar at the same time. The furniture was the same, but he had rearranged the living room in her absence. The sofa pointed in a new direction. The rug had been shifted, and bric-a-brac had been moved around.

"I like the changes," Samia said.

"Yeah," he said sheepishly. "I don't know why I did it. Let me make some tea."

While he was in the kitchen, she anxiously peered out the front window onto the dark street and saw a woman walking a dog. Her relief at landing in Boston was short-lived. At the Terminal E international arrivals hall, she had spotted a man with his back to her by the Dunkin' Donuts. Blond hair with a sharp part. Jeans. Black windbreaker. Joggers. She put her head down reflexively, and when she looked over again, he was gone. This couldn't have been the American from the hotel suite, the one Evan Cunliffe had called Mr. Spooner? The possibility that it was Spooner crashed her mood and led her to take two Ubers to Cambridge. She had the first one drop her at South Station in Boston, where she milled around for a couple of minutes, looking for a sign she might have been followed, before summoning a second Uber to Danyal's place.

"Here's your tea," Danyal said. "Sit, sit. You're a nervous wreck."

She took the cup from him, put it down, threw her arms around his thick middle, and began to cry.

"You're safe here," he said, returning the hug.

"My auntie," she sobbed.

"I know, I know," he said. "What's done is done, and she's with God. Drink your tea. Let's talk."

She took her jacket off and sat on the sofa. "I'm not used to the view," she said.

"Now you can see the kitchen," he said. He mentioned another couple they both knew. "Max and Bushra said they like it better this way. I wasn't sure when you were coming or even if you were coming."

"It's okay, isn't it?" she said.

"I told you to come. I'll make up the bed for you. I'll take the sofa."

"We can be together," she said.

He looked down at the floor and changed the subject. "Did you have any problems entering the country?"

"I was worried because of my expired student visa, so I bought a round-trip ticket. I told the customs officer I was coming for job interviews and would be returning to Egypt to wait for a work permit. He waved me through, no problem."

"That's good," he said. "Do your parents know you're in America?"

"I told them I was going someplace safe, but I didn't tell them where."

"What are you going to do?"

"I contacted Professor Donovan like you suggested."

"What did he say?"

"We haven't spoken yet. We have to meet. He's seen a photo of the papyrus."

"You have it?"

She took the Bible from her handbag and opened it to the page where the papyrus lay.

"That's it?" he said, looking over her shoulder.

"That's it."

"It doesn't look like much," he said.

She closed the book. "It wasn't worth my auntie's life, but it's of great consequence."

"What does it say?"

"You're safer if you don't know."

"No, tell me," he insisted.

"Saint Peter was the first pope."

"I know that," he said.

"He was married."

"I know that too. The Bible says he was."

"This papyrus says that his wife was Mary Magdalene."

"Is that such a big deal?"

"It also says she became the second pope when Peter died."

He sat back down, removed his heavy glasses, and rubbed his eyes. "Oh. I see. You said a wealthy man wants to suppress this. Who is he?"

"I won't tell you that, Danyal. It's better you don't know."

"What will you do with it?"

"Don't worry. I won't keep it here. I'll give it to Professor Donovan tomorrow."

"Will it come out—that you stole from the museum?"

"It has to," she said mournfully. "There's no way to hide what I did."

"What will happen to you?"

She broke down, sobbing.

"Never mind," he said. "I shouldn't have asked. You can stay here for as long as you like. I won't tell anyone you're back. I have to go to Providence tomorrow morning to give a talk at Brown. I'll be back late. Will you be all right?"

Through her tears, she said, "Yes, I'll be fine.

"When the troubles are behind you, we can get married, and you can get your green card. I just want you to be safe and happy."

She stood and held out her arms for him. "Come, we can sleep in the same bed."

He kissed her on the forehead and went off to change the sheets.

She got her phone from her bag and made a call. Cal was at home, halfway through a few fingers of ice-cold vodka, and he pounced on the phone when he saw the caller ID.

"Samia, where are you?"

"Professor, I'm in Boston. Did you get the photo I sent?"

"I got it. Are you somewhere safe?"

"I'm where I used to live."

"When can I see the original?"

"I can meet you tomorrow to give it to you," she said. "I don't feel safe with it. Tell me when is good."

"Tomorrow's crazy. I teach in the morning, then I've got a

lunch thing I've got to do, and a faculty meeting in the after-noon. Can you do dinner in the Square?"

"Yes, no problem," she said. "Text me the time and place."

"Samia—" he said.

"Yes, Professor?"

"What you have—it's important."

"I know it is," she said. "It's also dangerous."

She sat quietly for a few moments. Danyal called from the bedroom, asking if she had reached Professor Donovan, and she replied, "Yes. We'll meet tomorrow."

She wanted privacy for her next call. The only place for that was the bathroom. It was a mess, a bachelor's bathroom.

"It's me," she said, sitting on the edge of the bathtub. "I'm back in Boston. I need to see you."

The houses on Lawrence Street were cheek by jowl on small lots. Danyal's apartment in a Victorian duplex overlooked a park with basketball courts. They were empty at this hour save for a solitary figure concealed behind netting covering the chain-link fence. Spooner paced along the fence line, inspecting an app on his phone. It wasn't the kind of thing you could download from an app store. Possessing and using it without a Justice Department waiver was a federal crime. Spooner knew someone who knew someone at the Israeli company who made the Orion software. A large sum of money—Tommy Cunliffe's money—was involved. It was the kind of tactical weapon Spooner employed only in extreme cases. Getting caught with the spyware wasn't an option. He'd used it only twice in the past to identify employees suspected of stealing corporate intellectual property. His boss didn't like involving the Feds in these kinds of matters. To avoid a public airing of sensitive topics, he preferred that Spooner deal with such situations internally and quietly. Spooner decided that this business with the papyrus required extraordinary measures, and he pushed Orion onto Samia Tedros's phone in a no-click exploit of the phone's operating system. In the two days it had been in place, he'd been able to see all her emails, texts, and WhatsApp messages, every telephone number called and received, and her GPS location.

Tommy was using the elliptical in his home gym when Spooner called.

"Yeah, what's going on?" he said.

"I'm outside a house in Cambridge. She got here a half hour ago."

"She's got it with her?"

"I'm one hundred percent certain. We know she sent a picture of it to this guy, Calvin Donovan, from the plane. We know she didn't meet anyone at the airport because I had eyes on her. We know she took two Ubers to get to Cambridge with only three minutes between the dropoff and pickup."

"Why two?" Tommy asked.

"She probably saw something like that in a movie."

"And she's been inside since she arrived?"

"Yeah. She made two calls. One to Donovan. A second to someone named Gregory Kalogeras."

"Who is he?"

"I haven't checked him out yet. The only info in her address book is his name and number with a Boston area code."

"You can't just go in and get it?"

"There's someone inside with her. I saw him through the window. It's too risky."

"So, what's the plan?"

"Sit tight. See what her next move is. Hang on—"

"What?"

"She just got a new text from Donovan. It's setting a time to meet for dinner tomorrow at a restaurant in Cambridge."

"I had Bill Stearns look into Donovan. He's heard of him. He's a biblical expert at the Harvard Divinity School and was probably one of her professors. If he gets his hands on the papyrus, we've lost. Do you understand?"

"I do."

"By the way, the article on the nun is being published tomorrow," Tommy said. "First salvo in that war."

⊙━◆━⊙

A young woman, one of Silvio Licheri's employees at the Press Office of the Holy See, barged into his office as he was having his first coffee of the morning.

"What? You don't knock?"

She didn't apologize. "This just hit the internet."

"What did?"

"This article from *Il Grido dell'Aquila*."

"You read that rag?"

"You pay me to read it."

She put the printout in front of him, and he picked it up with distaste. *The Eagle's Cry*, an online paper, occupied a space of right-wing journalism just to the left of the real crazies.

219

Licheri's spine straightened as he read the headline, and his face contorted as he worked his way through the article.

"Christ," he said. "Has anyone else seen this?"

"Not that I know of," she said. "Do you think it's true?"

"How the hell would I know? I've never heard of this journalist. Look her up and send me every tweet about the article and every secondary pickup."

He gathered up his jacket and headed for the door.

"Where are you going?" she asked.

"Where do you think I'm going? You don't deliver this kind of news over the phone."

Elisabetta kept him waiting until she finished a call with the papal nuncio in Brazil concerning a priest in São Paulo who had been killed in a robbery.

"Silvio, how can I help you?"

He gave her the sheets. "This article was just published in an online newspaper called *Il Grido dell'Aquila*."

"Never heard of it," she said.

"You wouldn't have. It's quite obscure and ultra-conservative."

She rocked her chair as she read it, her lips pressed together, her jaw firm.

She looked up when she was done and simply said, "It's not true."

"Do you know this woman, Emanuela Sordelli?"

"She and I were at school together, and we were on the same volleyball team; that much is true. But we never had any sort of untoward relationship. We were casual friends, that's all."

"When did you last see her?"

"My goodness, it has to be twenty-five years. Why would she make this up?"

"In such cases, it tends to be in service of base motivations—revenge, jealousy, greed."

"I hardly know her," Elisabetta said. "I know nothing of her life. When we were kids, there was nothing between us to motivate revenge. Someone must have paid her to say these things."

Licheri nodded gravely and said, "Did the journalist contact you for a comment?"

"Not to my knowledge. We can check the call logs, but I'm sure this kind of inquiry would have been put through to me by my staff. There was no outreach to your office?"

"None whatsoever. It seems they had no interest in a counter-narrative."

"It's a smear campaign." She sighed. "How should we handle this?"

"We must be calm and deliberate," he said. "We'll prepare a statement, a denial. I'll make a draft, and you can edit it to your satisfaction. It probably will be short and sweet. However, we won't release it prematurely. We'll monitor the uptake of the story and its impact first. We don't want to create the story ourselves."

"What a stupid distraction," she said. "There's so much real work to do."

"I completely agree, but we shouldn't be shocked at the tactics of your opponents. I think we need to urge an investigation into the story's origin. I'll reach out to some journalists of caliber. I'm sure there will be considerable interest in exposing the conspiracy behind this."

She stood and smoothed her habit. "Does the Holy Father know about this?"

"I came to you first. Would you like me to speak with him?"

"I'll do it myself," she said.

Cardinal Tosi had his driver take him across the river to the Propaganda Fide Palace on the Piazza di Spagna. The triangular palace complex was home to the Congregation for the Evangelization of Peoples, the organ of the Vatican that coordinated worldwide missionary work. The office of the cardinal prefect was absurdly grand in scale. Even a man as prodigious as Cardinal Navarro appeared small in the voluminous space.

"Giuseppe, what was so important you had to run across town?" Navarro asked by way of greeting.

Tosi slapped the article onto Navarro's desk. "The tree we've planted is bearing fruit."

Navarro's reading glasses were dangling on a cord around his neck. With spectacles in place, he read the printout.

"She's a lesbian?" he said. "Is this true?"

"That's what the woman in the article claims," Tosi said, leering.

"Is it enough?" Navarro asked. "Will she have to step aside?"

"I'm sure she'll deny it, and there will be ambiguities," Tosi said. "Let's see how it plays out in the coming hours and days. I'd say it's a start. It shows that a man like Tommy Cunliffe is capable of delivering results. He assured me when we last talked that there would be more. And when her position becomes untenable, I will offer myself up to the Holy Father to fill the void in the Secretariat with a pair of safe hands."

"I'm sorry to interrupt your schedule, Holy Father," Elisabetta said, "but I need to inform you of a development."

She glanced at Monsignor Finale, who was standing to the side of the pope's trestle desk. Given the nature of the business, she might have requested a private audience, but Finale's position had been hers only weeks ago, and she understood that the papal private secretary had to be involved in these matters.

"What's the matter, Sister?" the pope said. "You look troubled. Sit."

She remained standing and said, "We were blindsided by an article that has just appeared on a rather obscure website. It's an interview with a woman I went to school with when I was a teenager. She claims she had a sexual relationship with me when we played on the girls' volleyball squad."

Finale remained poker-faced, but the pontiff arched his bushy eyebrows. "I see. In matters such as these, I am hesitant to press for the truth of the matter, and I must say, I have no interest in knowing intimate details of the life you led before you took your vows. However, our path forward will be undoubtedly easier if the allegations are false."

"They are false, Holy Father. The relations I had before becoming a nun were heterosexual."

"Why would this woman say otherwise?"

"I have no idea. I haven't seen her since we were young. I think we have to assume that someone has induced her to bear false witness."

"Vipers and serpents are among us," the pope mumbled. "You've met with Silvio?"

Elisabetta nodded. "He's working on a comprehensive plan."

"Good. Keep me informed, and keep your head down. I know you have great things to accomplish as the secretary.

Remember the immortal, albeit fake, Latin saying: *Illegitimi non carborundum.*"

She smiled and thanked him.

Don't let the bastards wear you down.

Spooner's phone rang at four o'clock in the morning and woke him from a light sleep. He had been curled up in the cargo area of his rented SUV parked on Lawrence Street near the Victorian duplex.

"Spooner here," he said, his tongue thick and dry.

"Mr. Spooner, it's Antonio Solla calling. I'm afraid I don't know what time zone you're in. I know you travel extensively. If I've awakened you, I apologize."

"I'm good. Anything to report?"

"I've just sent you an English translation of the article on the nun's school friend. I can tell you that it's getting a tremendous amount of attention. It's trending on Twitter. You know— 'Vatican Secretary of State's lesbian past exposed.'"

"Hang on, let me read it," Spooner said, putting the detective on speaker and opening the email attachment. When he was done, he said, "This isn't a knockout. It'll become a she said, she said type thing that the public will get tired with. You told me you were working on something a lot more explosive. Where are you with that?"

"I'm making good progress. The elements are falling into place. Soon I'm going to need you to authorize a six-figure expenditure."

"Just get it done. My boss wants to bury this lady."

17

Cal awoke with pleasant thoughts in his head. He had spent the previous evening reading and annotating some thesis chapters submitted by one of his grad students, an Israeli woman with an undergraduate degree in artificial intelligence from Hebrew University. She had come to Harvard to use AI and machine learning to analyze the handwriting and behavior of the scribes who wrote the Dead Sea Scrolls. Cal found the subject matter fresh and exciting, and she wrote well. That made her thesis advisor happy and so thoroughly engrossed that he wound up drinking less than his usual fill. As a result, his awakening moments were devoid of his typical dull headache, wooly mouth, and bleariness.

Clearheaded, he was enjoying the soft morning light filtering through his bedroom curtains and the promise of the day. That evening, he would lay eyes on Samia's miraculous papyrus. He had been sketching out a campaign to validate it. He knew which academics he wanted to invite onto a multidisciplinary team of physicists, chemists, papyrologists, and biblical scholars. He was hell-bent on moving fast, getting the pieces in place to authenticate it, and then publicly reveal it with a splash.

But mostly, he relished the prospect of using it to help Elisabetta. He understood the mutability of the Church as well as anyone. Roman Catholic doctrines had changed over two millennia, and practices and attitudes had evolved. But documentary proof that Mary Magdalene had succeeded Peter as pontifex maximus, as pope, promised to shift attitudes about Church women fundamentally. Catholic orthodoxy might still consider the ordination of women as a bridge too far, but how could anyone who possessed even a touch of enlightenment object to a woman holding the highest administrative office at the Vatican when there had been a Pope Mary?

He had come to grips with Elisabetta's decision. She had chosen the Church over him, and that was that. In the past, when one relationship ended, he immediately went on the prowl for the next. He knew what people said about him—and the word *serial* usually prefaced it. Serial womanizer. Serial monogamist. Serial commitment-phobe. He suspected a therapist would have a field day with him, but he got all the therapy he wanted from the clear, viscous elixir he kept in his freezer.

But Elisabetta was resetting something inside of him. They hadn't broken up. He'd never had her. She was, and remained, unobtainable, and there was something romantically appealing in that. Over the years, all his romances eventually devolved into one form of bitterness or another. Yet his love for Elisabetta was unrequited and thus timeless, and like an insect trapped in amber, it could remain in a state of perfection.

Cal had been the product of argumentative parents, a Jewish mother and a Catholic father. Even his name had been a negotiated settlement. Donovan, his father's surname, was Catholic. Abraham, his middle name, was Jewish. Calvin, his given name, was a compromise—neither parent had a strong dislike of Protestants.

Cal's upbringing was purely secular—parental stalemate meant that a religious education had not been foisted upon him. Only when he became a biblical scholar and Church historian did he gravitate to Catholicism. After he decided to become a practicing Catholic, he told his friend, the Harvard chaplain who would prepare him to receive the sacraments, that he was going all in, pushing all his chips onto the table. During his Catholic education, he had come to admire the discipline underpinning the celibacy of priests because it was a mindset opposed to his own. He had marveled how these men—the ones who truly stuck to their vows—did it.

Now Cal decided he would honor this unaccustomed state of unrequited love by giving celibacy a twirl. God only knew how long the vow would last, but it felt right and clean.

His fair-winds mood lasted only as long as his first glance at his phone and the headline in an alert from an Italian paper: WOMAN CLAIMS SHE HAD A LESBIAN AFFAIR WITH VATICAN SECRETARY OF STATE.

He flew through the article, which was based on reporting from an online site he'd never heard of. Then he dived into the Twitterverse and wallowed for a while in the muck. The Vatican had put out a brief press release stating that the article was false and defamatory and that neither the secretary of state nor the Vatican would have anything further to say. He didn't give a damn whether the story was true. What incensed him was its timing. This was a smear job, and it was probably only the first shot fired in a war.

While he made coffee, his phone dinged with a WhatsApp. Micaela Celestino had taken to casually texting him tidbits about Elisabetta. He was happy to keep an oar in the water with the Celestino clan and always answered promptly and cheerfully. This message was concise: Did you see the garbage about Eli?

He replied that he had, and moments later, his phone rang with a WhatsApp call.

"Can you believe it?" Micaela asked.

"Tell me what you know," Cal said.

Micaela, clearly upset, spewed in Italian, "This girl—she was in Eli's year at school, but I knew her a little. I don't think Eli had any contact with her for over twenty years. It's completely untrue. Eli says this is a complete fabrication. She's not a lesbian. She's never had any relations with a woman, even in the way some young girls like to experiment with their friends. They're trying to undermine her. These assholes think the best way to bring down a woman doing a traditional male job is to claim there's something wrong with them. It makes me crazy."

"How is she?" Cal asked.

"Angry, but resolute. She tells me she doesn't have time for this shit."

"I saw the press release the Vatican put out."

"I wish they had let me write it," she said. "I would have blasted those motherfuckers."

Cal laughed. "Maybe it's just as well they didn't. Is there anything I can do?"

228

"No, but there's something I can do."

"What?"

"I don't want anyone trying to convince me not to do it. If you read about me getting arrested, you'll know what I did."

"Christ, Micaela, try not to make things worse for her."

"I'll exercise my usual charm and discretion. Maybe you can send her a little message of encouragement. It could cheer her up."

"I was thinking about doing that."

"Good. I wish she had gone with you to America."

"I wish she had too."

It was a typical day in the life of a university professor. In the morning, he taught his undergraduate course, a sweeping history of Christianity that satisfied one of Harvard's core General Education requirements for undergraduates. He had a luncheon at the Faculty Club with the dean of the Harvard Divinity School to set the stage for a battle royale on a tenure decision for an associate professor in the department whom Cal adored but the dean did not. The decision turned on how much academic weight should be given to the popular books on religion the woman had published. In the afternoon, he attended a long and contentious faculty meeting on the emotive topic of graduate student unionization.

Finally, the time arrived for his dinner with Samia Tedros. He arrived a few minutes early to Henrietta's Table at the Charles Hotel in Harvard Square. He had the waitress give him a table tucked in the back corner so he could inspect the

papyrus free of prying eyes. Cal had never eaten there without running into university types. While waiting, he ordered
a bone-dry vodka martini and fiddled with his phone. When
Samia was five minutes late, he got miffed. After ten minutes,
irritation set in. A half hour later, he grew concerned and
texted her, waited a few minutes for a response, and then called
her mobile number. It went straight to voicemail.

Cal knew the waitress from dozens of meals. She was an
attractive young woman who was always flirty with him, but he
wasn't in the mood to reciprocate this evening. She swung by
again to see if he wanted another martini.

"I think I'm done. Looks like my guest was a no-show."

"Well, that's a bummer. Still have to eat, don't you?"

He tossed a couple of twenties on the table and told her his
appetite was gone.

It was a clear evening, and the square was bustling with
students and car traffic. Cal cut through Harvard Yard on the
way to the Divinity School and, as he always did, made sure
to pass by his freshman dorm, Lionel Hall, for old times' sake.
The lights were on in his rooms, and he flashed back to the day
he first walked in, a rebellious twenty-year-old who had washed
out of the army after punching his sergeant. He had missed the
admissions deadline, but he was given a freshman spot after his
star-professor father interceded with the university president.
The dorm suite had two bedrooms, a single and a double
with a bunk bed. A kid from California, a weedy applied-math
wonk, was making up the single bed when Cal arrived.

"You're not going to like that room," Cal had told him.

"Why not?"

"Because I just got out of the army, and I refuse to sleep in a bunk bed ever again. If you don't let me have the single, I'll make your life miserable."

The kid grew up to become a professor at Princeton, and to this day, he and Cal never missed an exchange of birthday phone calls.

Cal had a vague idea where the Divinity School kept these sorts of records. The records room was in the basement, and fortunately, his master key opened all doors. He found the drawers with files on former grad students through trial and error, and eventually put his hands on Samia Tedros's paperwork. She had spent five years at Harvard and had three local addresses on file, one in Allston and two in Cambridge. Her last address coincided with her last semester at the Divinity School. It was c/o Danyal Tamer on Lawrence Street in Cambridge. The listed phone number was the mobile he had been calling.

During the brisk walk to his house, he skirted Cambridge Common, trying Samia's number a couple of times along the way. His street was heavily populated with professors who drove Teslas, and he was no exception. Soon he was autopiloting along Storrow Drive.

The house on Lawrence Street was a mauve and white Victorian duplex. One side had D. Tamer's name on its mail slot. It was mostly dark with only a faint glow coming from one of the side windows. He rang the bell a few times, and in case it wasn't working, knocked. If he hadn't been worried about Samia's safety, he would have left it at that, but he was very concerned, so he tried the door. It was locked.

He called her phone again from the sidewalk, and as he considered what to do next, he failed to notice a man shrouded in darkness watching him from the park across the street. Cal took a look at the walkway between the Victorian house and a neighbor's and strode past the wheelie bins. At the rear, a staircase led to a deck. He climbed it and rapped on the glass door.

"Samia, it's Cal Donovan. Are you okay?"

He found himself grasping the doorknob. It turned freely. He opened it and gingerly stepped into an unlit kitchen.

"Hello? Anybody home?"

He found a light switch. The kitchen was in a dire state of disarray, with drawers open and contents strewn across the floor and countertops.

The living room was in no better shape, and he had to find his way through toppled belongings.

In the dim light of a hall fixture, he made out a pair of shoes with toes down, heels up, seemingly impossibly balanced. He cautiously drew nearer and realized there were feet inside.

Samia was stretched out on a hallway runner, lying on her belly.

He muttered, "Oh Jesus," and knelt beside her, trying to find a pulse under the cold skin of her purplish neck.

By the time the homicide detectives arrived, Cal had given statements to two sets of responding Cambridge police officers. A detective found him in the bedroom where the police had deposited him.

"I'm Detective Stella Caruso," she said without extending a hand. "I understand you broke into this apartment and found the victim? Is that correct?"

She was about Cal's age, platinum blonde with a stony,

attractive face, dressed more stylishly than he imagined detectives dressed. There would have been a time in the not-so-distant past when Cal would have sparked to her.

"I don't think I'd describe it as breaking in," he said. "The door was unlocked. I was worried about her."

She was scribbling on a pocket-sized notebook. "It doesn't matter how you'd like me to describe it. You told the officers that you tried the front door, then went around to the back, climbed the stairs, and entered a residence that doesn't belong to you. That's breaking and entering."

"Again," he said evenly, "I was concerned because she failed to show up for an important dinner."

She was relentless. "So every time you get stood up on a date, you break into the lady's house?"

Cal wet his lips with his tongue. "First of all, it wasn't a date. It was supposed to be a working dinner. Samia is—was—a former graduate student of mine."

"And professors never date their former students?"

"We weren't romantically involved, if that's what you're asking."

"That's exactly what I was asking. She looks like she was an attractive young woman."

"The answer is no. Samia left my department and returned to Egypt last year. She contacted me recently about a historical document she found in Cairo. She was going to show it to me tonight. She told me she was in trouble and needed help."

"We'll get to that. Had you been to this apartment before?"

"Never."

"It belongs to someone named Danyal Tamer. Do you know who he is and where he is?"

"I don't know him."

"She told you she was staying here?"

"She only said it was somewhere she used to live. When she didn't show up for dinner, I went to my office and looked up her records to find her last address. It was Lawrence Street."

"Do a lot of detective work, Professor?"

"To solve ancient puzzles, yes. To investigate murders, no."

"How do you know this was a murder?"

"Did you see her neck?"

"What kind of professor are you?"

"History of religion and biblical archaeology. Harvard Divinity School."

"See a lot of broken necks in your line of work?"

"More than a few. Ancient ones—skeletons."

"Funny guy," she said humorlessly.

Stella's partner, Brendan Davis, was a decade younger than her, a fleshy fellow in a Walmart suit and a loose necktie. He poked his head in and asked her into the hall.

"The ME's here," he told her. "His first impression is fractured neck by manual compression and torsion. Someone strong. She's been dead four to six hours."

There was a sudden commotion, a man screaming and crying. Cal went into the hall to see what was happening, and Stella sternly motioned him back inside the bedroom.

He heard her tell her partner, "That'll be Mr. Tamer. You take him down to the station. I'll take the egghead."

18

The Cambridge Police Department headquarters was in Kendall Square, a part of the city more MIT than Harvard. Cal was transported unceremoniously in the back of a cruiser and taken to an interview room with mucus-green walls and a bolted-down table. He was forced to cool his jets waiting for Detective Caruso, and when she finally breezed in, she launched into an aggressive line of questioning.

"You must have known that entering the house on Lawrence Street tonight was against the law."

"It didn't occur to me," he said.

"I looked you up just now. You're a pretty smart guy. It says on your bio that you're not an ordinary professor at Harvard. You're a University Professor." She read from a piece of printer paper, "You're an individual whose groundbreaking work crosses the boundaries of multiple disciplines, allowing you to pursue research at any of Harvard's schools. That's very impressive."

"Thank you," he said dryly.

"I would think that a University Professor such as yourself would have called the police to do a health and safety check of someone he was concerned about, not break into a house."

"The next time the situation arises, I'll undoubtedly do that."

She removed her jacket and draped it over her chair. When she turned and bent, the collar of her blue satin blouse picked up a dusting of makeup from her cheek. "We've got to deal with this situation first," she said. "We can charge you with unlawful entry."

"Do I need a lawyer?"

"I don't know, do you? Samia Tedros."

"Yes?"

"You told me the two of you had no romantic involvement."

"That's correct."

"But you're quite the ladies' man, aren't you?"

"I'm sorry, what?"

"A ladies' man. I spent all of fifteen minutes online, and I find you on the cover of *The Improper Bostonian*'s most eligible bachelor edition. I see you popping up in *Herald* gossip columns, stepping out with this lady and that. You're quite the player for a University Professor. You're a looker. Samia was a looker. Maybe things soured between you. Maybe there was an argument. You do something crazy in the moment. You tear the place apart to make it look like a burglary. I mean, you were there."

Cal was a bit unnerved by the detective's unflinching stare. "I can't say this clearly enough. Samia was my student. That was our only relationship. She was in trouble. She contacted me. I was going to try to help her."

"I need to know where you were between three and five o'clock this afternoon."

236

The question came as something of a relief. "I was in a faculty meeting."

"Can anyone vouch for you?"

"About seventy members of the faculty as well as the dean of the Faculty of Arts and Sciences. I made a few remarks. It's all recorded and minuted."

"And before that?"

"I had lunch at the faculty club from 12:30 to 1:30 with the dean of the Divinity School, then went to the faculty meeting at two."

Stella leaned back in her chair, looking a bit deflated.

"Well, we will check into that. Tell me what Samia found and why she told you she was in trouble."

"It was a first-century papyrus with several lines of text in Greek."

"Papyrus. That like paper?"

"Yes, an ancient form of paper made from the pith of the papyrus plant."

"I learned something new," she deadpanned. "And this thing that got her in trouble?"

"It was a biblical text that was very rare, very controversial, very valuable."

"Keep talking," she said.

"Samia had been working at the Cairo Museum. She recovered it from a mask. Used pieces of papyrus were sometimes recycled to bind the plaster of Egyptian burial masks. She stole the papyrus to pay for her sister's kidney transplant. She had an accomplice, a dealer, who sold it to someone she described only as a rich American."

"Do you know who it was?"

"I wasn't told."

"Go on."

"She found out that the buyer was going to essentially bury the papyrus, keep it hidden from the world, and that greatly upset her. She thought the world needed to see it."

"Why would someone do that? Keep it hidden."

"As I said, the text is very controversial. Samia was a good person who did a bad thing, then got cold feet. She made a forgery, and that's what the American wound up buying. She kept the original and wanted me to authenticate it and make it public. She called me last night to arrange a meeting. I was going to see it this evening over dinner. Apparently, the forgery was discovered, and the buyer's people went looking for her. She told me they killed her aunt in Cairo. Samia panicked and flew to Boston. Unfortunately, it looks like she was followed."

"So you think she was killed because someone got stiffed on a deal?"

"That's shorthand for what I think."

Stella puckered her mouth. "Maybe if I was a University Professor, I could put it more eloquently. How much money changed hands?"

"I don't know. I imagine it was considerable, given the importance of the text. Did the police find it inside the apartment?"

"What does it look like?"

"It's about the size of a three-by-five file card, tan-colored, irregular, torn edges, reddish lettering."

"Nothing like that was found as far as I know, but someone pulled the place apart looking for something." She let out a sigh of exhaustion and exasperation. "Listen, it's time for you to tell me what the hell was written on it. You do know, I assume."

Cal had been avoiding the camera on the wall, but now he glowered at it and said, "I imagine that whatever I say tonight is going to be a matter of public record."

"Potentially," she said. "As part of court proceedings."

"Here's the difficulty I have," he said. "We don't know whether the papyrus is authentic. It needs to be studied by experts. I wouldn't want its contents to get into the public domain if it's a fake. The university and I will be accused of perpetrating a hoax, and things will get very nasty. For that reason, I'd rather not describe it further at this point."

Cal never saw anyone come to a boil so quickly. "A young woman was murdered!" she shouted in his face. "I want to know why. I don't give a flying fuck that you'd rather not describe it further. Tell me what it is that got Samia Tedros's neck broken."

Cal kept his cool, didn't flinch, and didn't buckle. "I think there are two ways to go here. You can turn off your camera, and I can speak to you off the record, or I can stop talking and consult with a lawyer. She'll be someone you've heard of from Harvard Law School. It's up to you."

Her smirk lasted several seconds, then faded.

"Okay. For the sake of this girl, I'll play along. For now." She looked into the lens and said, "Brendan, kill the camera," and when the red recording light went off, she turned to Cal and said, "All right. Tell me."

"If it's real, it might be a lost passage from the Gospel of Mary."

"Never heard of it, and I go to church on Sundays."

"It's one of the biblical Gospels that wasn't incorporated into the New Testament. Mark, Luke, John, and Matthew are the principal Christian Gospels. However, there are also multiple so-called gnostic Gospels that were discovered in Egypt in 1945 that tell the story of Jesus and early Christianity from the perspective of other authors. One of these is the Gospel of Mary Magdalene. Several papyrus pages are missing from Mary's Gospel, but what is there gives the strong impression that Mary was an important figure among Jesus's followers, right up there with Saint Peter."

"Which brings us to Samia's papyrus," she said.

"Which brings us to Samia. According to existing biblical passages, Saint Peter was married. That's not surprising, because Peter was a Jew, and there was never a marital prohibition in Judaism. Samia's papyrus tells us that Peter was married to Mary Magdalene, which is interesting on many levels."

"Give me a break," she exclaimed. "You think someone killed her because they didn't want *that* to get out?"

"No, I think someone killed her because they didn't want the other part to see the light of day. It says that Mary succeeded Peter when he died. If the papyrus is real, it means that Mary Magdalene was the second pope."

Stella picked up her pen and began clicking it. "A woman pope?" she asked.

"That's what it says."

She snorted. "Well, that would chap my priest's ass."

"I think it would chap a lot of asses," Cal said. "We're at the moment in time where a new pope has just appointed a woman to the second-highest position at the Vatican. A lot of people are unhappy about that. My guess is that whoever bought Samia's papyrus was one of them, unhappy enough to pay a fortune to suppress it, then get mad as hell when they found out she passed off a fake and kept the original."

"So, find the buyer, find the killer—is that what you're saying?"

"More like find the buyer, find the person who hired the killer."

She stood up and adjusted her pencil skirt, and Cal asked if he was free to go.

"If you want to help find the killer, I'd like you to keep warming that chair."

He asked why.

"Write down the names and numbers of people who can confirm your whereabouts this afternoon. If I can eliminate you as the perpetrator, I want you to return to the crime scene and help me look for the papyrus. Will you do that?"

Brendan Davis pulled the car into an open space on Lawrence Street and said to his partner, "You sure you want to bring this guy inside? It's kind of irregular."

"He's going to sit there like a good boy, and if we find something, he'll tell us what it is."

The good boy was in the backseat of the car. Stella leaned over the seat and sought a confirmation.

"I won't touch a thing," Cal said.

It had taken an hour for Stella to call Cal's contacts and clear him as a suspect. While he was at the police station, the crime scene had been processed, and Samia's body had been removed to the morgue. Brendan confirmed that Danyal Tamer had been giving a lecture in Providence that afternoon, and after his police interview was done, he had cut him loose to stay with friends. Cal and the detectives ducked under police tape and, after donning booties and gloves, went inside.

Stella pointed to a chair in the living room and told Cal, as one might say to a canine, "There. Sit."

"What exactly are we looking for?" Brendan asked.

"Tell him, Professor," Stella said.

"I can show you," Cal said, drawing out his phone. "Samia sent me a picture of it."

"Why didn't you tell me that?" Stella barked.

"You never asked."

"There was nothing like that on her or in her handbag or suitcase," Brendan said. "Where would you stash something like this?"

"It will be brittle," Cal said. "I'd want to protect it between the pages of a book, preferably a hardcover book that didn't have any bend to it."

"Like a Bible?" Brendan said.

"Sure."

"She had a Bible in her shoulder bag. I went through it, but maybe we should have another look."

Brendan took the shoulder bag from a large plastic evidence bag and got the Bible for Cal, who carefully riffled through every page.

"Nothing," he declared.

Danyal had a floor-to-ceiling bookcase, but most of the books had been tossed onto the floor. "Looks like the killer had the same idea," Stella said.

"They could've found it already," her partner said.

"Yeah, maybe," she said, "but we still have to look. Forget what I said about not touching anything. Three pairs of hands will plow through these faster than two."

Danyal had a few hundred books, and it took a while to look through all of them. When nothing was found, Stella said to Cal, "If you were Samia, where else would you hide it?"

"I suppose she could have placed it between stiff pieces of cardboard and taped it inside or behind a piece of furniture. It definitely wouldn't have been safe under a cushion."

Brendan looked at his watch and yawned. "At least it's only a one-bedroom apartment."

They finished the search a little before midnight, finding nothing. As the detectives prepared to close the place up, Brendan had a thought and pulled out Samia's mobile phone from an evidence bag in his briefcase.

"Did you touch this when you found her?" he asked Cal. "It was right by her body."

"I don't think I even noticed it," Cal said.

"If you touched it, we'll find your prints," Stella said.

"I didn't touch it," Cal insisted.

"The SIM card's missing," Stella said. "Know anything about that?"

"I do not. I think it's time for me to go home."

Brendan locked the doors with Danyal's keys. Outside, the street was clogged with broadcasting trucks and reporters packing up from their live spots for the local eleven o'clock news. Brendan asked Cal if he needed a ride.

"My car's over there. Where does the investigation go from here?"

"The Egyptian consulate in New York should have contacted her family by now," Stella said. "We'll liaise with the police in Cairo to see if there are any links we can establish between Samia's murder and her aunt's. We need to see if we can find out about the guy Samia was working with, the one who sold the papyrus to an American."

Brendan said, "Uniformed officers have been interviewing Danyal's neighbors trying to see if anyone has video from doorbell cameras. So far, there's nothing. We'll need to retrace Samia's footsteps from the time she got off her flight to the time she was killed less than twenty-four hours later. We'll subpoena her phone records and location data and try to figure out where she was when she lost her SIM card."

"We're in the grind-it-out phase," Stella said.

"It's vitally important we find the papyrus," Cal said. "Its historical value is incalculable."

"Hopefully, the killer didn't get it already," Stella replied. For the first time since they met, she smiled. "Thanks for your help tonight, Professor Donovan. If we need you, we know where to find you."

Her phone went off, and she pulled away to answer, close enough for Cal to hear one side of a heated personal call about not telling someone she was going to be late.

Brendan said, "I hear you like to step out with the ladies, Professor."

"Who the hell told you that?"

"Detective Caruso. Who else?"

"I'd rather be known for other things," Cal said defensively.

"Just thought I'd warn you not to bark up Caruso's tree. She's not on the market."

"Sounds like the guy on the phone's not a happy camper."

"It's a she," Brendan said. "Her wife's name is Natalie. Personally, I'm never getting married."

"That, Detective, has been one of my guiding principles."

⁃───────⁃

"I want you to understand the depth of my disappointment, Joel," Tommy Cunliffe said.

Spooner pressed the phone to his ear, absorbing the full measure of his boss's quiet wrath. Tommy only used Spooner's first name when dressing him down, like a father reproaching his son.

"I completely understand that failure isn't an option," Spooner said. "I promise, I'll find it."

"I'm having a hard time understanding what she could have done with it," Tommy said. "We know she texted a photo of it to Calvin Donovan just before her flight landed in Boston. We know she went directly to Cambridge and stayed at the apartment until her noon meeting the next day. We know that, for some reason, during or shortly after that meeting, she disabled her phone by removing her SIM card. And that's when you say you lost her."

"I didn't have eyes on her," Spooner said. "I was nearby, but I was relying on the spyware. When I lost the beacon, I lost her. That was a failing."

"Yes, it was, Joel. How long was she missing?"

"From 12:21 when her phone went dead until 4:30 in the afternoon when she showed up in a taxi back at Lawrence Street. Her dinner with Donovan wasn't until six. When I lost her, I decided to go back to Lawrence Street in case she returned, which is what happened. I figured she either took the papyrus with her when she went to her meeting with Kalogeras or left it in the apartment. We knew she planned to pass it to Donovan at dinner in either case. So at that point, it was going to be inside the apartment with her. Her boyfriend's car wasn't back, so I made entry, and the rest, you know."

"One dead girl who wouldn't talk, and one missing papyrus," Cunliffe said. "Where is it, Joel?"

"I don't know. I went through the apartment with a fine-toothed comb."

"Could she have given it to Kalogeras?"

"Why would she? She was going to see Donovan in a few hours. What would be the point of leaving it with him? It doesn't make sense. Anyway, if she did, he would've turned it over to the police by now."

"Why?"

"Because it's all over the news. Every TV station in Boston is here."

"Well, it's got to be somewhere," Tommy said. "Where's Donovan now?"

"He and two detectives spent a couple of hours back at the apartment," Spooner said. "They just left."

"I'm sure they were looking for it," Tommy said. "Tell me again—you're positive it wasn't there."

"Hundred percent. She must've stashed it somewhere during the hour and three-quarters she was off my radar."

"Donovan will fully understand the importance of the papyrus," Tommy said. "I've been reading about him. Did you know that he was chummy with Pope Celestine and is said to be Pope John's closest lay friend? I even found a smiling photo of him with Elisabetta Celestino from a Vatican event last year. He's a danger. He's as progressive as they come. If he gets his hands on the papyrus, by God, he'll use it. He'll smear our faces in it."

"I understand," Spooner said.

"Make sure you do. The photo the girl sent him is useless to him. He needs the original. He'll be highly motivated to find it, and if he does, you need to make sure you're there to relieve him of it by any means necessary."

19

Rome, 64 CE

It is said that no one is as zealous as a convert. If so, Linus was the king of the zealots.

Twenty-five years had passed since his friend and fellow Pharisee, Paul, returned from the east. The Temple priests had sent Paul to Damascus to arrest a group of troublemakers, followers of the martyred Jesus of Nazareth who had the temerity to flout Jewish laws and customs in the name of their new sect. Yet something happened to Paul on his journey to Damascus, something he would preach and write about for the rest of his days.

Paul was born Saul of Tarsus, but as a Roman citizen, he also carried the Latinized name of Paul. He was more brains than brawn, quick to anger, quick to forgive, but first and foremost a dedicated servant of Jewish law who had been trained in Jerusalem by the famed rabbi Gamaliel. A diaspora of small bands of heretics was enjoying inordinate success turning Jewish heads away from the Talmud toward this messianic and populist cult. Paul's mission, and the mission of fellow Pharisees like Linus, was to arrest these people and return them to Jerusalem for trial and punishment according to Jewish law.

One day, on the road from Jerusalem to Damascus, Paul experienced a life-altering event. A vision of the ascended Jesus suddenly appeared to him and asked why he was persecuting him. Paul wished to know who this man was, and the reply came, "I am Jesus whom you are persecuting. Get up and go into the city, and you will be told what to do." The blazing vision left Paul blinded, and he had to be led into Damascus, where he spent three days in prayer, refusing food or drink.

Then Jesus appeared to Ananias, one of his disciples in Damascus, telling him to seek out Paul. Ananias feared this merciless Pharisee, but Jesus pressed him to obey. He explained that Paul was his chosen instrument to deliver the gospel to the Gentiles, their kings, and the people of Israel. Ananias found Paul and told him that Jesus had sent him to restore his sight and fill him with the Holy Spirit. When he laid on hands, the scales fell from Paul's eyes and Paul's sight was restored, and Ananias baptized him into the dominion of Christ. From that day forward, Paul traveled the land teaching the gospel.

He journeyed to Arabia, where he spent years in prayer and meditation, and finally returned to Jerusalem in the year 39. The Temple Elders heard of Paul's presence in the city and dispatched Linus to determine what should be done with the turncoat. Linus had long looked up to Paul with the reverence of a younger brother, but when he found his old companion by a ritual bath near the Mount of Olives, he addressed him harshly.

"Brother, I could scarcely believe the news that you have betrayed your fellow Pharisees. Tell me in your own voice. Is it true that you have become one of these wretches who has forsaken Jewish laws and customs in favor of the rantings of the dead magician, Jesus?"

Paul took Linus by surprise by grabbing Linus's shoulders and slowly drawing him into an embrace.

"My friend," Paul said. "How good it is to see you."

Linus fought to hold on to his anger but felt it slipping away.

"Your beard is longer and grayer, and you are thin," Linus said. "I hardly recognized you."

"It is me, and at the same time, it is no longer me."

Linus pulled back. "What can you possibly mean?"

"Are you happy, Linus?"

"Happy? Whatever do you mean?"

Paul said, "Think on the happiest moment of your life. Can you remember it?"

Linus furrowed his brow. "It was the time I first laid eyes on my newborn son."

"And did the moment last?"

"Alas, it faded, and nothing since has compared. As you know, my boy and his mother died. I am alone."

Paul gazed at him serenely. "Since accepting Jesus into my life, every moment of my existence has been filled with indescribable joy. I tell you, Linus, he is the true Messiah. He died for our sins, and God raised him to take his place beside him in Heaven. Though he has risen, his message of peace and love lives on in our hearts. He will come again. He told us so. Those who acknowledge him as Lord and Savior will ascend to the Kingdom of Heaven when he returns. Accept Jesus, and you will never be alone again."

Linus sat down on the trunk of a felled cedar. "I have heard that you tell your disciples that Jesus appeared to you in a vision and commanded obeyance. If what you say is true, have him appear to me."

"I am but a mortal man," Paul said with a wink. "I can no sooner make it rain in the summer than I can summon the Lord. What I can do is walk with you and talk with you and teach you what I have learned. Perhaps my words will have the power to convey the joy I feel within my breast. Will you walk with me, Linus? It is a beautiful day."

Linus spent days with Paul, hypnotically wandering the hinterlands of Jerusalem. He returned to the city a changed man and marched into the Temple and sought an audience with the Sanhedrin, the supreme council of priests. The old men muttered and sputtered from their soft cushions as Linus renounced his old life, condemned the Pharisees, and proclaimed that he had been baptized into the one true faith, Christianity.

"We could arrest you here and now," the high priest declared, thrusting a bony finger like a dagger.

The priests conferred among themselves and handed down their pronouncement. His life would be spared in deference to his service to the Temple, but he would have to accept banishment. And so, as Paul left Jerusalem for the first of his lengthy missions to the east, Linus left for Rome to minister to the pockets of Christianity residing in the imperial city.

In Rome, Linus found a small but ardent community of converted Jews. They were scattered throughout the city, largely hidden from the authorities, worshipping their Savior in private houses. Linus found lodgings in the slums of Subura and passionately threw himself into his new mission of turning hearts and minds to Christ. He set his sights on converting Jews. There were tens of thousands of them in this city of half a million souls. Unlike the Gentiles, the Jews were monotheistic, and it was easier to convince them than the polytheistic Romans that the Son of God had been sent to Earth to save their souls.

As a Pharisee, Linus had been trained in argumentation and disputation, and he went from house to house using his considerable skills to tell the story of Christ, Paul's conversion, and his own. In time, he established his own house of worship tucked away in a tenement on a narrow, filthy alley near the Pantheon, and as the reign of Emperor Claudius ended and that of Emperor Nero began, Linus's reputation as a teacher steadily grew, and with it the size of his congregation.

With reputation came danger. Claudius had forbidden religious proselytizing within the city, and from time to time he cracked down on Jews and Christians. Nero was more spirited in his persecutions, and he became adept at blaming Christians for all manners of municipal woes.

In the year 64, the day finally arrived when Nero's soldiers banged on the door of Linus's thriving house church. They dragged him before a magistrate, who accused him of fomenting rebellion.

"I have it under authority that you have become one of the high priests of Rome. Christians flock to your house of worship. You use your pulpit and your silvered tongue to plot against the emperor. You lead your minions in strange rituals and seditious rites. We generally tolerate the Jews, for their religion is ancient and ancestral and they are docile, but you Christians are rabble-rousers, and you spread like weeds. I think, perhaps, after your trial, we must acquaint you with the wild beasts inside Nero's Circus."

Linus listened with mounting terror and asked to speak with the magistrate privately in an uncharacteristically thin voice. Linus had attended the games at the Circus of Nero one time only and had been traumatized by the sight of men and women torn apart and left to die upon crimsoned sands. The elderly judge, dressed in a ceremonial toga, agreed and took him into his chamber, where he poured himself a glass of honeyed wine and asked what Linus wanted to say.

"I value my life," Linus said. "I wish to find a way to save myself."

"Will you publicly renounce your religion?"

"That I will not do."

Thin shoulders rose, then fell. "Then you will die."

"Perhaps there is another way. Perhaps I can help the emperor."

"How can you possibly help Nero?"

"I teach my worshippers to live peacefully and treat Roman laws and customs with the respect they deserve. You must have been informed that I only seek converts from among my Jewish brothers and sisters, not Gentiles."

The magistrate shifted on his divan. "Ah, but do you deny that there have been respectable Roman citizens who have succumbed to your sect?"

"That is so, but I have never baptized a Gentile, and I pledge to you that I never will."

"And you expect that meager pledge to save your skin?"

"Magistrate, I am in a position to know everything that happens within the Christian community of Rome. I know which priests convert Gentiles. I know when a Christian hot-head spoils for a fight. I know when Christ's apostles—the ones who were with him when he walked the Earth—sneak into Rome. I can be your ears and your eyes and alert you to the presence of the more rabid members of our flock. I ask only that you release me."

The magistrate smiled, displaying a ragged set of brown teeth. "Do you know of Simon Peter, the one the Christians call the bishop of Rome, their pontifex maximus?"

"I know him."

"When did you see him last?"

"He came to Rome five years ago."

"Where is he now?"

"Antioch, I hear."

"Our spies tell us that he has left Antioch and say he is coming to Rome. Give us Peter, and we shall let you live. What say you, Linus?"

On the night of July 18, a small fire started in a shopkeeper's storeroom inside a tenement on the Aventine Hill. The fire quickly spread through the timbered building and jumped onto the roofs of adjacent structures. Within the hour, across the Aventine, Palatine, and Caelian Hills, the slums of the poor, mansions of the rich, Roman temples, and public buildings were ablaze. The fire burned for seven days, seemed to abate, and then flared again and burned for three days more. When the last embers were cool, large swathes of Rome lay in waste.

The apostle Peter, his wife, Mary, and their entourage arrived in Rome a fortnight later to the acrid smell of a blackened and decimated city. Word came to Linus that they were in Rome, and he arranged for a feast to be held in Peter's honor at the house of a well-to-do Christian on the Esquiline Hill, which was untouched by the great fire.

When Linus arrived by horseback, the esteemed guests were lounging and drinking in the dining hall. He knelt before Peter, kissed the old man's hand, and then rose to acknowledge Mary with a fleeting bow.

Mary had never forgotten her first encounter with Linus when the choleric Pharisee appeared in Galilee those many years past to condemn Jesus and threaten them with arrest. Peter had long forgiven Linus and considered him a brother in Christ, baptized by Paul himself. But Mary's memory burned brighter than her husband's, and though a polished façade had supplanted the spiky arrogance of Linus's youth, she never rid herself of the suspicion that this was a man who could not be trusted.

"So, Rome is in ashes," Peter said. "Whose doing is this?"

"God only knows," Linus said. "We hear that Nero is fixing his eye upon us."

"A billowing curtain touches a candle, and Christians are to blame," Peter said ruefully.

"What will the emperor do?" Mary asked.

"We can but wait and pray," Linus said. "For now, let us eat. We are anxious to hear of your recent travels."

Peter and Mary had spent three decades crisscrossing the continent from Rome to Corinth and as far east as Antioch, preaching, teaching, and converting souls. Since the death of

Jesus, Paul had also spent much of his time in the east. The missionary work of the apostles had borne fruit. The young Christian Church flourished in the eastern hinterlands away from Rome and Jerusalem.

Yet Paul had made the ill-advised decision to return to Jerusalem to raise money to support his ongoing mission. There he ran afoul of the Jewish elders, who had the Roman authorities arrest him and haul him to barracks for questioning by flogging, a practice that often led to death. Paul asserted his rights as a Roman citizen to prevent a flogging and was held for two years under house arrest while the Roman governor and the Jewish high priests wrangled over the disposition of his case. Eventually, he was sent to Rome to stand trial for offenses against the order of Imperial Rome, where he was once again bound over for house arrest, and there languished for years longer as judicial procedures dragged on.

During the feast, Peter regaled his fellow Christians with tales of life in Corinth and Antioch and proudly spoke of how pleased Jesus would be when he returned to Earth and saw how many souls were in his flock.

"Tell me," Linus asked. "Why have you returned to Rome? Why now?"

"For one reason, and one reason only," Peter said. "To see our dear friend Paul one last time. He has been held captive these many years. We hear his trial cannot be avoided and that the outcome is certain."

Mary said, "We simply want to embrace him, laugh with him, cry with him, pray with him, and say farewell to him until we may meet again in Paradise. If we were in prison, he would do the same for us. Have you seen him? How is he?"

Linus replied, "His house is not far from here. The fire spared it. The Romans control access to him, but the soldiers can be bribed. I visit with him on occasion. His mind is strong, but his body grows weaker."

"Can you arrange for us to see him?" Peter asked.

"It is not without peril, but yes," Linus said. "I can make it happen."

"The Romans have branded me an enemy of the emperor," Peter said. "If they find out I am in the city, all is lost. They will arrest me, and they will kill me."

Linus spread his arm expansively, gesturing to all at the table. "Your secret is safe with us. You are among friends."

Paul's house of detention was a walled villa with a small garden where the captive grew vegetables and harvested hens' eggs. Peter and Mary came to him on a moonlit night. Their heads hooded, they avoided the gazes of people they passed along the rutted road. An acolyte of Linus, a young priest, guided them on foot to the villa, telling them that the bribes had been paid. The guards would turn a blind eye and let them convene with Paul, provided their stay was short.

When they approached the villa, they saw a single soldier illuminated by a torch set in the wall outside the iron gate. The young priest went to him, leaving Peter and Mary in the darkness. After a brief exchange, the priest returned, assured them that all was in order, and told them he would wait outside.

Once they were through the gate, Mary immediately saw that all was not in order. A phalanx of soldiers awaited them. A broad-shouldered young man who wore a breastplate of crimson armor accosted them. "I am Quintus Tatius, Praetorian guard. Simon Peter, I hereby arrest you in the name of the emperor."

As the drama played out around her, a shocked and dismayed Mary found herself absently staring at the ringlets of golden hair that flowed from under this soldier's helmet. She heard Peter begging for Mary's freedom and Quintus replying that he had no orders to detain her. She heard a man calling from a window, asking who was there, and her husband crying out to Paul that it was Peter come to see him, but alas, he was arrested. She heard Paul shout that Christ would protect them, before someone dragged him away from the window. And she heard Peter telling her he loved her as the brawny Praetorian pulled her husband into the shadows.

Nero let the Senate know in no uncertain terms that Christian extremists had set the fire that ravaged the city. Their pontifex maximus, Simon Peter, would have to pay for this outrage in a grim, predetermined sequence of justice. He would be confined to a dank dungeon within the barracks of the Praetorian Guards on the Quirinal Hill. He would be questioned under flogging. He would be found guilty at trial, and he would be publicly crucified. The tribune of the garrison of Rome personally charged Quintus Tatius, an immunis or corporal of the Guards, with the day-to-day supervision of the prisoner. Quintus obeyed his orders scrupulously, but he took no pleasure in the suffering of an old man. After Peter was flogged, Quintus gave him water to drink and axle grease to soothe his wounds.

Once Peter said to him in Latin, "You are very kind."

Quintus shrugged those big shoulders of his and replied, "You are human, as am I."

"Yes!" Peter said. "That is the essence."

"The essence of what?"

"Of Christ's message. Love God, and love your neighbor as yourself."

"Which god?" Quintus asked. "There are many gods."

"No, my son, there is but one true God."

As the date for the trial approached, Peter engaged Quintus in daily conversation. Quintus had an open, almost childlike mind, and he was naturally good-hearted. Here was fertile ground for the old man to plant one last seed and grow one last sapling before death. He spoke to the soldier about Jesus's life, his teachings, his death, and his resurrection.

"Jesus died for us," he told him. "If we wish to ascend to Heaven one day, our path is simple. We must believe in him, repent of our sins, and cry out to him for mercy. Do you wish for eternal life in the presence of God, Quintus?"

"What is Heaven like?" the soldier asked.

"Jesus spoke of Heaven in parables because man cannot fully comprehend the glory of Heaven. He said, 'The Kingdom of Heaven is like treasure hidden in a field. When a man found the treasure, he hid it again, and then in his joy went and sold all he had and bought that field.' This treasure can be yours, Quintus. All you need do is open your heart and receive the Lord."

Quintus heard his name being called from outside the cell and got up from his squat.

"I will ponder what you say. Tomorrow is the day of your trial. I am charged with taking you to the Forum."

"Will I finally be allowed to see my wife?"

"Each time I have requested on your behalf, it has been refused," Quintus said. "I will try again."

"Then will you tell her I love her?"

Mary had come every day to stand outside the barracks in silent vigil. The only one who would speak to her was Quintus, who, at the end of his shifts, passed along messages from Peter and let her know quotidian details of his incarceration: what food he had eaten, how he had slept, how were his spirits. In this way, a bond was formed between the jailer and the captive's wife. Mary was touched by the soldier's kindness, and in turn, her quiet dignity touched Quintus.

Quintus found Mary at her usual spot near the sentry post. "His trial is tomorrow," he said. "He wants you to know he loves you."

"How does he seem, Quintus?"

"He is peaceful. I have never seen a man at such peace."

The trial was brief and brutal. The charges were read. Sedition. Arson. The murder of those who perished in the great fire. Trumped-up witnesses testified. Peter's protestation of innocence was cut short by the magistrate. His sentence was handed down, and Quintus drove the cart carrying the old man back up the Quirinal Hill.

That night, Quintus brought Peter special rations, his own soldier's victuals. Peter ate the bread and meat eagerly, saying, "There were many at the table at Jesus's last supper. I have only you, Quintus."

Quintus hadn't cried since childhood, and he seemed embarrassed by his tears. "I will miss you, Peter."

"We can meet again in Heaven if you accept Jesus as your Lord and Savior. Will you do this?"

Quintus nodded and tried to hide his tear-streaked face. "How is it done?"

"Bring me that cup of water and kneel before me."

Peter anointed him with prison water and told the soldier that his sins had been washed away and that he would be saved. Quintus rose, the water dripping from his golden locks, and stumbled from the cell like a man drunk on mead. Peter sat alone and prayed until Quintus returned an hour later, still in a daze, to say that Peter had a visitor.

"Mary? Is it Mary?"

"Not her. A man called Linus."

Linus wrinkled his nose at the stench of the cell and stood over the broken old man. "I have come to pray with you in your time of need," he said.

"I have been praying," Peter said. "The Lord is with me. In the morning, I will be crucified as he was crucified. When my suffering is done, I will see him again. I ask you, Linus, was it you?"

"What do you mean?"

"Were you my Judas? The Romans were waiting for me at the house of Paul."

"How can you say such a thing, brother? You know I love you."

"Here you stand in a fine robe, a free man. Here I am in rags, awaiting my death. We are both Christians. Yet I have been convicted of sedition, arson, and murder, and you are blameless in the eyes of the emperor. How is it so?"

"I do not know why Nero does what he does. You will be

sorely missed, brother, but I will carry on as best I can, tending the Christian flock."

Peter raised his skinny arms. "You know the truth, and God knows the truth. I need not know."

"My conscience is clear," Linus said. "Pray listen. I come to you to discuss a matter of great importance. I hear that you have decided on a successor as pontifex maximus. I hear it is to be your wife, Mary."

"That is so," Peter said. "She was at Jesus's side from his early days. She was his favorite. She was by the cross when he died. She found his tomb empty. He appeared to her first. She has been at my side, ministering and teaching, for these many years. She is the one to carry our young Church forward."

Through clenched teeth, Linus said, "She is a woman."

Peter closed his eyes, as if remembering something sweet from the past, and said, "Yes, she is a woman, and she is a child of God, and she is our next pontifex maximus."

"I beg you to change your mind," Linus said. "It should be me. I have been a fine bishop. I have converted many Jews in Rome. I have found a way to honor Jesus and grow our Church without running afoul of the Romans. I have been the one who has kept Paul alive. Tomorrow, before you are hoisted upon the cross, tell all that I am your successor."

Peter shook his head. "It will be Mary. Serve her, Linus, as she served me. Now go in peace. I have a long night ahead and many prayers I wish to say."

Outside the barracks, Mary saw Linus leaving.

"Did you see him?" she asked.

"I did."

"And yet, they refuse me."

"You may see him at the Circus tomorrow and stand among the crowd. It will be quite the spectacle."

She fixed her brown eyes upon him. "How cruel you are, Linus."

"If I sound sharp, it is because his stubbornness vexes me."

"What did he say?"

"He said you will succeed him."

"It is what he wants. I will do my best."

"I told him it should not be a woman," Linus spat. "As Jesus was a man, so should the pontifex maximus, his agent on Earth, be a man."

"Jesus loved me as much as any man," she said, raising the hood of her cloak against a sudden swell of wind. "But you were not there, so you would not know."

Peter was crucified at the Circus of Nero, the chariot track and amphitheater built on the Ager Vaticanus, the alluvial plain on the west bank of the Tiber. The mob bayed and hooted as the nails went in and drank wine and sang bawdy songs while he suffered on the cross. As Peter's life ebbed, he seemed to take notice of only one person in the crowd, a woman in a brown robe who stood under him, fixed to a spot, like a statue. For the second time in her life, Mary stared up at a man hammered and strapped to a Roman crucifix, wordlessly telling him that he was loved.

And when Peter breathed no more, he was taken down and put on a donkey cart by the tearful soldier Quintus.

Quintus gave Mary Peter's silver ring in the shape of a fish and said, "He wanted you to have this."

Mary walked beside the young man until they reached the Roman tombs on the Via Cornelia. Three centuries later, Emperor Constantine, the first Christian emperor, would find Peter's tomb and build a basilica over it. The first St. Peter's Basilica would go to ruin by the sixteenth century. A new, grander basilica would be erected in its place. Peter's mortal remains would lay beneath its foundations until 1942, when workmen excavating the grottoes beneath the great altar would find a small tomb marked with ancient graffiti. *Peter is within.* And in that tomb would be the bones of a man aged sixty to seventy years.

Mary anointed Peter's body with oils, wrapped him in linen, and sat with him for a while until Quintus came into the dark tomb and laid a hand on her shoulder.

"My Lady, you must go. There is word that the emperor wants to question the new pontifex maximus."

Crushed by fatigue and grief, she said, "Go? Where?"

"Your followers have assembled outside the tomb. I have spoken with them about your safety. They say that Galilee is too dangerous. The rebellion between the Jews and the Romans has flared again. Antioch, they say, is better for you."

"Yes, Antioch," she said weakly. "Thank you, Quintus. You are a good man. I will miss you."

Quintus unbuckled his armored breastplate and let it slip to the floor. "You will not have cause to miss me, My Lady. Thanks to Peter, I am a Christian now. Wherever my pontifex maximus goes, I will go too."

20

Micaela Celestino finished seeing patients on the internal medicine and gastroenterology ward at the Gemelli Hospital, threaded her way through the midday crush of staff and visitors in the lobby, and retreated to the calm of her office. She was dictating a discharge note when her brother called.

"Okay, I got the number for you," Emilio said.

"Just text it to me."

"I don't want there to be a written record that I gave it to you."

"Why so cautious? You didn't do anything wrong."

Emilio didn't sound happy. "It's borderline at best. Do you want it or not?"

She took it down and thanked him as only Micaela could. "You're an asshole, but I love you."

Micaela had many talents, but tracking down unlisted phone numbers was not one of them, so she had turned to the head of the Vatican police for help. Her brother had pushed back, insisting that Emanuela Sordelli's accusation of an affair with Elisabetta was a public relations matter, not a criminal one, and they proceeded to have one of their inevitable shouting matches. In the end, Micaela convinced him that using his good offices to get the number was at worst a minor sin, and he asked a colleague in the Roman police for help. It proved to be a trivial exercise. Emanuela had multiple arrests for drug offenses, and the same mobile number appeared on each report.

Emanuela answered the unknown number with a suspicious-sounding "Pronto."

"Is this Emanuela?" Micaela asked.

"Who's this?"

"It's Micaela Celestino, Elisabetta's sister. Do you remember me from school?"

"How'd you get my number?"

Micaela looked out the window at an ambulance arriving in the hospital forecourt. "I looked it up."

"No you didn't."

"Look, it's not important how I got it. I want to see if we could meet for a coffee or a bite."

"Why?"

"To talk, that's all."

"I said what I said. We've got nothing to talk about."

"Come on. We were all friends in the old days."

"You were an annoying little brat."

"I'm still annoying."

Micaela thought that the laugh she elicited was a good sign, and sure enough, the woman agreed to meet in Ostia that evening.

Micaela knew the Ostia neighborhood of Rome well. When

she, Emilio, and Elisabetta were children, their parents had taken them to the seaside there to paddle during steamy summers. She chose a café called MIT Bistro located in an upmarket part of the city but regretted the choice as soon as Emanuela walked in. The bistro was trendy, and the patrons were fashionable. Emanuela was not. She was gaunt and unkempt, with a black-and-blue mark extending from her left ear to her chin. Despite the warm, clear evening, she wore a dirty, lined raincoat, and her tights had a hole above one knee. There was little in her of the schoolgirl Micaela had known, and she drew stares as the restaurant owner showed her to the table.

"Well, look at you," Emanuela said.

"And look at you," Micaela countered.

Emanuela sat and pulled her raincoat tight to her chest.

"Are you cold?" Micaela asked.

"I'm good. The guy said the reservation was under Dr. Celestino. You're a doctor, a medical doctor?"

"Yes."

"What kind?"

"Gastrointestinal diseases."

"Like the runs?"

"Yeah, like the runs."

"Cool."

"It has its moments—well, not the runs part."

"You don't dress like any doctor I ever met. Red hair. Miniskirt. Big earrings."

"Yeah, I'm not known for my subtlety."

"I didn't recognize you," Emanuela said. "You were such a skinny runt back then."

"We all grow up."

"How's your brother? He was cute."

"Some say he still is."

"He became a policeman, right?"

"Head of the Vatican Gendarmerie."

"Wow. Big deal. Married?"

"Single."

"Me too, but I'm probably not his type."

Micaela sidestepped that one. "Want a drink?"

Emanuela inquired about Micaela's glass of red and said she'd have the same. "You're paying, right?"

Micaela nodded.

"Then make it a bottle."

With the wine starting to flow, Micaela sought to build rapport by talking about school days. Emanuela was Eli's friend, but with only two years separating the sisters age-wise, Eli had often included Micaela when the older girls hung out. Emanuela's situation at home was fractious—her parents were constantly at each other's throats, so she often spent time at the Celestino apartment after school. Eli and Emanuela were keen volleyball players. Micaela loathed the sport, but she would tag along to the park for something to do and was given the job of retrieving balls slammed out of bounds.

"You couldn't even do that," Emanuela said. "We were always going, 'Where's Mic?' You were off somewhere, not paying attention, and we'd have to get the ball ourselves."

"It was boring," Micaela said. "I preferred looking for four-leafed clovers. I hated the game then, and I still hate it. When my husband puts it on the box, I have to leave the room."

"How long have you been married?"

"Twelve years. One husband. One kid. That's my limit. What about you?"

Before answering, Emanuela drained her glass. "Me? I'm a mess."

Micaela had already figured that much out. Her dishevelment. Her bruise. Pupils constricted, a little giddy, raincoat sleeves that probably hid track marks. "Want to talk about it?"

The waiter interrupted to take their orders. Micaela was starved as usual and went to town with the menu. Her guest ordered one small plate.

When he left, Emanuela said, "You didn't ask to see me to talk about my crap life."

"You're right. But here you are, someone I used to know very well, and, well, I have some concerns."

"Really? You and Eli probably wish I were dead."

"Then you don't know me, and you don't know her. What's been going on with you?"

"One shitty thing after another, I suppose you could say. You and Eli and some of the other girls I knew went to university. I went to work in a bar. I got involved with a guy, a real asshole. He turned me on to drugs, then knocked me up."

"What happened to the baby?"

"I got rid of it. I shouldn't have, but you can't undo these things. Maybe if I had a mother who wasn't a wreck herself, I would've kept it. Anyway, I went into a tailspin and started to develop a bad habit. I managed to hold down a job, but the asshole stole whatever I had to buy junk for himself. By the time I kicked him out, I was pretty far gone. The Celestino girls were in roses. I was in the sewer."

"Okay, maybe I didn't have any big obstacles in my life,

but you know what happened to Eli when she was in her late twenties, right? She almost died."

"I heard something about that. My twenties were hazy. I was out of it most of the time."

Micaela saw the opening and went on the attack. "What you missed was that she was stabbed and her boyfriend was killed. She spent months in the hospital in agony. She reexamined every aspect in her life, and when she recovered, she decided to change everything and become a nun."

Emanuela defensively folded her arms across her chest. "Okay, maybe next she'll become a saint."

"Eli told me that what you said is untrue. She never had an affair with you."

"Maybe she doesn't remember what I remember."

"And what do you remember?"

"We slept together."

"When was that?"

"At your apartment."

"Okay, tell me what happened."

"It was in our last year at school. She invited me into her bed. Your brother was at university, and you were in his room. We had sex."

"Eli told me the same thing, except that there was no sex. She said you were very upset one night. You couldn't stop crying. Things were bad at home for you. Your father was drinking and hitting your mother. She held you until you fell asleep. That's the only time there was even that small physical contact. But you told Chiara Falova there was an affair."

"Who's Chiara Falova?"

"The reporter."

Micaela had a copy of the story in her bag and showed Emanuela the byline.

"The woman who came to see me was named Monica."

"What was her last name?"

"She didn't say. She told me she was a reporter. She asked questions and recorded my answers. Look, I don't like to be challenged this way. Maybe I'll go."

She was distracted long enough by the arrival of scented bowls of zuppa di mare for Micaela to persuade her to stay and eat.

"Look, I don't want to make you uncomfortable," Micaela said. "My sister is under assault for having a job that some people say should only belong to a man. She's fighting for her dignity. If she had sex with a woman years ago, who the hell cares, and whose business is it? Do you know how many gay priests there are in the Vatican? They're left alone. These misogynistic assholes think they can bring a woman down by shouting about her sex life. If the accusation were true, I wouldn't be here. But Eli says it's not true, and she's never lied to me. Come on, let's have this nice soup while it's hot."

They slurped quietly for a while until Emanuela said, "I always liked Eli. I didn't mean to cause her so much trouble." She began to blubber. "I've had a lot of problems."

Micaela gave her a tissue and said, "How did saying these things help with your problems?"

Emanuela looked at her lap and said, "Monica paid me. I needed money for rent and food. I don't have a job."

"And maybe you bought some drugs too," Micaela said. "It's not to accuse. I can tell you're still using. So let me tell you

271

what I think happened, okay? This woman who called herself Monica, who probably isn't a real journalist, was sent by someone trying to discredit Eli. She finds a vulnerable woman with problems and pays her to embellish an innocent story about schoolgirls having a cuddle. The more it's embellished, the more she pays. Is that what happened?"

There were more tears. "Yes."

Micaela forked a mussel from a shell and said, "I'm going to offer to help you with your problem whether or not you take your story back. My friend is the medical director of a rehab clinic in Rome, a good one. I can get you admitted, and if you're motivated, you can get yourself clean. My brother Emilio knows a million people. If you can get off the drugs, he and I will try to find you a good job."

"You'd do that for me?"

"We were friends. We do these things for friends."

Emanuela's lower lip trembled uncontrollably. "How can I make things better with Eli?"

On her drive back to Rome, Micaela called her sister on her mobile.

"If everything's all right, let's talk later," Elisabetta said. "I'm still at work."

"Guess who I just had dinner with?"

"Come on, Mic. I'm busy."

"Emanuela Sordelli."

Elisabetta sounded angry. "I think you'd better explain."

As Micaela recounted the dinner, her sister's anger dissipated, and in the end, she had to admit that the result was a good one.

"She sounds like a lost soul," Elisabetta said.

"It's sad, for sure, but that doesn't justify what she did," Micaela said. "We need to have a real journalist interview her. How do we do that?"

"I'm dealing with too many crises right now. Our nuncio in China is in difficulty. An audit report on some Vatican-owned real estate in Paris is going to make unpleasant headlines. I don't need to say more. I'll have Silvio Licheri, the head of our press office, call you to get the details, okay?"

"Yeah, sure, no problem."

"I love you for this."

"Love you too."

"I don't suppose you told Emanuela that I'd pray for her?"

"For God's sake, Eli, the woman needs medical attention, not a blessing."

The nun tutted at her sister the way she always did when the topic of religion came up between them. "In my experience, medicine and faith can be quite synergistic."

Monica Magnani was getting her nails done near her office when her partner called.

"Where are you?" Antonio half-shouted into her earbuds.

"At the nail salon. What's the matter?"

"You haven't seen the story about Emanuela Sordelli yet, have you?"

"What? What happened to her?"

"I texted you the link."

"My hands are soaking in soapy water. Read it to me."

She had to listen to Antonio cursing while he punched it up on his computer.

"It's by a journalist named Analisa Paciolla who's the editor of something called *Women Church World*. Here it goes. 'Emanuela Sordelli, the childhood friend of Vatican Secretary of State, Elisabetta Celestino, who claimed she had a lesbian affair with her when they were younger, has now dropped these claims in a dramatic recantation. Contacted by *Women Church World*, Sordelli now says that she was paid to smear Sister Elisabetta by a woman she knew only by her first name, Monica, who represented herself as a journalist. An article carrying her accusation was published on a right-wing website, *Il Grido dell'Aquila*, written by the journalist Chiara Falova. When reached on the telephone for comment, Falova swore and hung up.'"

"Christ," Monica said. "They got to her. What else does it say?"

"Let's see. There's this gem: 'A poor woman with a history of substance abuse and addiction was seemingly preyed upon by unsavory elements from the political right who wish to persecute the secretary of state for the crime of being a woman.'"

"Yes, well," Monica said, looking at her submerged cuticles.

"Is there any way this can be traced back to us?" Antonio asked.

"She only had my first name. I gave her cash. I don't see how. Does the client know yet?"

"I sent it to Spooner. I'm waiting for the shockwaves from the nuclear explosion. It's a good thing we're making progress on the other angle."

"Don't say 'we,' Antonio. I told you I don't like what you're doing."

"How is it so different from your piece of work on Emanuela Sordelli?"

"I'd describe my work with Emanuela as embellishing the truth. They were friends. They were in a bed together. Your situation involves outright fraud."

Antonio laughed a little and said, "If that completely artificial distinction helps you get through the night, that's perfectly fine with me."

21

When Cal exited Sever Hall following his undergraduate lecture, the harsh autumn sunlight sent him into a squint. It took him a few moments to place the woman bearing down on him.

"Detective Caruso," he said. "How did you find me?" She lifted her sunglasses and treated him to an eye roll. "Right," he said. "You know how to find people."

"I had a harder time finding my car keys this morning," she said.

"How can I help you?"

He headed north toward the Divinity School, and she fell in beside him. The foliage in Harvard Yard was nearing peak color, and the walkways were crowded with students and gawkers.

"Do you know someone named Gregory Kalogeras?"

"I know Greg. Why?"

"How did Samia Tedros know him?"

"I had no idea the two of them knew each other."

"Tell me about him."

"We're acquaintances, not friends, so I don't know him all that well. He's in the Physics Department. He's an expert in magnetometry and LIDAR. He gives occasional courses to archaeology students. That's all I can tell you."

"Those things you said, I don't know what they are," she complained.

"They're techniques for detecting what's below the ground without digging."

"Like x-rays?"

"Sort of. Why are you asking about him?"

"We got Samia's phone records. She made three calls from her iPhone, from the time she landed in Boston to when she was killed. One of them was to you."

"Which I told you about."

"Yes, you did. Gold star. One was to Cairo to her parents' apartment—the Cairo police helped us with that. And the other was to this guy, Gregory Kalogeras, right after she called you. I'm seeing him at his office in half an hour. Want to help me kill time with a coffee?"

They were standing outside the Science Center Building, just outside the gates of Harvard Yard.

Cal checked his calendar on his phone, saw he was free, and gestured toward the concrete and steel building. "Sure. There's a café inside."

⊂══◆══⊃

Stella stirred her coffee and looked at the tables full of students. "It's funny," she said, "I've been in the Cambridge police for sixteen years, and this is the first time I've ever been inside a Harvard building."

"This is one of the more recent ones," Cal said, "built in the seventies. If you're seeing Greg Kalogeras at Jefferson Labs—that one's late nineteenth century."

"You're a regular tour guide," she said.

"If you'd like a walking tour of the campus one of these days, I can oblige."

She smiled and pointed out her wedding band.

"I wasn't hitting on you," Cal said in mock horror.

"Good, because until I find Samia's killer, you're a person of interest."

"I'd rather be an interesting person," he said.

She tasted the coffee, made a face, and added more sugar. "You Harvard types are pretty clever, aren't you?"

"We try."

"Tell me about Samia. What was she like?"

"She was a lovely young woman—quiet, studious, smart. She was a Coptic Christian, so she grew up as a discriminated-against minority in Egypt—only about five percent of Egyptians are Copts. She told me her family was middle-class, traditional, and conservative. I don't think she was very worldly. When she came to Cambridge, it was the first time she'd been out of Egypt. For her, it was a leap into the void. She was overly formal too. All my grad students call me Cal. She'd only call me 'Professor.'"

"Why did she want to come all the way to Harvard? She couldn't go to someplace in Egypt?"

"To be honest, I think she wanted to work with me. Some of my research interests overlapped with hers. I'm primarily at the Divinity School, but I've got a joint appointment with the Anthropology and Archaeology Department. Samia was looking to do post-doctoral work in biblical archaeology."

"And she was with you for five years?"

"That's right. She left a year ago."

"Five years sounds like a long time. Did she have a problem graduating?"

"No, she breezed through. Five years is typical for a PhD candidate."

"What do I know?" Stella said defensively. "I only went to a junior college you never heard of. What kind of research did she do?"

"Samia studied early Christian Coptic manuscripts, many of them discovered at Egyptian archaeological sites. She was good at what she did, and her thesis was impressive. I know she was proud of it. I think she wanted to get it published, but I'm not sure what came of that. She was disappointed she didn't land a faculty job in the US, and so was I. She wanted to stay in America, but she had to return to Egypt when her student visa ran out. My understanding was that the only halfway suitable job she could get in Cairo was in a papyrus restoration lab at the Egyptian Museum. It was more of a technician post than an academic one, so it was sad."

"Not as sad as getting murdered," Caruso said. "Why couldn't she get a job here?"

"She aimed too high. I encouraged her to broaden her search, but I think, in the end, she was unrealistic. Sometimes the students who come out of Harvard think they're God's gift and that people will toss petals in their path."

"Never one of my expectations," she said. "So, Samia's in a

shit job back home, her sister gets sick and needs a kidney, and Samia goes to the dark side."

"Except that, when push came to shove, she reverted to form. She was a scholar, a devout Christian, and, let's not forget, a woman. She couldn't abide the Mary papyrus and all its implications being lost to history."

"It was brave, but she paid one helluva price," Stella said. "Let me ask you something. Are you sure it's for real? Could Samia have pulled a double fake—a forgery of a forgery?"

"That would have been wildly out of character. No, I trust Samia's story about the papyrus's provenance. It didn't pass through multiple hands, as these texts often do. It was newly discovered in a mask. There's some funkiness about the supposed age of the mask that I won't trouble you with, but my guess is, if we recover the papyrus, tests will prove that it's an authentic missing fragment of the Gospel of Mary."

Stella looked at the time on her phone, mumbled that she had to be going soon, then said, "You know, I hope it's real."

"Tell me why."

"Because women are always getting shat on." She looked out the window and said, "I probably shouldn't be telling you this—"

He smiled. "Because I'm a person of interest."

She bookended his smile. "Exactly, but you're also an interesting person, and you're not her killer. I was going to say that I had to put up with unbelievable shit coming up through the police and detective ranks as a woman. I mean, here we are in one of the supposedly most woke cities in America, and I still had to develop armor-plated skin to make it through all the sexist BS. And don't even get me started on the Church. I met my wife at a Mass, of all places. We're both practicing Catholics, and we're both reasonably good people—well, Natalie is, more than me. Do you think we were able to have a church wedding?"

"Not unless you found a rogue priest," Cal said.

"My priest, Father Bonifacio, treated us like we were lepers, and I'm pretty sure the fucker is gay himself. So I like the idea that there was a woman pope. It'll put all these assholes in their place."

When Greg Kalogeras opened his door to Stella, he had the appearance of a man struggling not to vomit. He was thirty-five with curly black hair spilling over a wide forehead, and he had black stubble from a missed shave. His hand was damp, and Stella was obliged to wipe hers off on her skirt before pulling out her notebook. The office was typical assistant professor fare—it was tiny, stuffed with books and papers and electronic gadgets. He retreated behind his desk and looked at her plaintively as if waiting for something terrible to happen.

"You know why I'm here," Stella began.

"You told me on the phone it was about Samia Tedros."

"You do know what happened to Samia, don't you?"

"It's all over the news. It's very upsetting. Do you have any idea who did this?"

"It's an active investigation."

"I'm not sure how I can help you."

She pursed her lips, clicked her pen, and stared at him until he seemed to become smaller, as if he was collapsing under his own weight.

"Professor, can you tell me where you were yesterday afternoon between about three and five o'clock?"

"I'm not a suspect, am I?"

"This is just routine questioning."

"I taught a graduate seminar from two to four, then had a meeting with the post-docs in my lab from four to five-thirty."

"You have people who can confirm that?"

"Yes."

"And after that?"

"I drove home to Newton. The trip will be logged in my Tesla."

She remembered Cal Donovan's car, parked on Lawrence Street. "Jeez, do all you Harvard profs drive Teslas?" she asked. "Did you recently speak with Samia?"

"She called me the night before last, but you probably know that, don't you? That's why you're here."

She read from her notepad. "According to T-Mobile, she called you at 9:14 p.m. and was connected for fifty-six seconds. What was the nature of the call?"

His fidgeting made his chair roll a little on its casters. "Just that she was back in Boston and wanted to say hello."

Stella put on an expression of faux surprise. "That's it? 'Hello, I'm back'? Nothing else?"

"She mentioned that she'd like to meet."

"And did you?"

He had a prominent Adam's apple that shot up when he swallowed. "I'd like to help, but I'd rather not say."

Stella straightened her spine and raised her voice. She was

five foot five and weighed about a hundred twenty, but at that moment, at least to him, she must have seemed like a snarling giant. "Would you rather I park a couple of patrol cars outside the building, blue lights flashing, so all your students and colleagues can watch you being brought in for questioning? I might even give a heads-up to a few reporters. I can picture the headline in the *Globe*: 'Harvard Professor Questioned in Samia Tedros Murder Case.'"

"No, I'd rather that not happen." He opened a bottle of water and took a swig. "She came by my office yesterday, around noon. She stayed about half an hour."

"Okay, play that meeting back for me. What was its purpose? What did she say? What transpired between you?"

"She told me she was in some kind of trouble. She asked for my help."

"Why you? Who were you to her?" Stella asked.

"We'd been friends for a few years."

Stella found that sometimes in an interview, less is more. She simply repeated the word dryly. "Friends."

"We met at a wine and cheese talk I gave over at the Peabody Museum on imaging techniques in archaeology. We saw each other from time to time afterward."

"As friends."

"Yes, friends."

"Forgive me for being suspicious, Professor, but I get paid to be like this. Samia makes two calls the night she arrives while staying at her ex-boyfriend's house, and one of them is to you. You see her the next day, and a few hours later, she's murdered. You're sitting there looking like you're about to throw up or pass out or both. You're wearing a wedding band. If you're not forthcoming, I can and will do a deep dive into your personal life and interview your wife and your colleagues. This is a murder investigation, so no holds barred. What was the nature of your relationship with Samia?"

"We had an affair," he croaked. "I don't want that getting out. We broke it off when she moved in with Danyal Tamer during her last semester in Cambridge. If you're interested, the affair violated my marital vows, not university policy. There's no prohibition of a consensual relationship between faculty members and graduate students so long as the faculty member isn't supervising or teaching the individual. You can look at the policy. Here's the Faculty of Arts and Sciences Guidelines on Sexual and Gender-Based Harassment. I'm confident that the single lecture of mine she attended did not constitute a teaching relationship."

It was open on his desk as if he'd been consulting it. He looked for all the world like a beaten man.

"All right. So you had an affair with her. She goes back to Egypt, gets herself in some kind of trouble, as you put it, and wants to see you the day after she lands in Boston. What did she tell you?"

"She told me her sister had kidney failure and needed a transplant and that she'd probably die before the public hospitals had a kidney for her. She stole something valuable from her museum and sold it to raise money for a private clinic. She didn't give me details, but she said the deal went bad, and the buyers went looking for her and killed her aunt. She went on the run and flew to Boston. She was very emotional, extremely distraught."

"Did she tell you what she stole?"

"She didn't."

"You're sure about that?"

"Absolutely."

"Didn't give you anything for safekeeping?"

"Nothing."

"What did she want from you?"

"She didn't have any money, and I gave her what I had on me—about a hundred dollars. I would've given her more via Venmo, but my wife sees the credit card transactions linked to the site. I told Samia I'd give her more cash next time I saw her."

"Which was supposed to be when?"

He closed his eyes and said, "Today."

"Is that all? Is that all she wanted?"

"She asked me if she could stay at my ski condo in Vermont. She wanted someplace to hide. She thought she might have been followed and was panicked. She was going to take a bus to Vermont this afternoon."

"She'd stayed there before," Stella said.

He slowly nodded. "A couple of times, when my wife was abroad."

"What else?"

"That was it."

"You say she was here for about thirty minutes, right? According to her cellular provider, her phone loses contact with the nearest cell tower at 12:21. Know anything about that?"

"That was me," he said. "She was paranoid about being followed. She thought she recognized a man at the airport who was involved with the buyers of whatever she was selling. And this morning, when she left Danyal's apartment, she thought she might have seen him again, hanging out in a park. She was a mess. She didn't know what was real and what wasn't. People with enough resources can track cell phones. So, for peace of mind, I told her to remove her SIM card and buy herself a prepaid phone. She tossed it in my wastepaper basket."

Stella got up to look at the bin, but he told her not to bother—the cleaning people emptied them nightly.

"There's one more thing," he said. "After she ditched her SIM card, she said she needed to make a call. I let her use my cell phone and went to the restroom for a couple of minutes. When I returned, she was done. I hugged her, and she left. She was supposed to call me later on her new phone to set up a time to get the cash today. She never called."

Stella was on her feet now, leaning over the desk. "I need you to give me the number Samia called."

He meekly pulled the phone from his pocket, looked at the recent call log, and wrote it down for her. It was an 857 area code, a local number.

"Is that it?" he asked tensely. "Am I done with the police?"

"Here's my card," she said. "Text me about the people who can vouch for your whereabouts yesterday afternoon. If it checks out, you probably won't see me again. And Professor, I'd advise you to keep current on those university guidelines on affairs with students."

Cal was lacing up his track shoes for an evening run to test his mended leg when his phone rang. He'd already entered her into his contacts, so he answered, "Hello, Detective Caruso. How can I help you?"

"It looks like Samia called someone else. Does the name Greta Schenck ring a bell?"

"Greta's a current grad student of mine. I think she and Samia were friends—I used to see them hanging out together, so I'm not surprised she called her."

"Good Lord," Stella said. "Is there anyone involved in this case you don't know? Don't talk to her about Samia. Leave her to me."

"Did you see Greg Kalogeras?"

"Yep."

"The papyrus. Did he know anything about it?"

"Nope."

"Damn it. Maybe Greta knows something. Are you sure I can't ask her about it?"

Stella said, "If you do, I'll turn you into one of the most eligible eunuchs in Boston."

She didn't sound like she was joking.

22

Cambridge wasn't Spooner's kind of place, and Harvard wasn't his kind of school. Although he had never been on the campus before, what he saw fed into his stereotypic opinions on the kind of things that went on at an elite, Ivy League university. He bristled at the Black Lives Matter and pro-grad-student-unionization placards in the dorm windows, the smell of marijuana in the air, the stuck-up coeds who looked askance at his military bearing and gave him a wide berth.

And while he didn't know more than a bare-bones bio of who Calvin Donovan was, the more he followed him, the more he disliked him. He resented the way he confidently glided from one ivy-covered building to the next, buttonholed by adoring students. He resented his good looks and wealth, which he divined from his fancy house on professors' row. He resented the way he'd been able to insinuate himself into the heart of the police investigation. He watched through the windows of the Science Center café as Donovan and the pretty blonde detective shared a coffee and intimate conversation and guessed they were already sleeping together or would be soon.

And he imagined that a privileged jerk like Donovan would look down on a southern boy like him who went to a state college and wound up joining the military. His boss was a billionaire who lived a fantastically lavish lifestyle. Still, Tommy Cunliffe was "one of us" in Spooner's books—a God-fearing, country-loving, family man whom Spooner would take a bullet for. Tommy had told him that this piece of old paper he was looking for would be bad for Christians if it got out, and that was all he needed to know. He was going to try his damnedest to secure it, and if that meant putting Donovan down, then all the better.

Spooner was smoking a morning cigarette in his non-smoking rental car parked near Cal's house and picked up the call from Tommy on the first ring.

"Anything new?" Tommy asked.

"Nothing. He stayed in all night."

"No visitors?"

"No, sir."

"You slept in the car?"

"I didn't miss anything. It would be a lot easier if I pushed Orion onto Donovan's and the detective's phones."

Tommy used Spooner's first name, a sign of his irritation. "Joel, you know I don't want to be read into something like that. You do what you need to do to accomplish your mission."

"Got it."

"Good man. So, listen, I've decided to greenlight Antonio Solla's proposal. We've got to ratchet up the pressure on the nun. I'm authorizing you to transfer three hundred thousand euros to his account so he can pay the guy and set this up."

"I'll do it right away."

"You call me if there are any developments."

"Roger that, boss."

⊙━━◆━━⊙

Tommy Cunliffe found his wife in the breakfast nook off the kitchen watching TV and having an omelet.

"Looks good," he said, pouring a coffee from a carafe.

Barbara didn't turn away from the screen. "Want one?" she said.

"Wouldn't say no."

"Then make it yourself or ask the cook. He's downstairs in the prep kitchen."

"Very nice, Barbara," he seethed, "very nice. You know, you look like crap. How much did you drink last night?"

"Just about enough."

The TV was tuned to CNN—not his favorite channel— and as he was about to leave, a story began to air about the recantation of Elisabetta Celestino's childhood friend. He watched it for a while and grimaced as one of the talking heads described the initial accusation as part of an orchestrated smear campaign by reactionary right-wing elements within the Catholic Church.

"How can you watch this crap?" he said.

She ignored the comment and said, "I've decided to co-operate with your campaign."

He registered a look of surprise and said he was glad to hear it.

"I have some conditions," she said.

"Oh yes? Who've you been talking to?" he demanded.

"The little voice in my head," she said, muting the TV. "I want our old prenup torn up, and I want a new post-nup agreement drawn up. I want a substantial lump-sum payment now for being the good wife if you run, and another lump sum if, God forbid, you go for the presidency. I want all the deeds and titles to my family's houses, boats, and cars transferred to them. And I want a clause that expressly forbids you to enter my marital bed and doubles all payments if you violate it."

Tommy's nostrils were flaring as he silently listened to her demands until he heard the last of them and said, "That one, I can agree to."

She clattered her fork down and slid her plate away. "Not the others? It's only money, Tommy. You've got loads."

He took a seat opposite her at the breakfast table and slammed his coffee cup down hard enough to spill coffee and blemish the oak.

Given the violence of the gesture, his voice was surprisingly calm and even. "No, we're not going to be changing our arrangements. The prenup will stand. My lawyers have taken another look at it, and I'm told it's ironclad in the state of Pennsylvania. If you leave me, you get a million bucks, your jewelry, and your car. I know you can't live on that, so I doubt you'll be pulling the ripcord. Can you imagine yourself moving back to Houston, getting yourself a little two-bed, two-bath condo, playing golf on a public course? Going onto dating apps, looking for a rich fellow to take you in, at your age and the state you're in? I can't."

"You're a bastard," she hissed.

"Been called worse by better people than you," he said.

"No, you're going to pull yourself together as best you can, and you're going to be a picture-perfect political wife or suffer some unpleasant consequences."

"You're threatening me now?" she yelled.

"You bet I am. I've already gotten affidavits from every member of the staff at Heartland Manor about the extent of your drinking. I've got Dr. Ferris teed up to ask a court to initiate proceedings under the state's Mental Health Procedures Act to have you involuntarily committed because of your danger to yourself. I've even had my pollster test out the public perception of a gubernatorial candidate whose wife's been committed to the loony bin. Turns out there's a fair bit of sympathy, provided they like the candidate. So, my advice to you, dear, is to stop listening to the little voice in your head and listen to the big voice coming out of your husband's mouth."

Tommy ducked out of the way of the omelet plate she hurled at him and, on his way out, told her to have someone clean up the mess.

There was a small family-owned restaurant near the offices of Solla Investigations where Antonio took his lunch every day. He often dined alone at his usual window table with a newspaper for company, but today he asked Monica to join him.

They were tucking into their caprese salads when Antonio said, "Look, it was bad luck that this girl, Emanuela, was unreliable. I wanted to have lunch with you to tell you I hope you're not beating yourself up over it. I've noticed you moping around the office. The Vatican probably paid her more than we did to recant. The corrupt are corruptible. Someone smart once said that. Maybe me."

"Yes, but I'm not beating myself up," she said, leaning in, keeping her voice down. "I'm happy she took it back. For my first time as a private investigator, I was disgusted with myself. Usually, we're doing honest work, exposing cheaters and scum. When have we degraded ourselves like this? Every time I put another hundred-euro note down in front of Emanuela to make her story keep getting juicier, I felt a little bit of me dying."

Antonio looked over his glasses at her and said, "You're being melodramatic. We've paid for information before."

"Yes, sure, but for true information, not lies."

He sipped at his beer and said, "One man's truth is another man's lies."

"What does that even mean?" she said.

"I think I read it from a fortune cookie," he said. "I'm a better PI than a philosopher. All I know is that business has been way down, and we've got a client who is paying us handsomely to do work he regards as vital. Who are we to say whether he's right or wrong in his desire to take this woman down?"

"I've been reading about the nun," Monica said. "Her story is inspiring."

"Yes, well, I find Tommy Cunliffe's wire transfers inspiring. We received three hundred thousand euros today—two hundred for expenses for the thing I'm working on, a hundred for our special fee."

"What the hell? How can you possibly need so much for expenses? And what in God's name is a special fee?"

As he laid out his plans, she put her silverware down and twisted her face into a deep frown.

"So that's how it's going to work. This afternoon, I'm meeting with Cardinal Giuseppe Tosi. He's a big shot, the cardinal camerlengo. Tommy Cunliffe made it happen. The guy's got connections. With Tosi's help, everything comes together."

Monica got up and pushed her chair back, the legs scraping the tiles.

"Where are you going?" he asked.

"You've got one missing piece, Antonio. Me. I quit."

"Come on, be reasonable. Sit down and finish your lunch."

"What you're doing is illegal," she whispered into his ear. "You've already lost your dignity. Now you'll lose your license."

"Half the special bonus—it's yours," he said.

"Keep it," she said. "You'll probably need it to hire a lawyer when this blows up in your face. I'm done."

Antonio scowled at the diners at a nearby table, who were staring at the fracas, and they went back to minding their own business.

"The agency was going to be yours when I retire," he said. "What the hell do you think will happen to you without me?"

"I've already had conversations with the women who work at the agency. They're all enthusiastic about my idea."

"What idea?" he said.

"We're going to form an all-female investigations agency. Take care of yourself, Antonio. It was a hell of a ride."

⁓—⁂—⁓

Antonio and Cardinal Tosi settled on a discreet place to meet, the Bioparco di Roma zoo on the grounds of the Villa

Borghese. The detective spotted Tosi, incognito in the garb of a simple priest, admiring the lions basking in the sun within their walled enclosure.

"Eminence," he said, "I'm Antonio Solla."

"Ah, you found me. It seems you are a good detective."

"I recognized you from your photos."

One of the male lions chose to give off a booming, throaty roar, delighting a party of schoolchildren.

"They're magnificent, aren't they?" the cardinal said. "Come, let's walk. I can use the exercise."

This was perhaps one of the last of the truly warm weeks before winter began to nudge aside the autumn, and the park was teeming with visitors. The animals made music with their bleating, chattering, screeching, and roaring, and the children provided counterpoint with excited shouting and jabbering.

Pausing to look at the giraffes, Tosi asked, "Have you met our American friend?"

"Only on the telephone."

"He's a great man, a soldier for Christ."

"I can't disagree," Antonio replied.

"He told me to meet with you and bring you what you needed. I need to know how you intend to use it."

"Eminence, I can tell you the plan or not tell you. It's up to you."

"Yes, I understand the value of not knowing your intentions, but I feel I should exercise a certain diligence. A risk assessment, I think the professionals call it. I have no tolerance for being publicly linked to your endeavors. What will the seal be used for? Ah, look! The giraffes seem to be amorous. They shouldn't let the children see!"

Tosi started walking again toward the kangaroos. Antonio had to limit his stride to match the cardinal's mincing waddle.

"The endeavor, as you put it, involves the sale of treasures from the Vatican collection," Antonio said. "As you know, during this exercise, Sister Elisabetta was in charge of the Pontifical Commission for Sacred Archaeology."

"Those were dark days," Tosi said. "As the leader of the Pontifical Commission for the Cultural Heritage of the Church, I was obliged to participate in the farce. The nun was Pope Celestine's puppet."

"I have identified a buyer, a private collector, of one of the classical statues that the Vatican Museum chose to divest," Antonio said, "a Belgian who has since passed away. He paid about a million euros for the piece. I believe it currently adorns one of his country estates."

"Yes, so?" Tosi said.

"Would it not be fatally damaging to the nun if paperwork was discovered that demonstrated she received a kickback for ten percent of the purchase price?"

Tosi pointed at two kangaroos racing each other to get to a bushel of carrots, apples, and broccoli that a keeper dumped in their enclosure.

"Will you look at that!" He turned serious and said, "You can do this?"

"It's arranged. All I need is the official seal embosser from her Pontifical Commission."

"Is there any conceivable way this could come back to bite me?"

Antonio rubbed his lower face in thought. "How did you obtain the seal?"

"A trusted monsignor within the Commission, a man who was horrified by the sale of Church patrimony. I asked to borrow it for two days. He was sensible enough not to ask why."

"If you believe he will be deaf, dumb, and blind, then I don't see how you can be implicated in the affair."

Tosi reached into his leather messenger bag and handed over the small, heavy instrument.

"I need it back tomorrow," Tosi said. "Let's meet at the same time, at the monkey house. I do love the monkeys. The things they get up to!"

23

Robinson Hall, home to the History Department, was an ornate three-story building of red brick and limestone that matched the architectural aesthetic of the neighboring structures in Harvard Yard. Stella was getting used to the campus and had to admit that she was enjoying spending time with professors and students instead of her usual crop of witnesses and suspects.

Greta Schenck was a German national doing her graduate studies jointly with the History Department and the Divinity School. Her main office was at Robinson Hall, a shared space with two other PhD candidates, one of whom was there when Stella arrived for their appointment.

Before Stella could introduce herself, Greta, a dark-haired woman with the wiry physique of a long-distance runner, picked up her things and said in a strong German accent, "We should talk elsewhere."

They went into the hall, where Stella thanked her for making herself available. She delivered perfunctory condolences, unsure how Samia's death had affected Greta.

"Yes, a terrible tragedy," Greta said unemotionally. "I think Robinson 106 is empty. We can meet there."

Stella accompanied her to the seminar room with a long table for sixteen and a whiteboard. They faced each other, Stella kinetic, preparing her notepad and pen, Greta motionless, with clasped hands resting on the table.

"Samia called you on the day she was killed," Stella began.

"She did, yes."

"Were you surprised to hear from her?"

"Indeed, yes. I wasn't aware she was in Cambridge."

"How friendly were the two of you?"

"Quite friendly, I would say, in that when she lived here, we would socialize. She was two years ahead of me, but we found ourselves in the same seminars at the Divinity School, and we had much to discuss."

"You both had Professor Donovan as your thesis advisor, is that correct?"

"Yes, that is so. I have two advisors for my dissertation, Professor Donovan at the Divinity School and Professor Clarke at the History Department. I called Cal to inform him when you contacted me. I thought my supervisor should know that the police wanted to interview me. He advised me to cooperate with the police fully. Although we shared an advisor, Samia's research topic and mine differed. Samia studied early Christian biblical texts. My work centers on the schism of the German Church at the time of the Reformation and the rise of Calvinism."

Stella lobbed out a "sounds fascinating," without sounding the least bit fascinated. "Why did Samia call you?"

"She wanted to see if I was available to meet. I almost

didn't answer the call because it was from a number I didn't recognize."

"Were you available?"

"Yes. She came to see me."

"Where?"

"Right here, at my office. She came directly from Greg's office, I believe."

"Greg? You know about Professor Kalogeras?"

"Well, yes. I told you we were friends. I knew about their affair, if that is what you're asking. When a woman loves a married man, it's useful to have a female shoulder to cry upon. It was hard for her to break things off with Greg and move in with Danyal, but she hoped to get a green card through marriage. Danyal is a nice fellow, but she was really in love with Greg."

"When you saw her, how was she?"

"She was very emotional. She was scared, angry, sorrowful, a complete mess, I'd say. She told me what had happened in Egypt. I assume you already know about her sister's kidney disease and what Samia did to find money to help her."

"We know the rough outline, but it would help our investigation if you could tell me everything she told you. There may be details we don't know about." Stella leaned in for effect. "We want to catch the people responsible for her murder."

"Of course, yes. I have an excellent memory, and I talk quite fast when I get going. Would you prefer to record this conversation?"

Stella pulled out her pocket recorder and said, "Greta, you are my kind of witness."

Cal was reviewing PowerPoint slides for a morning lecture when his secretary rang to tell him he had a visitor, a Cambridge police detective. Stella appeared, ruddy-cheeked from a brisk walk across campus, and had a look around his modern office.

"This place isn't what I expected."

"What did you expect?"

She smiled at him. "I don't know—it's a Divinity School—maybe dark wood paneling, candles, chanting. Medieval stuff. I love that type of thing."

He chuckled. "You won't find many monks around here, but if you're looking for wood paneling and stained glass, Andover Chapel's got that going for it."

He poured her a coffee from a fresh pot at his conference table.

"I just finished interviewing Greta," she said. "Samia went to see her immediately after she left Kalogeras."

"Yeah, Greta told me."

"I thought I told you not to speak to her about the investigation."

"That was the extent of it. She asked me what to do, and I told her to cooperate with you. Did she?"

"She's something," Stella said. "She must have a photographic memory. She was able to recite both sides of her conversation with Samia, basically word for word."

"Yeah, Greta's off-the-charts smart. Did they talk about the papyrus?"

"Samia told her pretty much the same story that she told you, Kalogeras, and Danyal Tamer."

Cal extended his arms pleadingly. "Are you holding out on me? Did she show it to Greta?"

"She didn't. But Greta told me she left Samia alone in her office for a couple of minutes while she used the restroom. I wondered: Hey, what if Samia hid it inside Greta's desk? So I searched the hell out of this little student office, and—drum roll—nothing."

Cal cursed and sat back in his chair, defeated.

Stella had her recorder out and was fiddling with it. "But there was one thing Greta said that I didn't hear in any of the statements. Hang on. I made a note of the timestamp while she was saying it. Lemme jump to it."

She found the spot on the recording app and hit play.

Greta: *Samia told me that she met with the buyers in a fancy hotel in Cairo—well, not the actual buyer, his representatives. She said they were Americans who had some affiliation with a museum and one Egyptian who said little. She told me she liked one of the Americans, a man who seemed to be an expert in biblical texts. She disliked the other two men.*

Stella: *Did she tell you their names?*

Greta: *She did not, and I did not ask.*

Stella: *Did she give you any physical description of them?*

Greta: *Also, no.*

Stella: *Did she give you the name of the actual buyer?*

Greta: *No. She only said that he was a very wealthy man.*

Stella: *What about the name of the museum?*

Greta: *Again, no.*

Stella: *Did she tell you how much they paid?*

Greta: She did not know for sure because the Egyptian broker she was working with did not tell her. However, she had the impression that it was a lot of money, surely millions, she thought, given the importance of the text. She was disappointed that this broker, whom she also did not name, would not give her a greater share of the proceeds. She was paid twenty-five thousand US dollars, which was the precise amount required for her sister's kidney surgery.

Stella: Did she tell you what was on the papyrus?

Greta: She said she wished she could because it would be of great interest to me as a scholar and a Christian, but she thought it was better that I did not know. I accepted this and made no further inquiries.

Stella stopped the playback and said, "Is this the first you're hearing of a museum?"

Cal was lost in thought, and her question reeled him in.

"Samia didn't mention a museum to me," he said.

"Is it helpful for the investigation? Does it point us in any direction?"

"I wish it did. Lots of museums out there."

She narrowed her gaze and said, "You okay? You've gone a little funny."

"Nope, I'm good. I've got a few minutes before my next appointment. Let me show you Andover Chapel. If you like old churches, you'll love this one."

Elisabetta was fond of Silvio Licheri, but every time he showed up unannounced in her office, it was to relay another slug of bad news. She had developed a Pavlovian reaction to these spontaneous visits—to wit, a churning, acidic stomach. When her secretary informed her Silvio was on his way, she reached for her bottle of Brioschi antacids.

Within a few seconds of seeing his face, she knew he was bearing some extremely unpleasant tidings. "What now, Silvio?" she said.

He sat before her ornate desk and briefly closed his eyes as if to calm himself. "It seems we have a new problem," he said.

"Spare me the melodrama," she said. "Just tell me."

"I've been contacted by a journalist from *La Voce della Libertà*. Do you know it?"

"I know it," she said. "I don't read it. It's a bit too fascist for my tastes."

"They're preparing a story for publication in the morning, and they are seeking comments from you and the Vatican. They claim they have discovered a serious financial irregularity involving the sale and transfer of a statue from the Vatican Museum to a Belgian collector named Jules Maes during Celestine's charitable campaign."

She thought for a moment and said, "I remember him by name. We never met. He's the gentleman who purchased our third-century Roman funerary monument missing its arms and a nose. It wasn't all that good. I can't remember what we got for it offhand, but I do recall he overpaid."

"It was approximately one million euros," Silvio said, referring to some papers from his folder. "I'm afraid there's an accusation that you were paid a kickback of one hundred

thousand euros. They have produced certain documentation."

Elisabetta was suddenly standing as if her chair had a
mechanism that ejected her. She came around the desk and
demanded to see this so-called documentation, sputtering that
she'd never heard anything so absurd in her life. Silvio gave
her two exhibits to inspect. The first was a memorandum in
English, typed on stationery bearing the letterhead of the Pontifical Commission for Sacred Archaeology. The recipient was
Jules Maes; the sender was Elisabetta Celestino, director.

*This is to acknowledge that in conjunction with your
purchase of the statue of a Roman funerary monument,
c. AD 250 from the Vatican Museum (Accession Number
46B398777), you have agreed to make a donation of
100,000 euros to the Pontifical Commission for Sacred
Archaeology to support its mission of public education and
preservation of antiquities. Please wire funds to ARG Bank
(Malta) —Account BN987386754. We thank you for your
generous support.*

Elisabetta's name was typed with no signature. The memo
bore the official seal of the Commission.

"This is complete nonsense," Elisabetta said, her voice an
octave higher than normal. "I never wrote this or anything
like it."

Silvio nodded appropriately. "The journalist tells me he
has the original memorandum with the embossed seal of the
Commission. Then there's this."

The second document was a one-page summary statement

from a Maltese bank, ARG Bank (Malta) Limited. The account was in the name of the Pontifical Commission for Sacred Archaeology, Elisabetta Celestino, trustee, and the balance, as of the end of the previous financial quarter, was given as one hundred thousand euros.

She read it and angrily slapped it down on the desk. "It's a forgery, Silvio. It's completely absurd. I don't have a bank account in Malta. I've never engaged in any financial impropriety. All they need to do to expose this fraud is contact Jules Maes."

"The journalist told me that he died three years ago," Silvio said. "We have to get back to him this afternoon if we wish to have our response included in the article. What shall we say?"

"Deny it categorically," she half-shouted. "Say it's a forgery and part of the campaign we've been witnessing to destabilize my position. Demand to see the supposed original document with the Commission's seal. Write something, and let me review it. But let me tell you, Silvio, I'm not taking this lying down. Now, if you'll excuse me, I've got some calls to make."

Once she had sufficiently composed herself, she rang Monsignor Finale to brief him on this latest crisis. Pope John was attending a meeting with the Congregation for Bishops and couldn't be interrupted. Finale was his usual phlegmatic self and calmly assured her that he would pass the message to the Holy Father at the earliest possible time.

Her next call was to a woman she had first met in her capacity as private secretary to Pope Celestine. Fiona O'Reilly was a former governor of the Central Bank of Ireland whom Celestine had consulted from time to time on complex financial matters.

Elisabetta liked the small, pert lady immensely. She was formal to a fault in meetings, with the capacity to make difficult accounting principles understandable to non-specialists, and wickedly funny in private. Elisabetta had recently recruited her to become a standing member of the Vatican Council for the Economy, a prestigious group of outside expert advisors.

"Oh, hello, Fiona, this is Elisabetta Celestino calling from the Vatican. I hope I'm not disturbing you."

"Ah, Madame Secretary, how could you possibly disturb me? I positively get goosebumps every time I speak with the *female* Vatican secretary of state. Is there something I can help you with?"

"There is. You can help me from becoming a former female Vatican secretary of state."

When Stella left, Spooner lingered outside Swartz Hall, smoking a cigarette. He grumbled at the decision he had to make once again: Follow her or follow Donovan. His boss had no idea how difficult it was for one operative to cover a mission like this, but Spooner was the only one Tommy trusted to deal with this kind of situation. He wasn't about to bring in contractors. He was on the verge of going down a dangerous path. Orion wasn't something you sprinkled around like grass seed. It was twenty years in federal prison if you got caught deploying it. And using it on a law enforcement officer was wildly out of bounds. Tommy Cunliffe would disavow knowledge of it, and Spooner would take the rap. Spending his retirement years in prison wasn't how he envisioned life playing out.

He stubbed out his cigarette and let Stella disappear from view. *Fuck it*, he thought, as he opened the Orion app on his phone. A child could navigate the interface. He had Donovan's mobile number from Samia's phone. He got Detective Caruso's mobile by paying twenty bucks to a public records site, of all places. He entered the numbers in a field, hit the activate button, and the virus began infecting their devices through the ether.

In minutes, Stella became a moving dot on a Cambridge map, and Cal a stationary one, a few meters away. Spooner wandered off to find a bench and amused himself by reading their old emails and messages.

Cal sat alone, looking out his window at the students going to and from the Divinity School library, pulling up hoodies against a sharp wind, leaning forward to balance the weight of books in their backpacks.

Museum.

Since he heard Greta utter it on Stella's recording, the word had been rattling his brain. It had crystallized a germ of suspicion he'd been harboring about this rich American buyer of biblical texts. Everyone in the world of early Christian manuscripts knew about Tommy Cunliffe. He had a voracious appetite for acquisitions and was a logical buyer for rare material. But he was but one of several usual suspects, and Cal would never have been so reckless as to throw his name around in a murder investigation.

But to hear that the buyer had an affiliation with a

museum—well, that narrowed things down, didn't it? Cal had never visited the American Museum of Faith in Pittsburgh, although he certainly knew about it. Serious academics loathed the notion of a private museum that could outbid most public museums on important items, and that used its collection to fortify an overtly evangelical mission and drive enrollment to a second-rate outfit like the Cunliffe Catholic Bible College. Still, he couldn't accuse one of the wealthiest men in the country on the flimsiest of suspicions. He'd need a lot more before going down that road.

Cal found the website for the museum and jotted down the number of its director, William Stearns. He'd never met Stearns. They didn't run in the same circles. He'd been at conferences that Stearns had also attended, but that was the extent of it. Stearns's name appeared more frequently in newspaper articles about legal proceedings than in scholarly journals. The AMF had been accused of obtaining cultural artifacts without valid export licenses and had been forced on several occasions to return items to originating countries and pay heavy fines. However, the museum was represented by the best art lawyers in the country and had never been compelled to admit culpability. It was the kind of institution that Cal and his colleagues gossiped about at cocktail parties.

He held the phone to his ear and said, "Hello, this is Professor Cal Donovan from Harvard Divinity School. Is Dr. Stearns available?"

Usually, when he was kept on hold for this long, he'd swear and hang up, but he kept at it until the line came alive again with a voice that sounded tight and forced. "This is Bill Stearns. Professor Donovan. How are you?"

"Oh, hi, Bill, I'm fine. I hope I'm not catching you at a bad time. I don't think we've ever met, have we?"

"No, I don't think we have. I certainly know about your work. What can I do for you?"

"I know this is out of the blue, but one of my former grad students was killed a few days ago. Her name is Samia Tedros. She found an interesting first-century papyrus with biblical content in Egypt and attempted to sell it. I was wondering if she or a broker contacted you at the museum?"

Cal thought the pause on the line spoke volumes.

"No, I'm sorry. I don't believe we've been contacted about an item like that. Would it have been a recent query?"

"Very recent, yes."

"Well, I'm sorry I can't help you. If I hear anything about a piece that matches your description, I'll be sure to let you know."

The call ended with an awkward few exchanges, and Cal was left staring out the window again.

Spooner's heart was motoring as he speed-dialed Tommy. "Boss, Donovan just called Bill Stearns."

"Good God," Tommy said. "How do you know? No—don't tell me."

"He asked about the girl and the papyrus. I don't know if he knows something or was just fishing. I—"

Tommy interrupted him. "That's Bill calling me now. Let me take it."

A few minutes later, Cal was stuffing some papers into his

bag when his mobile phone rang from a 412 area code. A young woman asked if this was Professor Donovan, and then asked him to hold for Tommy Cunliffe.

Cal sat back down, preparing himself for the unexpected.

"Professor Donovan, this is Tommy Cunliffe," was the cheery opening. "I hear you and Bill Stearns were chatting."

"We were," Cal said cautiously.

"You probably know I've got a keen interest in early Christian texts, and my ears certainly perk up when I hear first century."

"Rare as hen's teeth," Cal said.

"That's right. Maybe rarer. Would you be free to come to Pittsburgh tomorrow to have a meet and greet?"

"What is it you'd like to discuss?"

"Rare biblical texts. Academic research. I promise you, you won't be disappointed. I'll send my private jet to make it as painless as possible. In and out in one day, what do you say?"

Cal ran through a decision tree in his head at warp speed and replied, "I say, I accept your invitation."

24

Northern Oasis, Egypt, 68 CE

Mary had been a guest in the House of Leah for eight months, and slowly but surely, she felt her health and strength being restored. Leah took on the role of doting daughter, feeding Mary's body with food and her mind with intellectual stimulation. Another woman might have grown sullen by being eclipsed within her community by a more powerful and more renowned guest like Mary Magdalene. But Leah was delighted to be hosting the Christian pontifex maximus and took pleasure in watching the community grow by word of mouth.

Christian pilgrims who came to the House of Leah, only to discover that it had become the House of Mary, could not believe their good fortune. They sat cross-legged on reed mats and listened spellbound as Mary transported them back in time to the days when Jesus walked the dusty roads of Galilee with her, Peter, and the other apostles.

In gratitude, they donated what coins they could, and thus the House of Mary began to prosper. When the pilgrims left the oasis, some of them carried copies of the Gospel of Mary and other Christian texts produced by the scribe Isaiah and his apprentices. And when they arrived at other corners of the Roman Empire, these pilgrims told others that Egypt—not Rome, not Jerusalem, not Galilee, not Damascus, or Antioch—had, by Mary's presence, become the center of the Christian world.

One day, after a communal breakfast of figs, bread, and honey, Quintus announced he would be riding to Bawiti to purchase supplies and asked if Mary finally would like to see the town.

"Will Mary be safe?" Isaiah asked.

Quintus laughed heartily and said, "With Jesus taking one of her hands and Quintus taking the other, no harm will come to the Blessed Lady."

"It is a lovely day," Mary said, "not too hot, not too cool, and my bones are feeling strong. All I hear from Quintus is that the people of Bawiti do this, and the people of Bawiti do that. I should like to see for myself. And perhaps we will find some Gentile we might convert to the faith."

"Tread carefully, Blessed Lady," Leah said. "The Romans do not much care what gods their Egyptian subjects worship, but the Egyptian priests do not take kindly to conversions. We should live in peace with them, lest we be forced to leave this pleasant land."

"You are wise," Mary said, kissing her forehead, "and I will refrain. When our Master took Peter and me into his fold, he told us we would become fishers of men. We will not bring our nets with us today."

They arrived at the busy market square of Bawiti mid-morning. Quintus helped Mary down from the cart, and the other men watered the horses from the communal trough. Mary had not left her tiny hamlet since she first arrived and was delighted to let all her senses sample what the oasis town had to offer. Bread was baking, meats were roasting, a pack of skinny dogs chased after a cat, children were playing in the dirt with wooden toys, and an old man with a lute was sitting against a rock, singing in the local dialect a haunting song he had learned from his father's father.

"So much life," Mary said, turning her face to the sun and closing her eyes in pleasure.

"Let us go, Blessed Lady," Quintus said. "We have purchases to make."

"What shall we buy?"

"We need a few bushels of barley for flour, grease for the cart wheels, tallow for candles, and most importantly, wine."

Quintus sent the men off in different directions and told Mary he would buy the wine, for he insisted on sampling the wares personally. "Will you come with me, My Lady? The wine merchant is Roman, and I enjoy speaking with him in Latin."

Flavius, the wine merchant, had a shop in the Roman district of the town on a street not far from the main square. The mud-brick store and warehouse were set between an apothecary and a harness maker. Quintus barreled inside with a beaming smile—for this was a place of happiness for him—while Mary hovered by the door, watching Flavius's young sons busying themselves with play and work.

Flavius, a big-gutted Roman with buck teeth, greeted Quintus with, "There is my favorite former Praetorian! You have come at a fortuitous time."

"Why is that?" Quintus asked.

"Because I have just received a shipment of excellent Albanum. Would you care to sample it?"

Quintus nodded eagerly, and Flavius began cracking the wax seal of a fresh amphora.

"That woman," Flavius said. "Is she your mother?"

"She is not, although I consider her to be my spiritual mother."

"I see," Flavius said. "A member of your Christian cult."

"Not a member," Quintus said. "She is our leader."

"Is that so? She doesn't look like she could lead a thirsty mule to the water. All right, try this."

Quintus sampled the wine from the beaker and hid his delight. "I think it is good, Flavius, but I am uncertain. Another beaker might help me form an opinion."

Flavius laughed and gave him a fill-up.

Quintus downed it and said, "Yes, fine. I will buy one amphora. How much?"

"Two denarii."

"I will give you one denarius."

"The price is two. The wine is fresh. The demand will be high. I will not haggle today."

Quintus grumbled and paid, and Flavius shouted to his eleven-year-old son, "Manius, bring me an amphora of Albanum from the storeroom."

The boy ran off and returned, lugging the ceramic jar.

"You are getting strong," Quintus told him.

The boy looked up at the tree trunk of a man and said, "One day, I will be as strong as you."

After the boy deposited the amphora in the cart, Mary asked

Quintus, "Is there a merchant who sells cloth in this town? I wish to buy some for Leah to sew her a new dress."

"Not in the Roman section," Quintus said, "but there is an Egyptian store."

The main street in Bawiti was straight as an arrow, lined on both sides by shops and stalls. Mary and Quintus had to navigate through the crowd, avoiding a donkey cart with a broken wheel, piles of dung, and a fistfight between two drunk combatants. She stopped for a moment to look at some painted funerary masks drying on a rack in front of a mask-making shop. The artisan, Shakir, saw that someone was admiring his work and left his workbench.

"You like my work?" he asked in Coptic.

Neither understood what he was saying, and Quintus stepped in between the mask maker and Mary protectively.

"We do not speak your language," he said in Aramaic.

"Christian scum," Shakir said, going back inside.

The cloth merchant knew a sprinkling of Aramaic words, enough to get by with passing Jews. Mary inspected a rack of linen bolts, from coarse to fine, but all of them white.

"Leah should have a colorful dress, don't you think, Quintus?"

"These are all white," Quintus said with a bored look.

"Yes, I can see that."

She tried to ask the shopkeeper if there were any colored cloths, but the fellow couldn't understand her question. In a moment of inspiration, she pointed to Quintus's eyes.

"Wic! Wic!" the man cried in Coptic, running off to another room. He came back with a bolt of sky-blue linen.

"Yes, that will do splendidly," Mary said. "It is a perfect color for a woman as lovely as our Leah."

It was evening when three young men walked the Roman street in Bawiti, asking the same question to anyone they saw. The harness maker told them he did not know, so they went to the wine merchant next door.

One of them, a tall and sinewy man named Levi, spoke Latin proficiently and asked Flavius, "Do you know where the Christians live? We are looking for a woman named Mary of Magdala."

Flavius seemed dejected that these were not customers. "They have a compound to the east of the city, one hour by foot. Follow the beaten path at the end of this street, and you will see it."

Levi told his companions in Aramaic, "We have found her."

The women were clearing up after supper, while outside, the children were playing tag in the fine evening air, and some of the men were sitting in a circle, discussing plans to build a church to serve the community better.

Three young men rode mules into their midst, and one of them, Levi, waved his hand hopefully and said in Aramaic, "Hello, friends. Is this the Christian House of Mary?"

The scribe, Isaiah, rose from his haunches and said, "Indeed it is. Why have you come?"

"We are Jews who hail from Jerusalem. We desire to become Christians."

Quintus, hearing the voices, came out of one of the houses and looked at them sternly, his arms folded across his broad chest.

"There are Christian priests in Jerusalem who will happily convert their Jewish brethren," Isaiah said.

"We are traveling men," Levi said, "traders, who were not long ago in Galilee. We hoped to receive our baptism by Mary Magdalene herself, the pontifex maximus. That was our fervent wish. The good people there told us she had gone to Egypt. As it happens, we had business in Cairo and Bawiti, and so here we are."

"What do you trade?" Quintus asked.

The three men exchanged glances, and Levi said cheerfully, "We are wine traders. We have concluded an agreement with Flavius, the wine merchant in Bawiti, for a future shipment."

Quintus perked up at the mention of wine and said, "A small miracle! We purchased an amphora of Albanum from Flavius just today. Would you care to sample it?"

"We would, friend. Thank you. May we see Mary?"

"She has gone to her bed," Quintus said, pointing to Leah's house. "Let us have some wine, and then I will get straw for you. It is a good night to sleep under the stars. In the morning, you shall see Mary."

Sicarii.

The word evoked fear throughout Judea. These skilled Jewish assassins first began to operate in Judea and then throughout

Israel, wreaking havoc among the Roman occupiers of the land. Their weapon of choice was the short-bladed knife, the sicae, carried under their cloaks and deployed with lethal effect against Romans and their Jewish sympathizers. They struck like lightning, and then disappeared into a daylit crowd or the darkness of night. While Romans were their avowed enemies, the wealthy would hire them to settle disputes or seek revenge for transgressions. Levi and his comrades had been unwilling to leave Jerusalem, where war was waging against the Romans, but an offer of the princely sum of one hundred gold aurei was impossible to turn down.

The three strangers whiled away the hours with Quintus, drinking wine, although unbeknownst to him, they watered down their cups.

"Come, good fellow," Levi said over and over, "drink some more of this excellent Albanum."

"Will you sell Flavius a boatful of wine this good so that my cup will never go dry?" Quintus asked, slurring his words.

"Your cup will remain full to the end of your days," Levi said.

Quintus finally staggered off, leaving the three men on their beds of straw, watching the moon wink in and out of the slow-moving clouds. They waited until the compound was still as a tomb, and when the moon went dark behind a cloud mass, they moved with stealth toward the house that Quintus had pointed out.

Levi crept up to a window. Leah had left a shutter open to let breezes cool the house, and with his comrades standing guard, he slipped inside without making the slightest noise. He found himself in a dining hall with bowls stacked on a long table. There was one door to his right and one to his left. He chose the one on the right and pushed it open ever so slowly in case it squealed on its pegs. A creature of the night, Levi had keen vision. He saw a solitary figure lying on her back, her head on a pillow. Drawing over her, ready to pounce, he saw she was a mature woman, not an elderly one, so unlikely to be his target. If she awoke, he would have killed her, but she remained asleep, and he withdrew as silently as he had entered.

In the other bedchamber, he saw another solitary figure lying on her side, her face fully on display. This woman was old. He drew his dagger, slid closer, and slowly extended his free hand. With a sudden move, he clamped his hand over her mouth and whispered, "Are you Mary?"

Mary's eyes sprang open, and finding she could not speak, she nodded her head.

"This is from Linus."

With a practiced move he had employed countless times, he cut her throat with his sharp blade and tasted a spray of hot blood that made it past his lips. When he was sure she would no longer be able to cry out, he took the ring from her finger and cut off a lock of her hair.

Mary faced her last moments without fear. Jesus had promised her he would return, and when he did and God's kingdom arrived on the Earth, suffering, pain, poverty, oppression, and hatred would end. She had waited for him to appear every day and place his hand upon her head again. But as the blood drained from her body, she knew that it was she who would be coming to him, and that the moment she arrived would be sweet indeed.

Mary was buried in a blue dress made from the cloth she had bought Leah. Her grave was a rectangular pit cut into bedrock a stone's throw from Leah's house, where others of the community were interred. Leah led the prayers at the ceremony, and no one wailed more than Quintus, who blamed himself for drinking himself into a stupor and failing to protect the Blessed Lady from these wretched strangers. When the earthen mound over the grave was patted down and smoothed and a coating of gypsum was applied, Quintus left the congregants and began walking into the desert, tears streaming down his face. He ignored calls to come back and kept going until he disappeared on the horizon. Leah and the others thought they would never see him again, but a fortnight later, he reappeared, gaunt and sunburned, to tell them that Mary had come to him in a dream.

"You did nothing wrong, dear Quintus," she said to him, "and you must not bear the weight of my passing. I am joyful and with the Lord, and one day, you will be with him too. Until that day comes, you must protect Leah and help her spread the glad tidings of Jesus Christ, our Lord and Master."

The winds were fair, and the voyage from Alexandria to Rome took only eight days. Levi, the sicarius, had been to Rome before. He had been told that Linus dwelled in a private home near the Colosseum. In the vicinity, he made discreet inquiries until one man agreed to speak with him. The man asked Levi in a hushed voice whether he was a Christian, and Levi assured him that he was and that he was carrying an important message.

The house of Linus was a fine villa with a walled garden. Levi found the priest conducting evening prayers in a large subterranean chapel, hidden from the prying eyes of the authorities. A pair of Christian bodyguards let Levi enter when he persuaded them that Linus was expecting him, and he watched the congregants celebrate the Eucharist and disperse.

The bodyguards whispered in Linus's ear, and the priest cautiously approached him.

"I am Levi," he said. "I have done your bidding in Egypt and am here to collect my payment."

"Prove to me you are who you say you are," Linus said. "Who hired you to perform the deed?"

"Aaron, son of Eli. He told me he had once, like you, been a Pharisee before converting to the Christian faith."

Linus sighed in relief. "Is Mary dead?"

"She is dead by mine own hand."

"How may I know you speak the truth?"

Levi produced a pouch and handed over Peter's silver ring of the fisherman that a smith had made smaller to fit her slim finger and a lock of her bronze-colored hair.

Linus closed his eyes, thanked the Lord for his providence, and thought, *An injustice has been righted. On this day, I am become pontifex maximus. Christians will long remember me and soon forget the impostor, Mary of Magdala.*

25

"Hi, I'm Paul," the captain of the Challenger 600 jet said. "You've got the cabin all to yourself. Snacks are over there. If you need anything, we'll keep the cockpit door open. Should have you in Pittsburgh in just under two hours."

"Do you have Wi-Fi?" Cal asked.

"This is Mr. Cunliffe's personal jet. We've got everything — a regular flying office. Can I get you a coffee before liftoff?"

"You fly the plane. I'll fly the coffee pot."

Cal helped himself to a cup, buckled in, and reflexively checked his Twitter feed. The day was starting badly.

Vatican Secretary of State May Have Received Kickback on Sale of Statue

He sat, stunned and angry, and as the jet began its taxi from Hanscom Field in the Boston suburb of Bedford, he wondered what, if anything, he should do.

When the jet pierced the clouds and the cabin filled with light, he logged onto the Wi-Fi and texted Elisabetta.

They want to stop you, but they can't. Samuel Johnson wrote that great works are performed not by strength but by perseverance. Keep fighting. Many people, including me, have your back. Cal

Shortly after the captain told him he could get up and roam the cabin, his phone dinged with a reply, a tiny red heart followed by Don't worry, I'm on it.

Tommy toweled off from his morning swim in the indoor pool and looked around for his assistant.

"Beth Ann?" he shouted. "Where are you?" He got miffed. He had calls to make and no one to make them, and when she appeared from the door to the main house, he yelled, "I got a sore throat from calling for you. Where'd you go?"

She ran across the slippery tiles and apologized. "You asked me to monitor the *La Voce della Libertà* website. The article you were interested in was just published. I printed it out along with a Google translation."

"Oh, good. Let me see," he said, grabbing it greedily.

He read it, bobbing his head and emitting soft grunts. "Get me Spooner."

"Right away. And Evan wants to see you before Professor Donovan gets here."

With the Orion spyware as his eyes and ears, Spooner had been able to relax a little. He had swapped his rental car for a hotel room and had his legs up watching TV when Tommy called.

"The article landed," Tommy said.

"I know. Solla just sent it to me. He's pretty pleased with how it came out."

"It looks terrific," Tommy exulted. "I think we've got her this time."

"Solla wants to draw down his bonus."

"I'll bet he does. Go ahead and authorize it. Anything up with the police?"

"Nothing more. I'll be monitoring the investigation."

"Well, at least you won't have to worry about Donovan today. He lands in about an hour. All right, got to go. Evan's here."

The cook had made Evan a smoothie, and he was noisily sucking the last of it through a straw.

"What did you want to see me about?" his father asked gruffly.

Evan loped over, collapsed on a chaise, and said, "I don't get you sometimes."

"What is it you don't get?"

"Why the hell—sorry—why the heck did you invite this Donovan guy to come here? This whole thing with the dead girl. You don't want to be getting anywhere near that. You've got the company, the college, the museum, and now you're running for governor. Meeting with Donovan's like playing with fire."

"It's so touching you're worried about my reputation," Tommy said facetiously.

"Okay, mine too. I did the deal with Shamoun. I went to Egypt. I'm in deeper than you."

Tommy shouted for Beth Ann to get him an orange juice. "Look, Ev, you haven't been exposed to the kind of business environment that your brothers and sister thrive on at CEG.

You've got to take calculated risks. You've got to seize opportunities when they present themselves. Donovan called me. He's a smart cookie. He already figured out that we might have been the entity that negotiated on the papyrus. It's incumbent on us to neutralize him, and the best way to do that is to invite the insect into the spider's web."

Evan did one last loud suck and put his smoothie aside. "Sometimes it's hard to understand what you're saying."

Tommy took his juice through a straw too—like father, like son. "No, I don't suppose you do understand. I'm going to give Donovan a new, shinier object to set his eyes on. I'm going to give him the one thing that academics want."

"What's that?" his son asked.

"An unlimited budget. Spooner will come through, as he always does, and he will find the papyrus. Once we have it, it will be as if it never existed. Donovan will eventually forget all about it. All he has is a photo, and that's like having smoke. It disappears."

Tommy got up and threw his towel on the tiles for someone else to pick up. "He'll be here soon. I'm going to do the business end of things one-on-one. Come to lunch, if you want, but you don't know anything about the papyrus. Never heard of it. Never heard of the girl. Understood?"

"I still think having him here is risky," Evan said petulantly.

"The risk isn't zero. I'll give you that. I don't want to jeopardize everything I've built. But I believe God has tasked me with a mission to protect our Church from those who would erode and profane it. The Mary papyrus is poison, and when you find a bottle of poison, you don't put it in the medicine cabinet. To protect your family, you flush it down the toilet.

And if Donovan becomes a liability rather than an asset, then Joel Spooner has the talents and resources to neutralize him permanently."

⌁━╫━⌁

Cal's first view of Tommy's estate was from the helicopter that whisked him from the Pittsburgh airport. At first he thought he was looking at a hotel or conference center, but the pilot gestured toward the helipad by the tennis courts and descended.

An attractive young woman in a pink cardigan with a string of pearls greeted Cal on the helipad. "Welcome to Heartland Manor, Professor Donovan. I'm Beth Ann, Tommy Cunliffe's assistant. I've got a golf cart to take you up to the house."

Tommy was waiting at the front of the house and seemed tickled to death that he and Cal had nearly matching outfits of gray flannel pants, blue blazers, and light blue shirts.

"Well, aren't we a pair? I'm Tommy Cunliffe. Welcome to my humble abode, Professor."

"Hardly humble," Cal said, matching Tommy's vise of a handshake. "Call me Cal."

"All new visitors get the full treatment," Tommy said. "Hey, Beth Ann. Lower the drawbridge."

Cal thought it was hokey, but he displayed the kind of admiration his host seemed to crave and entered the palatial residence.

"I've got a light lunch for us," Tommy said. "Let's head in."

Evan had traded his tracksuit for something business casual. After his introduction, he took his seat at the dining table without saying a lot.

"Evan's the one birdie of ours that hasn't flown the nest," Tommy said.

"It's a tough nest to leave," Cal said, giving Tommy the opening to provide vital statistics about the mansion and grounds.

Tommy suddenly frowned and asked his butler where Mrs. Cunliffe was.

Barbara Cunliffe arrived walking unsteadily in a bright orange Diane von Fürstenberg dress. Cal rose to shake her hand as Tommy made a pucker to Evan behind his back.

"I looked you up, Cal," Barbara said. "You are even more handsome than your photographs."

He smelled the vodka on her breath and smiled back.

It was clear to Cal that the lunch was going to be some kind of de rigueur prelude to something else, and he settled into a light social mode, answering questions from Tommy about his background and his academic interests while Evan clattered his knife and fork and Barbara drank from her very own pitcher.

Asked about his interest in biblical studies, Cal talked about the endless dinner-table wars between his Jewish mother and Catholic father and the inevitability that he'd catch the religion bug. Tommy asked whether the bug had infected his spiritual life as well.

"It was a slow virus," Cal said. "It took a while for it to get a toehold, but it finally did. I became a practicing Catholic."

"Are you, now?" Tommy said with a toothy grin. "I didn't know that. That's excellent. I'm a fan of clubs, Cal. Barbara and I enjoy our country club. We give a lot of money to the Boys' Club of New York. I'm a member of the Club for Growth and various other business clubs. But the finest club I belong to—if you want to call it that—is the Catholic Church. I don't know what I would do if I didn't have the Church in my life."

Cal was about to say something affirming when Barbara, who'd been sipping away and eating almost nothing, piped up. "Are you single, Cal?"

"I am."

"I can't believe no one's ever gotten you down the aisle."

Her husband tried to change the subject, but she was tenacious.

"Let him answer, Tommy!"

"Not yet," Cal said, "but you never know."

"Oh, if I were twenty or thirty years younger," she said melodically. "You should have seen my figure in the day."

Evan, who hadn't uttered a word in twenty minutes, said, "Mom, did you take an extra diabetes pill today by mistake? You get funny when that happens. Come on, let's go upstairs and do a test strip."

"I'm fine," she said.

Tommy stood up and announced that his son was right, that low blood sugar could make anyone loopy. He coaxed her out of her chair and gave her to Evan to sort out. He then returned to the head of the table, and as Barbara was led away, Cal heard her asking why she couldn't say goodbye.

"Come on, Cal, we'll take our coffee in the library," Tommy said. "It's time we got down to business anyway."

Cal was glad to put the excruciating lunch behind him. He complimented his host on the grandness of his library and his wall of dignitary photos and sank into a chair.

"Cal, I see that you're a good friend of our new Holy Father," Tommy said.

"We've known each other for years. It's great to have an American pope finally, don't you think?"

"I don't disagree," Tommy said, "though I'm more of a John Paul II type of Catholic, if you know what I mean."

"I do."

"I also see you know our new secretary of state?"

Cal was surprised.

"I saw a photo of both of you from a Vatican conference."

"I worked with her in her capacity of private secretary to Pope Celestine. She's a very capable woman."

"I'm sure she is. I don't suppose you've seen the scandalous news that came out today about her involvement in some financial irregularities."

Cal saw a flicker of glee across Tommy's face but remained politic. "The knives have been out for her. The last so-called scandal was bogus. I predict this one will be bogus too."

"Let's hope so. The Church doesn't need this." Tommy leaned in intimately. "So, Cal, I asked you here to talk about some matters of importance to me, but before I do, I wanted to clear the air about this papyrus you called Bill Stearns about. I know he told you he didn't know anything about it. That's not strictly true."

Cal felt the back of his neck prickle. "Oh yes?"

"Bill felt he wasn't authorized to speak about it, but we were contacted by an Egyptian antiquities broker who was offering it up for sale. Bill is a capable man—been with me for ages. He's careful and ethical to a fault. He queried this fellow about the provenance, and according to Bill, the story about it being late first century fell apart. Apparently, it came from cartonnage, and if you know anything about cartonnage, which I'm sure you do, you know that papyrus was no longer used in masks by then. I'm not in the habit of spending good money on fakes. Another red flag was the mask itself. I don't know the details, but Bill suspected it was pilfered from a museum, and you must know the problems the American Museum of Faith had a few years back about buying allegedly stolen materials. It was all nonsense, but we had to accept a Justice Department consent decree, and we don't want to fly too close to the sun ever again."

"Were you shown a photo of the text?"

"Bill saw one, yes. He translated it. It was some nonsense about Mary Magdalene. Jesus's wife type of hokum. Have you seen it?"

"As a matter of fact, I have. A former grad student of mine, Samia Tedros, found it. She sent me a photo."

"What was your opinion?"

Cal forced a laugh. "Well, anyone with a pulse would be interested. But what good is a photo? You need the papyrus to make a case one way or the other. Did you know that Samia was murdered a few days ago?"

Tommy nodded solemnly. "I didn't until you called Bill. It's shocking. Such a tragedy. Do the police know who did it?"

"Not yet."

"Bill and I were talking about it last night. He's got a theory. He thinks someone purchased the papyrus, probably for a fair bit of money, then found out they bought a fake. The buyers lean on the broker to get their money back, but the broker, well, maybe he thinks that what they found was genuine. Maybe this girl, Samia Tedros, forged a copy and ran off with the genuine papyrus to sell it herself and keep all the money. I mean, a first-century papyrus could go for life-changing money."

"I thought your opinion was that the papyrus was hokum."

"I do. This is Bill's theory about what might have led to this girl's murder. These international brokers have connections. He could have had tentacles that reached all the way to Cambridge, Massachusetts, and had her killed. Maybe he recovered the papyrus. Maybe it'll resurface on the market one day. Who knows?"

Cal felt like he was playing some kind of chess game. "If it did, and it was the real deal, would you buy it?" he asked.

Tommy thrust out his lower lip. "If it were authentic? I suppose I'd have to seriously consider it."

"I mean, I'm sure a piece like that would be a big draw at your museum—at any museum," Cal said.

"I suspect you're right. Curiosity value, if nothing else. The whore, Mary Magdalene, the successor to Peter? Some first-century scribe would have had to have a wicked sense of humor."

"Before she died, Samia told me that the buyer wanted to suppress the papyrus for political reasons. Didn't like the message it sent about women and the Church. If you owned it, you wouldn't do something like that, would you?"

"Absolutely not! Like you said, Cal, it would be an incredible draw at our museum. If you hear anything about the papyrus resurfacing, you'll let me know, right?"

"I'll do that."

"Good. That's good. Which brings me to the reason you're here. I wanted to pose a question to you. As a biblical scholar, what would you do if you had what amounted to an unlimited budget? All the resources you wanted and needed to pursue any line of research? Any archaeological expeditions that struck your fancy? Any acquisition of artifacts and desirable texts? As many staff as you required?"

"Sounds like divinity school nirvana," Cal joked.

"I'm being completely serious," Tommy said. "The Cunliffe Catholic Bible College and the American Museum of Faith are my babies. I love them as much as I love my children. Some would say more. It's a good college and a good museum, but they're not world-class institutions. Yet. Bill Stearns is a good man, Cal. A good, loyal man who's done well for himself. But Bill is no Calvin Donovan. The president of the college, Gareth Pfeiffer, is a good man, but he's no Calvin Donovan. With you at the helm of both institutions, we could take them to the next level and leave future generations something of incalculable value. I know it's tough to leave a place like Harvard, but if you did, I'd be willing to pay a sign-on bonus of ten million dollars, an annual salary of five million, and put that unlimited budget I spoke about at your disposal. I'm a very wealthy man, Cal, and I can use that money to rock your world. What do you say?"

Cal smiled and thought, *I didn't know it, but now I do. You had Samia killed, you son of a bitch.*

He said, "You're a very persuasive man, Tommy. I promise that I'll think about your offer, long and hard."

Tommy clapped his hands together once. "Excellent! Then my work is done. If you've got the time, we could swing by the museum on the way to the airport, so you can have a look at it."

Cal made a show of looking at his watch. "I'd love to, Tommy, but I'm afraid it'll have to be some other time."

26

Detective Brendan Davis was losing his mind. Stella knew this because every time she walked by his workstation, he told her, "I am losing my mind." As the junior lead on Samia's homicide, he had the unenviable job of sifting through a tsunami of video footage to answer the question: Where did Samia go after leaving Greta Schenck at Robinson Hall, and did anyone follow her?

Harvard University quickly complied with a subpoena to produce the video feed of on-campus cameras for the hours in question, but Harvard Yard and the surrounding university areas were swarming with security cameras. Brendan sensibly approached the exercise by starting with camera feeds from the other two buildings on Sever Quadrangle—Sever Hall and Emerson Hall, both with views capturing the entrance of Robinson. Unfortunately, several classes seemed to be starting and ending around the time Samia would have exited, and the quad was filled with students. Brendan knew what Samia was wearing that afternoon—jeans and a sweatshirt—but he kept moaning,

"They all look the same. It's like they're in uniform." Adding to that, she could have exited Robinson from the rear. So he kept drinking coffee, trying to find a needle among all that straw.

During Brendan's morning whine, Stella promised to lend her eyes to the operation, but first she had to appear at the Cambridge District Court at a domestic abuse trial. The testimony of the previous prosecution witnesses dragged on, and she didn't get back to the police station until late afternoon.

"All right, Brendan," she said, slumping into the chair next to his, "I'm reporting for duty."

"How'd it go?"

"The defense lawyer was a tool."

He nodded sagely. "That's what they're paid for, right? Hey, I bookmarked something I saw a little while ago. Tell me whether you think this could be Samia."

He threw up a clip onto his screen and hit play. "See this gal walking along the path? Same color sweatshirt as Samia's. Same slim build. Same shoulder-length black hair. The time-stamp is 2:41 in the afternoon, which kind of works."

"Is there an angle we can see her face?" Stella asked.

"This is the only one. It's from a camera on Lamont Library."

"I don't see anyone following her, did you?"

"Nope."

"What's the building she's heading into?"

Brendan pulled out his campus map. "It's Houghton Library."

"There's no camera at Houghton pointing out?"

"I called over to the Harvard IT people. They think that feed was down for a few days."

"I mean, it could be her," Stella said. "Is that the best you've got?"

"So far."

"What about footage of this person leaving Houghton?"

"I scanned a two-hour window. I couldn't see her. Maybe she left from one of the sides or the back."

Stella picked up her bag and said, "I guess we'd better jump on it. Call over to our buddy at Harvard Police CID—what's his name again?"

"Sergeant Detective Clifford."

"Tell him we're going over to Houghton. Have him grease the skids."

Houghton Library was a mid-twentieth-century redbrick building on the south side of Harvard Yard, dwarfed by the adjacent Widener Library that housed the main university collections. On their way over, Detective Clifford texted Brendan that the director of operations, Amelia Foote, would assist them. They asked for her at the welcome desk in a rotunda that displayed collection highlights in glass cases.

Foote furrowed her brow and asked how she could help. Stella laid out the problem. A murder victim might have visited the library on the afternoon of her death. If so, they needed to know what she was doing there.

"Oh my," Foote said. "Was she a student?"

"A former grad student," Stella said. "She left Harvard about a year ago."

"Then she couldn't have gotten in. The library is only accessible to current students, faculty, and visiting academics."

"No exceptions?" Brendan asked.

"We're very strict. Our collections are valuable. We can't have outsiders wandering around."

"There's no visitors' book or anything like that?" he asked.

"Students and faculty swipe in with their IDs. An outside guest, a visiting academic, for example, would have been issued a pass with a QR code that we scan on entry and departure. Would she have been issued a visiting researcher pass?"

Brendan said he doubted it from what they knew about her activities, and then pulled out his trusty map. "You've got all these libraries in this corner of the Yard. What's this one for?"

Foote patiently explained, "This one is Widener, our main library, with nearly four million books. This one is Lamont, the undergraduate library. Pusey is entirely underground. It houses the university archives. And we, Houghton, are the rare books library."

"What kind of rare books?" Stella asked.

"My goodness, where to start?" she said. "We have a famous collection of materials on Dr. Samuel Johnson, a large collection of English broadsides, pamphlets from the French civil wars, medieval and Renaissance manuscripts, large theater arts and photography collections, a collection of ancient papyri—"

Stella's eyes were glazed from her mind-numbing day at court, but she alerted to the magic word. "Papyri?"

"Oh yes, we have several dozen extremely rare and valuable papyri ranging from the third century BC to the sixth century AD—literary texts, biblical texts, all in Greek or Coptic."

The detectives immediately let her know that that's where they needed to go. Foote invited them onto an elevator, explaining that the papyrus collection was in one of the sub-basements. They exited into a central reading room with offices and archives at the perimeter. It was five o'clock, and Stella saw one of the staffers put on a jacket to leave.

Foote said, "Here we are. What now?"

Stella said, "I know it's an imposition, but we need everyone to stay here until we can ask a few questions."

"Is that necessary?"

Stella had Samia's official picture as a Harvard student and showed it to the woman. "If we want to catch the person who killed this girl, yes. I'd like you to tell your people they need to remain at their desks until we clear them to leave."

Foote made a hasty tour through the floor and assured Stella that the staff was prepared to cooperate.

Stella started at one side of the horseshoe-shaped row of offices and cubicles, Brendan the other, with the plan of meeting in the middle. The interviews were quick work. *Do you know this woman, who would have visited the library on this date and this time? No? Thank you. You're free to go.*

Stella was just starting with another employee when she heard Brendan calling for her. She found him in an office with a distraught young woman with ultra-short hair and a gold nose ring.

"Stella, this is Caroline Cook. She's an information research specialist. Caroline, tell the detective what you told me."

"I'm sorry," Caroline said, "is it true? Is she dead?"

"You didn't read about it in the news?" Brendan asked.

"This is why I don't do news. It's too upsetting."

"Go on, tell Detective Caruso what happened."

"I was here at work that afternoon. I look up, and Samia's standing right where you're standing. I almost jumped out of my skin."

"How do you know her?" Stella asked.

"When she was a student here, she used to come to Houghton to research some of our papyri. We got friendly. She was a super-nice kid. I can't believe she's dead. You said someone killed her? Why would someone kill Samia?"

"That's what we're trying to find out," Brendan said. "You might be one of the last people to see her alive, Caroline. It's important to tell us everything she said and how she acted."

"Okay," she said weakly.

"Before we get into that," he said, "how'd she get into the library? Did you let her in?"

"No. Like I said, she just showed up. I didn't think to ask how she got in."

"Why did she say she came to see you?" Stella asked.

"Just to say hello. She said she was in Cambridge for a few days and wanted to say hi. When she was in grad school, we used to chat about silly things, sometimes go and get a tea. I mean, we weren't close friends, but she was nice."

"That's it? 'Hello, how are you,' and nothing else?" Brendan asked.

"Pretty much. She wasn't here for more than a couple of minutes when she said she had to go."

"Go where?" Stella asked. "Did she say?"

"No."

"How did she seem? Was she happy? Sad? Stressed? Relaxed?"

"She seemed off. She wasn't her usual bubbly self. I didn't

ask why. We didn't have that kind of relationship. She hugged me by the elevator and left. That's it."

"Did she show you anything?" Brendan asked.

"Like what?"

"A papyrus."

"No."

"Are you sure?" he asked.

"Uh, look around at where we are. I think I'd remember."

They hooked up with Amelia Foote again, and Stella told her that the only thing that made sense to them was that Samia swiped her way into the library.

"Could she have used her old Harvard ID?" Stella asked.

"They're deactivated on graduation."

"Is it possible hers wasn't?"

"I don't know," she said. "It's not my area."

"We're going to need you to check your records. It would have been just after 2:41 in the afternoon," Stella said. "We'll wait."

They parked themselves in the welcome hall, both of them doing emails on their phones until Stella saw Foote coming back, shaking her head. Just then, her phone rang from Cal's number, and she let it go to voicemail.

"I'm sorry," Foote said. "There was no Samia Tedros on our logs."

⟜━◈━⟝

Paranoia set in on Cal's flight back to Hanscom Field, and he held off on using his phone. Who knew if Cunliffe had the cabin bugged? Or if he'd have access to the sites Cal visited on the plane's Wi-Fi? So he mostly looked out the window and helped himself to a vodka in the galley. It was a common enough brand, but the bottle of Grey Goose creeped him out. How much did Cunliffe know about him?

On the way back to Cambridge, he put his Tesla on auto-pilot, cruised down Route 2, and did what good drivers weren't supposed to do—he searched for stories about Elisabetta on his phone. By the look of it, she was having a rough day. He wanted to call to see how she was. He wanted to tell her about his suspicious day with Tommy Cunliffe. Mostly, he wanted to hear her voice. But it was nearly midnight in Rome, and he hoped she was getting some sleep.

Instead, he called Stella and got her voicemail.

She returned the call a few minutes later, and he said he had something to tell her.

"Oh yeah?" she said. "I've got something to tell you too. Samia was in the Houghton Library a little while after leaving Greta Schenck's office. We picked her up on a security cam."

"What was she doing there?"

"She visited a friend of hers, a girl who works with the papyrus collection. Caroline Cook. Heard of her?"

"I don't know her."

"Before you ask, Samia didn't show her the Mary papyrus. What we can't figure out is how she got into the building. She must've had an ID card, but her name didn't appear on their logs. It's just weird. What's your news?"

"I spent the day with a guy who might have been the buyer. His name's Tommy Cunliffe. He's a wealthy collector from Pittsburgh—"

"I've got another call coming in," Stella said. "It's my wife, and she's probably pissed off at me because I fucked our dinner plans. If it can wait, let's talk tomorrow, okay?"

⟡

Tommy's cell phone rang while he was having dinner with his wife.

"Got to take this," he said, getting up and moving to the next room.

Barbara told him she didn't care and caught the butler's attention by waving her empty martini glass.

"What?" Tommy asked.

Spooner said, "He just told the police he thinks you're the buyer. That's all he said. They're going to talk again tomorrow."

Tommy heaved his chest. "All right. I guess I've got the answer to my job offer. Joel, I want you to take care of him tonight. Without him, they won't be able to connect the dots. I don't want to know the details. When you're done, take a long, much-deserved vacation somewhere out of the country. Just let me know when it's over. It's a pity you didn't find the papyrus. Hopefully she hid it someplace it will never be found."

⟡

Cal had to stop at his office at Swartz Hall to pick up the books he needed to prep for his undergraduate lecture the next day. At this hour, the building had emptied out, but a few faculty members and students were still around. He passed by an open office used by grad students and skidded to a halt.

342

A woman in jeans was on her hands and knees under one of the desks.

Not recognizing her from her rear end, he said, "Hey, what's up?"

The woman backed up and said with a German accent, "Oh, hello, Cal. How are you? You're probably wondering why I'm under the desk." It was Greta Schenck. "I'm looking everywhere for a lost item."

"Oh yeah? Tell me what it is, and I'll keep a lookout for it."

"It's my Harvard ID. I can't imagine what I did with it. I'm always so careful. I didn't need it for a couple of days, but I badly need it now. Professor Albrecht had to let me into Swartz Hall."

Distracted, Cal put his bag down on one of the desks too close to the edge. It toppled off and thudded onto the floor. "When did you see it last?" he asked excitedly.

Greta didn't seem to understand why Cal wasn't interested in the fate of his bag. "I think the day that Samia came to see me. Yes, I'm pretty sure."

Cal bent for the bag and said, as he dashed off, "I don't think you're going to find it. You'd better request a new one tomorrow."

27

Fiona O'Reilly had a look around the spartan room at the Vatican Sancta Marthae guesthouse, told Elisabetta's private secretary Monsignor Thompson that it would do nicely, and said she needed only a few minutes to freshen up after her flight from Dublin. A short while later, she told the monsignor that the barebones office in the Apostolic Palace, down the hall from the Secretariat of State, would also do nicely.

"You are a most agreeable person," Thompson said, with a twinkle.

"Hardly what my ex-husband would say."

The English priest suppressed a chuckle. "The documents you requested are in the red folder," he said. "Madame Secretary will stop by when her teleconference has concluded. Line three is an outside line."

The last person to use the office must have been a foot taller, and Fiona had to adjust the desk chair. She promptly kicked off her high heels, wiggled her toes, and glanced out the window onto St. Peter's Square. If those who knew Fiona were restricted to a one-word description of her, most would come back with *formidable*. She had been formidable since she was a schoolgirl growing up in Dublin, but she began to be noticed at Trinity, where she was elected president of the student union and graduated with a first in economics. After receiving a PhD at the London School of Economics, she rose through the ranks at the Bank of Ireland, and then spent a decade as a governor of the Central Bank of Ireland. In her sixties, she was one of the most distinguished female business leaders in the country, sat on corporate boards and charitable foundations, and had recently joined the Vatican Council for the Economy.

The red folder had all the paperwork regarding the sale and export of the statue that Jules Maes, the Belgian collector, had purchased, as well as an attestation of the funerary monument's origin and provenance, written by an outside expert at La Sapienza University. Silvio Licheri had convinced the journalist at *La Voce della Libertà* to let him see the alleged original memo from Elisabetta to Maes, acknowledging a donation of one hundred thousand euros to the Pontifical Commission for Sacred Archaeology. The seal of the Commission was embossed on the memo. Fiona ran a finger over the seal and felt its rough ridges. She then inspected the summary page of a financial statement for an account in Elisabetta's name at the ARG Bank (Malta) Limited.

While waiting for her flight in Dublin, Fiona inquired into Jules Maes. She was friendly with a Dutch central banker at De Nederlandsche Bank NV, who told her, "Of course I knew Jules. We swam in the same pond. He died too soon."

She asked who handled Maes's financial affairs and was

directed to a partner at the accounting firm BDO. She rang the number and asked to speak with Stefaan Lempers.

When connected, she said, "Oh, hello. This is Fiona O'Reilly with the Vatican Council for the Economy calling concerning a deceased client of yours, Jules Maes."

Lempers said, "The Fiona O'Reilly?"

"Well, I know of several Fiona O'Reillys," she said. "It's not an uncommon name in Ireland."

"Ah, but I think that perhaps you are the one who was a central banker."

"Guilty as charged."

"I am at your disposal, madame."

When Elisabetta came in, Fiona looked up from her pad and got up to shake hands.

"Goodness," she said, "I'm greeting you in my stockings."

"I'm glad you're comfortable," Elisabetta said. "How wonderful of you to drop everything and help me with this humiliating situation."

Fiona rolled her chair so the two of them could sit on the same side of the desk. "It's no bother," she said, "and it's a darn sight more interesting than reviewing the audit report of a pharmaceutical company, which is what I'd been slated to do today. Besides, as I've told you before, you're my favorite nun."

"Yes, you told me about your primary school days. A nun that never rapped your knuckles with a wooden ruler was bound to be your favorite. So, Fiona, what do you think?"

"First of all, it goes without saying that I take you at your word that you didn't write this memo to Jules Maes."

"I did not."

"And you don't, to your knowledge, have a bank account in Malta."

"To my knowledge, no."

"The seal on the memo. To your eye, is it authentic?"

Elisabetta examined it once again. "It does appear to be the true seal of the Commission."

"How many seals did the Commission have?"

"Just the one, at least when I was president."

"Is anyone looking into this?"

"My brother."

Fiona frowned. "Your brother?"

"Oh, I'm sorry, I thought you knew. Emilio Celestino is the inspector general of the Vatican Gendarmerie."

"My goodness! There's an accomplished family. My brother sold double-glazed windows."

"I'm sure he was very good at it," Elisabetta said.

"Let me know what Emilio comes up with on that front," Fiona said. "I'm pursuing two lines of inquiry. I've made contact with the estate of Jules Maes, and if we can get the permission of the trustees, we'll try to see if there is a copy of your memo in their files."

"There won't be," Elisabetta said confidently.

"I expect not. I'll also be speaking with the ARG Bank in Malta. I rather doubt they'll be forthcoming. If not, we may need to get Interpol involved. How much time do we have until the article is published?"

"The Press Office people tell me it could happen anytime

now. We have told the journalist that the documents are somehow fake or manipulated, but he seems convinced by their legitimacy."

"Well then, there's no time to lose. Let's expose these bastards. Fraud is one of my least favorite crimes."

Emilio Celestino arrived at the Pontifical Commission for Sacred Archaeology unannounced. He drove a marked Carabinieri car from the Vatican to the Commission near the Roma Termini train station and parked on the sidewalk in front of the ancient building to make a statement about the urgency of his visit. For effect, he left his business suit in the closet that morning and opted for his full dress uniform.

The receptionist usually dealt with visiting scholars. The sudden presence of a stern-looking police officer seemed to unnerve her, especially when he demanded to speak with the Commission president.

"Is the archbishop expecting you?"

"He is not," Emilio said.

Archbishop Riccardo Gentile was a nervous man with a curiously boyish face for a man in his sixties. He fast-walked through the lobby and greeted Emilio with, "How can I possibly help you, Inspector General?"

"Let's talk in your office, Eminence."

Emilio had been consumed with outrage over attacks against his sister, and this latest one, arising from the heart of the Holy See, left him volcanic. Yet Archbishop Gentile seemed so flustered by the sudden appearance of the officer that Emilio had to ratchet down his approach lest the fellow suffer a medical emergency.

Emilio accepted a coffee from Gentile's pod machine and sniffed at the moldy mustiness the old building gave off. "Where do you keep the Commission's seal embosser?" he said.

"Our what?"

"The clamp device that stamps your official documents."

"I've no idea," the archbishop said. "Why the interest?"

"Someone has forged a document, purportedly arising from the Commission, relating to the sale of a statue to a private buyer during Pope Celestine's divestiture campaign."

"That was before my time here!" Gentile said with relief, as if suddenly off the hook. "Elisabetta Celestino was president then. Isn't she your sister? Perhaps you can ask her about it."

"The seal, Eminence. Who keeps it?"

"My secretary, Father Galiotto."

"Please summon him."

Emilio listened to one side of the phone conversation. "How many seal stamps do we have here? Just the one? Bring it to me. The police are here!"

Galiotto was about the same age as the archbishop, taller, fleshier, with watery eyes that darted around the room. He extended his arm.

"Here is the seal, Eminence."

"Don't give it to me. Give it to the inspector general."

Emilio took the small rectangular box and opened it. The brass handle of the seal had the patina of age and use. "You say this is the only seal possessed by the Commission?" he asked the priest.

"It is."

"Where is it kept?"

"In a cabinet in my office."

"Is it locked? If so, does anyone besides you have the key?"

"As far as I know, I have the only key, but I have only been in my post for five years. There could be other keys floating around, I suppose."

"What do you say, Eminence? Do you have a key? Have you ever taken the seal from its cabinet?"

"No, to both questions."

Emilio didn't love the way the priest had been avoiding looking at him directly. He had the original memorandum in a plastic sheath, and he showed it to him. "Does this look authentic to you?"

The priest took it and was about to pull it out when Emilio told him to inspect it through the plastic. "Fingerprints," Emilio said. "This is a criminal case. Please don't touch it."

"It looks like a true Commission document."

"Have you ever seen it before?"

"No. Why would I have?"

"I assume you keep photocopies of these kinds of documents in your archive."

"That would be standard procedure."

"Would you check to see if there is a copy in the files?"

"What, now?"

"Yes, now."

Emilio engaged the archbishop in strained conversation while the priest went about his search. Over the years, Emilio had heard enough about archaeology from his sister to carry his own, and they spent a quarter of an hour discussing a restoration project in the Catacomb of Callixtus. Father Galiotto finally returned, empty-handed.

"I looked through the files on the statue, and there is no corresponding document."

"I'm not surprised," Emilio said. "It seems we have a mystery. I believe that someone has forged a memorandum and gotten access to your official stamp. The questions are how and when."

"Look at its date," the priest said. "It could have been done years ago."

"Possibly," Emilio said, rising, "but I don't think so. I think it's quite recent. I'll be taking the seal into evidence. I hope you won't be too inconvenienced. I'll need both of you to come to the Carabinieri headquarters at the Vatican later today to have your fingerprints taken."

"Whatever for?" the priest asked.

"We call them elimination prints. That way, we can eliminate yours from the other fingerprints we've been able to lift from the memorandum."

Fiona was able to jawbone her way to a timely telecon with the chairman of ARG Bank, a Maltese national named Temi Misura. He seemed to be pretending that he knew who she was, but she suspected he had looked her up in the interval since her initial call to his office.

"Governor O'Reilly," he said, "it is such an honor to speak with you."

"Likewise," Fiona said. "I sent your man an email with one

of your bank's statements. It's a matter of utmost importance that I validate the authenticity of the account and its holdings. The account is in the name of the current Vatican secretary of state. You are also in receipt of a signed statement from Elisabetta Celestino authorizing the release of information to me. I make this request as a member of the Vatican Council for the Economy. I've been commissioned to investigate the matter."

"Why doesn't the account holder log onto the bank portal and access her account information in the usual manner?"

"Because, Mr. Chairman, this is a fraudulent account."

Misura affected a pleading tone. "But, Governor, you must know how our privacy and data security procedures work. We would need original copies of a duly notarized request from Mrs. Celestino. Upon receipt and review by our regulatory department, we could provide the account holder with copies of her account statements within several days."

"Not Mrs.," Fiona said. "She's a nun."

"My apologies, but the point stands."

"What a pity," Fiona said. "As this is a highly time-sensitive matter, we're going to have to get Interpol involved on an emergency basis. I do hope you didn't have supper plans for this evening."

The pleading continued. "Governor O'Reilly, I pledge my help, but isn't there anything we can do to forestall the involvement of Interpol? You can't imagine the complications."

"Tell you what," Fiona said. "We'll get you all the signed and notarized materials you need by morning courier and hold off on Interpol if you'll simply look up the account and tell me the date it was established. A memorandum that we also believe is a forgery suggests that one hundred thousand euros were transferred six years ago."

Fiona heard a sigh. "In this day and age, even that is irregular, but hold the line, and I will check."

Fiona spent a few minutes sipping water, wiggling her toes, and tapping her gold-plated pen against the desk.

Misura came back on the line and seemed like a different man. No longer pleading, he sounded leaden. "Well, there is something odd going on," he said. "We may need to get Interpol involved after all. This account was opened and populated with funds only two days ago."

Fiona slipped her high heels on and clipped her way over to Elisabetta's office just as Silvio Licheri arrived. Father Thompson looked up from his desk in the anteroom of the Secretariat and seemed to be wondering whom to announce first.

Silvio apologized to Fiona, whom he didn't know, and said to Thompson, "Please tell her that the article has just been published and that all hell is breaking loose."

28

Spooner was in his hotel room with one eye on the TV and one eye on the Orion app when Cal called Stella from the vicinity of Swartz Hall. He listened to Stella's voicemail prompt and Cal's message to call him right away. When Cal's location beacon started to move away from the Divinity School at a vehicle's speed, Spooner put his shoes on.

He wouldn't be coming back to the hotel, so he packed his roller bag, double-checked all the drawers, opened the safe, and scooped up its contents, starting with his pistol and tactical holster. He had carried a Beretta as a special-ops officer, but his shooting-range buddies had turned him on to the new military standard issue, the SIG Sauer M18 in coyote brown. Spooner didn't operate in deserts these days, but he liked the camo color nonetheless. He had two passports. The fake one was a master-piece. The best money could buy. He'd used it before in test mode, and it did its job on three continents. Name-matched credit cards were linked to an account shielded by an offshore limited liability company. He'd used one of the cards at this hotel, The Charles, located just off Harvard Square. Finally, he retrieved Greta Schenck's Harvard University ID. He had found it in Samia's purse at Danyal's apartment and took it in case it came in handy. He'd destroy it later.

He climbed into his rental car, mounted his phone on the dashboard, and drove toward the beacon position. It looked like Donovan was heading home, the best possible news.

The minute he got through his door, Cal tried Stella again and got voicemail again. By force of habit, he opened the freezer drawer where he kept his bottle-in-progress, but shut it and got a Diet Coke out of the fridge instead.

Outside, a rental car pulled into a space across the street from Cal's house. It would be dark enough for comfort in an hour.

Cal called the Cambridge Police Department and asked for Stella and Brendan Davis, but both were off duty. He resorted to throwing a frozen meal in the microwave, but watching the timer count down made him crazy, and he called Stella's mobile one more time.

"Jesus," she answered. "How many times have you called? Is this about the guy you think is the buyer? Can't it wait till the morning? I'm having kind of a thing with my wife."

"That can wait," he said. "The other piece of information I found out just now could be more urgent. I know how Samia got into Houghton Library."

"How?"

"She stole Greta Schenck's ID from her office."

"How do you know that?"

"I just saw Greta at the Divinity School. She was looking for it everywhere."

"Holy crap," Stella said. "If Samia used it to get into one Harvard building, she could have used it at another one. If she did, we can fill in the gap in her timeline between about 2:45 when she left Houghton and 4:10 when she got a taxi at Harvard Square for Danyal's place."

"How do you know she took a taxi?" Cal asked.

"Detective Davis only looks dumb. He figured she couldn't get an Uber or Lyft because she had pulled her SIM card. It was too far to walk, so she must've taken a cab. He called the taxi companies—there aren't many left—and found the record."

The microwave dinged, and Cal said, "First thing in the morning, we've got to get Harvard's IT department to go over the keycard logs."

"Fuck the morning," she said. "Let's do it now. My wife's ready to kick me out anyway for being the worst spouse in history. I'll make a call and get one of their IT people teed up over there. I'll pick you up in a quarter of an hour. Did I hear your microwave go off?"

"You did."

"Then you've got time to eat your delicious dinner."

Spooner lit a cigarette, blew smoke out the car window, and screwed a suppressor tube onto his SIG. Fifteen minutes was more than enough time to do what needed doing. Enter through the rear door, deliver two perfectly placed shots to the head, retrieve the casings, and drive off. He would toss the weapon into the Charles on the way to the airport. He'd already been thinking about destinations. Something tropical. There was a reasonable connection out of Logan to get to Panama.

But now he was paralyzed by a sense of duty. It sounded like Donovan had found the missing puzzle piece. Tommy Cunliffe deserved the full measure of his devotion to the original mission. He would play the game for a while longer and try to deliver not one but two trophies on a platter—the papyrus and Donovan's head.

Stella pulled into Cal's driveway and honked. He climbed in, and she told him that the Harvard police had gotten a university technician to come back into the office and assist them with their inquiries. On the brief drive to the IT department on Memorial Drive, Cal gave her a synopsis of his day in Pittsburgh and was disappointed by how little weight she gave it.

"You could be a hundred percent right in your hunch," she said, "but it's speculative at best. Give me one shred of evidence directly connecting this Cunliffe guy to Samia's murder. I couldn't even get a search warrant based on this. You going to take the job?"

He exploded. "Hell no! What do you take me for?"

"I don't know," she said. "You've got a nice house, you've probably got more money than I'll have in ten lifetimes, but he's cutting you a check for ten million? Come on, man."

The IT headquarters set on the Cambridge side of the Charles River was locked, and Stella leaned on the bell until a young man opened up and asked if they were the police. Stella showed her badge.

"What about him?" the young man said, pointing at Cal.

"He's one of your eggheads," she said.

They climbed the stairs to his workstation, and the technician, named Jim, logged in and asked for the name and university ID number for the badge they were interested in. Stella asked if Cal had the number, he replied with why would he, and that precipitated a brief bicker.

"Can't you look it up, Jim?" Stella asked.

"Not without the permission of the student or faculty member," he said. "Privacy guidelines."

Stella didn't like the response. "Tell you what, Jim. If someone tries to roast you on a spit over the fire for this, you tell them that I held a gun to your head."

"You're kidding, right?"

She pulled her jacket back to show him the butt of her Glock. "I never joke about pulling my service weapon."

Jim rolled his eyes and said, "What's the holder's name?"

"Attaboy," she said. "Greta Schenck. I'll bet you there's only one by that name. And here's my card. If you get into trouble, call me."

It didn't take long for Jim to find her. "Here she is," he said, scanning a database. "Schenck, Greta, Divinity School and HU History Department."

"That's her," Cal said.

"All right, give me the date and the times to search on."

He told them it would take a few minutes—something about retrieving data from individual access points and combining them into one file. Stella mumbled that they didn't need to

358

know how he made the magic and proceeded to ask Cal's opinion of who was right and who was wrong in the domestic argument with her wife.

Cal wasn't interested one way or another but would have come down in favor of Stella's wife if pressed. It was fortunate that Jim had an answer before it came to that.

He pointed to a spreadsheet column on the screen. "The HUID—that's Harvard University—"

"Got it," Stella said, crowding in.

"Okay, Greta's ID was used at 2:41 p.m. to access the front entrance of the Houghton Library."

"Told you," Cal said.

"Yes, you did," Stella agreed.

Jim squinted and said, "It looks like it was used once more that afternoon, and not since."

"Where?" Cal said, leaning over.

"At 3:10 p.m. at the front entrance to Swartz Hall."

Cal straightened his spine and said, "Are you sure?"

"Definitely," Jim said, looking around. Cal and Stella were already at the door.

"You've been very helpful," Stella called back. "I probably wouldn't have shot you."

In the stairwell, Stella said, "She must've come to see you."

"I don't think so," Cal said, skipping down the stairs. "She knew I was tied up. I was at a faculty meeting all afternoon. We were meeting for dinner. Why would she have gone to Swartz?"

"Maybe to see another friend?" Stella said, reaching the lobby first. "She makes a social call at Houghton, then does the same at Swartz."

"I don't think so," Cal said. "All the evidence tells us that she had the papyrus with her when she left Danyal's apartment that morning and didn't have it when she returned that afternoon. She told Kalogeras she was scared she was being followed. She's almost at the finish line. In a few hours, she's going to give it to me. For peace of mind, she goes to the building on campus she knows the best and puts it somewhere for safekeeping. She probably planned on taking me there after dinner. Maybe she would've given me Greta's ID."

"The killer's got the ID," Stella said, unlocking her car. "I don't know if you're right, but you talk a good game. Where are we going to look?"

"I don't know," Cal said, buckling up. "Let me think."

Francis Avenue was littered with autumn leaves blowing about in the gusting night air. Stella pulled up and parked outside Swartz Hall and turned to her passenger. They hadn't talked much on their drive from the IT building, and now she said, "So?"

"I still don't know," Cal said. "Let's go inside."

Cal swiped them in, stood in the entrance hall, looked right and then left, and started to think out loud. "She couldn't have left it in my office. I always lock my door. She wouldn't have hidden it in any common spaces. Too risky. Current grad students share her old office. Also, too risky. Christ, it's a big building."

Stella's phone rang, and she told Cal to keep cranking.

He heard one side of her conversation. "You're kidding me.

How'd you miss it? Yeah, you said. I wasn't paying attention. What time? And that was the last one? You'd better be sure, or we're going to have a serious talk."

"What?" Cal said.

"That was our buddy, Jim. He's still there, writing a memo to his boss about our visit. He printed out the search on Greta's card and realized he missed an entry importing this or doing that—I didn't understand what he was talking about. The card was used again inside Swartz Hall. At 3:12, she used it to get inside the Divinity School Library."

Cal started down the corridor apace. "The library. Why the library? Come on, think. Why the hell would she go to the library?"

Spooner listened to Stella's call with Jim and slipped on a balaclava. Francis Avenue was dark and empty. At the entrance to Swartz Hall, he used Greta's ID card to swipe himself in. A sign on the wall pointed toward the library.

Cal entered the library at the first-floor level, flipped on a set of lights, and stood, hands on hips, looking around.

"Okay, the third floor has classrooms, the Rabinowitz Seminar Room, staff areas, collection management. Doesn't fit. The second floor has circulating collections, public computers, seating areas. Could she have slipped it inside a book? And risk someone checking it out? That doesn't fit. This floor is mostly staff areas and current periodicals. Can't see it. That leaves the ground floor. It's mostly reference collections. You can't check those books out, so she would've seen it as less of a risk. I don't know. Let's go downstairs."

He switched on lights and looked down row after row of library stacks—thousands upon thousands of books. He began walking through the stacks with Stella following on his heels.

He turned a corner, started down another row, and said he didn't even know where to begin.

"Look for a book with her name on it." She laughed.

He stopped and looked at her. "What did you say?"

"I was making a stupid joke."

He took off, and she ran after him. "Where're we going?" she called after him.

He pulled up somewhere near the center of the room at a long row of shelves of thick books with identical black bindings. "Here," Cal said. "We're going here. This is where we keep archival copies of the PhD dissertations of all our grad students. Other students can use them for research, but mostly we keep them to honor our graduates. Samia was so damned proud of her thesis. Help me find it. It'll have her name on the spine."

Stella went to one end of the row, Cal the other, and they worked toward the middle.

After a minute, she heard him say, "Hey," and then saw him reaching up, just as her phone rang again.

"What now?" she answered. "Oh Christ."

She looked over at Cal leafing through Samia's thesis, stopping on a page, and staring in wonder.

"Stella—"

"Cal, quiet!" she whispered. "That was Jim. Greta's card was just used again. Someone's in the library."

29

T he lights," Cal said, heading toward a cluster of light switches near the restrooms. He carried Samia's thesis like a running back tucking a football.

He flicked every switch on the plate. The stacks went dark, but the lights over the study carrels remained on.

"Can you kill the others?" she whispered.

"Other wall," he said.

They would have to exit the stacks at a lighted area to get to the main stairway and elevator. She asked if there was a second set of stairs, and he pointed toward another set of lighted carrels.

It must have been a rapid maneuver because Cal missed Stella's Glock draw, but it was out now, in a two-handed grip.

"I'm calling this in," she said. "Then we're going to move."

Cal nodded. His experience with close-quarter maneuvers in the army led him to the same conclusion. You wanted to keep moving, avoid being a sitting duck. Stella didn't carry a police radio. She used her cell phone to call dispatch.

"This is Detective Stella Caruso, badge number 88701," she said, low and breathily. "Officer needs assistance. I'm trapped with one civilian, ground level, Harvard's Swartz Hall library, Frances Ave. Potentially armed assailants. Send all available units. Use this number for communications." She slipped her phone into her jeans, neglecting to set it to vibrate.

Spooner stopped by the first-floor circulation desk to listen to Stella's call, flicked off the SIG's thumb safety, and then moved toward the stairs.

Cal and Stella chose to cross the room via the darkest row in the center of the stacks. Cal whispered, "Wait," and made a space on one of the shelves for Samia's thesis.

They crept toward the end of the row. The coast was clear for a dash to the north stairs.

Then Spooner called Stella's number.

The ringtone from a blocked number startled her. She declined it and switched the phone off, but it was too late. Spooner's ears were his homing device. He had come down the north stairs and was listening from the stairwell.

He barged into the room, saw Stella at the end of the row, and began firing. Two suppressed shots, then two more. The firing produced nothing more than muffled clicks, but they didn't need to be loud to be lethal.

Cal heard Stella groaning on the floor and police sirens in the distance.

The human brain is a marvel. In the span of a single second, Cal played all the angles in his head. He could drag Stella away from the end of the row. He could try to stanch her bleeding. He could run. Or he could do what he did.

Her Glock was beside her, and he grabbed it. It was a simple weapon to use. There was no safety. Police officers keep their guns chambered, so he didn't need to rack the slide. Army training never leaves you. He lunged forward, toward the light, toward the danger, spraying rounds, until he caught sight of a man in a balaclava in a shooter's stance with a long suppressor tube on his barrel.

A round from Spooner's SIG twocked into a book by Cal's shoulder.

Cal was in an out-of-body state, inside a red mist of rage.

Samia dead. Stella shot. Eli tormented. Cunliffe smug. A stranger trying to end my life.

He yelled at the top of his lungs and pulled the trigger again, and again, and again, and again.

Cal slowly opened his eyes to the sounds of a beeping cardiac monitor and whooshing ventilator. There was the faintest sliver of light through louvered blinds. His body felt heavy and stiff, and it took a few moments to get oriented. He shifted in his chair, felt Samia's thesis pressing against his side, and pulled off the thin hospital blanket someone had used to cover him.

"You're awake."

He turned toward the chair beside his. Stella's wife, Natalie, a delicate-looking Puerto Rican woman, held out her hand, and he took it.

"How is she?" he asked.

"The nurse told me she's stable. They thought she might have to go back into surgery, but they don't think so now."

"Good."

"Brendan wanted to speak with you when you were awake. He's outside."

Brendan was in the ICU waiting area with the Cambridge chief of police and other detectives holding vigil.

"You hanging in there?" Brendan asked.

"I'm fine," Cal said. "Who was he, do you know?"

"He didn't have any ID on him. We were waiting for his prints to come back when one of our units found his rental car. He had two sets of IDs, one real, one fake. His name's Joel Edward Spooner. He's ex-military, currently—or rather, formerly—employed at Cunliffe Energy Group in Houston as head of security. We're making inquiries, but it's the middle of the night in Houston."

"It's not as early in Pittsburgh," Cal said.

"Why Pittsburgh?" Brendan asked.

"Let's sit down. You're going to need your notepad."

After an hour, Brendan had filled up half his notebook with his oversized scrawl. He told Cal to wait while he conferred with the chief of police, and when he returned, he said, "The chief buys it. I'm contacting the FBI to get an arrest warrant issued for Tommy Cunliffe."

Cal looked in on Stella again, asked Natalie to call him with any developments, and trudged out of the Cambridge City Hospital. He took a dose of crisp autumn air from the sidewalk and shivered in his thin shirt. The best way to warm himself was to jog home.

To the few people out at this hour, he must have looked a sight—a tall man in dress pants, button-down shirt, and loafers, running through Cambridge Common at 5:30 in the morning with a large black book under an arm. His street was in sight when his phone rang, and he slowed to a walk to answer her.

"Cal, we read about a shooting at the Harvard Divinity School," Eli said. "Tell me it didn't involve you."

"I'm afraid I can't tell you that."

"Oh God, are you all right?"

"I'm unhurt. Eli, I found it. I've got the papyrus."

"Oh. That's good, but I'm more concerned about you. You sound shaken."

"Good word for it. I killed a man. A very good cop is in critical condition. I'm trying to figure out if it's too early or too late for a drink."

"Oh, Cal."

He closed his eyes, touched by those two simple words.

"I'm concerned about you too and those false accusations. I swear, we're going to expose every last one of your tormentors."

"I'm blessed with wonderful supporters like you. Fiona O'Reilly, a financial expert, came to my aid from Dublin. She's made some shocking discoveries. Emilio has also been marvelous. It's a fast-moving situation, but today will be a good day. I'll call later when I can say more."

"I'll be waiting."

"And, Cal, please don't drink."

GLENN COOPER

Tommy Cunliffe was having his morning coffee in the breakfast nook when his assistant Beth Ann rang him from her home. He figured she was calling in sick.

"Don't tell me you're not coming in today," he said, laying his irritation on thick.

"No, I'm coming. I got an alert on one of the searches I've got running and wanted to make sure you knew."

"Know about what?"

"The article in the Italian paper on Elisabetta Celestino."

"What does it say? No, just send it to me, translated."

Tommy shouted to his butler for his laptop, and the computer was duly retrieved from his office. As he clicked on the link in Beth Ann's email, his wife padded in, in her bathrobe and slippers, and without either of them exchanging good mornings, she turned on the 9 a.m. news.

The article was from the financial pages of the Italian daily *Corriere della Sera.* Tommy winced at the headline.

Kickback Allegations Against Vatican Secretary of State Fall Apart Under Scrutiny

Tommy skimmed the long article, his nostrils flaring in anger.

Fiona O'Reilly, a former governor of the Central Bank of Ireland and a Vatican consultant, had found definitive evidence that an employee of the ARG Bank of Malta recently accepted a bribe to establish a fraudulent account in the name of Elisabetta Celestino and deposited one hundred thousand euros into it, using backdated paperwork. Interpol was questioning the employee.

The Vatican Carabinieri established that an alleged memorandum from Celestino arranging a kickback on the sale of a Vatican statue to a private buyer was a forgery. An employee of the Pontifical Commission for Sacred Archaeology, a Father Galiotta, admitted to the Carabinieri that he had provided the official seal of the Commission to make the memo appear authentic. A prominent Vatican cardinal, so far unnamed, was also under investigation, and a private investigator from Rome, Antonio Solla, was being detained over his role in the scheme.

Tommy slammed his laptop shut and became aware of the TV playing on the countertop. He was about to demand that his wife shut it off when both of them heard the news anchor say the name Joel Spooner.

"Following the shooting at the famed Harvard Divinity School last night, police have identified the dead shooter as Joel Edward Spooner of Houston, Texas. A Cambridge police officer was critically wounded in the incident. There's no motive for the shooting at this time. Tune in for further details at six o'clock."

Barbara looked up from her eggs and cackled. "Spooner was a creep, always cleaning up after you. What mess have you gotten yourself into, Tommy? Is this the one that's finally going to bite you in your ass, Governor?"

Tommy stood up so suddenly that his chair tipped over backward. His jugulars filled with blood and popped out of his neck like purple snakes.

"We're finished!" he shouted. "I'm done with you! You're even a shrew when you're sober. I'm a good Catholic. I abhor divorce, but I've reached my breaking point with you. You're getting nothing! I'll even fight you on the prenup. You were nothing when I married you, and you'll be nothing again. I'm going to shower down in the summerhouse, and when I get back, I want you gone."

He stalked past the stunned cook and butler, marched outside through his drawbridge door, and began walking through the chill air. He was halfway down the hill when he heard the whirr of the electric motor.

He turned his head and saw a sight that hitherto had been something he always enjoyed—a gleaming electric golf cart, speeding almost silently over green grass.

The cart was going as fast as it could when Barbara plowed into him, all four wheels thumping over his torso and head. She braked, made a wide turn, and saw him crawling away. She pressed the accelerator to the floor and struck him again. And for good measure, she backed up, left the rear wheels planted on his lifeless body, and sat in the driver's seat until the FBI arrived a short while later to serve an arrest warrant on Tommy Cunliffe.

30

Six months later

Cal carried it in his briefcase, sandwiched between two panes of framed glass, snug inside a foam-lined wooden box that had been specially built. The occasion was a formal papal audience in Pope John's library, but any notion of formality melted away the moment the pope entered with Elisabetta.

The pontiff went straight for Cal and reached as far around Cal's back as his bulging belly allowed, and Cal matched the bear hug.

"It is so good to see you, Cal," the pope said.

"I feel the same way, Holy Father."

Elisabetta was next. She looked radiant and strong. She had weathered the storms and gotten on with her job brilliantly. Most no longer called her the female secretary of state. They called her the secretary of state.

Cal reached out his hand and smiled at her.

"The Holy Father gets a hug, and I only get a handshake?" she said.

It was the first time he had embraced her. It lasted only a few sweet moments, and it was over.

In the audience, Micaela elbowed Emilio in the ribs and whispered, "Did you see that?"

He whispered back, "Fortunately, the photographer was too slow. She doesn't need more trouble."

Elisabetta asked the Egyptian ambassador to the Vatican and the papal nuncio to Egypt to come forward.

Cal handed the wooden box to the ambassador, an elegant, balding man, who opened it and presented it to the pope.

The ambassador said, "We are thankful to Professor Calvin Donovan for authenticating this Egyptian treasure. Not only is it the earliest biblical papyrus ever discovered, but it is also certainly the most important and revolutionary of them all. Two thousand years ago, there was Mary Magdalene, a female pope! Now we have Elisabetta Celestino, a female secretary of state! And we are so very thankful to the professor and to Harvard University for brokering this historic agreement whereby the Mary Papyrus will be on loan to the Vatican Museum for ten years, after which it will return to Cairo as one of our most valuable cultural treasures, to be enjoyed by Christians and Muslims alike."

The pope studied the reddish Greek letters for a few seconds and passed the box to Monsignor Finale for safekeeping.

The pontiff whispered something to Cal, who left his side and approached two women wearing beautiful new dresses and black mantillas over their heads.

"He wants you to come forward," Cal said.

Stella and Natalie stood in front of Pope John, holding hands.

"You were very brave, Detective Caruso," the pope said,

presenting her with a papal medal. "Thanks to you, good has triumphed over evil."

Stella curtsied and wiped a tear with a gloved finger.

"How long have you been married?" he asked.

Natalie said, "Two years next month, Holy Father."

"Still newlyweds," the pope joked. "Although we are not at a point in the history of the Church where we may bestow a sacramental on same-sex unions, I would like to offer a blessing on the occasion of your second anniversary."

The two women stood in shock as the pope bowed his head, raised his hands, and whispered a few words.

At the reception, Elisabetta clinked glasses with Cal and asked how long he was staying in Rome.

"Not long. I've got to finish up the semester—couple more lectures to give, papers to mark."

"And then?"

"Then I've got to sit down and write a monograph on the discovery and authentication of the Mary, Pontifex Papyrus. The working group generated a mountain of scientific data."

"That should be a most pleasurable task," she said dreamily. "Tell me, how is Cambridge this time of year?"

"Winter's on the ropes," he said, looking deeply into her dark eyes. "Spring is coming."

"I should like to see spring in Cambridge one day," she said.

ABOUT THE AUTHOR

GLENN COOPER is an internationally bestselling thriller writer. His previous books, including his bestselling Library of the Dead trilogy, have been translated into thirty-one languages and have sold over seven million copies. He graduated from Harvard University, magna cum laude, with a BA in Archaeology. Cooper attended Tufts University School of Medicine and was an internal medicine and infectious diseases physician in hospitals, clinics, and refugee camps in conflict zones before joining the biotechnology industry, where he was the CEO of several publicly traded companies. Now he writes full-time.

Learn more at:
GlennCooperBooks.com
Facebook.com/GlennCooperUSA
Twitter @GlennCooper
Instagram: Glenn_Cooper